KRUGER'S GOLD

A novel of the
Anglo-Boer War

Sidney Allinson

In loving memory of my aunt,
Nursing Sister Dorothy Maddison,
who tended soldiers in two wars,
and
Pte. William Wilfred Collins,
19th Hussars,
who rode far across the veld.

GLOSSARY OF UNFAMILIAR WORDS

Afrikaans: Boer-Dutch language
Afrikaner: Afrikaans-speaker, of Boer stock
assegai: stabbing spear
baas: master
biltong: dried meat
bint: young woman
bittereinder: fighter to the bitter end
Blighty: England
Blighty-one: serious wound, invalided home
Boer: farmer, Afrikaner
boojer: army slang for Boer
braai: barbeque
buckshee: obtained free
burgher: citizen
Canuck: Canadian
cobber: friend, buddy
Commando: military unit, individual member
Creusot: French artillery gun
Digger: Australian
donga: ravine
doolali: insane
dorp: village
fizzer: offence charge-sheet
funk: fear
Geordie: born in County Durham
Gerries: Germans
glasshouse: military prison
gun-cotton: cellulose explosive
hensopper: hands-upper, surrendered Boer
Hoosier: born in Indiana
Johnnies: Boers
joiner: Boer in British service

Joodje: Jew
Judge Advocate General: army legal corps
kaffir: black African
kakie: British soldier
khaki: colour of British uniforms
Kiwi: New Zealander
kleinbaas: young boss
knocking-shop: brothel
koppie: hill
Krupp: German artillery gun
laager: defensive camp
lekker: nice
mamba: venomous snake
mampara: fool
Mauser: German rifle
meisie: pretty young woman
MG: machine-gun
moordenaar: murderer
MP: Military Police
mufti: civilian clothes
mujik: peasant
n.c.o.: non-commissioned officer
Okhrana: Russian Imperial Secret Police
Oom: uncle
opzaal: mount up
Out Of Bounds: forbidden to enter, off-limits
penkop: under-aged boy commando
pom-pom: automatic light cannon
Pommy: Englishman
predikant: church minister
prottie: Protestant
Provost Marshal: military police chief
PW: prisoner-of-war
quid: one pound sterling
roer: rifle
RSM: Regimental Sergeant Major

schantze: rock shelter
scouser: Liverpudlian
sheila: young woman
shebeen: drinking-den
shell-shock: nervous breakdown, battle-fatigue
sjambok: whip
skelm: villain, crook
slim: crafty
smous: Jewish peddler
snoep: stingy
Springbok: South African (also, antelope)
squaddie: low-rank soldier
stoep: verandah
subaltern: lieutenant
Swart Gevaar: Black Peril
Tommy: British soldier
Transvaal: across the valley
uitlander: foreigner
veld: open plain
veld-cornet: commando-leader
verraaier: traitor
verkenner: reconnaissance scout
Vierkleur: Transvaal flag
volk: people, nation
Volksraad: Boer Parliament
vrede: peace
vrou: wife, woman
wit baasskap: white supremacy

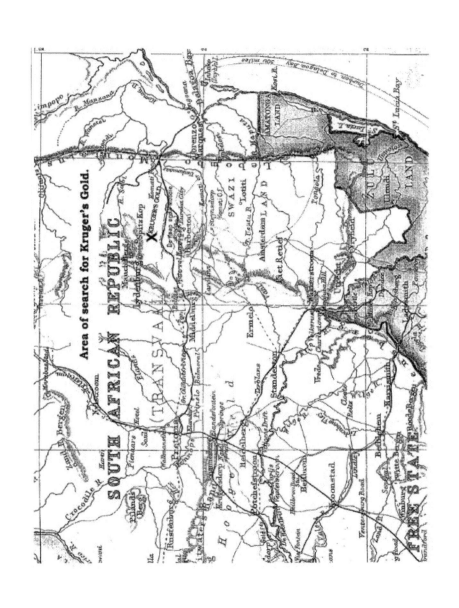

Area of search for Kruger's Gold.

CHAPTER ONE

"*A aaaaak!*"

Frantic screams rasped from the tall Boer woman. She stamped in a small circle, tearing hair out of her scalp and throwing tufts towards the burning farmhouse. Her shrieks pierced the roar of crackling wood and flapping sheets of flame that were almost invisible in the clear African sunlight. Dry as straw, the white-painted walls fueled the pyre, destroying a lifetime of hope in minutes, mesmerizing the vrou.

Her glazed stare could not focus even on the small girl who crouched at the steps, cradling a gut-shot brown dog, kissing it's muzzle. All that existed was this sudden evil that descended at daybreak an hour ago; the raiders' bullying voices, yells for Henk to stop being a cowardly hands-upper and come out on commando duty. Though they ransacked every room and shed, her husband was not to be found, having ridden off when he heard them coming.

So they dragged poor Jessoo the houseboy into the yard and beat him with sjamboks to make him betray where his baas had gone. The black could not tell, so they tired of the sport, and took Jessoo out of her sight. The veld-cornet brought Henk's bible from the house, pressed it into her hands, and explained carefully why she could keep nothing else.

Her husband's stubborn refusal to obey the Transvaal Military Service Law that required every burgher between 16 and 60 years of age to fight made him a traitor, so all his worldly possessions were now forfeit. They torched the homestead, slaughtered all livestock, then shot three kaffir field-hands and the family dog. The job was all done when a *verkenner* came with warning of a British patrol on the way, and the Boer commandos left.

Only minutes later, soldiers rode in from three or four

directions at once, over forty of them. Some came galloping fast, others slow and cautious, watching for ambushers. The first two thundered ahead on big horses, spinning to abrupt halts in the yard, recklessly close to where she stood. They were off their saddles in a blur, standing back to back, hefting Lee-Metfords, eying the outbuildings. She began shaking, no longer ashamed to show fear of the Volk's enemies, keeping her head down but glancing to take in everything.

They were clean-shaven young men, in chocolate coloured shirts, whipcord riding britches, and high boots laced at the ankle. Each bore a leather bandolier across his chest and two holstered pistols. Their khaki Stetson hats had the crown pinched to a high point and a bronze maple-leaf badge in front. These soldiers' hairless faces looked boyish compared to the fully-bearded men she was used to, but she had heard many stories of how dangerous the British could be. Perhaps they would turn even worse now without a woman over them, since their old Queen Victoria died last month.

Harry Lanyard could feel the heat from here, and wondered how the kid could stand it so close. The other Scouts spread out quickly among the farm buildings, looking for Boers or loot. So he slung his rifle, nodding at Piet van Praage that the coast looked clear, and trotted over to the stoep. His move startled the woman to notice her child again, and she called pleadingly for him not to hurt her. Piet calmed her with a few words of Afrikaans, but told her to stay where she was.

"Come on, honey. Best be moving." Harry smiled and tried to keep his voice gentle to reassure the child, but had to pitch it loud against the roaring blaze. Yet he could hear her quite well, a tiny voice crooning a lullaby to her pet. Wisps of smoke were coiling off the back of her dress, so he started to move her away.

She cried, "Ne! Ne!", pulling against his hand, still

cuddling the whimpering dog. The roof collapsed suddenly, folding the house inwards and roiling thick smoke into the azure sky. A flare of heat struck the child's back, crisping her dress, and her scream mingled with her mother's. The kid slid up one step, and the agonized dog dragged itself after, trailing thin blood across her bare feet.

Harry stroked the mutt's head, looking into its stricken eyes. "Okay, feller," he said. He gently turned the child's face away, unholstered his Colt .44, and shot her dog behind its ear.

The little girl flinched, then she skipped up the steps, screaming, fleeing crazily along the flame-licked verandah.

"Watch yourself, buddy!" Everybody started yelling, trying to call him back, but he jumped after her without thinking much.

His boots thumping behind seemed to scare her more than the fire, and she scampered to the far end before he caught up. He pushed her below the flames, ignoring his hair frizzling and an arm starting to blister, busy slapping at the burning dress. He scooped her up and rolled over the charred rail, falling hard on his rifle but managing to cradle her landing.

Five or six troopers pulled them to safety, checking to see how the kid was. Others flailed with their tunics at his smouldering shirt, while Jiggy ran to fetch a bucket of water. Everybody got out of the way when the vrou pushed forward to tend her daughter.

Harry felt foolish being rolled over and over in the dust, and stood up to show he wasn't on fire. The woman was yelling again, frantic while she ripped off what was left of her girl's pinafore, and some skin came away with it. The kid was pretty brave, barely made a sound.

"Oh, Christ!", Jiggy Mendip called out, not about the child. He was leaning over the well wall, shading his eyes to look down inside. "We can't use this now."

Piet caught on right away, and detailed a native

Auxiliary to guard the well. Harry unslung his water-bottle and gave it to the couple of RAMC orderlies treating the burns with zinc oxide cream from their wound kits. The medics' care seemed to calm the mother and she finally stopped her racket, holding the infant's head in her lap, humming a psalm quietly. For the first time, she looked the soldiers straight in the face. She still knew all kakies were accursed of God, but these ones did show some Christian feeling.

Ned Coveyduck brought a bandage for Harry's arm, and said that was enough of playing silly buggers, seeing as he didn't fancy a slice of barbied Canuck anyway. Being the biggest trooper in the outfit, Ned towered over Lanyard, who was a medium-sized man.

Coveyduck gave Harry his canteen back, though there wasn't much left in it. Harry gulped a few mouthfuls, until Ned held up his hand. "Better save it, mate. They tell you Jiggy found a blackie down the well?"

Lanyard corked the bottle and glanced over at the guard standing shaded by the well canopy. "That's a new one."

"Main column's taking its own sweet time, as usual." Ned squinted up at the sun. "Only a day since we left Derby, and the Boojers've hit-and-run three times already."

"Poor bastards." Lanyard meant the straggling column of weary British infantry; 1400 men humping 50-pound packs under the brutally hot sun, marching steadily over rough ground for ten hours a day.

All along their route, soldiers fell out to the side, either collapsed with enteric fever or squatting miserably, trousers down, straining with dysentery. Scores of dead and dying horses littered the line of march, piteous victims of over-work, neglect, or starvation.

In the army's wake, a dozen pillars of black smoke roiled up to form clouds across the windless sky. They marked where farms had been set afire in Kitchener's new scorched-earth policy to starve out Boer guerilla fighters.

The column of troops moved slowly from valley to valley, herding away cattle and sheep, looting and burning, and turning out women and children to weep in despair beside the ruins of their once beautiful homesteads.

Heads down, close to exhaustion, the plodding Tommies were easy meat for snipers and darting flank attacks by burgher horsemen. A few quick kills, then a short gallop away into the rock labyrinths before infantry could react. "Gat'll turn us loose sure enough today."

"Better we got a move on, sharpish. Ride the buggers down before they gain a lead." Ned laughed quietly. "Charlie'd never dare to send us off ahead, though. Gat'd go doolali if he missed a fight."

"Crikey." The big Australian looked at the ruined house and stopped smiling. "Never ever get used to this part, do we?" Harry just shook his head. They had both burned their share of farms lately, but seeing Boers do the same thing didn't make him feel any better about it.

"Makes you wonder why these bitter-enders don't just pack it in," Ned shook his head. "Old Oom Paul's been snug in Holland nearly a year since his government surrendered. 'Cleared out the banks while he ran, they say. Nice work if you can get it."

"Kruger left his sick old wife behind, too, without a pot to piss in." Ned squinted at the surrounding hills, alert for movement. "No better off than those crazy commandos roving the veld with their arses hanging out of their pants. Too stubborn to give up, even while we herd their families into those bloody camps."

"They still manage to run rings around us, though." Harry gave them due.

"Well, round Pommy generals, anyway." Coveyduck pulled a face. "They're thick as planks when it comes to anything not laid down in King's Rules And Regulations. Strewth! My cobber Breaker always says Rule Three-O-Three's the only way to deal with Boers."

"Yeah, well . . ." Harry didn't see much point in mentioning that a few Canadians in his old regiment held the same opinion. Word had it some of Lord Strathcona's Horse lynched six Boers at Twyfelaar after they put up a white flag then shot two Canadians coming to take their surrender.

Ned slapped his knees and stood up. "It takes wild Colonial boys like you and me to really hurt guerillas. Mind you, Aussie's moved out of the colony category now." He was still full of the news that the Australian colonies had Federated into a new nation just a few weeks ago.

Harry joshed, "Canada beat you there by thirty-odd years." Ned grinned and faked a punch with his over-sized fist. He loped off to check for heliograph messages and see if there was anything tasty in the way of tucker.

Harry went to his horse, standing by the stone shed where he left her, reins down. She whickered softly, bunting his chest. He stroked her satiny flank. "Still got a long day ahead of us, gal."

He dug in the blanket-roll for his spare khaki tunic. Like the other, it had no sergeant's chevrons on the sleeves. Boer snipers watched for badges of rank, shooting officers and n.c.o.s first, so he'd inked three faint lines on a sleeve, to just show up close.

He stripped to the waist, sun-tanned face and hands contrasting with his pale torso. After months on horseback, he was pared to lean muscle. Harry slathered some ointment on his burned arm, bandaged it, changed shirts and folded the ruined one.

He patted Molly's neck, fed her half his breakfast apple, and loosened the big California saddle he brought when he left the Strathcona's. He gave her sleek coat a quick rub-down, and checked for back-sores or ticks. To finish, he unsheathed the Enfield bayonet from his boot, and scraped grit off her hooves.

He wet his bandanna to squeeze a drink for the big chestnut, and moistened her mouth. It was just past eight o'clock but the sun was fierce already, so the polluted well caused a big worry. Without the tank-wagon, no fresh water was to be had for the long ride ahead.

Everybody read the same signs, and took care of their horses quickly, as there wouldn't be much time after Gat turned up. They chatted casually, easily confident, not at all concerned that enemies were nearby. With sentries at alert, native lookouts on nearby hills, and signalers watching for flashes from the main column, the anti-guerillas were able to relax for now.

You could see their self-reliance in their gait and swagger, the way they held their heads up and looked straight at you when they spoke. They were Howard's Canadian Scouts, and didn't give a shit for anybody; certainly not Johnny Boer, or even General bloody Kitchener himself.

Howard recruited his new unit mainly from demobilized Canadian soldiers, but welcomed any man who could ride well and shoot straight — Australians, New Zealanders, British, plus Springboks from the Cape, some renegade Boers, and a few Americans. Valued as one of the few outfits able to fight Boer commandos on their own terms, all troopers in the unit held the rank and pay of sergeant. At Colonial rates, not Imperial, that came to a buck-seventy-five a day.

Harry saw Charlie Ross had ridden in, and stood with Jiggy questioning a scared-looking native girl. Even from here, you could see she was barely able to talk, rolling her bulging eyes towards what else the commandos had done.

In the cow-pen, three natives lay in a row. Two men and a woman it looked like, but their head-wounds and ragged clothing made it hard to tell for sure. Behind them, a few cattle lay dead as well, and the raiders had taken time to carve sides of beef from some. A big bull ox knelt on its knees, lowing in agony through his slit throat.

Charlie waved for the two senior sergeants to come over,

and Harry joined Coveyduck at the wall. "Housemaid. She managed to run and hide, but says there's about fifty of them. Headed towards Rusplaats farm." Charlie jerked a thumb at rugged hills behind the Basuto girl.

She was no more than sixteen or so, face greyed with shock, tears running through grime on her cheeks. Her dress was badly torn, no more than rags, and Jiggy was smirking at the glossy patches of skin that showed here and there.

The dying ox was so loud, Charlie couldn't hear what Jiggy was translating, so the captain went over to put the beast out of its agony. It took two shots. During the interruption, Harry caught the little man living up to his nickname with the maid. "Like to jiggy-jig with me, darlin'?" Then he mumbled something oily in the Sotho language, and slid his hand inside a rent at her front.

Lanyard gave him a nasty look, and the Yorkshireman stepped back, palms up mockingly. "Easy on, Harry. We all enjoys a bit-of-the-other where we finds it." He laughed, "Shagging a Boojer bint, yourself, I hear."

Lanyard would have decked him, but Ned stepped between. "Watch your mouth, short-arse." His finger jabbed Mendip in the chest. "And it so happens the lady's Dad's a septic." At Harry's puzzled glare, Ned grinned, "Just Aussie talk. Septic tank -- rhymes with Yank!"

"Cut it out, guys!" The captain sounded more tired than mad. He reloaded a couple of .303 rounds into his rifle. "She really sure about how many and where?"

"Yes, sir," Mendip was ex-British cavalry, and more inclined to military courtesy than most of the Scouts. "Says they split into two parties, up both sides of t'valley."

"We're getting close to the Swaziland border." Ross turned a recently-issued map to show their position. "Too strongly patrolled for them to go that way, so they'll try to get around Derby and cross the Combies River." He traced the red dots snaking west from the town of Piet Retief. "Some of those new-fangled blockhouses are just beyond, so maybe we can drive the commandos against the line." He caught the sergeants' faces, and nodded, "Yeah, if they don't dance around us as usual."

"What about that helio report of gunfire?" Harry asked Jiggy.

The apple-cheeked soldier was in charge of unit signals, though he looked too young to have been out here two years. He addressed the captain, "In t'valley directly behind us, sir. Stopped as soon as it started."

They heard sentries yippee-ing, and the clatter of wheels. A four-wheeled water wagon came rattling up the track, with Gat waving his hat at the lead. Close behind, rode his orderly, Sergeant Northway, a couple of troopers, and some armed native Auxiliaries. Another black drove the surviving two horses in the traces, straining at pulling the water tank with a machine-gun carriage hooked behind. Everybody came running, grinning like idiots in relief to see Gat was okay after all. They crowded around their commander, who stayed mounted so everybody could hear him.

"Sorry I'm late, boys, but a sniper got my lead horses." Major Arthur "Gat" Howard, DSO, slapped the Colt machine-gun's breech and chuckled, "Took half a beltful to settle his hash." The troopers laughed like schoolboys. Old Gat was indestructible, for sure.

Unassuming as ever, he wore a private's uniform, with no crowns of his rank on the shoulders. "Looks like more hot work for us today, too." He took in the corpses and burning house at a glance. "But, first we'll need to borrow some nags from you, Charlie!"

Everybody roared at the dig, Ross being well known for collecting captured horses and cattle to sell illegally on the side. While native handlers ran to get fresh mounts, Charlie explained the whereabouts of the enemy. Howard listened impatiently, often standing in his stirrups to peer across the terrain like the old Indian-fighter he was.

He looked the part; wearing his gray hair long these

days, with a white drooping mustache like Buffalo Bill Cody. Howard was originally American himself, having served in the U.S. Cavalry on the frontier for six years before retiring. He'd still be a Saturday-night soldier with the Connecticut National Guard if he hadn't fallen in love with the Gatling, the first machine-gun. Howard brought three up to Canada to demonstrate them in action during the Riel Rebellion of '87, then settled in Quebec and never went back to the States. People called him "Gat" ever since.

Captain Ross told his plan of herding the Boers towards the blockhouse line, careful to make it sound like just a suggestion. Howard tapped his map-case and nodded, ahead of events as always."Looks like we can scupper the whole damn pack of 'em, lads." At fifty-four, he had a chesty, old-man's way of talking. Gat was way over the official age-limit for active service, but the Royal Canadian Dragoons were glad to accept him, and he soon earned the Distinguished Service Order for bravery.

"Don't want to scare 'em away before we get there, though." He laughed deeply, and waved for the horse-wranglers to get a move on. "I'll just ride ahead with Dick and take a look. Soon as you've watered the mounts, follow up on both sides in a pincer movement."

"Hell, Gat, shouldn't you just hang on 'til we're all ready to come?" Charlie didn't look too pleased with the plan, and a few others murmured support. "Remember how the Crees jumped those two Mounties out on their lonesome?" Ross had soldiered alongside Howard in Canada years ago, and they shared many a hairy experience.

Gat did not respond to the reminiscence, just hitched his belt, checking his two six-guns were snug for the ride. He seemed more interested in how quickly the native handler fetched his horse a drink than discussing tactics. "Ready, Dick?"

Sergeant Northway hesitated, not wanting caution to seem chicken-heartedness, then spoke in his modulated

English way. "Yes, sir, but more than likely they're watching us through opera-glasses right now." He had two prior years in country with the Canadian Mounted Rifles, and respected Boer alertness.

"True enough, Sergeant, but they'll pay more attention to our gun's location than just a couple of riders." Gat's switch to using formal rank showed his irritation. "Let's go."

He called out, "Listen here, fellers! Captain Ross'll lead up the valley to catch the Johnnies between you and the gun. Keep an eye peeled for my signal to attack."

As always when leaving, Gat Howard stood in his saddle to wave and call, "Good luck, boys!" He cantered off ahead of Northway and the Auxiliary. As they disappeared over the rise, Harry wondered how many Boer binoculars were paying particular attention to that black man with a rifle on his shoulder. Nobody thought to warn the three females, so they jumped and screamed when Coveyduck's gun-cotton charge exploded with a hollow clang to seal the well-shaft. Lucky they didn't know the houseboy was down there.

Lanyard felt badly about the kid's dog, and got a shovel to bury it. Then he tore the charred sleeve off his shirt and took it over for the little girl. She was sitting in the shade, with nothing more than bandages on her upper body. Her mother looked up from her Bible, straight-faced, and took the shirt from him without a word. She put it around her daughter and whispered something. The little girl squinted up at the horseman, and said solemnly, "*Dankie, rooinek*".

"Shhh!" The vrou was as worried at seeming impolite as about how the soldier might react to the insult. Harry just smiled and waved farewell. The kid had picked up the word, with no idea "redneck" was the Afrikaans sneer at all British settlers and soldiers.

The Royal Army Medical Corpsman shrugged when asked how things looked for the little girl. She'd probably be all right, so long as her burns got treated every few hours and she was able to rest. Not much chance of either though. They both knew how rough a cart journey it would be to the nearest refugee concentration camp, at Barberton, a hundred miles away.

Charlie put Lanyard in charge of the Colt m.g., telling him to take five men as gun-crew and escorts. He picked Art Furby and Terry Bramah for Number One and Two, with Piet and two ex-cowpunchers as outriders. He made a quick check to see the Dundonald cart's two wheels were well greased and that six boxes of belted ammunition sat snug in the panniers. Everybody had a lot of faith in the American Colt. It was air-cooled and seldom clogged, unlike a tetchy water-jacketed Maxim.

"Okay, move out fellers!" Captain Charlie Ross never was much for correct military orders. The Canadian Scouts rode away in column of threes, breaking into a canter without being told to. They set off fast, keen to catch up with Gat and nail the Boers before they got away again.

Lanyard had a couple of steady men for his gun-crew. Bramah was the only fat guy in the outfit. Nobody knew how he kept all that weight on, with their diet of Maconachie's canned stew. Art Furby was a hard-faced Alberta rancher from up Peace River way. He could handle the wildest stallion that ever bucked, so to get over his boredom with a placid draft horse this morning, he was riding it bare-back. He kept the gun-cart close behind Lanyard, clattering along the farm track until they reached Piet Retief road.

Harry waved them to a trot, making good time to be in position for close support-fire. Piet brought up the rear, while the two point men loped ahead on each side, well away from the road, heads turning all the time. They mostly watched the higher koppie to the east, where mist still hung in shadowed clefts, but they had to also watch the open ground that sloped gradually ahead. Boers were so clever at concealment, they could be lying anywhere in the sniper-pits they favoured.

After a while, though, the peaceful scenery reminded one of the Alberta cowboys of riding the range back home, and Bronco Fontaine started to yodel.

> "Moseyed down to Calgary, to see my gal,
> Found that already she'd married my pal.
> Singing ki-yi-yippee, yippy-yi, yippee-yay,
> Ki-yi yippee, yippee-ay."

Harry shouted at him to put a sock in it, so the rest of them could listen out for trouble. Since that insinuation by Mendip, it was hard enough for Lanyard to keep his mind on the enemy. He thought of Beth. Her beauty, laughter, and sweet lips. She could help birth a cow as well as she played the piano. He used to ride in to the Blenkarn farm every chance he got off patrol. Harry told her he loved her, wanted to marry her.

That last night in the garden, she let him get as amorous as long skirts would allow. Addled with lust, he chuckled and whispered, "This what 'hands-upper' means?"

Fiercely, she pushed him apart, flouncing her petticoats down. "That's no joke to any Afrikaner!" She spat, "The most hateful word of all. And just what our friends would call me and father if I married a kakie. I was stupid to get involved with you in the first place!"

Before long, they were arguing bitterly, and Beth sent him away. She made it clear there could be nothing more between them until the war was over or he quit Kitchener's army for good. When he left the next morning, she would not even come out of the stable to kiss him goodbye.

Now, Harry jerked from his reverie as a crackle of rifle shots sounded. The distinctive *pick-pock* of Mausers. Somewhere nearby, their exact location muffled by folds in the ground.

Lanyard punched his fist ahead, signaling to ride towards the gunfire. Sergeant Furby hauled reins left, whipping his horse to a gallop. The carriage wheels bumped over ditches, hit open country, then clattered up the slope after Harry. Already, Piet van Praage had raced to join him, yelling he'd spotted a few Boer horseman coming around behind them. The Canadians halted just before the crest, below the skyline. Lanyard crawled forward with van Praage to look along the valley.

"There!" Piet pointed at where four wagons were parked under trees, no horses or men to be seen nearby. Right then, the first of Captain Ross's troopers charged over the opposite hill, curious about the deserted laager. They were only 20 yards away when Boers sprung their ambush. Shots rippled from trees near the wagons, emptying a half-dozen army saddles by close-range shooting from concealment.

Without spotting any enemy yet, Harry shouted over his shoulder, "To me! Unlimber!"

Furby steered to the crest, unhitched his horse, and ran it aside. Bramah stamped the gun's recoil-plough into the ground. Harry opened an ammo box, and his Number Two latched it to the Colt's left side. Lanyard flipped the breech open, laid the tip of a canvas ammo belt in place, and racked the cocking-handle.

Mausers kept cracking, but he could still only see faint puffs from smokeless powder down there, "Come on, Number One!" he yelled. He whirled, "What the hell's keeping you?"

Bullets spanged off the gun-shield, and one caught Art Furby in the open, halfway back to his post. He moaned "Mother!", then blood gushed from his neck and he lay down to die.

Bronco and the others started firing at a couple of Boers sniping somewhere from the rear. "See to 'em, Piet," Harry called, and straddled the Colt's iron seat. "There's a lot more buggers down here!"

He waved Terry Bramah to take Number Two position at the Colt. They crouched low, flinching while lead splattered the shield. Lanyard span the elevation wheel, tilting the barrel to bear on the distant trees. He guessed the sights at 500 yards, squeezed the brass pistol-grip, and loosed off ten rounds rapid. *Tak-tak-tak!*

"Fifty short!" Bramah reported yards, calm as if at training practice.

Gat's gravelly instructor's voice sounded in Harry's mind. "A machine-gun's like a garden hose, son. Ignore how the stream arcs, just watch where the tip touches down."

Gauging from dust puffed by his test rounds, Harry tilted up the muzzle slowly. He triggered five-round ranging bursts to kick up dirt, gradually marching his shot-fall towards the hidden ambushers.

"Target gained!" Terry Bramah bent to feed the chattering belt.

The Colt settled into a steady yammer, 600 rounds a minute in short aimed bursts, as Lanyard raked the trees with suppression fire. Leaves and branches and flesh tore, men screamed, gray shapes slumped out of bushes, then other Boers darted in retreat from this copper-jacketed rain. Even through the gun's racket, he heard Molly squeal in agony.

He turned to look behind, and a Mauser slug cracked where his head had been. More rounds vibrated close, and the Colt stopped dead. He yanked the cocking-handle but it was jammed solid, the ammo-belt fabric smoldering where a bullet had hit. Rifle-fire stopped down below anyway, so Harry ran to his horse. She whickered when he arrived and petted her to be calm. Molly had a neat hole punched through one ear, and a long gouge along her ribs, but was still steady-legged. He wiped most of the blood from her eyes, but had to get to the scrap in a hurry. He rode her pretty roughly, kicking her ribs, plunging down the slope, a six-shooter in his fist.

He was halfway there when one of the column officers, Major Beatty, galloped towards him, waving his arms. "Too late! They've got Gat!"

That couldn't be true, but Harry used spurs on Molly for

once, raking her in his agony of mind. While she raced towards the wagons, skipping to avoid a dozen Scouts and horses on the ground, Lanyard could see Captain Ross standing with a bunch of men.

Up close, he saw some were crying over two still bodies at their feet. Major Gat Howard and his native scout. Both had been shot several times, at close range judging by powder-burns on their clothes. Harry's throat hurt as he knelt and touched Howard's dead face, just to convince himself.

He looked up dazedly, and saw Ned nearby giving a drink of rum to Dick Northway, propped against a wheel. There was blood all over the Englishman's stomach, ripped by a dum-dum, but he managed to speak clear enough.

"Laager looked deserted. Gat wouldn't wait. Insisted we look in the wagons. He was just pocketing a buckshee box of matches when they shot us." Rum bubbled back into Northway's mouth, and he sucked it weakly.

"Pinked Gat first crack, wounded. I got off a few rounds before they downed me. Pack of 'em came up and riddled Sambo with his own gun. Thought I was a goner, so they rolled Gat over, still alive. All started to jabber, somebody recognized him, I think." Dick's voice faded, "Rotters pumped him full of lead, point blank." Troopers wiped away tears, growling in their throats, and barely noticed that Northway died.

"You heard, guys." Charlie Ross called in a flat voice. "Gather round and raise your right hand. I want you to make a solemn oath. Repeat after me."

So on the afternoon of February 17, 1901, Howard's Canadian Scouts stood bareheaded and vowed
together, "Because of what was done here today, this outfit never takes another Boer prisoner alive."

CHAPTER TWO

The subaltern caught another fly. He watched one hover close within reach, then snatched it out of the air, quick as a mamba. He cupped the blue-bottle buzzing in his fist, stepped over to the high window, and threw it to freedom between the bars.

After four weeks' practice, Harry Lanyard was getting good at fly-catching. The un-glassed window let every kind of winged pest come swarming in, day and night. Maybe they were attracted by the warmth and smells. The square three-storey blockhouse was put up only a month ago, an afterthought to protect the railway station long after there was much danger. Its offices, barracks rooms, and cells alike were filled with the stink of creosote, sawn wood, and fresh concrete baking in the unseasonably high temperatures.

Late April, autumn here, but summer heat hung on, baking the dusty streets. After the morning train arrived, there was not much sound outside, just the occasional rattle of a supply-wagon or crunch of boots when a platoon marched by. Belfast was a dead-and-alive hole. 'Bit like me, Harry thought.

He caught the despair seeping in, and glanced at the narrow army cot, but started to pace the room instead. Back and forth, nine steps between the outside wall and the barred corridor. He did this a few times every hour, a break from lounging in stupefying boredom. He scratched his brownish hair, kept cropped short against lice for a year, but growing in now he was off patrol. His ordinary-looking face was losing its deep tan, too; more like the tennis-court sunburn on the scores of young officers who lounged around town.

Harry stopped pacing, but resisted lying down for a spell. When he was first put in here, he used the bunk a lot. After living rough on the veld, he rediscovered the simple pleasures of a comfortable bed and sleeping undisturbed all night. Pent-up combat strain and exhaustion, followed by arrest, had knocked him out, so that he slept twelve hours at a time. Even then, he tossed and twitched, shouting himself awake, holding his ears in pain at explosions still heard, cheeks wet with tears he could never admit.

When rest eased his shell-shocked nerves and he finally caught up on sleep, the hopeless brooding began. He lay on the bunk by the hour, hands behind his neck, staring at the raw ceiling. He saw the faces of dead friends; over a score more comrades gone during the year since Gat had been killed. Even Molly was taken from him, probably ridden to death by now. The remorse came back; that young Boer, Beth lost forever, concern for his mother and father in Victoria when they eventually heard of his disgrace. Word had not reached Canada yet, though. He could tell that from today's routinely nasty letter from his sister in Montreal.

"You should be ashamed to be a soldier there," Dora wrote. "Every day, we hear evidence of the horrid atrocities you Imperialist marauders are committing in South Africa. Burning the roofs over those innocent housewives' heads, disgraceful accounts of mass assaults on women's virtue, and deliberate extermination of helpless mothers and babies in your concentration camps. All just to protect those mittel-European mine-owners who exploit slaves to gouge wealth out of the Rand's native soil."

Speaking of which, Dora, he thought, Britain's stated aim was to abolish racist laws in the Transvaal's Constitution which forbade any equality between blacks and whites, either in church or state or employment. Once, he had tried to explain to her there was more to the Afrikaners' cause than a romantic crusade for independence. They were also fighting to keep foreign immigrants excluded from citizenship, claim a larger share of goldmine profits, and preserve Boer tyranny over the natives. That view only infuriated Dora even more, and in the end he stopped replying to her angry letters.

This time, his sister's passionate idealism engraved her

blue pencil-point into the paper. "Eye-witnesses from South Africa address our public meetings of the Friends Of The Boers, showing lantern-slides of children like little skeletons. They display ground glass and fish-hooks they swear had been discovered in prisoners' rations. Surely proof that British doctors are waging genocide against the Boer nation." There was a lot more along the same lines, but he had just crunched Dora's letter and thrown it in the bucket.

Boots clattered upstairs, and a Cockney voice bawled instructions across the orderly-room; the army unable to even push paper without making a noise. Harry pulled the wool undershirt over his head, and started doing some Swedish drill. Twenty-five knee-bends. Stand hands on hips, swivel left and right repeatedly. Flop down, body and legs stiff, sideways one-arm pushups. Up, down.

"Well, wonders never cease!" Acting First Lieutenant Glendon Scayles, Army Provost Corps, called ahead through the outside door. That big Regimental Police corporal was behind him as usual, the faithful pit-bull. The Redcaps strode down the corridor, firm-heeled, in perfect step, uniforms crisply starched.

"Up and about for a change." They cracked to a halt in front of the cage. "Healthy exercise is good for a chap." Scayles waited, expecting some response to his rare approval. Harry ignored them, flipping to change arms so he faced away. Up, down.

"Dammit, Lanyard, get to attention when I address you!" The lieutenant was a beefy, rugby-playing sort of young man, not used to being defied. "Or should I just knock some respect into your thick Canadian skull?"

Harry stopped in mid-press, still not looking. He had enough trouble already, but couldn't resist saying, "You could try, I guess." Transferring his weight to tips of his fingers on one hand, he held the body-slant and twisted to look up. "Two of you." He glanced at the big Webley in the corporal's holster. "Armed."

The two-striper screamed, "No insolence when you talks to an officer!"

Harry got up. "I could say the same to you, Corporal." He toweled his armpits, and pulled on his tunic. The RP glanced at the single pip of a second lieutenant on the jacket shoulder, but sneered anyway.

Scayles sounded a mock-groan. "Corporal Gudger has too much regular army service to respect a Colonial amateur like you. In a scallywag mob of irregulars at that. And it's well known you Canadians are the worst looters in the entire army."

He nodded at Gudger to use his keys. "Likely be losing that pip soon, Lanyard, anyway. You're due for the firing-squad, like those murdering Australians."

"Morant was English. Like you."

"Well, he lived Down Under long enough to act like an Aussie. Finally wrote a confession note to Reverend Canon Fisher just before he was executed. Morant was guilty as sin!"

The recent executions of two Australian officers in the British-run Bushveld Carbineers had caused an uproar. Three lieutenants were tried by court-martial and found guilty of killing 12 Boer prisoners and a German missionary who witnessed things. Their defence was that General Kitchener himself had ordered any Boers caught disguised in British uniforms be shot out of hand. Truth be told, Lieutenant "Breaker" Morant had gone on a rampage of revenge, half-crazed with grief after his best friend had been kicked to death by Boers while their prisoner.

General Kitchener was already in political trouble at home over reports of other excesses by anti-commando units, mainly Colonials, and he refused to commute the death sentences of Lts. Morant and Hancock. The other accused, Lt. Wilton, was sent to serve a long term in Gosport Military Prison, where he confessed that Morant had in fact ordered the killing of PWs. But pride was wounded in the newly-formed country of Australia. Most Diggers started to believe the executed men were scapegoats, sacrificed as a sop to soft-hearted critics of the war in Britain.

Now, Lanyard was facing a similar charge, but it was obviously being kept quiet, judging by the silence from Canadian authorities. He could expect no help from them, anyway, as they probably considered it best to leave his predicament as a British affair. His only hope was that Kitchener's fury over yet another undisciplined Colonial would be curbed by reluctance to face some more criticism.

The barred gate clinked open, but Scayles gestured for the prisoner to stay well back. "For some reason, I was told to personally keep a special lookout on you. Can't imagine why. I've put in to go back to the Mounted MPs, and wish I was out on the veld, again. Troops're getting away with too much there. Insolence, desertion, looting."

"Not to mention burning."

"You'll laugh on the other side of your face, soon! The brass have come for you at last."

"Can't say I'll miss your company, bud."

"I'm your superior officer, Lanyard, and you'll address me as 'sir'!"

"Respect goes both ways — Scayles."

The MP glowered and rubbed his heavy jaw, shaved pink and smooth. He looked around the barely furnished cell with a jailer's distaste. The cement floor was swept clean, and there was nothing on the walls but a 1902 calendar with black mourning-crepe around Queen Victoria's picture. "Pigsty. You'll see nobody until you get that unmade bed squared away."

He stood at the cell gate while Harry took apart the three mattress biscuits, stacked them at the bed-end, and folded blankets tightly around the sides. Scayles wrinkled his nose, and snarled at Gudger to have the sanitary bucket changed. A barefoot Basuto fetched a replacement from the storeroom next door, and sidled out with the used one. The native cringed each time he passed Gudger.

Lt. Scayles eyed the taut bedding. "Bit of an improvement. Now if you're smart, you'll mind your manners for once." The policemen stamped away.

A few minutes later, Scayles led in two men, one in a new-looking uniform and carrying a dispatch-case, the other a middle-aged civilian. They stood in Harry's cell, looking around for a place to sit. There was only two chairs beside the small table, and the civilian indicated the officer should take one.

The captain said, "Do, sit down, Mister, er, Lanyard." He looked at the policeman hovering in the passage. "Thank you, er, Lieutenant."

"This officer's still under close arrest, sir. I'll post a man just outside, in case."

A crumpled green packet of Wild Woodbines was on the table. Harry pulled the remaining fag out and tapped it on his thumbnail. "I'm not allowed matches." He looked meaningly at the captain. The man did not offer a light, just frowned, but Harry didn't feel like asking for permission. This wasn't the regimental dining room. Besides, he suspected now would be an appropriate time to smoke his last cigarette.

The civilian leaned over and flicked a gold lighter. Harry nodded thanks, the pair of them weighing each other up through the smoke. The older man was immaculate in a well-cut suit of gray barathea, with a high stiff collar, striped tie, and a monocle dangling from his lapel.

The captain said, "My name is, er, Barlow. I'm with the, ah, Judge Advocate General." He had thick glasses, a moon face, and a small slit of a mouth. "This is Mister, er, Smith. An, ah, observer." He waved at the smoke. Woodbines were five for tuppence and they smoked awful, but Gudger claimed no other brand was available.

Harry blew out another long plume and tapped ash into his palm. "Are you my Prisoner's Friend, defence attorney, or whatever they call it?"

"Good God, no!" Barlow looked shocked. "I'm here only to be sure you fully appreciate the gravity of your, ah, legal situation."

Harry spat a tobacco flake off his lip, "Near as I figure, my situation is I get a fair trial then be taken out and shot." The legal officer leafed through a buff file. "You are facing very serious charges. Pretty, ah, beastly ones." He paused when the Basuto padded in silently, carrying an extra chair. Smith remained standing, watched the black leave, then nodded for Barlow to go on.

"Your alleged offences include murder of a wounded enemy prisoner, contrary to the rules of war." Barlow's mouth went tight as a hen's arse. "Committed in a barbarous manner. What puts a particularly bad light on things, the alleged incident was witnessed by two Belgian military attaches."

"In the middle of all that shellfire? Even if they'd been close enough to see what I did, they could never hear why." Harry walked over and threw his fag-end into the bucket.

"Have a care!" Barlow stammered. "It's best you don't make any, er, incriminating comments at all. This isn't a privileged conversation, so we could be called to witness against you."

"Won't make much difference, with everybody else so keen to swear my life away."

"No question, you are in very difficult circumstances, indeed. Facing summary court-martial for a capital offence. With apparently overwhelming evidence, unbiased believable witnesses, and past association with similar, ah, proclivities."

Harry knew the lawyer meant those prisoners rumoured to have been lynched by his old regiment. He was about to point out that nothing had ever been proved about the incident, when Barlow went on. "And of course, the unfortunate, er, blood oath you took."

"That was in the heat of the moment. Christ, we'd just

found our C.O. shot out of hand!" He tried to get the man in civilian clothes to say something. "You'd understand, sir." Despite the Burlington Bertie get-up, Smith had British Army written all over him.

The stubble mustache twitched, and he spoke for the first time, "It'd be helpful if you let Captain Barlow finish." His voice was quiet, precise, but with a steely edge of command.

"I want to make clear just how strong the case is against you." The lawyer would look anywhere but at Harry. "Most of your original regiment have returned to Canada, and you subsequently served in two different units." He glanced at the file and frowned suspiciously, "After you received a commission, Howard's transferred you to Rimmington's Scouts for some, ah, reason."

"Normal procedure. The army doesn't like new officers to stay in the same outfit where we've served in the ranks. Afraid the men might act too familiar."

"Ah, I daresay, but both units have been re-organized since. So, any defence lawyer would be unable to locate character witnesses in your favour."

"Hell, just call Charlie Ross up from Cape Town! He knows I never condoned his reprisals."

"Captain Ross has also returned to Canada", Barlow cut in. "Rather quickly. To avoid prosecution on charges of stealing Crown property, um, cattle-rustling."

Loud mechanical noises jangled outside, as the morning train from Komati Poort passed close by the cell window. In the quiet that followed, Mister Smith strolled to the gate and looked left and right along the corridor. He came back and offered a black-lettered cigarette tin. "Perhaps you'd prefer one of these." Harry took it, a Balkan Sobranie. He nodded thanks, and the pair of them lit up.

Smith, or whoever he was, sat down and pushed the round tin of fifty close to Harry, along with a box of Swan Vestas. The lawyer turned his attention to straightening papers in the dispatch-case.

"I hear you were engaged to a nice young local gel, Lieutenant." This cool Englishman seemed hardly the type for idle conversation, but Harry decided to just enjoy the rich tobacco.

"Almost, but it didn't come off in the end."

"Oh, too bad. Someone mentioned you used to visit her father's place every spare moment." Smith turned the lighter end over end on the table, and said casually, "Enormous spread, near the Mauchberg Range. What was it called, now?"

Harry said, "Farm Vincennes."

"Ah, yes. I understand you were based around there for some time, chasing Johnny. Probably know the ground well."

He flicked ash towards the bucket, and went on in a harder tone. "Lieutenant, we wanted you to know first how badly it could go for you at any field court, before we offered a possible alternative."

Harry nodded slowly, "I catch your drift. Something to save Kitchener the embarrassment of executing another Colonial. Maybe I agree to plead guilty, and get off with a mere ten years' hard labour in Gosport?"

"Listen to me, man. I'm offering you a chance to avoid the firing-squad!" Smith bit each word for emphasis.

Despite himself, Lanyard felt the hope rising inside. This guy seemed straight enough, and anything would be better than being shot at dawn for a shameful crime. Still, he couldn't bring himself to show his sick, almost squirming, relief at the possibility of reprieve. To gain time to think, he carefully stubbed out the Sobranie on his boot-sole. Nothing came to him, though, so he met Smith's waiting stare.

"Well, okay, what is the offer, sir?"

Barlow answered instead, speaking formally. "Er, all charges to be dropped, contingent upon you being reduced to the rank of private, and guiding one last patrol." He read wording carefully from a slip of paper. "Also, should you, er, return, you will be released from His Majesty's service and, ah, repatriated to Canada without delay."

"That's it, your wonderful deal?" Somehow, Harry felt more disappointment in Smith than he did about the shabby terms. "Bust me, deport me, after I do some dirty-work?"

"Perhaps we could look at things more from a soldier's perspective." Smith's comradely tone excluded the legal officer. "Consider, the patrol we propose could help save a lot of lives, on both sides. And you're best equipped to pull it off."

"Yeah, as a private, facing dishonorable discharge!" The scorn in Harry's voice made Barlow recoil. "Listen, I volunteered to get into this war, remember? All the way from Victoria, British Columbia. A pokey little corner of the Empire you probably never even heard of!"

His outburst seemed to embarrass Barlow more than anything, but Smith took in every word when Harry went on. "I even signed up with a new British unit, Strathcona's Horse, when his Lordship's recruiting agents came over to Canada. Our regiment cost him half a million as his personal donation to the British Army."

"A fine regiment, of course." Smith jerked an approving nod. "Hear one of your Strathcona chaps got a VC at Wolve Spruit."

"Yeah, and he's back home in bed, now!" Harry laughed shortly. "If I'd wanted a short war, I could have just joined the Victoria Field Artillery for a one-year tour. When the Canadian contingents left, I stayed on instead, and joined Howard's Scouts. I've been in the thick of it for over two years, and I Goddam-well earned my lieutenant's commission!"

"No-one denies you're a good soldier, Lanyard," Smith said quietly. "Though you made a bit of a black mark when you did away with that prisoner."

"Speaking of which, Kitchener's own orders for shooting prisoners are posted on the orderly-room wall upstairs."

"Ahem," Barlow chimed in. "They specifically refer to the lawful, er, execution of enemy caught disguised in British uniform, or with expanding bullets in their possession."

"Yeah, sure, circumstances alter cases. Except for me."

"Not entirely," Smith said. "Hear me out, and perhaps it'll change your mind."

"Sure, when pigs fly!" Then Harry stopped himself, sat down, and reached for another fancy fag.

Smith laid something on the table with a hard click. "Know what this is?"

Harry turned it over idly in his hand, a small smooth disc that looked like gold. It could have been a coin, except for its lack of any embossed design. "Haven't the foggiest."

"*Kaal ponde*, the Boers call 'em. Naked pounds, because they're unmarked." Smith bounced the disc in his palm. "Thousands of these have started turning up all over Europe, then recently in South Africa. First clear signs we've had of Kruger's gold. You were out here when he did a bolt. 'Must have heard all the talk at the time."

"Yeah, Oom Paul's treasure." Harry sucked his cheek mockingly. "That story's so old, it's got hairs on it."

"His gold's real enough, Lieutenant!" Smith snapped. "Filched all along his escape-route. President Kruger cleaned out the Jo'burg mines, the National Mint, and every bank vault between Pretoria and Machadodorp. A fortune in blank sovereigns like these, plus *veld ponde* stamped coins, bullion bars, and paper currency."

"Sounds like a ton weight. How much dough are we talking about?"

"All indications are, he decamped with well over three million pounds Sterling aboard his private train."

Harry blew a silent whistle. "Fifteen million dollars!" A huge sum of money; nigh impossible to even imagine when ten dollars a week was considered a good wage.

"Quite. You can imagine our interest." Smith said dryly.

"We ferreted out a chap who rejoices in the name of P.J. Raubenheimer, one of the ex-train guards. He turned over to us a receipt signed by Senhor Machado, the Portuguese station-master at Lourenco Marques. It was dated the twentieth of May, Nineteen-Hundred, acknowledging the import into Mozambique of three million in Transvaal state gold. For a goodish time, we assumed it all went with Kruger aboard the Gelderland, that cruiser the Dutch sent to take him into exile."

Harry shrugged, "So it's long gone." He wondered where this conversation was headed.

"Most. But by no means all." Smith held up his hand for a moment, ear turned towards the corridor, before continuing. "A German ship-chandler in Delagoa Bay now informs us that around the same time up to fifty cases of gold were also put aboard two German liners there, consigned to Dresdner Bank in Hamburg."

"Rhodes' financiers, how about that. Cashing in from both him and the enemy."

Smith ignored the comment. "Granted a million quid's worth of the loot's been spent in Europe for Boer military supplies. And though Kruger's living comfortably enough in Europe, he has just fifty thousand in his own bank account. So we asked, where's the rest, pray?"

He lowered his voice to a half-whisper. "From what Intelligence has pieced together, perhaps half the total loot was left behind, hidden here and there before his train passed through Komati Poort."

"Could be the Boers're pulling somebody's leg. They do that a lot."

The flinty eyes glinted with irritation, but Smith managed to go on calmly, "Last week, our agents located a chap called Schwartz, who was Kruger's personal coachman. He boasted that while the Presidential train was at Nelspruit, Kruger personally ordered him to take two ox-wagons loaded with gold and bluebacks and bury the lot somewhere near the Devil's Knuckles."

Smith paused for emphasis. "Schwartz refused to say

exactly where, and he's managed to disappear on us again, before we could, ahem, question him a little more forcefully. Best indications are, though, it's hidden on or near that Vincennes place. Your old staging-grounds."

"Anyone who thinks those crafty locals wouldn't have sniffed it out long ago must be pretty stupid." Harry didn't care about military courtesy anymore. What else could they do to him now?

Smith waved impatiently. "They haven't, yet. More to the point, imagine the ramifications if President Burger, say, or General De Wet, got their hands on even a fraction of that much money. It could prolong the war for Lord-knows how long. Help them buy new weapons and provisions, not to mention bribing politicians and newspapers for Boer support all over the shop."

"If."

The unruffled way Smith kept taking all Harry's lip hinted there was still something left unsaid. "Plenty of German and French arms salesmen certainly think it exists. Including some British scum, too. Just the hint of new Boer funds has brought them all flocking back to Mozambique in hopes of profit from smuggling supplies across the frontier."

He rubbed a tiny *mopane* fly out of his eyelid, then said reasonably, "You know every mile of the region where the treasure is. You can find it if anyone could, and help knock Johnny out of the war."

"How big a patrol would a private command?"

"Over-large a force would draw too much attention. Eighteen men with two officers should do it. We've rounded up some chaps who were in the Scouts with you. Pick anyone else you think'll be useful as well."

Smith cleared his throat. "You've already met your assigned patrol leader. Lieutenant Scayles."

Harry slapped the table hard, and scraped to his feet so fast the chair went flying. "So that's the nigger-in-the-woodpile you've been hiding!"

Not looking into Harry's angry face, Barlow explained

primly. "With, ah, so much money involved, this must be an army police matter, kept entirely under Provost Marshal protection."

"Yeah, and entirely madness! I get busted down to a shilling-a-day private to guide a patrol into the mountains where every Boer's out to plug me personally, while Scayles of all people gives me orders?" Lanyard forced a laugh, and jerked his thumb towards the gate. "Let's call it a day, gentlemen. Even a court-martial offers better odds!"

The civilian shook his head slowly, then Barlow threw up his hands. "Very well, C.M. proceedings will start against you tomorrow morning." He looked Harry up and down. "If you have a more, er, presentable uniform, you'd be well advised to wear it in court." He snapped his briefcase shut and walked out.

Smith turned stiffly in the gateway, "I do wish you'd reconsider, my boy, if only for your own sake." He sounded genuine. "By the by, Lieutenant Scayles was not told of our plans for him. Best keep it that way, now."

He left the Sobranies and matches on the table.

CHAPTER THREE

Dead on noon, the ceiling thundered to hob-nailed boots stampeding from the three-storied blockhouse. Soldiers hurried downstairs, jingling knives and forks, calling jokes, pushing like schoolboys to be the first outside. They joined the sudden throng in the street, as the entire garrison headed for the cookhouse.

Even in wartime, Tommies seemed to set their clocks by tea-breaks and meals, but the hour for dinner at mid-day was their favorite. It was more a social habit than hunger, as what they were served was awful. Poor quality food further ruined by bad cooking. Harry thought that rations were the worst aspect of being stationed in a British garrison town. The soldiers all complained about it continually, yet shoveled the slop down readily enough. They knew to eat whatever was served, or starve. Portions were small, no seconds allowed.

There were still plenty of veteran Regulars among them, but most infantrymen in South Africa now were green young recruits with an average of six months service. They had volunteered for the duration of hostilities, either out of patriotism or because sailing off to war seemed rather a lark. It was the ordinary Tommy's endless cheerfulness that always struck Harry. Rigidly disciplined, constantly bullied by n.c.o.s, flung wastefully into battle by thick-headed senior officers, they were paid a miserly shilling a day. Yet the English troops kept up a sort of joint merriment in each others' company, quick to make a joke out of almost every daily incident.

Harry could also sometimes hear Canadian voices among the passers-by. Their familiar tones mixed with other Empire accents, Aussies and Kiwis and Springboks. They were sent to the Holding Depot here from various re-organized regiments and disbanded irregular units. Halfway along the eastern railway line to the frontier, Belfast was once briefly in the news during a British victory over the

Boers at Elandspruit just up the road. Now it was just an administrative backwater, the ideal dumping-place for every odds-and-ends soldier who lacked a parent unit.

The war was in its third year, being fought in a grimmer style. Even though the governments of the Orange Free State and Transvaal had officially surrendered in 1900 after six months of formal war, the bitterenders continued to fight on as guerillas. Whitehall was impatient to close the tiresome business, while the Boers knew only to prolong their struggle as long as God gave them breath.

While he was part of it, out there on the sharp end, Harry had enjoyed an odd exhilaration, pitted against worthy opponents every day. He figured those commandos were among the most effective mounted infantry ever. But after being taken out of the excitement of combat, he wasn't sure he liked soldiering as much. In his own experience, there were not even that many perks to being a junior officer.

Normally, Lt. Lanyard would have a batman, a private assigned as a personal servant to look after him, like every other British officer. The privilege was often dropped while out on the veld, but he normally could expect it now he was in garrison. Probably it was being withheld because of the murder charge, and the closest thing to a batman he had was the Basuto cleaner.

Silent as ever, the native came in with a tin plate holding the main course, watery boiled potatoes and slices of gray beef. Having no tray, he had to bring each dish separately, in and out several times. Gudger stood by the gate irritably, scowling at the delay. Next came a chipped enamel mug, with a china teapot as faint concession to Lanyard's commissioned status. A yellow dollop of what might have been custard pudding was last to be fetched.

Corporal Gudger left the gate unlocked. "Better get that grub inside you, uh, sir. You've more visitors upstairs."

Harry stopped trying to chew a slice of boiled leather, and looked questioningly. The corporal did not explain, other than sneering, "One's a lady, so you mayn't want to keep her waiting, you being an officer and gentleman."

He stamped outside, and started yelling. "You idle bloody nig-nog! Always hanging about with your ear-holes open. Bugger off and do something useful!"

Lanyard slowly ate what he could stomach, in no hurry to meet his callers. Salvation Army workers were the only visitors ever allowed into his cell. They always spoke kindly and brought him little treats, like Fry's chocolate biscuits. Grateful to them as he was, he did not relish it when the Sally-Anners insisted he join them in long prayers. The door opened and he braced himself to be polite.

Three people came into the corridor, escorted by Gudger. Lanyard couldn't believe she was here. Bethany Beatrix Blenkarn handed her parasol to the black maid, then stepped towards him. She was grave, unsmiling, but with a flush to her cheeks.

"Hello, Harry." Her voice was low, a nice mixture of American and Afrikaans.

He stammered something, reaching to take her in his arms, but she offered her hand instead. He felt her small firm grip in the white glove, and wanted to kiss her until her ears fell off.

In the corridor, Gudger said politely, "I'll look after that for you, shall I, sir?" Nikki tried to look puzzled, so the corporal chin-motioned to the bulge in the alpaca jacket and opened and closed his fingers insistently. The Russian sighed, but handed over a chrome-plated revolver from his inside pocket.

"You can pick it up when you leave, sir. In fifteen minutes." Gudger herded the Basuto attendant outside, away from giggling with the maid.

The last time Harry saw Beth, she was in an old frock and sacking apron, tending a sick foal. Now, she wore a smart traveling suit of blue silk-weave cotton. Its short embroidered jacket with leg-of-mutton sleeves was open to show a pleated white blouse that swelled agreeably. Her starched collar had a tie patterned in green, red, white, and blue, like the Transvaal Vierkleur flag. She had a little slouch hat with the brim curled up on one side, held atop her blonde hair by pearl-capped hair-pins. The skirt was cut fashionably short, revealing her ankles above blue walking shoes. She bought all her town clothes from Lord & Taylors, far away in Chicago, a taste she developed during four years' education in the 'States at Terre Haute Academy.

Beth's elegance made him feel aware of his own scruffiness, in stocking feet and singlet. He had paid the Basuto five cigarettes to take away his tunic and boots for cleaning. "It's swell to see you, Beth. How the heck did you know?"

"Oh, you're famous on the veld, the King's Cowboy who rode a big mare with a hole in it's ear." She smiled wanly. "Everybody knows where you are now. And why."

"Some would even call you infamous, old chappie." Feliks Nikolai strutted in, tall, athletic, shooting the starched cuffs of his shirt. The two men didn't bother to shake hands.

She saw Harry's face had thinned, but his eyes seemed a clearer blue-green than ever. She forced her voice to sound harsh. "You know why I came."

"Just couldn't stay away, right?" He tried to smile. "Here, sit down."

"As your comrade said, we only have a few minutes."

"Yeah, let's catch up, Beth. How's Hiram?"

"Dada is well, thank you, and would have sent his regards. But ..." Lanyard imagined the tough old Hoosier's dilemma, unable to bridge their friendship now, considering the murder accusation.

Hiram Blenkarn had never been back to Vincennes, Indiana since he arrived in South Africa thirty-odd years ago and married a fine Boer girl. She died of puerperal fever in giving birth to their son, but Hiram stayed on the big farm they developed together. After a lifetime spent here, he no longer thought himself still a uitlander like most other settlers did. He was so proud of his adopted country, Blenkarn even gave up his American citizenship to become a legally enfranchised Transvaaler. He boasted he had sworn the loyalty oath to President Oom Paul Kruger himself.

"Send him my best regards, anyway. Irkie okay, then?"

"Dirk," she corrected, and tilted her chin proudly, "He's away, with friends on the veld. I hope with all my heart he does not meet you out there."

"Me too. Be a tough decision for us both if we did."

Harry could tell the boy had gone out as a penkop, an under-age soldier serving with a commando. He'd known Irkie well, a skinny kid with a big grin and the fondness for killing animals. He carried that little slide-action Marlin .22 everywhere, shooting any living thing; song-birds, snakes, wild dogs, antelopes. Harry had seen him plink a running leopard in the eye from two hundred yards away. Now, the boy would have graduated to bigger game in his sights.

She made a quick brush at her flaxen hair, trying to erase the image of this man and her brother firing at each other. "The story about you is horrible. You refuse to bargain to get off, so there must be another explanation. I came to hear it from you." She hesitated, "Harry, did you really do what they say?"

Behind her, Nikolai pouted mockingly, and rolled his head in denial like some circus clown. Harry held her gaze as steadily as he could. "Yes."

Beth went pale, and swayed, so he rushed on, "I've been wanting to tell you the whole story ever since it happened."

Yet where could he find the right words to describe that hellish morning? The column he'd been escorting was caught in a gully by Boer artillery firing point-blank from both sides in a sudden blast. Krupp and Cruesot guns pumped heavy shells into a zone of death. Deafening explosions numbed the brain and loosened the bowels; choking yellow clouds of lyddite, shrapnel like razors, a sleet of bullets from Maxims and Mausers. And everywhere the screams of ripped and dying Devonshires who crouched between the rocks.

A crafty pom-pom gunner kept alternating short and long belts, picking off soldiers who made a run for it during what they thought were pauses for re-loading. Harry was pinned down by the Nordenfeldt, shaking, covering his head. He had lost his firearms in the scuttle to cover, but when he heard that young Afrikaner yelling, Harry knew he had to crawl out and get him.

She managed to say, "But how could you do that, deliberately kill a helpless wounded boy?" She was shaking, the pain in her face changing to rage. "In the name of Heaven, *why*?"

"I had to! Listen." He reached out to calm her, but she wrenched away angrily.

"Had to? Had to come all the way from Canada to burn our homes, murder our women and children!" Spittle flew from her beautiful, twisted lips. "Had to hate one Boer youngster who stood against the might of the British Empire!" She half-sobbed, "And had betray me, all along!"

Bethany flung back her arm, giving him plenty of time to block it, but he just stood there and let her slap his face hard as she could. "*Skelm!*" She hit him again, weaker this time. She turned away, almost blind with loathing and sadness, banging the gate-bars as she ran out, pushing her maid ahead into the street.

"Not wise, Lanyard." Nikki sighed loudly and sat down, crossing his long legs. "Always, when a woman offers you an opportunity to lie, she wants you to."

"Yeah, advice from an expert liar. Why don't you just shove off?"

"Such crude manners. But, then, you've been in the army far too long, just dumbly obeying orders. Forgotten how to watch for the main chance."

The Russian leaned back, cocky as ever. "England will

never really win this war, you know. Its troops are brave, but too soft and poorly led. Parliament sends a powerful army, then gets cold feet when things drag on and turn nasty. Now, your politicos pay more attention to wailing women and cheap newspapers than to your generals." He picked lint from his sleeve. "A few regiments of Cossacks would have ended things here long ago."

Harry only half-listened, feeling the welts rising from the stinging hand-print on his cheek. The guy always did like the sound of his own voice.

"The British Empire, phooi! Russia conquered most of Asia in twenty years, from the Urals to Kamchatka. We slaughtered millions of savages and razed their primitive cities. Not like you here, wasting troops in return for a few farm hovels and penny-packets of enemy dead. Even when the commandos do surrender, your spineless government will hand this country back to them, anyway!"

"Anybody would think your time with Maximoff's commando prejudiced you against us," Harry drawled. "One good thing, the MPs tell me the Czar's stopped paying you to stir up the locals."

Nikki shrugged, "I admit, I had certain sub-rosa duties, but it seems our Holy Emperor's enthusiasm for interference in South Africa has faded. Time to look after oneself now." He stared unblinkingly, "As you should, too. We have a common problem to solve, and an uncommon opportunity."

"There'll be no problem if you just stop sniffing around Beth."

Nikolai preened his Macassar-oiled black hair. "My interest is on more important things than Miss Blenkarn's pantalettes." He held up a calming hand. "Escape for you, profit for us both." His English was near perfect, but the way he mouthed every word like a bon-bon always irritated Harry.

"How come you're here with her?"

"Hiram asked me to escort her when she insisted on

coming to see you." He leered, "As protection from all these rough British soldiers crazed with lust for innocent Boer girls."

"You plan to keep her in town overnight?"

"Bourgeois morals, Lanyard. If you must know, we stayed well apart at the hotel overnight, and have tickets back to Alkemaar on the afternoon train." Nikki slowly looked around the bare cell. "More important, you could be off and sleeping far away on the veld tonight."

"That's funny, considering I spent weeks around Vincennes watching my back against you bush-whacking me."

That was after they came to blows over the man's continual sneers that Russia would soon lead a European consortium to force British troops to leave Boer homelands. Czar Nicholas II seethed with anti-British hatred, which said something about his attitude towards his grandmama, Queen Victoria. Even after she died, the Czar kept threatening to send his troops against India while the British were safely occupied in South Africa. Though there was not enough evidence to deport him, the Military Police were sure Nikolai had originally come to the Transvaal as a secret agent of the Okhrana.

The day Harry finally took a poke at Nikki, Beth stopped them before the scrap got interesting. Maybe she knew that the real reason they fought was over the Russian hanging around her. He had plenty of opportunity. Despite the Russian's periodic drunken binges, Hiram Blenkarn for some reason still allowed Nikki a semi-permanent berth at one of the guest cottages.

It was explained a moment later, when Nikolai sneered, "Like everybody else in Transvaal, that crippled old Yankee lost his life-savings when Kruger robbed the banks. So I lent him a considerable sum from certain operational funds, to keep Vincennes going, purely out of the goodness of my heart. At wartime interest rates, naturally." Nikki gave his man-of-the-world shrug. "Shortly after which, my regular stipends from Saint Petersburg ceased arriving. Now Blenkarn says he can't repay anything for a while, leaving me temporarily embarrassed for cash. But a cartload of bullion, aah, that could solve all one's future needs."

Harry managed to keep poker-faced, hiding his shock that the Russian knew. Nikolai tapped a finger to his lips. "From what that kaffir let slip while we were cooling our heels outside, you and I can reap both our salvations. A key easily stolen from the stupid Tommies upstairs, a horse standing by. You could be away soon as it falls dark. Together, we surely could find Kruger's gold. Split fifty-fifty like gentlemen, naturally."

First Beth's informed remark about him not bargaining, now this. Harry saw the way Smith's plan was compromised by what they'd uncovered on their visit. Having learned about the patrol to recover Kruger's loot, both would know the hunt might fail without him to lead it.

Rum situation. He could expect no help from her, who had loved him, yet this man who was his enemy was offering to arrange a high-risk jailbreak. If Beth heard of any attempt to get him away, she would feel it her duty to turn him in to the British, to ensure he faced punishment for murder. She would not only want him tried for the crime itself, but also to keep Kruger's gold out of British hands.

Nikki's motive was not as complicated, if just as obvious. While a Russian agent, he had ridden the area around Vincennes for months, spreading bribes and sedition, and was on good terms with the locals. Probably he could track down the bullion himself without any help from Lanyard, so the plan would be simply to put him out of commission permanently.

"You must think I'm crazy, to risk my neck out there with a prick like you," Harry said. "Anyway, I've already made up my mind. I'll take my chances with a court-martial, if K allows one."

"Ah, the faithful soldier's touching faith in his superiors." Nikolai did not try to hide the triumph in his eyes. A military prison or firing-squad would keep Harry away from the gold-hunt just as effectively as an assassin's bullet. He sighed like a stage actor. "Well, our last farewell, I think. Nothing else for it but to call your lummox corporal to return my Nagant, and be off." He rattled the tin cup back and forth along the bars.

The commotion brought Scayles and Gudger down in a hurry, and they glared their annoyance at Nikki for alarming them. The corporal showed the Russian out, returning his shiny pistol with the cylinder open and bullets removed.

Nikki waved a jaunty hand without looking back, and crooned, "'Bye-bye, Harry. I'll be sure to take good care of Beth for you."

"Distinctly dodgy cove, that Russky, from all I hear." Scayles pulled back his cuff, checking a wrist-watch. Another affectation, Harry thought. Any man wearing one of those new ladies-style timepieces would draw snickers from real soldiers.

Scayles penciled a note about the visit in a small notebook before he locked the gate. "Obvious you're not choosy about your acquaintances, Lanyard. Though I must say, your farmer's daughter looks toothsome enough."

He brayed a boys-together laugh, "You did well to get organized with a white popsie out here. Most Boer girls spit at us." He leaned close. "Is it true they never wear—?"

Harry's hand snaked between the bars, caught Scayles by the collar, and slammed him forward against the ironwork. There was a satisfactory crunching noise, and blood spurted from the policeman's nose.

CHAPTER FOUR

"Stupid kakies are easy to kill!" Dirk laughed harshly, but was annoyed at how boyish his voice still sounded. He tried to deepen his tone, and kicked wood into the campfire. "They march in straight lines, or ride without keeping watch, and when they stop, they're too lazy to dig proper rifle-pits. We just have to kill enough, and the rest'll run off with their tails between their legs."

Dirk Blenkarn thought even the dullest kaffir could act with more sense. All you had to do was hide behind a rock while a British patrol rode by, and shoot the last man at the rear, then be off and away before they knew what hit them. Those rare occasions when soldiers did know where Boers were, snug behind little schantzes of rocks, Tommies would still come charging upright, and you could pick them off, pop-pop, just like that.

"There's more to our struggle than the shedding of blood," Wim Hartsma said. He must be at least forty, and sounded a bit soft in the head sometimes. "It is a serious thing to take the life of any white man, and a matter for prayer afterwards. It would be the Lord's blessing if this killing stopped."

"We can't do that, until all the rooineks go back where they came from."

"You're a brave boy, but wrong-thinking. Better you were still in school."

"That's over. I'm a penkop for General Botha, now!"

"You come from a good home, with a rich father. He is not here, so why are you?"

"I came in his place."

Hartsma's servant leaned to pour more coffee into the boy's tin mug, and Dirk scowled at him. Filthy kaffir. He had one of them to thank, though, for coming out on commando. This all started with Christmas, only five months ago.

The farm's head boy had come galloping into the yard of Vincennes, yelling that soldiers were wrecking the Hertzog's farm. Dirk heard from the stable, where he was shooting rats. He ran to hold the bridle of the horse that was plunging, foam-flecked from the run Christmas had put it to.

The elderly black man waved naked arms, shouting, "The good Lord save us, Master Irkie! Soldiers are coming!" Spittle flew from the nest of his gray beard. "If they know what Baas Blenkarn is doing, they'll burn us out next!"

"Ag, get off there!" Without having to think why he must go, Dirk pulled the Zulu down roughly, and swung himself into the saddle. A wrinkled brown hand reached out and laid hold of the .22 he was still holding. "Best leave that, klein-baas." Dirk felt the Marlin pulled from his grip, and was not able to snatch it back. Silently pleading, Christmas's frown was a mix of fear of arguing with the young boss and concern for the boy's safety.

Dirk kicked the faithful face he's known since babyhood and shouted, "Interfering old bastard!" He lashed the horse and raced away, ignoring Tannie Marthe's voice calling him back.

He found at least thirty soldiers milling around Hertzog's place, some of them bashing rifle butts through window panes to create a better draught. Others were busy at bayoneting sheep, while a corporal yelled at them to get their backs into it as practice for giving commandos some stick. A group of women and children stood huddled on the grass, near a mounted officer who studiously did not look at them. Herzog himself sat on a kitchen chair by the barnyard midden, his back to his home.

It was a little daub and wattle farmhouse, carefully whitewashed to cover green damp stains. Whoops of laughter sounded inside as the Tommies enjoyed themselves at mindless vandalism. Army discipline was relaxed at such times, to distract them from the enormity of destroying a family's home.

A sideboard crashed over with loud smashing of crockery, greeted by cheers. "Whoa, Eliza!" A soldier yelled, "Give us a tune, Archie!" Piano-keys tinkled and twanged from blows with an axe. That set Mrs. Herzog off, and she shouted reproachfully at the young officer, who looked almost embarrassed.

"Hurry them along, Sar'nt," he called. "That's enough fun for one day." He scratched his hair below the white sun-helmet, and Dirk noticed a red diamond patch sewn on its side.

"Cowards!" Dirk shouted. "Frightening grannies and babies! Go pick a fight with commandos, they'd soon kick your arses!" The officer just glanced at him, and he realized he'd been speaking Afrikaans. He switched to English, "You want a scrap, take me on! I'll fight any of you red-necked bastards!"

The lieutenant seemed amused for a moment, then said, "Look, laddie, they're getting what they deserve. So just toddle off."

"I'm not your laddie!" He yelled and stood high on the stirrups with rage.

A spyder cart drove in, Hiram Blenkarn at the reins, with Beth beside him, calling comfort to the Hertzog women. Christmas crouched behind, blood on his whiskers. His father said quietly, "Hold your horses, Dirk." He had never used his son's proper grown-up name before.

"Outside at the double, you perishers!" A strident voice brought troops hurrying through the door, wisps of smoke curling behind them. Herzog looked at the flames and picked up his chair, herding his womenfolk to the far end of the yard.

A boyish soldier went over to the farm-wife, "Here's your family pictures, Missus." She threw the photographs in his face, screamed with indignation, and pointed to something under his tunic. At the lieutenant's command, he reluctantly pulled out two silver picture-frames.

"Take that man's name, Sergeant."

The farm people stared. The officer had turned his soldiers loose to smash and burn their entire home, but now he would punish one of them for looting keepsakes. Boers would never understand these British.

Until a few years ago, Herzog had been a bywoner, a poor tenant worker with no land of his own. It was Hiram who lent him the money so he could get this farm, and been pleased at the way it prospered. "What are the Herzogs supposed to have done?" Blenkarn challenged. "They're good souls."

"Queer thing for a Canadian to say."

"But not for me, being American-born and bred, I'm proud to declare!"

"Ah, I hear some Yanks're in the Irish Commando."

"And I heard Kitchener's supposed to have halted his scorched-earth policy!"

"Quite so. However, these good souls as you call them are reported to have stored weapons for the enemy. Now they must take the consequences." Flames came roaring through the windows.

Bethany challenged, "But did your search find any actual evidence at all?"

"Not this time, miss, but our informants are reliable."

"With 'Occupiers' as new neighbours, I'd doubt the word of anyone hereabouts these days!" Many farms north of the railway had been cleared of commando sympathizers and taken over by Loyalists.

"Please," Beth said, "Can't you at least let the Herzogs move in with us?"

The lieutenant was about to reply, when hundreds of rifle cartridges started to cook off, hidden inside burning walls of the house. A sergeant bawled, "Take cover!" Ammunition popped and cracked, sending bullets flying everywhere, and one man yelped with a flesh wound.

The officer threw the silver frames into the fire. "A

concentration camp will obviously suit them rather well."

Beth would not even look at her brother during the ride home. After they helped Hiram down, she snapped, "Irkie, you have something to say to Christmas, I think."

Tannie Marthe watched with her arms folded while he spoke with the black. She slapped Dirk's ear when he walked past to go inside, "Shame on you!".

Hiram was seated on the back stoep, looking west towards the smoke. The house itself was not visible, as Boer settlers on the veld preferred to build out of sight of any neighbours. He peeled the band off a Henry Clay, and said, "Well, son, did you apologize like a man?"

"Yes, I acted foolishly."

"Every man does in his life." Blenkarn shifted his hip with a grimace, and scratched a match under the chair. After a few puffs, he examined the cigar at arm's length, and spoke more gently than usual.

"Christmas was a great lion-hunter in his time, did you know? Gutsy as only a Zulu can be. When I first arrived, the veld was swarming with lions that ate farmers' cattle like peanuts. The Boers set out to exterminate every one, and Christmas and me would go along to help bag a few. So talking of foolish, I had only one round left in my gun when I treed a wounded big cat. He was making a meal of my backside and would have ate the rest of me soon, if Christmas hadn't killed it with his spear.

" Hiram puffed thoughtfully. "I reckon he may have saved another Blenkarn's life today, holding on to that gun of yours."

Hiram saw the story made the youth feel only more callow, so gave a chuckle and added. "I was laid up with that lion-bite for weeks, and President Kruger came by to wish me well. I said something about my having been foolish. Oom Paul just laughed, and held up the stump where he blew off his own thumb in a hunting accident ages ago. So you're no different."

Dirk might not have heard. He said, "Father, why won't

you let me go and fight the kakies??"

"The law says you have to be sixteen."

"But penkops don't. There's kids as young as eight out on commando."

"Yes, but with their fathers or big brothers." He thumped his hip. "With this, I could never keep up. Besides," He gave a sly smile, "They consider I'm more useful here."

Vincennes had been covertly supplying food to bitterenders for over two years, by leaving produce at hidden places on far reaches of the property. Because no armed Boers ever were seen visiting him, Blenkarn's farm was left unmolested by British patrols.

His son tossed in his seat and glared, and Hiram said, "Wait 'til you're of age, and we'll see."

"But the war might be over by then!"

"In which case, what'll it matter?"

When the house had been quiet for hours that night, Dirk dressed himself in a thorn-proof jacket, corduroys, and heavy *veldskoen* boots. He crept downstairs, and there was enough starlight through the kitchen window to show him where to grab some cheese, bacon strips, and corn biscuits. He stuffed them in his pocket, and walked to the barn. The dogs barked before they smelled who it was, so he had to hurry.

He felt behind the manger box for his Marlin, kept there handy for ratting. Working by touch, he had his pony saddled and was strapping on his bedroll when he saw the lantern coming from the house. Beth held it up at the doorway, Hiram limping in behind.

She said, "Where do you think you're off to, Irkie?"

"To join the Crocodile Commando, of course. And I'm not a kid anymore. My name is Dirk, hear? Don't ever damn-well call me Irkie again!"

He despised their anxiety while they tried to persuade him to delay until he was old enough. Beth pleaded, "We are so proud of you, Dirk, wanting to go, but you are still a boy."

"If you try to stop me tonight, I will only go tomorrow, or the night after that." His voice cracked with determination.

After a long moment, Hiram said simply, "I figured as much, son." He held out his own favorite Mauser, the fine custom-made Plezier model with a sterling silver butt-plate he won years ago at the shooting competition in Jo'burg.

Dirk took it as if in a dream, hands shaking as they caressed the polished stock. There were two filled bandoliers to go with it, and he draped them criss-cross over his narrow shoulders. They were too long for his body, and hung level with his hips.

The sight brought a cry from Beth and she hugged her baby brother close for a long time. She stepped back, brushed her eyes, and pressed a bagful of food into his hands. "Here, without me or Marthe, you'll never eat decent meals out there."

That same bag was beside Dirk now, filled these days with biltong, mealie corn, and strong Arabian coffee. A bite of food and his horse and rifle were all any commando needed. They had no military uniform, just dressed the same as they would on any hunting expedition. A wide-brimmed hat, rough trousers, moleskin coat with the Testament in a pocket, and home-made leather boots.

He had brought a good strong pony from Vincennes. Like every Boer, he considered it part of him, a faithful companion a man took good care of. All his fellow commandos' mounts were the same Cape breed; small and wiry, able to jog along for fifty miles without tiring. They bore any kind of weather, thrived on wild grass or handfuls of hay, but could keep going two and three days without any food if need be. A fighting burgher's horse could carry him anywhere under God's heaven, to raid and shoot and ride away, like a Centaur no kakie could ever catch.

Dirk liked not having to follow any drills or discipline or roll-call. Every Boer was free to come and go from duty whenever he felt like it. Cornets and korporaals were elected by the men themselves, and held rank only as long as the others were content with an officer's performance. If he somehow stopped being popular, he could be demoted right away, and another man chosen in his place.

Dirk had fitted in with the life from the day he first rode into the Crocodile Commando's laager. He made a good start by arriving with a plump antelope across his saddle to share when he reported to Veld-Cornet Vilberg for duty. Veterans four times his age accepted him seriously as a volunteer without any comment about his youthfulness. They were called '*takhaars*', wild hairs, because they let their beards grow so thickly, swearing they would not shave again until the last invader was dead or gone.

The penkop fairly hugged himself with pleasure at being part of this brave company. He listened enthralled as the men spoke of this or that battle or their experiences in the wider world. His new comrades were from all walks of life and backgrounds. City burghers who had previously never been closer to a horse than one pulling an omnibus now rode alongside big-game hunters and tobacco-farmers.

Dirk met doctors, clerks, miners, sheep-herders; men from towns or isolated farms. Among them, was Gabriel Boergaard, the Pretoria lawyer who'd left a well-paid practice in London's Inns of Court to come home to fight, and struck up a friendship with Ino van Kettel, a farmer from Natal who thought the world was flat. They accepted each other as equals in their brotherhood for the Volk's crusade.

Some of the veterans were amused at young Dirk's youthful fierceness but impressed by his skill at shooting, and took him under their wing. Men like Wim Hartsma, the farmer from Orange River, and Ox van Antwerp, the huge blond Fleming, who made him welcome beside their fire.

Ox was inclined to dominate conversations, and spoke mainly in diatribes when their fight for freedom was discussed over every meal. "I put all this war down to the

Randlords, those rich mine-owners," he was saying. "Big financiers, German Joodjes like Alfred Beit and Julius Wernher. And the greedy English, of course, especially Cecil Rhodes. That Barney Barnato's another prize crook, both English and Jew into the bargain."

"Verdomde smous!" Van Kettel growled. "People like them got Milner to start the war just as an excuse to get their dirty paws on our gold and diamonds." Boers grunted agreement, some spitting at mention of such hated names.

"Even the British themselves are finding out too late they were maneuvered into this war." Boergaard fished out a tattered newspaper. "Last month's 'Manchester Guardian'. Here's what their John Hobson had to say."

He read slowly, stabbing an oratorical finger to emphasize certain words he quoted. "We are fighting in order to place a small international oligarchy of mine-owners and speculators in power in Pretoria. Englishmen will do well to recognize that the economic and political destinies of South Africa are, and seem likely to remain, in the hands of men, most of whom are foreigners by origin, whose trade is finance and whose interests are not British.'"

"Yes, men like the Rothschilds and their pocket Prime Minister, D'Israeli!" Van Kettel wrinkled his thick brows, "Another one of those."

"D'Israeli's British-born, and was prime minister long since, Ino, thirty years ago," Advokaat Boergaard corrected mildly. "Lord Salisbury's their Prime Minister now. He's in here, too." He snapped open the paper again. "Listen to the latest what Salisbury says, 'Once victory is secured, steps will be taken to improve the treatment of those indigenous races of whose destiny I fear we have been neglectful.'"

The commandos guffawed, "Indigenous—ooh, lah-de-dah!"

Ox sneered, "Ag, man. Easy for him to say, when there's not a single kaffir within thousands of miles of Parliament!"

"Anyway, the prime minister's nowhere as powerful

here as those London money-lenders or the Dresdner Bank." Boergaard shrugged.

Ox snatched the paper and threw it into the flames. "Scum of Europe hold all South Africa's purse-strings these days, backing both sides against the middle!"

Boergaard said, "There's no point singling out any one group for blame. We've plenty of enemies to go around."

"And some Joodjes have been among our best fighters," Wim chimed in. "Especially the Russian ones. There's Commandant Isaac Herman, and those scouts, Wolf Jacobson and Jackal Siegel. They were on commando from the start, and sent many a Tommy to Heaven."

Ox did not like his bigotry undermined, and switched aim. "We never needed any of those foreign volunteers, either. Kruger told them so himself. But they still came swaggering down here from America and France and Ireland, all flash and big mouths. Expecting we'd make them generals while they showed us ignorant Dutchies how to make war. Ag, I tell you man!" His audience chuckled at the conceit of non-Boers, to think they knew more than God's chosen race of the veld.

"But, Oom Paul did make one of them a general," Boergaard pointed out. "That clever Frenchman, Count de Villebois-Mareuil. He might have helped us win the war, if he hadn't got himself killed making some brave last stand. Same foolishness wiped out that fine Scandinavian Commando, too. Didn't have the sense to run away at Magersfontein, and died to a man, instead."

"Next you'll be praising Rhodes, himself!" Ox snorted, "That gold-grubbing skelm would still be Prime Minister of the Cape, if he hadn't sent Doctor Jameson to raid us, and got sacked for it by the British Parliament!"

"Now, Jameson, there's a man due every Boer's thanks," Boergaard chortled. "Without his raid showing us Britain intended to annex the republics, Oom Paul might never have declared war. All those Uitlanders would have kept pouring in, and they'd outnumber us in our own country by now."

Hartsma clapped Dirk on the back. "Hear that, youngster? Maybe we should put up a monument to the bungling Doctor Jameson someday!"

That drew a laugh, and conversation turned to lighter things. "You want another good joke?" van Kettel chuckled. "Last time I was home in Durban, I saw Brit immigrants shoveling cow-shit and digging ditches. White men doing kaffir-work!" More laughter boomed, just at the stupid picture of such a thing.

"That sort of thing's funny now, but the Swart Gevaar's going to be our biggest problem ahead," Boergaard said. "The black peril could swamp all whites one day, if we Volk don't keep an iron hand."

Trying to keep his end up, Dirk put in, "I read an American paper that says the English intend to give blacks the franchise."

Everybody hooted, falling about at the youngster's naivety. "Man, that's a good one." Ox slapped his thigh. "Our kaffirs will never be allowed to vote — not even if they wait a hundred years!"

Mealtimes passed merrily like that for Dirk in camp, but he started chafing at the lack of contact with the enemy. He spent as much time as he could going after game, always bringing back something for the flesh-corporal, who's job was to share out meat for the pots.

The new penkop's success as a hunter often drew attention to his fine rifle. It was a rarity these days, as Mausers were seldom used anymore because of lack of ammunition. Most commandos had adopted Lee-Metfords, captured from British supply-columns along with thousands of .303 cartridges.

Ox was the sole other commando to still carry a Mauser. He found a fresh supply of 7mm. rounds during a raid, a box of Kynoch bullets, labeled 'Mark IV Soft Nosed. For game hunting only'. They were the type called Dum-Dums, after the factory in India where they were made. Ox was running a risk, as using expanding bullets against white men was considered an atrocity. Anyone caught with them invited summary execution by the kakies.

Dirk had been thrilled at the chance to fire his Plezier in anger within a month of joining the commando. They were awoken one morning at dawn, and allowed only a half hour for coffee and the singing of psalms that started each day. Veld Cornet Laurens Vilberg told them of a good opportunity to attack an isolated column of beaters the British had sent out to drive Boers against the army's barbed wire obstacles that now criss-crossed the veld.

On the way, Ox and Corporal Schippers came to ride on both sides of Dirk. "This is your first time, boy," Schippers said, "So pay attention to what the others do. Don't shoot until I give the command. And most important of all, stay hidden like we do."

"Ja," Ox added seriously. "Remember, you don't have to impress anybody how brave you are, boy. No jumping up to cheer. And always keep one foot turned behind, ready in case we tell you to run away."

They saw the soldiers coming from far off, easily hid from the Lancer scouts probing ahead, and snuggled down with good fields of fire. Vilberg signaled start to the attack by shooting an officer off the lead wagon.

Boer marksmen felled soldiers dead where they stood, until the rest responded to sergeants' orders and took cover. Their discipline under fire was more sensible than it had been in the early days of war in South Africa. There was less emphasis on senseless bold charges, and more attention paid to lying down before returning enemy fire. But the bare killing-ground chosen by the Boers had few rocks to hide behind, and the khaki targets were easy to hit.

Dirk realized he was gawping at the scene like a lumpen visiting his first traveling circus. Eighteen-year-old Boschie Petersen called, "Hey, penkop, don't you want to get your nice gun dirty?"

He snapped out of his trance, and worked a round into the Mauser's chamber. He noticed a soldier hopping on one foot from a wound, and took a careful bead on him. He squeezed gently, the Mauser bucked against his shoulder, and the soldier fell down. Killing a man was simple, no more difficult than shooting game for the pot.

Dirk yelled a primitive sound, and started working the bolt quickly. Back, forward, squeeze. He emptied the magazine in less than a minute, picking targets and shooting in a crazy blur of excitement. Sweat and heat-haze and cartridge fumes blurred his sight, and he lost count of how many men he shot. A new cloying pleasure surged through him, and he felt gloriously powerful.

From somewhere, he heard Hartsma shouting, "Stupid kid, come the blazes out of there!"

He only noticed then the others were scrambling back the way they'd come. Vengeful yells sounded close beyond his sheltering rock. He caught sight of big Englishmen in sun-helmets lumbering uphill, bayonets twinkling. Cold steel in battle was something all Boers detested. They thought it barbarous for white men to spear each other like savages. Dirk ran for his life, but carrying with him a new feel of power he had never known before.

Since then, he had taken part in three more commando ambushes. Once, he went out on his own, and managed to snipe a careless kakie riding too far behind his comrades. Each time he killed brought a God-like feeling of exultation. The blasphemous thought made him guilty now when he heard the impromptu chorus of psalms start up around the campfire before they moved off.

They would be at worship for half an hour at least, and Dirk reached for his Mauser. He oiled it, then carefully filed the six notches in its stock more evenly.

"It is not seemly to keep score of the men you kill," Hartsma said. "Besides, it could be dangerous to be caught with a tally cut on your gun. Tommies would think it as bad as if you carried dum-dums." He pointed a finger at his temple, "Then, *phut*!"

"They have to catch me first."

Hartsma tapped out his pipe, and grunted. "Time for services, youngster." He used the word in mischief, amused at how references to his youth always made the lad flush angrily.

The Boers often played little jokes on each other, like an egg in someone's blanket, or gunpowder sprinkled in a tobacco pouch. Under their rough humour, was quiet scrutiny of how well a man took teasing, or if he lost his temper easily. They had noticed already that Dirk's constant smile could sour in a moment if he was the butt of remarks, and how quickly he flared up.

Dirk dragged his feet to the choir group, moving his mouth without voicing proper words of praise to Jehovah. Ever since he was a small child, he privately disliked having to take part in the religious activities that filled every Boer's days. He always jibed at being taken by cart miles each Sabbath to church-meetings, and standing by the hour singing eternal psalms. \

He had expected to escape piousness when he joined the takhaars, but discovered they were, if anything, even more deeply religious in their feelings out here. Burghers studied their Testaments at all hours, squinting to read by firelight, and even during lulls in a battle.

They took up humming praise to the Lord again now when they rode off in the moonlight, headed north to the main laager. Dirk chafed at the doleful tunes, and set other youngsters snickering when he imitated the droning. That devout old Huguenot, Lucien Languedoc pulled his horse alongside,"If you truly want to be part of our brotherhood, rich boy, let us hear if your voice is strong as a man's yet."

Others growled mockingly, agreeing with the challenge. He could not remember a single full verse of psalms, but he hated to be humiliated by staying silent. After a moment, Dirk threw back his head and began to sing in a clear light voice.

> "My Sarie Marais is so far from my heart,
> But I hope to see her again.
> She lived in the district of Mooi River,
> Even before the war had begun."

The others rode listening, pleased at how well he carried the traditional song that had almost replaced the 'Volksleid' as the Boer national anthem. Every man and boy of them stirred and joined in the next verses, proud words that echoed the commandos' defiance far across the mountain crags.

> "O bring me back to the Old Transvaal,
> there where my Sarie lives,
> Down where the maize grows,
> next to the green thorn tree,
> There lives my Sarie Marais."

CHAPTER FIVE

Despite the heat, Feliks Nikolai hurried to the Belfast Merchants Bank, pressed for time before the train left. The assistant manager knew him and cashed his cheque for one hundred pounds. The withdrawal left just five pounds thirteen shillings and sixpence ha'penny in his local account. Nikki asked for the money in sovereigns. His experience found gold was more persuasive than paper money. Especially since Kruger's theft of the bullion reserves devalued the Transvaal's blueback notes. He divided the coins into two canvas bags, each to separate pockets.

It was a fast ten minutes' walk to the town abattoir, where he found Cockeye sitting outside on a wall. He was bald and thick-bodied, wearing a splattered rubber apron and swilling his lunch of beer from a billy-can. He grunted a greeting without any surprise when the Russian arrived, but the wild roll of his cast-eye signaled some greedy interest. Nikki had paid the slaughterhouse man for wet-work once before, to permanently silence a Bolshevik settler who made too many speeches against the Czar.

He told Cockeye who the target was this time. "First, you keep close watch. If the army does away with him, prison or the firing-squad, fine and good. You just send me the details immediately, and nothing more. Money for jam, as the English say. But if he somehow gets returned to duty, you must make sure he never leaves town."

Nikolai bounced a money-bag in his hand, chinking it temptingly. "Forty five sovereigns for you, in advance. To keep, either way." He spoke in English, as he never could get his tongue around that gargling Taal, or Afrikaans, or whatever they called it.

"You'd be lucky, man!" Cockeye held out his blood-caked palm, head tilted sideways to bring his skew-wiff gaze to bear on the money. "I'll need sixty."

"Here's what you'll get, fifty pounds, cash." The

Russian nodded towards screams inside the abattoir as sledgehammers cracked cows' skulls. "A routine job for you." Nikki handed over the cash, and told the thug exactly what he must do.

To celebrate, Nikki bought a case of Polish vodka before joining Beth in the railway station buffet. He noisily put it on the floor beside her table. Stern-faced diners close by glowered their teetotal objection. He peeled foil from a bottle-top, amusedly eying Beth. She sat with untouched sandwiches, dabbing a handkerchief at her eyes.

"Come, princess, he's hardly worthy of tears." Nikki poured Wodka Wybrowka into a water-glass, holding it up to admire the small flecks of bison grass swirling in the drink. He tossed it down his throat and smiled at the weeping girl.

He idly turned an edge of the bread, winkling his nose. "Ugh, tinned corned beef. Another British delicacy. Just think what dinner-time horrors you've escaped by not marrying him."

"He's Canadian."

"Worse still." He shuddered comically, "Bear-paw soup and fried beaver-tails!"

Beth burst out laughing, despite herself. She became aware of her blotchy face and disarrayed hair, and went to the ladies' lavatory to repair the damage. When she came back, her beautiful face was composed, the tendrils pinned back under her hat. Nikki was draining another glass, reveling in scandalizing the respectable folk who glared from other tables.

He was about to make some gigolo flattery about her appearance, when she held up an impatient hand. "We have to find it ourselves, before Harry or anyone else. It is our duty!" She seemed to have freshened her resolve along with her appearance.

"If we did, then what?" He was busy refilling his glass Beth signaled for him to keep his voice down, and said in a half-whisper, "We take it to Acting President Schalk Burger if we can. At least turn it over to one of our generals. Anything to keep it from the British."

"Anything?"

"What? Not keep it for ourselves, if that's what you're hinting!"

"Not just a spare coin or two that might drop off the back of a wagon? Would even your darling Harry be that scrupulous if tempted?" He smirked, enjoying her flush of annoyance.

"My relationship with him has nothing to do with this. He is our enemy! I know that now, and we'll not let him or anyone else steal away the Volk's gold. Nobody. You must give me your promise on that."

Nikki raised his glass to toast the room, and gulped vodka. "Aah, the Poles can do something right." He smacked his lips. "Needless to say, if we are successful, it must end up in the right hands. You have my solemn word on that as a Russian officer."

He opened the door, and Beth strode out to brave the gauntlet of ogling she faced every time she came into town. Burghers' wives examined her smart clothes in detail, until annoyedly noticing their husbands' slack-jawed admiration of the girl. Young officers gave dashing smiles as she passed, then turned to watch the roll of her haunches. Tommies on the platform nudged each other, "Bit of all right, eh!"

Hetti jumped up from the plank bench set aside for natives. She strained to lift the leather portmanteau that held four changes of Beth's traveling-clothes. She needed to bump it against her leg to lug it to their door. Having paid First Class, they had a compartment to themselves. Nikki threw his jingling crate in and held out his arm for Bethany to climb aboard. He stepped up without a glance at the maid. Her mistress leaned out and took one end of the luggage so they could hoist it aboard together.

Nikki belched deliberately, "No real lady would lower herself to peasant's work."

"No real gentleman would make it necessary."

He scowled at her rebuke in front of a servant, "She's like your shadow. Couldn't get away from her in the hotel last night." Beth gave him a level look. Even in this modern new 20th Century, no respectable Boer woman was going to travel without a chaperone. He scowled and turned his attention to sucking a bottle as the train moved off. She stared out the window for a while, scheming, impatient to get back and start the search.

"From what we've heard, Oom Paul's wagons were last seen somewhere between Spitsdorp and the Devil's Knuckles," she said after a while. "Most of that's Vincennes property. We must organize the boys to track over each section in turn."

"Not without us to watch against thievery, though. I'd trust these black mujiks about as far as you can throw them."

Hetti did not understand English. She sat opposite, watching her mistress's every mood. The girl read sadness in Miss Bethany's eyes, and said something encouraging about the war being surely over soon and her soldier lover could return. She was hurt when Bethany snapped she was a stupid girl, and to mind her own business or she'd get twice the chores to do for a week. Hetti sulked, and soon went to sleep.

"That's better, snoring away." Nikki was leaning over Beth, smirking drunkenly. "Can't have your tame monkey watching while we play."

He grabbed her face, squeezing her cheeks, and delivered a slobbering kiss. She tasted his rancid mouth, felt his tongue probing her throat, sliding lewdly, and thought she would vomit. She squirmed, unable to call out, gagged by his tongue, and felt his hand fossicking in her blouse. He encountered only stiff whalebone there, so slid his hand to her thighs.

Beth twisted free, pulled a long pin from her hat, and stabbed his cheekbone. He reared back, hand to the puncture that had just missed his eye. She held the six-inch needle firmly, making little poking
motions at him.

The maid stirred awake and focused on them sleepily. Nikki swore vilely in Russian, *"Eb tvoju mat!"* He flounced into his seat, deliberately kicking the maid's legs. The two women stared at him warily, but after finishing the bottle, he fell asleep.

He awoke in no better mood at Alkmaar station, and half fell out of the carriage. Petta was waiting, a Hottentot with big smile for Beth on his yellow face as he carried the bags and helped her aboard their cart. As soon as they were on the road north, she pulled off her tie and celluloid collar, and breathed in happily.

She had escaped from the squalor of town, back out here where the setting sun turned the grassland to amber, and shot mauve and ochre splashes against the mountain peaks. It was where she belonged; in the volk's homeland, the free domain reached by Boers on their Great Trek sixty years ago.

As a child, she heard all the stories how her mother's ancestors had crushed the black inhabitants, and gained this land with sacrifice and blood, courage and sweat. Boers made the Transvaal theirs, then cleared it of dangerous wild animals to keep their farms safe. Only twenty years ago, Afrikaners defeated even the British in the First Anglo-Boer War. Surely they could do it again, even now, financed by Uncle Paul's legacy.

A hand on her shoulder made Beth flinch. "My dear, I seem to have had a leetle too much Polish potato-juice earlier on. Forgive my admiration for you running away with me."

Without looking round, she pushed his hand away. "It was embarrassing." Beth would not say anything more.

She leaned well away from him to wave back to some

navvy workers who whistled at her as they passed. Beth hid her resentment that they were uitlanders, foreign immigrants. This bunch sounded English at that, here to build the new railway spur up to Lydenburg.

She ignored Nikki completely, preferring to chat with Petta about the farm. It was run entirely by natives now, all the bywoners having left for the war long since. Lack of enough help made it ever harder to manage the cattle and crops. Perhaps worse, there were fewer workers available to keep watch against thieves.

Night was falling when the horse team veered left off the road, and they were on her father's land once more. Petta mentioned another five cows gone missing, and his suspicion they were taken by those bandits from the mining camps up north. Then her worried frown eased as they came around the trail's end and she saw the lights of Farm Vincennes.

The long white house was strongly built, its wood and stone seeming to have taken root. The wide windows still had their iron shutters, folded back and painted ochre now, but once as important against native attacks as the rifle slits that pocked the walls. Dogs barked welcome and chickens scattered under the cartwheels. Field-hands on their way to their quarters called softly, "God brought you back from safe journey, Miss Bethany."

Nikolai left his valise to be carried by a house-servant, and staggered away across the farmyard without a backward glance. He veered unsteadily towards his cottage, fumbling to unscrew the cap of another bottle.

"All the fuss, you'd think you were gone months, instead of overnight." Hiram tried to growl, but there was too much pleasure in his voice. He stood on the verandah, bent over to one side.

"Dada, why will you never use a cane?" She kissed his cheek, and caught his familiar smell of cigars. Lately, though, there was an added sour odour of shirts worn unchanged too long, and from the stubble, he had not shaved since she left. Personal neglect by so proud a man was a new sign of his inner despair.

"What, deprive my sassy daughter of a chance to nag?" He looked closely at her in the house-lights. "Things Orl Kerrect with Harry again?"

"Not OK at all. He's in very serious trouble, Dada, but brought it on himself. He confessed as much to my face. I shall not speak with him again."

"Mighty sorry to hear. I'd hoped he was straight as he seemed." He cleared his throat. "Well, glad that's off your mind. Now, a buyer's here about the prime of our tobacco. Best I go settle prices with him tonight."

"You and I must talk. Right away."

He looked anxiously across the yard. "Well, if it's that urgent. Let me grab a few minutes with him first."

Tannie Marthe came out of the kitchen. "There's some sliced meat and quinces if you fancy. You're never a one for eating after a trip. Or any other time, come to that, lately. Be skin and bones before long. Pining does that to a girl."

"Oh, Tannie, who would I have to pine for? I'll eat like a horse if you want."

"Let's not go too much the other way. Before you get fat, we have to marry you off first."

She led the way into the big kitchen, then shouted, *"Wat die hel doen ji?"*

Two young field-hands jumped up from chairs and headed out the door, with the cook fleeing behind them. One other, a good-looking youth with a shining blue-black face, did not move from the table. He lounged comfortably, looking the women's bodies up and down, and gave a lazy smile. "No offence, baas-ladies."

Marthe snatched her bamboo cane from behind the door, and swished it threateningly. "You too, Simius!"

She slapped the frayed end hard on the table in front of him, and screamed, *"Voertsek!"* She ordered him out contemptuously, as if he was a dog. She screeched more threats in a babble of Sotho about what would happen if he ever dared sit in her kitchen again, but even then he took his time leaving.

Beth did not know whether to be amused or shocked when Marthe muttered some very un-Christian words under her breath. She had never seen the dear woman so indignant.

Marthe was not really Beth's aunt, but had been housekeeper at Vincennes ever since her mother died, close as any relative now. Dada once said Marthe was "a fine figger of a woman", and Beth still sometimes teased him about marrying her. There was no sign of any such intentions, however, and watchful servant-girls were disappointed they never once spotted the Baas making any late-night visits to Marthe's bedroom.

"It's getting worse like this all the time with the blacks. Loss of proper respect, without a firm hand. Something bad's going to happen, mark my words. They see us as weak, no men to protect us, and money getting short. Losing this war will be terrible for all Afrikaners."

Beth hugged her, and said perhaps instead something might make a turn for the better for General Botha soon. She made a great show of enjoying the ham, and Marthe Keller went back to her earlier theme.

"So, nobody to sigh over now, you say. You cried in your room for months when you two broke up last year." Tannie's sharp eyes scanned the girl's expression. "It's really finished between you two forever, then?" Beth mumbled something dismissive through a mouthful.

"Did he do what they say?" Marthe asked. Beth nodded numbly.

"War does strange things to a man." Marthe smoothed her white cuffs, and said casually, "Oh, well, I've seen better looking ones."

"But you always did fancy him, Tannie."

Cook came back, and Marthe started to give her the rough side of her tongue about letting field-hands into the kitchen. Hiram came limping along the hall and she joined him at the dining-room table. It was a fine big room, that before the war was often crowded with friends, toe-tapping to concertinas and banjos

playing cheerful *boeremusik*. But the family seldom used it these days, without either money nor leisure to entertain.

"Now, what's so all-fired important?"

He listened without interruption while she told how a fortune on Transvaal gold was hidden somewhere on or near their property, and the urgency that they organize a search to retrieve it. She was annoyed but not surprised when he pooh-poohed her excitement.

"That's the tale we heard two years ago, after Kruger was holding court in his railway carriage just up the line. 'Always regretted he moved on before I got to say goodbye. But he'd have sent word for sure if he wanted me to hide any funds on Vincennes."

"But would he? President Paul was old, defeated, on the run. Besides, he wouldn't have wanted to risk a friend getting involved."

"Must admit, if it's around here, I'd like to dig it up before the Limeys do. Like you say, it could help President Burger hold on and maybe swing a better deal with Kitchener."

"And there's Irkie! Anything that shortens this war helps bring him home safely."

"That'd be best of all pay-offs, gal." He shook his head, "But it's a pipe dream. We don't know hide nor hair where it is, and we ain't got enough bodies to look under every rock."

"I'm going into Spitsdorp tomorrow to ask around. Somebody must have seen something. Remember the talk of wagons heading in our direction from the president's train that night?" She leaned forward to grasp her father's hands, willing the force of her determination. "And Nikki and me can organize the field-hands in shifts to search."

"How come he's in on this?"

Beth explained how the blockhouse cleaner had told both of them about the treasure, and the old rancher's face grew more worried. "I get the feel lately he's not a guy to be trusted. Never mind why."

"I had a bit of a shock myself today, and you never mind what either. But he's the only ally we have. And, Dada, a British search-party is on the way here! It'll arrive any day."

"Still time to let me sleep on it. We'll talk in the morning."

Beth knew she had done all she could for now, and ran up stairs. Two mirrored oil-lamps threw a soft glow in her room, bedclothes turned back ready. She threw aside her blouse and camisole, and called, "Oh, Hetti, come get these awful stays off me before I die!"

They giggled as she grabbed hold of the bedpost and made loud puffs of relief when the maid loosed the strings of her whalebone corset. "Hallelujah, free again!" She laughed and span around, making a show of scratching madly at her ribs under the shift.

"Ugh, I'm so sticky from the trip! Quick, lots of hot water."

Hetti fetched a heavy bucket up the steep stairs, and filled a washbowl and ewer with water. "Careful, it's still scalding, Missie."

"Never mind, I want to feel clean as can be tonight." She felt almost light-headed, the relief of homecoming so joyous it drove unhappiness from her mind for now. "You can go now, Hetti, until morning." She laughed, "I bet Simius will want to show how glad he is to see you again."

The maid ran down the back stairs, too eager to notice she left the door unlatched behind her. Beth pulled off her last garment and stared in the mirror at herself, stripped to the waist. She removed the pins to let her hair fall, and combed the ripe-corn tress loose with her fingers, so that it hung past her shoulders. She turned her head critically, one way then the other. Her arms were nicely taut from farm exercise, and her thrusting breasts were flawless, though still red-striped from whalebones.

She wet the face-cloth and enjoyed a slow sponge bath of her torso, wiping away the sweat and grime of two days' journey. She moistened her face with toilet cream, then used the new Gillette safety razor her father bought for her, after she read shaved armpits were all the ladies' mode in America. When Beth
lifted one breast to wipe its soft cleft, Nikki slurred, "Charming."

"Get out!" She snatched a chemise to cover herself, so shocked and angry, her neck-sinews went tight as ropes.

He leaned insolently against the door, closing it with his back. "Only a British cad would turn away from such a pretty sight. But no Russian who appreciates a well-fleshed woman could be so, what's the best word? Boorish?" He hiccoughed a chuckle at the pun, and put a shaky finger to his lips.

"Just re . . . realized, why you said you were embarrassed. Of course, a crowded train's no place for l'amour." Nikki reeled closer, stupefied with vodka, and reached out cupped hands. "Come, little milkmaid, I tip-toed up the back way. Your shadow won't be back tonight, judging how fast she ran into the barn to rut with that stable-boy. Nobody will disturb our long-overdue rendezvous."

"I said get the heck out! If my Pa finds you here, he'll . . . He'll blow your Russian balls off!"

Nikki massaged the puncture she'd made in his cheek. "Such talk from a young lady. But then, you're not really, hmm? More of a little Afrikaner white savage."

He stalked closer as he spoke, she backing away to the window. "Besides, if you did call out, what would everyone say? Naked with a man in your room? Could it be you cried out only because you'd changed your mind?"

"We'll risk that, you pig." She reached to throw open the curtains.

"But will your father want to risk his business arrangement with me?"

"What?"

"The two thousand pounds he owes me, and not one shilling returned yet. You could easily pay down a month's interest tonight."

"You think I'd fall for your cheap melodrama threats, man?" She gradually circled towards the wash-stand.

"Try to laugh it off all you want. Fact is, I could get legal possession of Vincennes in less than a week and throw you all out on the veld, penniless. Then try being nice to some fine big Basuto stud, instead."

Bethany dropped the chemise, and he leered at her dazzling white breasts. They bought her time to throw the hot water in his face. Then she smashed the pitcher and lunged at Nikki with the broken handle's razor edge.

CHAPTER SIX

Two second-lieutenants came for Harry just after he finished his breakfast of soggy bacon and fried bread. They were big 20–year-olds in checkered side-caps, bum-freezer jackets, and scarlet tartan trews. On the way to HQ, the subalterns chatted about their homes in Scotland, as pleasant as could be, but walked close on each side and had their revolver holsters un-buttoned.

The streets were thronged with soldiers hurrying from cookhouse to duty, eating-irons rattling in tin cups held in the left hand to free their right one for saluting. There were so many squaddies about, the three officers had to windmill their way, returning salutes every few yards. Harry responded to the passing troopers automatically, but was more aware of the civilians they passed.

A lot of Belfast residents were out strolling before the streets got too hot. Women and men alike, these Boer townees were well-dressed, unlike the scarecrow takhaars he fought on the veld. Some Anglos strolled just as elegantly, but most of them and uitlanders hurried about in work-clothes or house-dresses, and none give the Canadian a second glance. The only ones who did pay attention to him were the Afrikaners, watchful even while forever shaking hands with whoever they met.

It was not just his battered Stetson and ill-pressed trousers contrasting with the band-box uniforms of the Scots. The Boers all knew exactly who he was. Most showed it by following him with flat stares, but some of the shabbier bywoners cursed him as a *"Moordenaar!"*. One lout who looked like he stepped out of a butcher's shop walked close behind Harry for a while, and a couple of urchins threw stones from a safe distance.

When they reached the commandeered school building,

the Scots remarked that Harry was lucky they arrived ahead of the nosy warcos. A large Union flag on a staff in the front garden marked the site of District Army Headquarters, Eastern Transvaal. There was even more bustle than usual about the place since "K of K" arrived yesterday. Two sentries stood on the front steps, their bayoneted rifles at the slope, and a noticeable extra number of military policemen stalked around in pairs. Probably Lt. Scayles would have been among them, but he was being re-examined by the MO in sick-bay this morning.

The sentries slapped palms on their rifle-butts in salute as the subalterns strode up the front steps. The Orderly Officer signed a receipt for Lanyard's delivery under close arrest, and the Scots took their leave. DHQ had the usual relaxed atmosphere of a British army senior domain, where it would be bad form to show signs of too much professionalism. Red-tabbed staff officers spoke quietly to each other amid the rattle of typewriters and jangling telephone bells, but without any of the usual bursts of collegial laughter.

Under their casual pose, everyone from colonel to warrant officer kept a nervous watch on the door to the Inner Sanctum, where General Kitchener had been at work since 6 a.m. Except for some brief mid-morning exercise on horseback, "K" would be at his desk for the next twelve hours, evaluating reports, planning, ordering the course of the war single-handedly.

Harry was nodded at to wait, while a staff-sergeant announced him through a speaking-tube. He took off his Stetson and closed the hook-and-eye clasps of his high collar. The Basuto had done a good job at polishing his boots and brass buttons, so he guessed he looked as presentable as any accused murderer could. After a half hour, two men came out for him, a good-looking young captain and Smith, the civilian from yesterday.

"Sorry to keep you, Lieutenant," The captain smiled

charmingly and smoothed the middle parting in his hair. "We've been making some last-minute arrangements on your behalf. Turned out quite well, actually. My name's Maxwell, the ADC." He wore a row of medal ribbons, good ones, including the DSO and a couple of Indian war campaigns. What drew Harry's eye, though, was the crimson ribbon of the Victoria Cross, Britain's highest award for bravery, and he stiffened to attention to show respect.

The aide-de-camp gave a modest half-wave, and nodded to his companion, "You've already met Colonel Faulkner, I understand. These Field Intelligence wallahs get about everywhere."

The colonel in mufti nodded calmly, not in the least ruffled about his previous masquerade. "An interesting day ahead for you, Lanyard."

The gymnasium hall had been made into a command centre, with a half dozen tables smothered in papers, and maps tacked on every wall. A group of staff officers clustered in the corner, taking notes of orders growled by "K" himself. Harry recognized one as being the Canadian railway expert, Colonel Percy Girouard, said to be the only man who briefed Kitchener first-thing every morning.

Something was off here, though. Harry had expected a seated row of legal inquisitors, MP guards, maybe even the traditional sword of judgement lying on a table draped with the Union Jack. Instead, nobody paid any attention to his arrival.

Maxwell led the way to his desk, and opened a buff dossier folder. Though unlikely to be heard over the loud conference voices, Maxwell spoke in lowered tones. "Not to beat about the bush, Lanyard, the CM against you has been dropped. Pleased to say."

He flashed his practiced aide's smile. "Turns out those Belgie witnesses have been recalled home. Their government's not too keen on them testifying, shouldn't wonder. Actually, some of the things they did say pretty well corroborate your own explanation. So, the general has personally quashed all charges."

Harry felt the relief flowing through his gut, and realized just how much dread had been stretching his nerves for weeks. But now something else started to bother him. Bank clerking had taught him the skill of reading numbers upside-down, and he could see the date beside Kitchener's signature." Great, sir. But, when was this made effective?"

Maxwell went very still, and casually closed the file. Faulkner answered instead. "You've Captain Barlow to thank for the reprieve, Lieutenant. 'Been beavering away on your behalf in more ways than one."

Harry kept focused on Captain Maxwell. He figured a guy who'd earned a VC would be the most inclined to level with him. "General Kitchener signed me off the hook the day before yesterday, didn't he, sir?"

When Maxwell pursed his lower lip and nodded gravely, Lanyard turned to Faulkner. "Before you came offering that so-called deal of yours."

"'Fraid that was more our chaps' fault down at Pretoria, Lieutenant," Maxwell drawled. "GHQ wasn't quite as quick at passing word to you as we might."

Faulkner said, "And we were in urgent need to sound you out anyway. Catch your slant on things."

Harry was about to blurt how he felt about his reprieve being left delayed under English tea-cups, when the Intelligence officer said, "Barlow not only found evidence to wriggle you out of the charges, he learned that Scayles' rank is only an Acting First Loo. So we can just move you up a notch to substantive First Lieutenant, making you his superior. That suit?"

Harry felt his head spin, trying to come to terms with this sudden turn-around. Faulkner allowed himself a glimmer of amusement. "It seems your new second-in-command was in some sort of fracas at the jail. Refuses to say exactly what about. Anyway, congratulations on your field promotion."

The telephone rang on the ADC's desk, demanding that Maxwell deal with some irritated brigadier needing a fresh supply of boots for his footsore troops. During the break, Harry started listening to the steely voice from across the room, dominating the staff officers.

"Done my damndest to ease the train situation for you, Percy. I've ordered against taking in any more refugees," Lord Kitchener was saying. "I wonder how that turnabout'll go down with their General Botha. He just finished telling the world he's only too thankful that Boer wives are under British protection. Well, it's up to you now to take full advantage of any extra carriages available."

"Thank you, sir. After all, we only have the one single-track rail line, and the enemy still cuts it at least once a week. Never seem to care that delays food to their own families in the camps as well as our chaps." Colonel Girouard jotted numbers on his pad. "Not needing to transport civilians to the camps could gain us another six percent of rolling-stock. Enough to bring fresh battalions up from Simonstown before month's end."

"Should hope so! I need every man for the big drives. We've got thirteen columns quartering the field now, so our mass pushes are starting to work. Going well, but all too slow. Still bagging only about seven hundred of the blighters a month." He waved across the room. "Faulkner here tells me there's still twenty-odd thousand of them swanning about. At this rate, we'll wait 'til Kingdom Come before they're all rounded up and a finish put to things."

An infantry colonel murmured that perhaps the gradual method was best, in view of the increasing criticism by Parliament and the British press. Kitchener's heavy face purpled, "Those bloody women!".

All started with that busy-body old maid, Miss Emily Hobhouse, who set the world into an outrage against Britain with her exposure of wholesale deaths in the refugee camps.

Kitchener had no sooner barred her from re-visiting South Africa, when the Secretary of State For War also started to question civilian concentration policies.

'Sent his own damned Parliamentary Committee Of Ladies on an inspection tour; formidable society women who were determined to get to the bottom of things, and Heaven help any mere general who dared interfere. Dame Millicent Fawcett's outspokenly critical report last year had listed measures to improve living conditions in the camps, which an embarrassed Parliament insisted must be applied immediately. Ever since, Kitchener had been the government's handy scapegoat for how Britain conducted the war.

"Those damn scribbling warcos are as bad, toadying to the do-gooders back home!" A heavy fist bashed the conference table, as Kitchener's temper burst through the iron mask of calm. He focused his anger on journalists and anti-war protesters, carefully avoiding criticism of his political masters. He had his heart set on being appointed the next C-in-C of India by year's end, if the secret peace negotiations led to a treaty quick enough.

"The news-rags used to support us, but now they're forever writing tosh about our gallant foes. True, except for a few white-flag violations, Boers fight clean. Usually treat our prisoners well, as we do theirs. Different matter entirely, those commandos who disguise themselves in our uniforms. There's the devil of an uproar when we only give them what they've asked for."

The table shook with the general's pounding and, oddly, a bird somewhere close by made a piercing whistle of alarm. "But God help any blacks the Boers find lawfully wearing khaki, though, or show too much co-operation with our side. Here's Faulkner's report on their General Smuts massacring a couple of hundred natives at Modderfontein just last month. Those sanctimonious Friends Of The Boers never mention that, you notice!"

Nobody replied, as it was clear the C-in-C's outburst signaled the morning conference was over, and the knot of staff officers unraveled. They hurried out with minimum fuss, stern-faced, minds set on their latest orders how to continue the war within the hour.

"Pretty girl! Pretty girl!" Harry stared at the sight of General Sir Herbert Horatio Kitchener, Earl of Khartoum, Commander-in-Chief, British Forces in South Africa, leaning over a bird-cage, making chirping noises. Maxwell looked at his pocket watch. "Tweety's calling it's time for your morning gallop, sir."

Kitchener pushed a stick of toast through the bars to the bedraggled-looking starling. It whistled again, and Harry could have sworn a faint smile lifted the general's trademark huge mustache. Kitchener grunted and reached for his cap and riding-crop. He was a massive man, well over six foot, thick hair parted in the middle, strange pale eyes glaring under bushy eyebrows.

The three officers stood up when he walked by their table. He waved his hand irritably for them to be at ease, and handed a wad of notes to his ADC. "Cobble these into daily orders, ready for my signature at noon."

Maxwell sighed comically, "No rest for the weary, sir." Behind his back, jealous fellow officers called Maxwell 'the Brat', because of his easy familiarity with the most feared general in the British Army.

"What else'll you be up to while I'm gone, eh?"

"Seeing what we can do about Oom Paul's nest-egg, sir."

Maxwell introduced Harry by name and regiment, but the general barely acknowledged him beyond a sharp glance. "This the chap we're sending? The Canadian who was in so much hot water? Don't know what it is about these Colonials. Their regular contingents put up a good show, none better, but once away from discipline, they turn into hooligans."

"Actually, sir, we're recommending Lanyard for his full second pip."

Kitchener's porcelain-blue eyes bulged at the faint ink stripes still visible on Harry's sleeve. "Good God, the man's nothing more than a jumped-up n.c.o!" His voice quivered with outrage. Kitchener was never known to have ever spoken directly to any other-ranks soldier.

Faulkner made his throat-clearing noise. "He's a well-experienced officer now, sir. We're just briefing Lieutenant Lanyard on the Kruger gold business."

Kitchener made an obvious effort to rein in his temper. "Vital job. Think he's up to it?'

"Yes, sir. I am." Harry said levelly, a bit louder than he intended.

"Eh?" The fearsome stare took in this impertinent subaltern, speaking up before he was spoken to. There was a shocked silence, then Kitchener said grudgingly, "Hmm. Like an officer to be confident about his objectives. Tell him, did you, it's crucial we keep that money out of Boer hands just now? Burger and De la Rey keep making hole-in-the-corner overtures for a peace settlement, but nothing's come of it yet."

Lord Kitchener actually looked puzzled. "Damned if I know what to make of 'em, Faulkner. We've offered the same terms we did two years ago, full compensation for war losses, millions of pounds for reconstruction, even self-government like Canada and Australia, but they still won't give up."

"Perhaps they'll have come round by the time we get back to Pretoria tomorrow, sir." Maxwell was ever the diplomat.

"Hmph! More like I'll still be cooling my heels in Melrose House while those Free Staters keep haggling. Oddest thing, Bloemfontein never had any grievance with Britain in the first place. The OFS only got into this war because of its defence agreement with Kruger. Yet now they're holding out for more concessions than any Transvaaler."

Kitchener searched the three officers' faces. "But, y'know what's the real sticking point, gentlemen?" He tapped the side of his nose. "Negroes! The Boers simply won't agree with our condition that natives must be given the franchise to vote. Those pig-headed burghers never will consent to that, mark my words."

The general clapped on his side-cap, "Still, they're poor as church mice now, so keeping funds out of their hands'll speed up our victory." He nodded curtly at Harry. "That's where you come in, Lieutenant. Good hunting!"

Thought of an early triumph made him almost cordial, and he said to his aide, "Looking forward to coming back to India, my boy?"

"Absolutely, sir." Maxwell glanced fondly at the desktop photograph of his wife and little daughter. "With time for some England, home, and beauty first."

"'Course." Rumour had it that years ago then-Lt. Kitchener had been engaged to an 18-year-old girl, but she died on him. He never did marry, and as far as anyone could tell, career success was his only passion since. "Carry on, gentlemen. Orders typed by noon, mind, Frank."

Maxwell nodded towards the rising babble of war correspondents outside. "Perhaps you'd prefer to avoid them through the back door, sir."

"Hah!" Lord Kitchener slapped his leg with the crop, and strode into the front lobby. Everybody in the building could hear him calling upstairs for his horsy companions to get a move on.

"Actually, you stood up to His Lordship rather well, Lanyard." Maxwell chuckled, and sat back for Colonel Faulkner to take over.

"Now you're back on duty, it's no longer a question of volunteering, of course. Written orders for the patrol will be issued, but for secrecy's sake it's best you don't carry them." Faulkner smoothed a map on the table, screwed in his monocle, then traced the railway east from Pretoria.

"All along Kruger's line of flight to Mozambique last year, his train kept stopping for him to make never-surrender speeches. Middleburg, Machadodorp, Waterval Onder." A nicotine-yellowed finger tapped the rail-line close to the Crocodile River. "He delayed longest there, at Nelspruit Siding. Five days. Plenty of time for Schwartze to unload gold onto ox-carts and squirrel it away."

Harry took in the familiar ground, where Farm Vincennes sprawled at the foot of mountains. "Rough country up there, all canyons and jungle and fever before the upland plain. Local settlers die like flies from malaria every summer. That many ravines, it could take a year to find the Bank of England itself."

"Yes, that's why we'd rather like to get a move on, Lieutenant." Faulkner said casually, "Early tomorrow, say?"

An outburst of men's voices sounded from the front steps as the scrum of war correspondents barred Kitchener's way. One louder than most called, "Horace Skulnik, New York Herald-Tribune, General. Your scorched-earth policy burned thirty thousand Boer homes. Now you've finally stopped it, can you explain to the U.S. public what all that destruction was intended to achieve?"

"Hah! Can you explain to them why just this month your own government's set up a Congressional Committee to investigate American military atrocities in the Philippines?"

"Two wrongs don't make a right, General. My readers need to know if your recent cancellation of farm-burnings is admission you were wrong to start them in the first place."

"They'd be better off reading the circular sent out by Commandant-General Botha two years ago. It ordered his commandos to do everything possible to prevent burghers from laying down their arms. He warned any Boers who surrender that he'd confiscate everything they own, burn their houses, and leave their families on the veld. And so he has ever since!"

Choking fury at having to explain himself to newspaper reporters made Kitchener's loud voice go almost shrill. "I personally offered him that if the commandos would spare harm to neutral or surrendered burghers, I would leave undisturbed all families of Boers who were out on commando. Commandant Botha refused, so I had no option but to sweep inhabitants into the protection of our lines."

"Protection's a funny word to use, General," another voice called in Cockney barrow-boy tones. "Edgar Wallace, here, London Daily Mail."

"I'm well aware of your scurrilous personal attacks on me, Wallace," Kitchener snapped. "From what I hear, you'd be better off scribbling penny-dreadful thrillers than muckraking for scandal-sheets!"

"I'll keep that advice in mind, sir, but my question remains. What action have you taken to stop the continued deaths of over a thousand Boer women and children every month in your camps?"

Captain Maxwell winced at Harry as they heard Kitchener's bull-throated roar, "Idiot, that's the Civilian Refugee Department's bailiwick, not mine! I'm more concerned that a thousand of my soldiers still die every month on the veld! Now, out of my way, you damned swabs!"

CHAPTER SEVEN

"Nice cushy way to fight a war."

Glendon Scayles glanced around the crowded Officers Mess. Many of the lunchtime crowd were subalterns awaiting assignment to units in the field, at a loose end meanwhile. They were boisterous young men, barking varsity enthusiasms like "Top hole!", "Good egg!", and "Ripping!", as they chatted about sports or prospects of a spot of leave in Cape Town. Politics, women, or soldiering were never mentioned, being taboo subjects in the Mess.

Harry shrugged, more interested in enjoying the first decent meal he'd had for months. "They'll get to chance their arm out there soon enough."

Meeting Scayles again was made all the more awkward by the raw gash on the policeman's nose. It was badly swollen, yellow-painted with iodine, and Lanyard avoided looking at it. He noticed Scayles already wore the badges of the Military Mounted Police in anticipation of his transfer going through, so he was probably even more disappointed at being assigned to Lanyard's little patrol instead.

"Lost no time putting your second pip up, I see." Scayles was calling on all the stiff-upper-lip manner he could muster to mask his resentment. "Bit of a stumer, being ordered to serve with you of all people, Lanyard."

"Same here, but we'll have to make the best of things."

"Oh, I will. For now." Scayles glanced around to be sure he was not overheard. His tight words came out like venom from a spitting-cobra. "But one day, you little shit, we'll meet behind a building for round two and ranks be damned!"

"Fair enough. After this is done with." At least it seemed their difference would be settled fairly with fists, rather than with a bullet in the back. "Did Colonel Faulkner fill you in?"

"The big picture, anyway." Scayles spoke coolly, as if his outburst had never happened. "You could certainly use a copper along, from the sound of it."

"Only if we find the you-know-what." He spoke guardedly, aware of senior officers seated nearby. The mutton with applesauce tasted very good. He waved over a Malay waiter to bring some rice pudding for dessert.

Scayles blew out his pink cheeks irritably, "Dash it all, having to go with you misses me off a big case. Our men are pulling all the stops out to collar this spy feller. He even turned up in our front lines during battle once, bold as brass, and issued false orders for retreat."

"Lax security?" Harry couldn't resist the dig.

"Our people actually did catch him red-handed, stealing some documents from H.Q. Killed a couple of MPs, though, and got clean away. Looks, behaves, and sounds like an officer, so he could be a turncoat." Scayles squinted around the room. "Might even be one of these chaps, for all we know."

"You'll have enough excitement, helping run our patrol. Just don't sweat the small stuff. I prefer the minimum of petty discip."

"Obviously." Scayles fingered his sore nose. "But we won't find so much as a farthing if the men are allowed to act like rabble."

"We're taking only well-experienced men." He kept his face straight, "Colonials, mostly."

"Oh, bloody marvelous."

A tight-faced major loomed over Scayles. "I'm Mess Sec'try. You know talking shop is not permitted in the dining room." He took in Harry's private's tunic. "And you are improperly dressed. Cut along, the pair of you!"

They signed chits to pay for their meal and went into the main bar next door. Harry lit a cigarette and asked the white-coated barman for a Bass Pale Ale. Scayles settled himself with a double whiskey and sparklet, then mused, "Have you any idea exactly what we're in for up there?"

"Well, I have met the occasional commando before."

"They'll be the least of our problems, where we're headed. Far worse, the whole area around the Lydenberg goldfield's swarming with bandits. Mixed bag of armed riff-raff, foreigners, Boojers, British deserters. Sort who'd kill you for your shoes, much less a lorry-load of bullion."

"Lucky we'll have a cop along to deal with them."

"I need to watch our own men too, considering the temptation. You picked all of them yet?"

"Intelligence has arranged most, but I've a couple of other guys in mind." Harry drained the warm ale. "I'll arrange weapons for you to issue. Look after the nominal roll and pay-parade, too, would you? We don't know how long we're away for, so indent to pay them three weeks in advance."

Scayles jotted down his list of duties."I have to pick up the slush-fund to pay informers, as well. A thousand quid, I'm told."

Harry pulled the corners of his mouth down, impressed. Notoriously tight-fisted Army Intelligence must be really feeling the heat from upstairs, to provide five thousand dollars in bribes for information received. "Well, that should loosen somebody's tongue."

Scayles shrugged, "Assuming those farmers actually know anything. Still, that's another reason I'm coming, to guard the funds."

"You'll be less conspicuous doing it if you get rid of that red cap."

Scayles just nodded without another word and strode away quickly. An abrasive man, but the sort who got things done.

Harry reported to the Army Pay Corps office and drew thirteen pounds sterling, two months' back pay owed to him, after deductions for kit and mess dues. At the officers' Tuck Shop, he bought some slabs of Rowntree dark chocolate, 400 Player's Capstan Full Strength Navy Cut, and a handful of souvenir ostrich feathers.

With his letter of authorization from Col. Faulkner, Lanyard was able to indent for equipment quickly, without the usual form-filling delays. Over at Central Stores, a disapproving clerk issued Harry with two new private's uniforms. As an officer, Harry was really supposed to pay for clothing out of his own pocket, but the rules were bent for bushveld service, so long as items were signed for. He also drew a haversack, underwear, socks, and calf-high black boots. He topped things off with one of those new-style bush hats that had the brim rolled up on one side. He shoved his belongings into the pack and went looking for weapons.

The armoury sergeant was more cheerful, promising to have 20 rifles ready by dusk, along with 500 rounds per man. He proudly held up one with gleamingly polished woodwork. "Look at this, sir. Brand new Lee-Enfields for your lot."

"Be a lot better if they loaded with clips like Mausers."

"That'll be coming with the Mark Two model." He cranked the bolt open and shut with almost personal pride. "Just listen, sir. Smooth as greased owl-shit."

"I generally use gun-oil, myself."

"But there is one thing, sir. This first batch have a problem with the sights set over five-hundred yards. Beyond that, best aim off right to compensate."

"Swell, so any Boers in the distance are safe as houses."

The armourer was puzzled when Harry turned down the offer of a standard bayonet to go with it. Harry hated the things now. He did take a big .455 Webley revolver, secure in its closed leather holster.

The Field Intelligence Department had not been able to locate the n.c.o. he had in mind, but it took just one quick question to a passing Kiwi to find who he was looking for. Ned Coveyduck was mooching about the stables, critically watching some horse-handlers.

"Well, stone the crows -- look what the cat's dragged in! I thought they were going to scrag you for sure, like Breaker.

Nice to see you've gone up in the world, instead." The Aussie nodded at Lanyard's new insignia, and punched his friend on the bicep. They were not demonstrative men, but the wide grins they swapped told more than any amount of fuss.

"Feel like working for a living again, Ned?"

"Too right! I'm going barmy, stuck here. Cheap Pommies decided it was too expensive to fork over a sergeant's pay to every man in the Canadian Scouts. So they booted us out on paper, with the option to re-enlist as privates or take release. 'Til now, I couldn't make up my mind whether to quit."

He jumped at Harry's offer of sergeant's rank again, even though he could only offer corporal's pay. "Cut-rate special for you, cobber! What's the game we're on this time?"

Lanyard told Ned about their patrol's assignment, not needing to mention the need for secrecy. "Our own special train's heading east at dawn, so we have to get weaving. There's parades for you to handle, so put your tapes back up right away."

Harry stopped by his room at Officers Quarters to get into a fresh uniform. He came out feeling the new clothes were as stiff as the holster riding high on his belt. Ned just raised an eyebrow at the plume Harry had stuck in his rolled hat-brim.

They went to join Lt. Scayles, who was on the parade-ground checking off the nominal roll of the men ready for patrol. Harry knew most of them, trail-mates from Howard's Scouts; Bramah, Cameron, Fletcher, Fontaine, McKay, Parkin, Rimmer, van Praage, and Wignall. He tried to weigh up the unfamiliar seven new men as they responded. When called, each shouted his name and the last three of his regimental number.

"Abbott, eight-three-nine."

"Baxter . . . iss hardt to rememper."

"Haywood, eight-one-five".

"deKrieger, seeks-seeks-sivvin."

"Lascelles, neyn-debble-too."

"O'Malley, tree-tree-foive." Harry had met the man before, and knew him to be a hard-case Regular.

"Schammerhorn, yo! Foah-wuun-foah."

When the muster was completed, Sergeant Coveyduck bawled, "Senior officer on parade! Atten-shun!" The troops jerked erect smartly, for Harry's benefit, and to further make their point. Before, they had deliberately acted slovenly to irritate Scayles, who they detested at first sight as an MP.

"Riiiight-dress!" They snapped heads sideways to face right, pushed fists against the shoulder of each next man, extended arms for even spacing, and shuffled their feet into straight lines.

Ned gave Lanyard an elbow-vibrating salute, then called, "Pah-rade, stand at, ease!" They stamped their boots apart and clasped hands behind backs.

Right away, van Praage, Fontaine, and other ex-Scouts called good-naturedly ribald greetings to Lanyard. Bramah's fat face creased in a big grin. "Great to see you again, Harry. Maybe now we can get on with this war!"

Scayles scowled at their Colonial unruliness, and looked Ned over critically. He took in the replaced stripes held by safety-pins, but just drawled the standard officer's comment, "Carry on Sergeant." He handed the duties-list clipboard towards Coveyduck.

Harry shook his head, "I need him to help pick horses."

He raised his voice to order, "Stand easy." The men's slouch barely changed. "I'm glad a lot of us know each other, because this isn't going to be any ordinary patrol. For once, we're not going out on a simple search-and-destroy. We have a different job to do that's even more important. I'll fill in the details once we're on the veld, but for now, get it into your heads our mission is to go find something, without picking any fights."

Lanyard walked slowly along the two ranks, looking into each man's face. "So, tough as you are, I don't want any showing off. If you come across any commandos, just keep your heads down and high-tail it out of there."

"Hey, come on, Harry!" Wignall called, "You really want us t'skedaddle anytime we see one lousy Boer?"

"I mean exactly that, Barney! You will not fire unless fired upon or directly ordered to shoot. Understood?"

Some nodded, but most looked puzzled at the unusual mission of a non-aggressive patrol. They showed even more surprise when Harry produced the ostrich feathers. "Half the commandos're wearing khaki now, but all wear beards so they can identify each other from a distance. We'll do the same thing, with these in your hats." He handed the plumes to van Praage. "Pass them out afterwards."

"Okay, men, it's payday, so raise all the hell you want tonight, but be damned sure to keep your lips buttoned about the patrol. I expect you here at six o'clock tomorrow morning, fully saddled up and equipped for a long trek, ready to take the train. God help anybody who isn't. Carry on, Lieutenant Scayles."

On the way back to the stables, Ned said, "You got anybody picked for signaler?" He looked sideways. "Maybe you could see to springing Jiggy for the job. They slapped the horny little bugger on Number One."

"Ah, Christ, what next?"

Even after Coveyduck told the full story, Harry took his time over choosing the horses. The stable-sergeant saw a fellow expert in Ned, an ex-stockman, and was apologetic about the poor selection on offer. "Fair disgrace, the rate this army's killing off the poor beasts. I hear tell Kitchener's knackered over four hundred thousand horses up to now."

The Veterinary Corps n.c.o. hawked and spat to show his disgust. "No wonder, the way they gives some London shop-boy five minutes training with the first horse he's ever seen in his life, then turn him loose to ride it to death."

He led out what was available, from tall English thoroughbreds to Hungarian cobs and shaggy Cape ponies. The British army sent purchasing agents all over the world, buying up any horseflesh available for service in South Africa. The attrition rate from harsh field service killed them off as fast as they were being bought, so their breeds and condition were a mish-mash at every garrison stable.

When Ned opted to take Basuto Cape ponies, the farrier nodded his approval. "No poncy cavalryman looks twice at 'em. None much over fourteen hands high, but those little nags keep going forever, and never catch a sickness." There were not enough ponies to supply ten re-mounts as well, so Harry made do with Argentine horses. For pack-animals, Ned insisted they go with five Missouri mules, as he did not want the sickly Italian donkeys they were offered.

The farrier asked, "Can I make a suggestion, sir? All these remounts and mules'll be a handful. A couple of Griquas along could help no end."

"Not armed Auxiliaries are they?" Harry was thinking of how blacks with rifles had drawn the attention of the Boers who killed Gat.

"No, sir. Strictly horse-handlers, and the best there is, I reckon. Two good un's are hanging around here looking for jobs."

"Okay, have them report to Lieutenant Scayles. If he approves, they're hired."

Harry was reluctant to take time away from readying the patrol, but he could not ignore this side-errand. He signed out two ponies for immediate use, while Ned went to scrounge a snack to eat on the way.

They clattered down the main road from Belfast, past tall stacks of the coal-mines fuming thick smoke, then took a short-cut between shanties of the 'Location', as the native township was called. Sight of the Tommies brought out swarms of picaninnies, black infants with remnants of their umbilical cords waggling from swollen bellies as they scampered alongside, begging for food. The soldiers hurriedly threw their jam sandwiches among the urchins and cantered away along the north track.

As Ned had ridden by the concentration camp before, he took the lead. "Easy to find, sport." He grinned crookedly, "Might say, just follow your nose."

The trail had deep ruts in it from heavy wagon traffic, and turned muddy when it reached the wetlands just beyond town. Otters splashed, blue herons croaked, caracals called, and bright puff-tails, barbets, and louries sang everywhere. Harry felt good to be outdoors after so many weeks of confinement, a horse between his knees and the pure scent of pine trees wafting down the slope.

Coveyduck was enjoying the same feeling. "This is the life, eh? After the shooting's over, it'll take civilian life a bit of getting used to. Don't much fancy myself going back to catching wild brumbies in Queensland. Hard to imagine you behind a bank counter again, either."

"I try not to think about it. I'm all for peace breaking out, but my prospects in civvie-street are best described as piss-poor."

Harry handed a chunk of Rowntree bar to Ned, and they chewed the sweet chocolate in contented silence. After a half-hour's riding up-hill through woodlands, the wind turned cooler, a hint of the bitter cold that would arrive on the Eastern Highlands within a couple of months. They rode out of the trees, and the Steencampsberg rose ahead in a sudden wall of rugged crags poking high into misty rain-clouds.

Harry took in the alpine beauty and said, "Looks a lot like back home in B.C."

Ned jerked his head angrily, "Except for that!"

Rows of grubby white bell-tents, hundreds of them, were set in straight lines up the sloping hillside. The camp had no barbed-wire fence or walls, but a separate clump of tents showed a big sign, "Armed Guard Post. All Visitors Must

Report Here". Considering Harry's unauthorized intention, it seemed a good place to avoid, so the newcomers took a short-cut off the track.

The steady mountain wind fluttered thousands of bits of soiled paper and menstrual-stained cloth that littered the ground ringing the camp. Then the breeze shifted, wafting a stink so bad it made Harry gag. The nauseating stench of human waste was fouler than anything Harry had ever smelled. Ned dead-panned, "'Wouldn't dismount if I was you, sport."

Excrement lay everywhere on the open ground. People had used the entire area as an outdoors latrine, and left an unbelievable stinking mess that fed swarms of buzzing flies. "Strewth, nothing but shit and jam-rags!" The Australian hawked and spat a gobful. "I bet old Kitchener never visited this particular hell-hole!"

The horses snorted and shied at the odour, and the men reined back onto the track. A young lance-corporal in a blue uniform hurried out of the guard post. He was what the Afrikaners called a Cape Coloured, part Hindoo, part Malay. He saluted smartly. "Good afternoon, gentlemen. May I ask your business, sirs?" Harry identified himself, and bluffed that he was here to take back a man from the camp for urgent duty. "Oh, dear. Completely impossible, sir. No soldier is allowed inside the women's camp without express written permission." The Guard Service n.c.o. hitched his old Martini rifle proudly. "Even I, myself, the perimeter commander, must ask permission to enter, sir."

Ned shouted and galloped ahead to the man drooping against a fence. Luckily, the Provost squad who put him there had given Mendip a Wolseley sun-helmet to protect against the glaring afternoon sun. Harry was shocked to see the state Jiggy was in otherwise. His whole body shook, and big patches of sweat and dried salt on his tunic showed how much he was suffering from heat-stroke.

The trooper somehow managed a grin, cracked lips and

all. "Sorry I can't salute, sir." Field Punishment Number One had him pinioned with both arms strung sideways, roped by the wrists to the fence-rails, two hours on, two hours off, for three days.

"Hope she was worth it, Jiggy."

Harry had been told by Ned the charge was 'Publicly performing an indecent act in a posted OOB area.' There was no officer around to plead for the prisoner to be released into his custody, so Harry just nodded for Coveyduck to start sawing with his clasp-knife at the ropes.

"Ta, Ned. Who'd've expected fookin' Redcaps to come up here at night and nab me shaggin' under a wagon?"

Trying to sound stern, Harry said, "Careful you don't put it quite that way to my new second-in-command. Now, how'd you like to go off in the blue with us tomorrow?"

"Oh, sir, this man was put here as an example to obey Refugee Camp rules. He is not to be released, please!" The lance-corporal's six Coloured guards had turned out as well, looking nervous in case they had to back him up against a white officer.

"Regulations are very strict about keeping troops away from the refugee women, sir."

"This man is required for special duties, Corporal". Harry showed his stores priority letter, though it had no relevance to this situation. The HQ letterhead seemed to impress the lance-jack well enough, and he led his men away. Mendip was groggy on his feet, grey tongue sticking out. Ned said, "We should get him to sick-bay, soon as poss."

"Best not, Harry." Jiggy panted. "I wouldn't pass the short-arm exam, and the M.O.'ll put me on a fizzer. It'd mean thirty days in the glasshouse, not to mention the medics reaming me out with that umbrella tool every morning."

Harry sighed loudly, "Christ, what else?"

The British army punished the contacting of venereal disease as a similar offence to getting drunk. 'Placing himself in such a condition as to be unable to carry out his duties'. If the MO put Jiggy on a charge, the painful medical treatment would be far worse than the month spent in detention cells. More important, there was nowhere else Harry could find another signaler who was also able to translate with Bantus.

"If you've caught a dose, think you could cope with being in the saddle?"

"Only a bit of clap, sir, not syph. Just give me a chance to flash t'old mirror again for you, and I'll ride anywhere, right as rain."

A horse and cart rattled out the camp's entrance and headed along a side trail. Two blanket-rolled adult bodies lay in the wagon, beside five tiny shapes wrapped in baby shawls. A dozen gaunt women held the cart sides, and tried to shush the noisy infants who skipped behind unaware. The soldiers pulled their hats off as the funeral cart went past, but women shook their fists in reply. A mourner limped over to Harry's stirrup and cursed, "Enteric seize you!"

Lanyard sat watching the procession until Ned said, "These hands of his look in a bad way."

"Yeah, maybe they'll dole out some first-aid at the field-hospital." He had spotted the black "H" on a marquee inside the camp.

CHAPTER EIGHT.

Lanyard put Jiggy on his horse and walked into the camp, ignoring the stares of hundreds of silent women. They watched out of curiosity, with no boldness at all, and looked down modestly if the foreign men met their gaze. Females of all ages halted in mid-step or crowded tent openings, gaping at the sight of three kakies among them. It was tough not to stare back.

These women looked like corpses, parchment skin stretched over cheekbones, black-rimmed eyes, shabby dresses loose on emaciated bodies. They moved unsurely, with an odd jerkiness, like figures in Biograph picture films. It was worse when you noticed the kids. They swarmed everywhere, too quietly, with unsmiling little skull-faces and pot-bellies, some bow-legged with rickets. One small boy aimed a stick at the soldiers, "Ping, ping!" Other children and adults peered though windows of the school-hut, and Ned gave them a friendly wave.

"What's this merry idea, then?" A middle-aged woman in a white cap, apron, and striped blue dress stood on the hospital steps, fists on hips.

Harry saluted and introduced himself. "Ma'am, I have an injured man here, and would appreciate a medic taking a look at him."

"I know very well who he is, Lieutenant, and FP Number One is scarcely an injury." She had sharp eyes and a no-nonsense Durham accent.

"Maybe so, ma'am. If somebody could just attend his needs, we'll be on our way."

"I'm perfectly aware of his condition, too. Considering I went out to check his state whenever I could." She looked at a stop-watch pinned to her bodice, sighed, and turned away. "Oh, very well. Quickly now."

No amount of carbolic could mask the sour odours of

sickness wafting into the dispensary. There was a loud babble of female voices behind the canvas walls; crying, talking, moaning in various levels of pain, and repeatedly calling, "Nurse, nurse!"

A whiff of smelling-salts brought Mendip out of his swoon, and he gratefully drank a pan of water. He lay back with a wet compress on his head to bring the feverishness down. A couple of harassed young Englishwomen in badly-stained whites kept darting between the ward and the matron, asking for supplies or advice. They always addressed her respectfully as "Sister". It was the British army term for nurse, not meaning a nun.

She seemed able to handle a dozen other medical tasks and enquiries at once between applying temporary bandages to the raw rope-gouges on Mendip's wrists. She noticed how Jiggy perked up when the girls came in, and pulled the knot-ends tight to curb him. "You're dehydrated mostly, feller-me-lad. So get this tea down and you'll soon be fit as a fiddle. But don't dare come near my camp again."

"Oh, I was with a chocolate-baby that night, Mum, not one of your ladies."

"It's your blame all the Boer women insisted the girl was sent away. I managed to get her into the black concentration camp at Middleburg, but conditions're worse still there."

"Sorry, Mum, it was only a bit of slap-and-tickle."

His turn of phrase brought a ghost of amusement to Sister's tired face. "Well, repeat it, and you'll have more than MPs to worry about. I'll deal with the problem myself." She scissored the bandage ends with meaningful snips.

"Ta, Mum."

She looked up and snapped, "Get away from there!" The big Australian jumped like a schoolboy away from peeking through the partition. "Leave our women some decent privacy!"

"No offence, Sister. I was only wondering how many patients you have."

"Two hundred and twelve in the ward. Excepting the ones who'll sneak back to their tents this afternoon."

Coveyduck wrinkled his brow. "Why would they do that?"

"Distrust of modern doctoring, mostly. Veld women prefer 'doppels', their traditional old remedies. Like horrible cow-dung poultices to cure pneumonia. Red body-paint or laudanum for child illness. Dogs' blood and sulphur drinks against typhoid." She sighed loudly. "Not that our own medicines are much help, either. Often it comes down to patients just wanting to leave the ward and die in company of their loved ones."

Sister breathed out shakily and ran chapped hands through her neat bun of reddish-gray hair. "So many here do, you know. Die I mean."

"Thousands of our fellers are dying of typhoid, too", Coveyduck said. "I've seen Tommies lying outside a hospital in the rain without so much as a blanket. Not a doctor in sight, blokes just left to kick the bucket."

"I know, poor lads. The RAMC can brag all it wants about its marvelous new X-Ray machines, yet there's still not enough doctors or orderlies to go around. That's why army medical care's really not much better otherwise than it was in the Crimea fifty years ago."

She gestured towards the cries beyond the canvas. "But all I can think of are the innocent civilians. Over two thousand lie in our cemetery alone. There's over ten times that many dead in the camps altogether. Children mostly, the lambs. Adults die of enteric, infection carried by flies from human waste. But it's measles, diarrhea, and starvation that take the little bairns."

Harry said carefully, "There's talk of, uh, harmful stuff being put in their food."

"That's all-my-eye-and-Betty-Martin!"

"Lies," Jiggy translated. "What Geordies say when they mean something's been made up." He gave Sister a fellow-Northerner's wink.

She managed a slight smile and a Durhamite's riposte. "And you can always tell a Yorkshireman, but you can't tell him much!"

She turned back to Harry. "No deliberate poisoning of food could ever match the thousands of deaths that we've caused by simple incompetence and stupidity. Nobody in charge seemed to have any conception of what epidemics you'd get from concentrating people into camps without adequate food, sanitation, or staff."

"Surely there's not just you three looking after things here?"

"Oh, we've six nurses altogether, now. I did have three others. Canny lasses, well-trained, but they died within a month of arriving from England." She fastened her starched cuffs briskly, and went on, "We've our camp physician, of course. One, to look after four thousand human beings. Doctor Wilkie's off doing rounds in the tents, where most of our patients stay even after coming down with something dire." She hurried at filling shoulder-packs with prescription bottles.

"The women here are always trying to help each other. Unfortunately, that includes slipping dangerous little treats like dates and meat to loved-ones who're deathly-ill with typhoid, which makes things only worse."

She explained that Superintendent van der Busche ran the camp, but the inmates didn't trust him at all. "He's an Afrikaner who changed sides, you see, and they swear he has a spite against commando families now. They keep asking for an Englishman to be put in charge, instead, if you can believe it. I swear Boers hate handsuppers even more than they do us British, and loathe the ones they call joiners most of all."

She changed another wet compress for Jiggy, then stood up in a rush. "Let him rest a few more minutes, Lieutenant, then please leave. Good day." She slung two medicine satchels, lifted a big bundle with a gasp of effort, and stepped towards the exit.

"Let me, Sister." Lanyard took the load from her arms, "Where do you want this?"

"Well, if you insist, thank you. These're our first new blankets to arrive in months. I want to distribute them before going on shift."

Before she could lift the other bale, Ned grabbed it. "Lead the way, ma'am."

A crowd was forming outside the stores tent opposite, mainly women, both native and white, but with a sprinkling of men. Their sunken eyes never left the storekeeper who stood on a platform yelling names from a list. Wives stepped forward in turn to collect their allocation, many helped by black servant girls.

A couple of Belfast civilians doled out each adult's weekly ration. Seven pounds of bread or flour, five pounds of meat, four pounds of potatoes or carrots, a handful of tea or coffee, a tin of milk, some sugar and salt. Children aged under 12 got about half the adult rations, and infants seemed to be expected to live on oatmeal and syrup plus one bottle of milk a day.

"There was no milk at all for children when I arrived." Sister read the look in Harry's face. "Mister Shapiro sent us some dairy cows, which was nice of him, but they all died from lack of fodder."

She had a way of raising her shoulders, as if to summon strength. "No medicines, soap, hot water boilers, or toilets, either. Not even beds. Much less any cloth squares for babies' nappies or women's monthlies. Providing bare necessities of cleanliness never occurred to the people who were supposed to be in charge. All men, of course!"

She moved quickly to each tent she considered was in most need, peeling blankets from the bales and quickly enquiring about the occupants' state of health. Along the route, she kept up a monologue of scathing opinion to her rare audience of soldiers. "Come to that, Boer menfolk are just as stupid. Riding around playing Cowboys-and-Indians. Abandoning their families to fend for themselves, or rely on the tender mercies of our gormless politicians."

"I guess commandos aren't the sort to give up." Harry was surprised to hear himself almost defending them to her.

"Hmph! The worst they face is an ocean voyage to one of our PW camps in Bermuda or Ceylon or some such nice spot. Twenty-five thousand captured enemy troops, who get as well fed as our own Tommies, plus adequate medical care. Meanwhile, we neglect their innocent families so much, they're dying in droves. That seems to me a very topsy-turvy way to run a war. But then, of course, I'm a mere feather-headed female, not credited with enough sense to even have the vote!"

The few male inmates they saw on the walk seemed to find nothing to do. They sat on chairs quietly, smoking a pipe, reading the Testament, or staring into small campfires. Some waved courteously, "Hello, English!". Each insisted on shaking hands, with a sentence or two about the change of weather.

"Gooi dag, Suster." Women greeted her all along their route between the tents. Though walking on steadily, the head nurse had a word or two for each in passing, "How're you, hinnie?" She asked after numerous ailments, sometimes in stilted Afrikaans, and often calling, "Hello, pet!" to a child.

Harry held out some chocolate to a youngster with the pinched face of an old man. "For Heaven's sake, no!" Sister snapped, "That could kill him! Diarrhea is chronic enough already." Lanyard winced at his mistake as they walked away. Unseen, Ned handed candy to the boy, anyway. The poor kid didn't look like he had much longer on earth, so what difference would it make?

A haggard-looking little man with a black bag came out of a tent and said quietly, "Two more SP cases in here, Sister." He leaned so close, the soldiers could detect the cloves he sucked against the odours in the tents. "A septic pneumonia epidemic is sweeping through every town in South Africa. It's usually fatal. Now some infected visitor must have brought it here. Will you lend a hand with moving a few patients to isolation?"

Harry hesitated, worried about getting back on duty. "Ah, don't lower yourselves!" Dr. Wilkie sneered, "I'll rent a couple of our fireside-idlers, instead. They won't raise a finger to help, either, until we pay them first."

Harry tried to explain, but the medico looked him up and down contemptuously. "Huh, it was some brilliant army officer who selected a sloping hillside for this campsite, too!" Wilkie scowled at them, patted his pockets for loose change, and hurried away to hire part-time bearers.

"Why, aye, man!" Weariness thickened Sister's Geordie dialect. "Every time it rains, we're plodgin' up to our knees in water, and tent floors're all clarty with mud."

She took some blankets from Ned and went inside another tent, her voice very firm. "Ladies, I keep saying, roll these wall-flaps up again! Sharpish, please!"

She came out looking cross, "I can't convince them that lack of ventilation helps spread disease. Along with the overcrowding. Twelve adults to a tent. Half a dozen kiddies put in one bed to keep warm at night, sick and healthy bundled close together."

A big schoolboy shuffled down the middle of the street, giggling. His pants were open and he pumped himself in a frenzy, red raw. The two soldiers glanced uncomfortably at Sister, but she did not turn a hair. "Now, Jacob, stop that foolishness this instant!" she called. "Put it away like a good boy, or I'll have to tell your pastor!" She watched him walk on, shoulder still jerking. "Poor lad. Lots of people go mad here, young and old. Only the Boers' strong religious belief keeps down the suicides."

"They seem to get on with you well enough."

"Easy to gain respect if a body's just ready to roll her

sleeves up. There's plenty of scope for elbow-grease here."

Harry thought about his sister and her protesting friends. He wondered if any of them ever thought of coming out to South Africa themselves to actually help relieve the horrors they so deplored before going home for high tea.

"We look after Loyalists as well as commandos' families," the weary head nurse was saying. "British settlers who've been driven off their farms. Orphans too young to know what their origins are. Mixed up refugees of every political stripe still keep coming in voluntarily, despite conditions here. The women are absolutely terrified of what black men might do to them if caught on the veld."

While waiting outside another tent, Ned nudged Harry. Some infants with trousers down were balancing themselves on a log laid over a foul-smelling pit. The smallest boy slipped backwards and fell in. The men were about to go to his rescue, but laughing playmates pulled him out. He ran on short match-stick legs towards his tent home, spluttering, "Ka-ka, Mama, ka-ka!"

"We've simply nobody to dig fresh latrines." Sister chewed her lips. "Any funds to pay labourers are not seen as being medically related. Even though the faeces that's trod onto every tent spreads enteric."

She moved ahead more quickly, almost trotting to reach the children's hospital. It was nothing more than a long marquee with makeshift wooden walls. Anxious mothers crowded around the entrance, and some tried to force their way through when anyone came out the door. You could hear a constant noise of hundreds of children crying and calling, so loud and pitiful that Harry wondered how anyone could ever sleep in the nearby tents.

A nurse opened the door to let out a tiny woman, red-faced with grief. She cuddled a small shape wrapped in brown paper, and walked away unseeingly.

Sister asked, "Not Missus Ruyter?" The nurse nodded.

Without looking at the soldiers, Sister almost whispered,

"She buried eight children on her farm before the war, all from dysentery. Now it's taken her only baby." Sister bustled inside to tend all her bairns. No time to say goodbye.

Back at the dispensary, they found Jiggy having his face sponged by one of the nurses. She perched on the chair edge, his arm casually around her waist as if to steady her. He was saying, "When's your next night off in town then, darlin'?"

The girl scampered away, and Ned led Mendip out to the horses. "Don't expect any bits of crumpet where you're headed, Randy-Balls!"

Harry stood by the hitching rail, helping Ned to swing Mendip up behind his saddle. Somebody called in a low voice, and it took a moment before he figured out the guttural words were English. At first, he did not recognize who he thought was an elderly woman standing on the classroom steps. She shaded her squint against the setting sun, repeating herself, "Mister Maple Leaf?"

The vrou looked about twenty years older since they met at her burning farm, fifteen months ago. "Oh, uh, nice to see you again, ma'am. Er, how's it going for you?"

"I am very well, thank you," she said carefully. "I study English and geography at our so good school." She nodded at Mendip. "I am thinking you would come here, when your comrade was punished. It is my maid they found him lying with, the girl you saw at our farm. He rode by and called her out. Now they have taken her away from me as well."

"That's too bad." He glanced around. "Where's your . . . ?" He smiled apologetically because he did not know the kid's name.

"Gone to being an angel, long ago. My husband Henk is with her, too, I think." There was no feeling left in her voice. "Measles, it was. Before even her burns had time to heal. I am too ill to go when they laid her at rest. Nobody recalls which one was hers, so is no cross on her grave."

"You were nice to her. I must tell." The vrou spoke quickly over Harry's regrets, gabbling to get her words out.

"There was a young woman here, Vrou Osseboom. Pretty girl, well-along with baby, but ill with fever. Her husband bringed her to the infirmary. Just a corporal, but talked like an English milord to the doctor. He is very handsome, but some of our ladies called him a *soetpiel.*" She blushed, and covered her mouth.

"He very angry at you. His wife died. Before her baby could be born. So sad it was. Her husband comes back to bury her. He is crying, the kakies first tooked his little brother and now his dear wife is gone also. He rides away, shouting and vowing by the Virgin Mary he will kill you."

"Too bad, but he'll have a job on, trying to snuff our entire army."

"Ach, not all. Just you, the Canadian called Lanyard. Mister Osseboom says you killed his brother. I will offer prayers to the Almighty for your soul."

"Hoer!" An old man with a shovel called something coarse about her dallying with a kakie, which drew the attention of other mourners coming back from the funeral. They crowded forward, spitting, shaking fists, and the wagon driver yelled, *"Fok jou, rooineks!"*

The vrou blushed again. *"Ag,* how bad you British will always seem to us Afrikaners now." She threw the apron over her face and ran away into the maze of tents.

CHAPTER NINE

Chilly drizzle started to fall as they rode back to Belfast, not speaking much. Lanyard dropped Jiggy behind the barracks, and told Ned to hide him until reveille at dawn. He had a harder time with convincing Scayles to pull some strings with the Military Police. The lieutenant reluctantly went to get Mendip excused further punishment, on grounds his signaling skills were required for active service.

Harry made a stop at Stores, to indent for heliograph equipment and two pairs of binoculars, one for Jiggy. Then he strolled over to the Mess, and picked up his mail. The porter handed him a yellow message chit with orders to attend a last-minute Intelligence briefing at 2100 hours. Harry checked his pocket watch. Enough time to visit Benjamin's for the ritual last big dinner before going on patrol.

Like all better-quality eating places in town, it had an Army Provost Marshal card on the door: OUT OF BOUNDS TO OTHER RANKS. He un-clipped his holster for the receptionist to lock in safe-keeping, and joined the warm gaiety inside. All bright chandeliers, mirrored walls, chiming cutlery, and merry conversation, the popular eatery was enjoying another packed Friday night. Benjamin Shapiro himself came forward, tall, saturnine, in full evening dress. He greeted Harry by name, and led the way to a wall cubicle.

"Congratulations on your promotion, Lieutenant. And your vindication." The restaurateur heard everything in Belfast. He handed a typewritten menu, his dark eyes sardonic. "Justice can prevail in this world. Not often, true, but sometimes."

"Thanks. Pity those cows you sent to the camp didn't prevail. They all starved to death."

"Ah, unfortunate. One would do more to help, but too much sympathy might be misconstrued." A Levantine shrug.

"The authorities, you understand."

"Yeah, might be bad for business."

Shapiro spread his hands resignedly, snapped fingers for a waiter, and hurried away. Many diners tonight were prosperous-looking gents of the army-supplier type and their women. There was a sprinkling of army officers taking a break from the Mess. Some fat-faced contractors recognized Lanyard and called "Hear-hear, only way to treat Boer rebels!" He studiedly ignored them. Some fellow officers did not even nod to Lanyard. He ordered a beer, which made the waiter look down his nose. The meal took its time being served, letting Harry savour the drink and a rare moment of ease.

Champagne was being drunk by the magnum at the contractors' tables, fueling loud talk of profitable deals still to be made from supplying both sides. Naturally, barring any inconvenient peace being signed to spoil everything. "Don't worry, chaps, this jolly war could go on for years." one brayed. "Haw-haw! That's if Burger gets that extra spending money his lot're hinting about."

"Nay, talk's cheap! Yon Boojers'll get nowt off my firm on credit, big promises regardless."

Harry decided to not let these vultures spoil his evening, and tuned them out like a Marconi wireless. He lounged comfortably, looking forward to the well-cooked roast beef he'd ordered, but felt uneasy somehow. Within a few minutes, he sensed being watched. Not just from idle curiosity, but stared at intently. It was the alertness you developed out on the veld, where detecting a covert gaze could save your life seconds before a shot from ambush.

His glance roamed as much of the room he could see without turning around, then scanned mirrors to cover the rest of the place. Nobody seemed particularly interested, now the novelty of his arrival had worn off. Still, the feeling would not go away. It was only the quick jerk of a diner's head turning away that caught his attention.

The man wore a dark suit and high collar, sitting alone on the far side of the dining-room. He sipped from a full glass, evidently having followed Harry in. The civilian kept his head turned, but the reflection showed his face, straight nose, a blue-black jaw. After a moment, he looked up again and started when he found Harry meeting his gaze. He smiled faintly, and half-raised his drink. The man was a stranger, yet there was a vague familiarity. Harry shrugged, probably just one of those hopeful cruising poufters.

When the meal arrived, he sat looking at the fragrant pile of meat and baked potatoes. It made him think too much of the starvation he had seen this afternoon. So he called for his bill, paid the puzzled waiter, and sauntered away without eating a bite. It came to him then who the starer was, one of the patrol's reinforcements, what's his name, deKrieger.

In his well-cut suit, lolling at a table in these surroundings, he looked unrecognizable as a rough-and-tumble trooper. "Good evening, sir." He squeaked the words in that almost parody of a Cape accent of his. "Care for a Bols?" DeKrieger indicated the bottle of Advokaat, and pantomimed for a waiter to bring another glass.

Harry managed to keep his voice level and low. "What the Sam Hill are you playing at?"

An easy smile. "Oh, just enjoying a final slap-up dinner, you know."

"If we weren't going off at dawn . . ." Harry sat down for a moment, so as to not draw attention. "By rights, I should put you on at least two charges. Dressed in civvies, and out of bounds. You'd be in the glasshouse for weeks, but I'd be left one man short."

"Sorry?" DeKrieger looked honestly puzzled, though there was something else in his response. Almost relief at Harry's focus. "But, surely, when I'm off duty . . . ?"

"How long've you been in the army? No private's allowed to wear mufti unless he's home on leave. Never on active service, much less in an O.O.B. café."

"But, I hadn't realized."

"Cut the BS! Get yourself in uniform and back to barracks before midnight. Clear?" DeKrieger made an apologetic smile, but as Harry walked away, he caught a mirrored look of naked malice on the man's face. It was a baffling reaction from such a mild-mannered man.

The owner stood at the front desk to hand his holster back. "Off your appetite, Lieutenant? Tell me it wasn't tonight's special." The sleek head cocked shrewdly. "Which reminds me, I was thinking of donating a few more spare cows to Sister. With weekly fodder this time. Or would that look too un-businesslike?"

"Not at all, Mister Shapiro." Lanyard shook hands, which he did rarely. He walked into the dusk, feeling a bit better about mankind, even if he had kept himself hungry.

St. Steven's Church was chiming eleven o'clock when Harry left the Intelligence briefing at H.Q. He paused outside, mentally repeating heliograph cipher codes he was not allowed to write down, then set off walking back to quarters. A score of street-walkers showed themselves under the gas street-lights opposite Headquarters. They were native girls mostly, starving refugees, with a sprinkling of desperate white women on the game. Each murmured, "Want a short-time, Tommy?", as he walked by.

Artificial lightning flickered off the low clouds, where naval searchlights signaled Morse code instructions to units far out on the veld. He noticed the glisten of a wet oilskin cape where a man stepped back into shadow. Some pimp, probably; or maybe an MP lurking to nab any officer stupid enough to get caught picking up a prostitute.

The Redcaps would be busy in Belfast tonight. Twenty-three hundred hours was curfew time for the pubs and shebeens, last drinks gulped, and boozed-up patrons sent staggering outside. The more abstemious type of soldier chose to avoid town on pay-night. Their drunken comrades crowded the rowdy streets, yelling, swearing, and spewing in gutters.

Community singing was the favorite entertainment of the times, and none enjoyed it more than soldiers. Especially when drunk. Groups of squaddies staggered about, laughing like hyenas and harmonizing music-hall favorites, "Carry Me Back To Dear Old Blighty", "My Bonnie Lies Over The Ocean", and "The Man Who Broke The Bank At Monte Carlo". Others bawled obscene stanzas from "Abdul El-Bul-Bul Emir", and other barrack-room ditties.

They were drunk enough to pick fights with beery coal-miners, and quarrel with the roving pairs of Redcaps who broke up the brawls. Harry saw a group of Scotties start a shoving match with two MPs, and decided to avoid the inevitable punch-up about to start. To get around them, he turned off down a narrow side-street.

The alley muted fading yells of "Bluidy Sassenach coppers!" There was only the loud clack of his heel-plates on cobble-stones, and something about the narrow place made his back hair prickle. He stopped to light a Players, and heard a boot scrape nearby. Lanyard whirled, fists up. The dim glow from the sky revealed a man and woman writhing in a nearby shop doorway.

He took a relaxing drag of smoke, then walked on through the gloom, blaming his jumpiness on shell-shocked nerves. Rain pattered heavier on his hat, and he tried not to think of Boer mothers struggling with a chaos of water-logged beds in pitch-black tents. Then his attention jumped at hearing the sudden crackle of oilskins behind. That moment, brighter reflections from a searchlight threw the enormous shadow of a man in a long flaring cape, running with his arm raised.

Harry put his back to the bricks and lashed out with a boot. He felt it connect solidly and the man cried in pain but continued to swing his arm. Harry danced sideways, and heard the attacker grunt with effort. A knife-blade grated on the wall, inches from Lanyard's throat, and fell to the cobbles. Double clicks sounded as the man cocked both hammers of a stubby shotgun he swung up from nowhere. Harry reached for his Webley, felt only stiff leather, and scrabbled to unbutton the holster. The twin barrels glinted, rising towards his head.

That goddam flap resisted his fingers, no time to draw the pistol, so he grabbed the shotgun muzzle instead. He shoved it away in a reflex. *Blam!* The blast lit up the alley for an instant like a photographer's magnesium flash. Warm wetness splashed his hair, and the attacker flew backwards.

Harry needed the wall to hold himself up while he breathed deep to settle the nausea. Police whistles shrilled in the streets, and hob-nails clattered into the alley. A bulls-eye lamp caught him, and a hard voice yelled, "Hands up, you!" When the MPs got closer, their tone changed. "You all right, sir?"

Some civilian police arrived, who were less respectful and demanded his identity. One late-arriving Redcap leaned over the body. "Looks like you've nailed another one, sir." Harry recognized the sarcastic voice of Corporal Gudger.

An Afrikaner detective was going through the corpse's pockets. "What happened, please?" Harry explained as briefly as possible. The plain-clothesman found a small bank-bag and chinked gold coins. "Hmm, successful at his trade, it seems." The 'tec was curious. This didn't play like some ordinary street hold-up to him. Odd the fellow was carrying a sawn-off shotgun on a string under his cape. "Did you know him, perhaps?"

"We never met, but I think his name was Osseboom."

"How so?"

"Somebody warned me about him a few hours ago."

"We must make further inquiries."

Gudger rolled the corpse over with his boot and shone his bulls-eye at the ruined face. "Well, whoever he was, his own mother wouldn't recognize him now."

CHAPTER TEN

"You Lanyard? Welcome aboard, sir." The Royal Navy sub-lieutenant on the roof gave a perfect salute, then slid backwards down the iron ladder's handrails without touching a step.

"Anybody tell me what the hell's going on?"

"'Been a bit of a change of plan, I'm afraid. The powers-that-be decided to borrow your private chuffer to send some needed squaddies along the line as well."

"I wondered why my men got stuck on the back of a troop-train." Harry glanced at his watch. "How much longer will the trip take now, with the extra stops?"

"Least another hour, I'd say. They've cobbled a carriage on for civvies, too." He seemed no older than a schoolboy, with his pimpled face and mouthful of horse-like teeth.

"Situation normal. Hurry up and wait." Harry nodded towards sounds of his men in the distance, shouting curses, hooves drumming up wooden ramps onto horse-cars. Two Griqua handlers called shrilly in Afrikaans as they pulled each mount aboard, settling them nose to tail.

The day had dawned clear after the rain. Cooler with the nip of autumn, but the sun was warm enough already to raise steam from the wet platform. The brass-bound little locomotive hissed to itself, free-wheeling pistons clanking slowly. Two Basutos shoveled coal into the fire-box fast as they could, sweat polishing their faces. The engine-driver watched his gauges, eager for the steam pressure to build, while his mate snarled at the stokers for more effort.

"Not to worry, the RN'll get you to Alkemaar quick as dropping off those other pongos will allow. I'm Galliano, by the way." He drawled his name as though it had ten final As. His peaked cap and webbing pistol-belt were snow-white with fresh Blanco. He wore a khaki uniform, but with gilt anchor-badges on the collar to let soldiers know the Naval

Brigade was in charge of this particular train.

"You can ride topsides with me if you like, to keep a look-out for any trouble. Quiet run, usually, though." He twisted a wry face. "I fancy the most excitement we can look forward to this trip is if those Jocks ever get a go at the Scousers. From what I've seen, you brown jobs fight each other more than you ever do with the King's enemies."

Lanyard said he'd best go and make sure his horses were shipshape. He quickly walked back along the jammed platform to check that his patrol was fully boarded. Indian tea-sellers with urns on their backs moved through the crowd, calling shrilly, "Most excellent Darjeeling, only a ha'penny per mug!" Tobacco hawkers did a particularly good trade, selling out all their stock of cigarettes and pipe-tobacco. About everybody in this man's army smoked.

Among the throng, Harry exchanged nods with a Scots officer, one of his breakfast escorts yesterday morning. Two companies of infantry were boarding, men of the Highland Light Infantry and The King's Regiment (Liverpool). Their officers took care to keep them well separated, as both had a fearsome reputation for quarrelsomeness with rival units. They were put in cars each side of the single carriage occupied by civilian passengers bound for towns along the Delagoa line.

Lanyard saw some of his men were still dallying with young women who has turned up to kiss their boyfriends farewell. Many were natives, but several white girls were there as well. Lt. Scayles was striding back and forth impatiently, all creaking leather and trousers pressed sharp enough to draw blood. Harry explained the train situation, then turned him loose to herd the stragglers aboard. Lanyard was grateful for the policeman's bullying efficiency in moving the troops along. One of them was deKrieger, drab again in uniform.

Jiggy turned up just in time, escorted by two adoring Basuto meisies. He gave each a quick parting feel, drawing obscene hoots from less enterprising troops at every window. He pinched the glowing end off his cigarette, tucked the stub behind an ear, and stepped aboard wearing a wide grin. "No way to talk about my sleeping dictionaries, lads."

He leaned out to call, "Keep it warm for me, girls. I'll be back soon to give you both a good seeing-to!" Burghers on the platform watched his performance with outrage, to see any white man behaving so with native women. Well, in public anyway.

Ned waved from the last carriage, and Harry pushed through hurriedly. The Australian handed down a wrapped ammunition belt, and said almost shyly. "After last night, I figured you need a decent shooting-rig."

Lanyard grabbed it quickly. "Thanks. Make a note, soon as we arrive, I want every man to practice-fire twenty rounds with those new Enfields." He took a last quick look around. "Sure our lot's all here?"

Ned held up both thumbs, "Bright-eyed and bushy-tailed, every mother's son. Mind you, I think some of the horses have hang-overs."

The engine loosed a shriek of steam, and Harry trotted back to swing into the command-car as it moved off. While the train rolled away from the station, Tommies waved to girls from every window and burst into the self-mocking tune they always sang at parting:

> "Good-bye, Dolly, I must leave you,
> Though it breaks my heart to go,
> Something tells me I am needed,
> At the front to fight the foe,
>
> Hear the soldier boys are marching,
> And I can no longer stay,
> But I hear the bugles playing,
> Good-bye, Dolly Gray!"

The sentimental words reminded Harry of when he first sang them himself. Dizzy with excitement, he had stood on deck among fellow volunteers aboard the Canadian Pacific ferry as they sailed from Victoria harbour a week or two before Christmas, 1899. His parents were there, pale-faced but proud, as the whole city turned out to wish the volunteers God-speed for a quick victory against the Old Country's foes in far off South Africa.

Sun sparkling off the Straits of Juan de Fuca and the snow-capped Olympic mountains beyond added to the glorious atmosphere. Ships' hooters blared as a great cheering crowd of relatives, lovers, and well-wishers called farewells across the widening water to their Brave Boys from Vancouver Island. Every recruit tingled with patriotic resolve as they sailed away, stirred by brass bands playing "Dolly Gray", "Auld Lang Syne", "The Maple Leaf Forever", and "God Save The Queen" over and over 'til they could be heard no more on board.

The Empire's cause had all seemed so noble and certain back then. Most of his companions of that day were returned home safe to British Columbia long since, hailed as conquering heros when victory was prematurely thought to be gained in 1900. That early unquestioning support for Britain against Boers had radically changed in Canada now.

But not out here, Harry thought. In the distance, he caught sight of the Witkloof escarpement, where the hell-for-leather Royal Canadian Dragoons had won three VCs in a single hour, saving the guns at Leliefontein. He wondered if anyone back home these days even knew or cared about such heroism.

He ripped open his father's latest letter and read its puzzlement and cautious criticism that had never been there before. "Of course we know that decent lads like you would never do anything to harm Old England's reputation, but 'The Victoria Colonist' is full of most disturbing reports by Miss Hobhouse and other observers about ill-treatment of civilians in South Africa. Dora has such a bee in her bonnet about it she can be quite tiresome. Worse still your dear mother has been hurt by cruel remarks from neighbours about your staying on where those barbarisms are said to be committed . . ."

It's how things were starting to seem to everyone back home. Revealing the truth of wholesale deaths in the camps was one thing, but that malarkey about fish-hooks showed just how much distorted propaganda was also being put about now. Still, Harry wasn't about to debate the issue with his father by mail.

He slipped the letter back in his pocket, and looked out at Africa's passing reality. The track followed the course of the Crocodile River, close enough that he could hear its roar above the engine. He looked straight down at the torrent that smashed over wild rapids, through deep gorges, racing eastwards across the high Transvaal towards Mozambique.

That could give him something interesting and neutral to write about in an overdue letter home. He used the back of a yellow message sheet, and quickly scribbled a reassuring page to convince his parents he was well and in no danger. Harry deliberately used the sort of carefree boyish language they would remember him using before he left, to chat about unit sports and beautiful autumn weather.

In case any rumour of the CM filtered back to Victoria, he wrote, "I got in a bit of a mix-up lately, but it turned out okey-doke, and now I'm off sight-seeing aboard a comfy train to a very quiet sector." He folded the sheet carefully, and wondered when he'd have a chance to mail it.

He noticed the thick belt he had snatched from Ned, and unrolled it with sudden pleasure. He recognized the duck's-neck butt of a Model '78 Colt six-shooter like all his old outfit once carried as gifts from Lord Strathcona. Harry lost his pair that day of the artillery ambush, and felt naked ever since. He threw the buttoned-up army rig aside, buckled the Colt's cartridge belt, and practiced a few quick draws from it's well-greased open holster. The curved grip fitted his palm perfectly, and he hefted it like an old friend.

The train's English-style passenger carriages had self-contained compartments with no corridors, so Lanyard could not move along to visit his men as he would have preferred. Isolation from them made him uneasy, heading into a war zone. The train-commander's compartment had a stair to the roof, and Harry climbed up. He found Galliano crouching in a waist-high ring of sandbags, with two straw-hatted ratings who crewed the Maxim. A big White Ensign flew stiff in the wind above the machine-gun nest.

"Hard to see much for long, up here," Galliano shouted above the noise. His chin-strap was fastened, and he wore a pair of those goggles that motorcar drivers used. Harry understood why when the coal-dust hit his eyes.

There being no point trying to talk over the racket, Lanyard squatted beside a seaman to look around. A flatcar layered with sandbags was coupled ahead of the locomotive as a buffer against sabotage. He turned away from the flying grit to look back, seeing Naval Brigade men hunkered down around two big signal searchlights, half-way along the train. His men were in the last carriages, next to a calaboose that carried the rear machine-gun. He made out the Griquas crouched among the ponies that stood in four open cars.

All along the train's curving length, he could see the rapt faces of young soldiers staring out, mesmerized by the scenery's overwhelming beauty. After the rain, breath-taking vistas of the high veld showed crystal-clear, before melding into lacy mist that swathed the peaks. Rolling slopes of dried grass lay like carpets of gold, rising into green foothills and towering purplish mountains.

More jaded Tommies barely gave outside a glance, interested in playing cards for a quick gamble, having a chin-wag, reading old newspapers, or exchanging insults with the blockhouse guards they passed. There were 8,000 of the little circular forts of corrugated iron along the 3700-mile

Imperial Military Railway.

One built every mile and a half, each blockhouse had a small garrison of eight bored soldiers. Their job was to protect the rail-line from sabotage and turn back any commando infiltrators on the run from flying columns. The daily train made a welcome diversion, and the isolated soldiers lifted two smutty fingers towards HLI jeering from windows.

Ten miles ahead, Dirk lay within earshot of other Tommies clattering around their pill-box home. They seemed strangely domestic, preoccupied with tending little vegetable gardens inside their compound, feeding goats, or playing with pet dogs. Dirk had heard them call it "Getting stuck in".

He snickered in their direction on the other side of the embankment, but Ox van Antwerp shook his head for caution. Careless as they looked, the guards always had rifles within reach, and one quick crank of the field-telephone could bring reinforcements from other posts nearby in either direction.

Commandos easily managed to cut their way through the barbed wire at night undetected, despite searchlights and trip-wire flares. Once, Dirk had sneaked close to deliberately jangle the empty jam-tins hung on the fence as alarms, so he could enjoy a fireworks display from nervous sentries firing into the darkness.

There was no bravado this morning among the commandos who arrived before dawn to position themselves along the railway. It was serious business, assigned to them only last midnight by a special message from Acting President Burger's Enemy Intelligence Department. Having been sent through the British-controlled telegraph office at Belfast, the wording came coded in an apparent commercial message about agricultural supplies. It was deciphered by the Morse clerk at Machadodorp Station, a Boer sympathizer. As soon as his shift ended, he had galloped two hours through the star-lit night to deliver the orders personally to the local veld-cornet in charge.

Laurens Vilberg read the flimsy by light of an oil-lamp. The instructions were terse and cold-bloodedly to the point. No explanation why, and none needed. It was sufficient for the Crocodile commando to be handed another opportunity to smite the invaders. Vilberg did worry about one thing, whether the sixty-eight men in his force were sufficient. Every one of them was a crack shot and usually more than a match for rooinek soldiers in any ambush. But these orders were different, a virtual mass-extermination, but with no clear information about how many targets there were.

The cornet sighed, rolled his blankets, and rousted everyone out at two o'clock in the morning to hold a quick conference. No attack was made by a commando until all members first discussed it. There was a lot of yawning and moaning among the sleepy gathering, so he had to shout to read the instructions aloud. "You are to kill or capture all Mounted Infantry aboard the Saturday morning train headed eastward."

He got no further when Saul ter Hoven hooted, "Put like that, they want us to shoot crazy kakies riding horses inside a train!"

Vilberg let them enjoy their laugh, then went on, "For purposes of this order, any ordinary troops also aboard may be ignored beyond normal fighting considerations at the time. Your priority targets are distinguished by ostrich feathers in their hats."

Van Kettel interrupted to ask if any of those fools at headquarters stopped to think that nobody wears his hat while in a train. The cornet stolidly finished reading out the orders, "Choice of attack-point is left to the commandos' judgement. However, it is imperative to act before the train reaches Alkmaar, where the patrol intends to disembark. This contingent must not, repeat not, be allowed to carry out its mission. Any surviving prisoners must be brought to

Acting President Burger's headquarters without delay."

"How many Tommies are there? Be nice to know!"

"Prisoners? Fat chance of time for those!"

There were more yelled arguments, the main reason Vilberg had grown to dislike his rank. He was just a farmer, after all. He always dreaded these wrangling discussions before a raid, and often wished his fellow Boers had at least enough discipline to listen politely to instructions.

Laurens lost his temper, and shouted, "You heard, it says 'without delay'! So we have to stop jawing if we're to reach the line before dawn. We'll need that much time to prepare Tommy's hot breakfast."

His men laughed, made in a better mood already. "We can plan on the way where's the best place to serve it. *Opzaal!*" It was an order his commandos agreed with, so they kicked out the fires and ran to saddle-up.

By dawn, their horses were hidden in a donga half a mile from the railway, guarded by 80-year-old Languedoc and the youngest penkops. At first, it looked as though Dirk would have had to stay behind with them as well, but he adamantly refused to miss the attack. Corporal Swarte Schippers probably was thinking of the youngster's safety, but no man had the right to tell any Boer what to do against his will and he shrugged permission. Now, Dirk was crouching on one knee beside the iron tracks, watching Ox van Antwerp closely to see how such a thing was done.

Ox slid a rat-trap snug under a rail, pulled back the spring of the killing-bar, and held it there taut by a copper wire he wound over the rail. He ran another wire from the trap-bar to the trigger of a shotgun that was jammed beside the sleeper. He wedged the muzzle to point at the explosive inside a half-buried artillery round that had been opened by removing its projectile. Finally, Ox scattered dust and cinders over the components to blend with the roadbed.

The giant Fleming grunted at the admiring boy, *"Goed genoeg"*. Good enough. Dirk shook his Mauser in silent applause, pleased at this new deadly skill he had learned. He crawled away to a place he could lie concealed without the morning sun in his eyes.

For all Sub-Lt. Galliano's optimism and the loco's fierce belching of smoke, they crawled along at 25 miles an hour. A horseman rode out from one of the isolated farms, whooping as he rode alongside to pace the train in a short race. They passed a score of tiny hamlets, where school-children waved from playgrounds when the driver tootled and Tommies threw sugar candies for them.

Progress was interrupted by brief whistle-stops en route, then longer at Machadodorp station to unload supplies, soldiers, and civilians. Harry was amused to notice only the English troops were debarked there. Commanders did not want the risk of posting a mix of scrappy King's Liverpudlians with HLI in one small community, and the Scots were bound for a separate garrison further east. The Highland Light Infantry were terrors, mainly recruited from Glasgow city slums. Despite their title, few had ever seen a sprig of highland heather in their lives. Nor were they a kilted regiment; just wore ordinary khaki trousers bound with puttees from knee to ankle

As the train slowly pulled away, an agitated-looking clerk dashed out of the telegraph office. The Boer agent stared at the unexpected additional passenger-load of infantry and civilians. He made to run back inside, then stopped, flapping his hands in a what's-the-use gesture.

With grit flying in his eyes, Harry spent the next hour atop the observation post, crouched with his back to the coal-heavers, trying to watch the veld for movement. The train came down into a green cup-shaped valley, where a small town nestled. The engine-driver blew a long blast on his whistle, and Galliano announced, "Watervaal Onder, old Oom Paul's last capital. Alkmaar's just three stops after this, then you'll be back in your saddles again."

Harry stared curiously as they approached some

corrugated-iron houses huddled around a large building emblazoned, 'Hotel Mathis'. Then Galliano focused his binoculars off to one side, and shouted, "Those are ours I hope?"

Harry squinted, and made out the backs of a big herd of horses down in a donga. When he saw the way they were saddled, he yelled, "Theirs, more like it! Look out!"

Galliano started blowing his whistle to catch the driver's attention. The gunner primed the Maxim and palmed its spade-grips, while Harry ran for the stairwell to get his rifle.

Dirk was the first to hear the train coming, long before it started up the hill. He called excitedly to the others, and they nodded casually, but some took time to kneel for a final prayer. The train dipped down a long slope, gathered speed, and entered the culvert with sheer sides. It met a patrol of City Imperial Volunteers pedaling from the opposite direction on a rail-car. The contraption looked like six over-sized bikes bolted together, and their swaying efforts to pump the pedals delighted the oncoming trainload of soldiers. "Yoo-hoo, Daisy!" Squaddies warbled, "But you'll look sweet, Upon the seat, Of a bicycle built for two . . ."

One pedeler yelled back cheerfully, "Up your's, you Scotch twats!" Next moment, he reared in his seat, pointing at something on the other rail close ahead. His mates could not make out what he said over the train noise, before he fell off with a Mauser bullet through the head. The CIV's wobbled and missed their strokes, puzzled what was wrong with him. Then the train wheel cut Ox's piano-wire, the rat-trap snapped shut, and pulled the shotgun trigger.

A blast of lyddite ripped out seven feet of rail under the train and flung the front buffer-car sideways. The locomotive and first few carriages corkscrewed in turn, sending bogie-wheels spinning, splintering brittle wood and shattering glass into shrapnel that shredded the men seated inside. The engine-crew were smothered under an avalanche of coal.

Lanyard was halfway down the steps when the blast hit.

As it threw him off, he had a quick sight of Galliano falling past the window in a cascade of sandbags and sailors. Harry's head slammed against the wall, and he shouted with pain as he lost consciousness.

There were roaring noises, shaking bangs that set his teeth grinding, and he whimpered loudly. He had not been rescued from that artillery ambush after all. He was still there, Creusot heavy shells crashing, that bloody Nordenfeldt pom-pom spitting one-pounder rounds, seeking him out.

Hurray, here's the stretcher-bearers after all. "This one's near a goner. Blubbering like a babby." Now they're officers with red tabs on, sitting at a long table. "Neurasthenia, my foot! All this sick-artry twaddle is simply a fad. Never had shell-shock in my day. Castor oil always worked wonders. Haw-haw! Feller's in a blue funk, just malingering. Small wonder, facing murder charges. So, agreed gentlemen? Medicine and duty, after which, turn him over to the Provosts!" Their cavalry boots seemed to tramp across his chest, and Harry's world shut down.

The Boers reacted fast when a crowd of fierce men in tartan side-caps came boiling out of the train like angry wasps. At first, the dazed unarmed Highlanders bunched near the train, trying to cope with the crash and this sudden hail of bullets. Others jumped out with rifles and began to shoot back cooly at the difficult targets above. There were none of the plumed troopers they'd been told to expect, but these other kakie targets would do well enough. Commandos fired steadily, picking off soldiers with care, and calling leisurely to each other. "See that shot, Jan? It went through two of them."

"Can you toss me a couple of clips, friend? I've used mine up."

After a couple of minutes, they spotted that civilians were in the middle coach, and carefully aimed away from it, but by then at least twenty rounds had hit inside. Screams told that a few folk had been hit, and the rest kept their heads down even after the firing their way ceased.

First, Dirk enjoyed shooting at the big searchlights. It was fun how they made loud popping explosions when the lenses blew out. After that, he sent shots into the nearest carriage choked with struggling Highlanders until the bolt clicked empty. He pressed another charger into the breech, and looked around carefully. Best to shoot the next rounds off more slowly, so he could select his targets.

He saw a splash of colour, and lined up on a tall man wearing tartan trousers, which he knew were worn by officers. The young second-lieutenant looked up and their gaze locked across fifty feet. The Scotchman pointed his revolver, and Dirk shot him in the heart. He scratched another mark on his rifle butt, and glanced around to see if anyone had noticed his kill. Not a bearded face was turned his way. Some commandos were busy lighting pipes before they settled in to finish sniping the rooineks trapped below.

When he came round, Harry heard himself moaning, and wondered if was from his dream or because his chest hurt. He had a bad headache, too. The staircase had fallen on him, clamping his chest tight so he could not move. It pressed him to the floor, and his lungs were not working very well. He heard the steady fusillade of rifles close by outside. Now and then, bullets punched through the sides and buzzed within inches of him.

He twisted his head to see what his chances were. There were broken spikes of timber all around, where the cabin had folded in, so he could see the sky. He strained again to try to lift the weight off his chest, but slumped with the effort. Black splotches swam across his vision as he tried to inhale more than a thin seep of air.

Nails and wood screeched close by, somebody tearing at the coach wall, but he stopped himself from calling out. There was a chance one of the attackers could get in here and find a sitting duck. He tried to stifle the loud gasps he was making like a landed fish. Then a quarter-deck voice called,

"I say, you still in the land of the living, Lanyard?"

Harry felt relief at hearing so many A's in his name. He wheezed, "Nothing feels broken, but I can't breath much."

"Not to worry, the Navy's here!" Sub-Lt. Galliano was covered in black grime except for pale rings around his eyes. "Sorry I'm late. Had to dig myself out of a coal-mine." He squirmed inside and examined the wreckage. "Ah, there's the culprit." He cleared jammed metal, grabbed the staircase, and heaved. Some pressure eased, and Harry sucked in air, able to breathe properly again.

"Best I can manage for now. We'll need some help to get you free." Splinters flew, and another slug thrummed between them. Galliano patted Harry on the shoulder, leaving a sooty imprint. "Just wait a tick, would you? Must give your chaps a hand with Johnny first." He pulled his Webley and vaulted out through the opening.

Within ten minutes, faint cheers sounded, and the firing died away. All Harry could hear was the rattle of the RN flag blowing in the wind. Soon after, Scayles and Coveyduck arrived with a half dozen troopers to drag Harry out.

"It was a good scrap, sir! Too bad you missed it." Scayles still panted with the excitement of his first combat. He was openly thrilled to have been in charge while Lanyard stayed out of sight for reasons he privately considered suspicious. "The dozy blighters didn't spot us back there around the bend, 'til we'd unloaded our horses and circled behind 'em."

"Tough on the Scotties and sailors, though," Ned said.

Blue-jackets and Highlanders lay everywhere. Harry counted over thirty dead and wounded. Hanging out of searchlight-posts and windows, sprawled around the train, some draped halfway up the culvert walls. The ambushers could have completed the massacre, if Scayles' men had not made their sudden flank-attack. Despite being surprised, most of the Boers got clear away, as they always considered heroic last stands to be pointless lunacy.

A lot of dead soldiers lay with no rifles, having lost them when kit tumbled down from overhead luggage-racks on impact. The ones who had found theirs put them to as good use as possible. Harry counted eight still bodies in shabby veld clothes.

"Good going, fellers. Now, where's that navy Subbie? I owe him."

"Hard lines, Lootenant," Schammerhorn twanged. "Sailor-boy got nailed plumb through the head. Blackened up and all, they likely figured he was just some coon."

CHAPTER ELEVEN

A double rainbow arched above the Mauchbergs far to the north-east, where the patrol was headed. The blockhouse system had quickly sent medical aid and repair crews, but it was obvious no trains would be running east before tomorrow. So Harry had changed plans and ordered his men to disembark right there. Scayles was the only one to bring a tall cavalry horse, saying he'd be hanged if he'd ride one of those Cape pygmies. They rode off in column of threes, cross-country towards Farm Vincennes.

The ponies were so eager to stretch their legs after being cramped in rail-cars, they had to be allowed to trot. There was a comforting sound to the jingle of metal accoutrements and muffled hoof-beats. It seemed even more like old times when Bronco Fontaine gave voice to one of his nonsense songs, about a ten-dollar saddle and a five-dollar horse. Grass crisped beneath the hooves, sometimes tinkling against a dried-out bone. Hundreds of horse skeletons gleamed everywhere along the slope, sad relics of past military columns advancing on Lydenberg.

Harry looked back at his darkly-tanned irregulars, sitting their mounts loosely, rifles canted on hips, not saying much because they were watching the skyline for any trouble. He felt a surge of pride to be leading such a fine troop of fighting-men. They watched his every move, and responded in a moment when he signaled to rein in to a walk. He tried to ignore a throbbing headache and painful ribs from the fall, letting the steady pace of his pony calm his nerves while his thoughts roved.

The tranquility out here made the morning ambush seem remote already, and raised his spirits. The open veld was where he always wanted to be, free as those vultures circling in their cobalt sky. Within twenty-four hours, he had escaped death three times. Life tasted all the sweeter after you have almost lost it. Yet despite the sense of peace now, he felt a nagging concern about the outcome of his patrol's objective.

He tried to concentrate on strategies to find the gold, with only the skimpy clues given him at the Intelligence briefing as guidance. Instead, he found thoughts of Bethany crowding his mind. His cheek stung again in memory where she had slapped it and called him a low-down crook. When she left the cell yesterday, he feared she would never look at him again with love. He had become just another persecutor of the volk, out to filch a hoard of money she believed rightly belonged to the Boer cause.

Before his accusation of murder, Bethany could have kept her love for him at least luke-warm, until the war was resolved one way of the other. Now, she thought she had two reasons to loathe him, murdering a commando and seeking the gold. Fueled by revulsion and patriotism, she would make a dangerous enemy.

The thought startled him, seeing her as an obstacle to his assignment. Worst of all, she had that Russian bastard as an ally in the search. With Harry out of the way, Nikki would try to worm himself into her affections, maybe bed her as well as loot the gold. The picture made Lanyard twist angrily in the saddle, and he wrenched his thoughts back to duty.

Because of what the Basuto cleaner relayed to them, Nikolai and Beth knew a patrol would be assigned to locating the treasure. Since then, they had gained two day's march ahead, ample time to organize a search. The train ride having been cut short gained the opposition even more of a lead.

Alerted by Farm Vincennes, the burghers of Spitsdorp could be tough opponents if it came to a showdown. They knew every yard of the surrounding area, and probably had at least one rifle per man. He had no real knowledge of their political commitment, but disarming them would have to be his first precaution anyway.

In mid-afternoon, Harry raised his fist for the troop to halt in the shade of a small clump of Australian gumwood trees. There was a rare stream there, and the horses slurped with pleasure. The Griquas had an almost magical way with horseflesh; piping orders, slapping hides and pulling manes, so the stubborn mules did as they were bid.

The Boers called all Griquas *'Bastaards'*, because of their mixed white and Hottentot blood, even though they were an Afrikaans-speaking people. The Griquas were among the finest horsemen in Africa, and Harry was glad he had hired a pair. The round-faced youngster named Rao had a huge squashed-looking nose but otherwise European features. Middle-aged Bertil looked more like a Hottentot, lemon-skinned and narrow eyed, yet with russet hair. He wore a ragged uniform coat of some kind with yellow facings. As Harry went by, he clapped their shoulders to show he was pleased with their work, and they grinned in response.

He often wondered about the docility of natives in this country. Not thirty years ago, fierce black warriors were the scourge of southern Africa. They resisted white invaders every step of the way, and ably fought British and Boers in a half dozen wars. Then in less than a generation, ruthless suppression by whites' superior arms abruptly changed them into being meek serfs in their own land.

Blacks out-numbered European settlers ten to one, yet they allowed themselves to be exploited with scant sign of resentment. They had not even taken advantage of this war between whites to retaliate against Boers who had persecuted them so long. Like most folk he knew, Harry took the social inferiority of blacks for granted, without feeling any particular animosity towards them. Lately though, he could not help puzzling how long it would be before the mass of African natives rose up to claim equality.

Troopers broke out some bread and canned stew for a quick meal. Not one let his rifle be out of reach. Harry told

Scayles, "All that firing, better hold weapons inspection soon as they've eaten."

Harry got his own Lee-Enfield and raised the lid in its brass butt-plate. He shook out a small oil-bottle, a pull-through cord, and squares of flannel. He opened the breech, flipped up the sear, and pulled the bolt out. He smeared oil on a two inch square of flannel, put it in the cord's loop, and dropped the weighted end down the barrel. He pulled it through slowly, careful not to rub on the muzzle rim, to avoid metal burn, then repeated the process with a dry patch. Harry's rifle not having been fired recently, there was no pressing need for cleaning, but it showed the men he followed the routine.

Coveyduck had them copy his example a few minutes later. When they were done, Ned told each soldier to present his weapon, slanted up with the bolt open, his thumb in the breech. Ned squinted down the barrels at reflected light, to check the rifling lands were cleaned to his satisfaction. Anyone caught with a fouled weapon in this outfit was asking for a royal tongue-lashing and an extra stint of guard-duty.

Satisfied, the sergeant ordered four troopers to be look-outs, all reliable ex-Scouts he knew personally. That reminded Harry he should get acquainted with some of the new men. He crouched on the stream-bank beside Lascelles, the plummy-voiced Englishman, and scooped some water with his hand. "I hear we used to be almost neighbours on Vancouver Island."

"That's right, sir. Duncan, just a day's ride up the Malahat trail from Victoria."

"How'd you get here?"

"Usual thing. Half the chaps in Duncan are from the Old Country, and they were joining up like Billy-oh. Weren't enough fellows left to form a decent cricket team. So I thought I might as well join the show, too."

Harry mentioned a few of his acquaintances in the little

town, and noticed some replies didn't fit right. He said casually, "Sounds like you kept to yourself a lot."

"Not really, sir. Oh, lummy, I see what you're getting at." Lascelles grinned ruefully. "Fact is, I'm what you BC-ers call a 'kangaroo', a Brit who hops about a lot. I'd just arrived in Duncan when the balloon went up with the Boers." He lowered his voice, nodding at Baxter and deKrieger. "I hardly expected some of them to be invited along on a sensitive job like this, though."

"Sensitive?" Lanyard felt a prickle of suspicion, as he had not briefed the rankers about their patrol's mission.

"Gossip has it we're after some spondulicks old Kruger left behind. That so, sir?"

"Well, yes, it is. I'll be filling you all in later."

Harry went over to Baxter, who was giving his pony's back a good rub. "Her saddle fit okay?"

"Oh, ja. But they always liking their spine done, you know." Baxter spoke with slow dignity, his Taal accent so thick, Harry could barely understand.

"Unusual Boer name, Baxter."

"My Pa, he was an English. He did die when I was young, and Mama was Volk, so to talk your way is hardt."

"You manage just fine." Harry noticed the man was wearing brown corduroy trousers, not British serge. "With the N.S., were you?"

Baxter did not reply for a moment, watching for signs of condescension. "Ja, a National Scout. I swore the neutrality oath first, then signed up to serve the British. Like van Praage."

"Not exactly. Piet enlisted in the Cape Mounted Rifles the day after Kruger declared war. He wouldn't appreciate being called any kind of handsupper."

"An Afrikaner, still. We both can be useful following Oom's old spoor, I think."

"Sure. Glad to have you."

Another hint the whole troop knew already what they

were out here after. He wondered how much info his men had spilled along with beer in the pubs last night.

He went to ask Scayles' opinion, but saw the MP barge in ahead of troopers waiting their turn in line for coffee. Unaware of resentful looks, Scayles relaxed on a log, sipping his mug. After a moment, Schammerhorn asked innocently, "Sir, you got the time?"

Scayles turned his wrist to see, the mug tilted, and hot coffee slopped on his trouser crotch. "Bloody hell!" He jumped up, slapping at his steaming pants, and the men snickered, wiping their eyes.

"Gee, Lootenant, I'm right sorry about that."

Harry gave Scayles a few minutes to calm down, then joined him where he lounged, idly watching Jiggy cooking a meal. The signaler looked up at Harry with a boyish smile, mixing the stew. He sang in his weak voice,

"There is a happy land,

Far, far away,

Where they all eat eggs and ham,

Three times a day."

When told about the rumours, the MP snorted, "Typical! Rankers can't keep from gossiping for five minutes."

"Guess it's about time I told them officially."

"Suit yourself. Frankly, I've some rum feelings about this lot." Scayles could speak softly without his lips moving, like a prison inmate. "Can't quite put my finger on it. Call it a copper's instinct, but there's something not quite right about some of your men. How do we know they're really who they say they are?"

"Forget it, I can vouch for most of them personally."

"Is 'most' enough?"

"I checked the other's pay-books myself."

"ID papers can be forged easily enough. Anyway, intend to ask for positive vetting of the lot."

"Background checks will be a waste of time. Look, Abbott and Haywood are definitely from Toronto, and Jiggy served with them. I've come across O'Malley myself, before. And nobody could fake being what Schammerhorn says he is."

"That still leaves Baxter, deKrieger, and that toffee-nosed Lascelles to worry about."

He watched Fontaine and Rimmer loading dry wood onto a mule. "You've been away from field service too long. This lot's true-blue as they come. Brains as well as guts."

"We'll need both, with these crafty Boers. They've got spies behind every tree. One less now, since you knocked off that Ossie-whatshisname."

"Spy? He was just some poor mad sod trying to take revenge."

"'Don't think so. I've been going over what you told me." Scayles thumbed pages of his notebook. "Handsome chap who sounds like a British officer. That description matches that top Boer agent we were all after. The one who talked his way inside HQ and killed two MPs when they rumbled to him. I'd say you did everybody a big favour."

"Yeah?" Harry was tired of the man's eternal suspicions. "Now, do me one, and order the men to saddle up. And from now on, I expect you to make your own dinners. Get me?"

They rode on for a solid four hours, dismounting often to walk for ten minutes at a time to spell the horses. After they forded a river north of Elandshoek, Harry decided it was far enough for the day. He wanted the horses dried and rested when they made a fast run to complete the trip tomorrow morning. There were three long hills just ahead, and he headed for the nearest to make camp.

His men were seasoned campaigners, and organized themselves without fuss. The grass was soaking-wet up here, so troopers cut out strips of sod to uncover dry earth for sleeping on. Within half an hour, latrine pits were dug, rations doled out, and camp-fires lit. There being scant fuel in this treeless region, each man had brought along whatever wood he could scrounge. Ned produced what looked suspiciously like fence-rails from some Belfast garden, and Bronco Fontaine added his gumwood branches to feed the cooking-fires. They made smoke, but it could not be helped, and Harry figured their progress was being watched by distant Boers all along, anyway.

Jiggy got out his Maunce equipment, spread the mahogany tripod-legs and screwed the mirror onto its brass head. He squinted at the low sun. "Should still be enough light, sir."

Harry scribbled on a message pad, giving HQ a SitRep on their whereabouts and ETA at Vincennes. Jiggy carefully transcribed it into the cipher Harry told him was for day one. He used the sliding alphabet pre-arranged with Faulkner's staff to encode the message. It would be changed every day and sent at expected time schedules. He gripped the key between his knuckles, and clattered out Morse. The helio mirror jerked, sending flashes of reflected sunlight across the valley.

Jiggy focused his Galilee binocs to watch the reply that winked back a few minutes later. "Shit." He wrote quickly on his pad, and handed it to Harry. "YOUR MESSAGE GARBLED STOP. IF BRITISH COMMA REPLY IN CLEAR STOP IF BOER COMMA PISS OFF."

Harry sucked his teeth with annoyance at himself, then shrugged. "I forgot we're not scheduled to be sending anything until tomorrow. They won't be looking for our codes yet. Just signal in clear that we'll check back on sked."

Within minutes, Mendip saw another mirror flickering from a koppie halfway to the army signal post. "Cheeky bugger. Know what he said, sir?"

"HAVE HAD MY REFRESHING PISS AS SUGGESTED. LOOK FORWARD TO READING YOUR NEXT ATTEMPT TO COMMUNICATE WITH OLD K."

Jiggy quickly flashed something rude back, and Harry did not bother to ask what. Now it was confirmed the Boers were watching, though they would not be able to read any enciphered messages. Still, it was worrying, and when he told Scayles, the MP took his rifle and field glasses up on an outcrop while Harry briefed the men.

"Gather round, fellers." They formed a circle, cigarettes glowing and tea mugs held comfortably. "You've heard enough gossip by now to have a good idea of what this patrol's about. But I want to properly confirm it. Our orders are to recover a stash of gold that Intelligence believes was left hidden by Kruger."

Clearly, it was not news to them. They nudged each other, rubbing fingers and thumbs together, nodding thoughtfully at their boots. Harry went on, "Our job is to dig it up before the Boers do, and its recovery is important to the war effort. We'll be doing a lot of hard riding to make a thorough search. At the same time, we have to keep an eye out for commandos who'll be sniffing around for the same thing. Any questions?"

As ever, Barney Wignall spoke up, "How much of this here gold is there?"

When he told them Intelligence's best guess, they whooped and shouted. "Holy-moley, fifteen friggen million bucks!" Drawn-out whistles followed, with loud jokes about how they could do with a slice of that pie, bud.

"Don't even think about it, guys." He said it flatly, and nodded at Scayles. "Now you know why our Provost's come along. Just keep in mind, if we recover the boodle first, it'll be a stick in Johnny's eye."

Piet van Praag put in, "That's a big area, Harry. Unless we know exactly where, it'll be like looking for a grey tick on a rhino."

"True, but wagons with a heavy load like that wouldn't stray far from trails, or go up any high ground. So the possible areas to search aren't all that many. Anyway, we'll start looking soon as we reach the area, noon tomorrow."

The Griquas had ankle-hobbles on the animals and were putting out oats for them. Harry believed in feeding his own mount, to make a closer bond. He slung a nose-bag for the pony, and used the glowing tip of his cigarette to burn off ticks around its eyes. He stroked the bristly ears. "Well, you're no beauty like Molly was, but you'll get us there, won't you feller?"

The aroma of sizzling McConochies and baked chapatties made him hungry. He made himself a quick supper of canned stew, then took his plate and enamel mug to join one group around a fire. He poured some coffee, added a dollop of sweet condensed milk, and nodded to a pair of the new men. Rimmer and Haywood had taken their discharge from the departing Canadian Field Artillery in Cape Town, so they could re-enlist with a British unit to see more action.

Jiggy pulled a fag-end from behind his ear, lit up, and said to Haywood, "Go on, Derek, tell Harry about those two posh popsies you met."

Haywood soon had them all smiling at his tale of how he and Rimmer celebrated demobilization by picking up two mature British ladies on the Promenade. "We were all tricked up in straw boaters and striped blazers, like a couple of swells. 'Course, if they'd a'known, they wouldn't have given us common troopers a tumble. Anyway, those two old darlings didn't waste any time, and took us home to a real mansion. In half a tick, we ended up in bed. We were all going at it like rabbits, when we hear this motor car come banging up the driveway."

The troopers howled, and O'Malley said, "I bet that put you off your stroke!"

"No, but it sure speeded the pistons up a bit," Haywood chuckled.

"Anyway, here's the best of it," Rimmer added. "My popsie said, 'Ooh, that was heaven, Canada, but you really must leave now. You see, that's my husband outside, and he's a brigadier!'"

It set them all guffawing, and Jiggy said, "Tell

the rest of it."

"We dived out that second floor window, lickety-split, and skedaddled down the Coast Highway carrying our pants!" The troopers roared, and the new men felt their acceptance.

In the mood for more bawdry, Jiggy called across the fire. "Hey, Sith-o, you're a Cape Towner. Bet a well set-up feller like you has some horny tales to tell, what with all those hot tarts in the Fishing Fleet."

He meant the shoals of British women who sailed to South Africa, trawling to catch a husband among lonely officers.

"Not me, I was, am, a happy married man."

After they hooted disbelief, Ned said, "Don't let these jackaroos get you down, deKrieger. And what's all this 'Sith' business, anyway?"

"Go on, Sith-o. Say it. You know. Let the sarge hear."

Others urged him on, so deKrieger finally said slowly, "I'm S'th Ifrican."

Troopers laughed and slapped their thighs, "Hear, Ned? It's the way he talks."

"Reckon near everybody has a funny way of saying things." Schammerhorn put in dryly. "'Cept me, of course."

Fontaine scoffed,"Hah, listen to our crazy goddam Yank!"

"Brother, call me sunnuvuh-bitch, but don't ever call me no Yankee. I'm Southern-bred in the bone, and Texican to boot."

Harry lit a Navy Cut and offered one to Schammerhorn. "Thanks Lootenant, but I chaw mine."

"Texas, eh? You're certainly far from home."

"'Come here the long way round at that. Few months ago, I was a buck private stuck in the boonies outside Manilla, civilizin' runty brown goo-goos for Uncle Sam."

Harry had not much time to read newspapers, but knew vaguely the American Army was fighting its own savage campaign against independence guerillas in the Philippines. Even Kitchener, of all people, seemed to disapprove. "Well, we need all the experienced soldiers we can get."

"That, I am. Old 'Howling Jake' Smith, my general over there, he ordered us doughboys to take no prisoners and turn Samar into a howling wilderness. Said shoot on sight and burn every hooch. Which we did in spades, yes-sir. Last I heard, the U.S. Army's put paid to two hunnert thousand of them Flips."

"Well, our style's a bit more selective here."

"For damn sure. Thang is, when I moseyed over to sign up in Africa, I thought I'd be shooting me some more niggers. Hadn't no idea the Limeys was in a white man's war." He spat tobacco juice sizzling into the fire. "Guess the joke's on me."

"What have we here?" DeKrieger drew attention to himself again, holding a ration tin at arm's length. He read its label aloud in a comical sing-song. "Contents, four ounces concentrated beef pemmican, four ounces Van Houten cocoa paste. To open, pull tab, separating items, exercising care."

He chuckled, incongruous with the deep way he sounded while using Afrikaans. "Is that care against spilling it, or eating it?" When speaking English, the man always pitched his voice higher. It occurred to Harry that deKrieger was almost deliberately making a fool of himself.

"If you read the other side, Sith-o, you'll see that's emergency rations," Sgt. Coveyduck snapped. "Not to be eaten unless previously without food for thirty-six hours. And only then by permission of an officer. Didn't that Cape outfit teach you anything about the army?" The n.c.o. obviously thought little of whatever unit deKrieger may have served in before.

"Nothing wrong with local regiments, Ned." McKay spoke with an edge to his strong Springbok accent. "I joined the Natal Mounted Rifles with most of my neighbours, and we know our way around the veld better than Tommies ever could. Good as commandos, for that matter." He glared at deKrieger. "From how they talk, you'd think Boers were the only whites who've been here long. Hell, my grandmother came from Scotland to settle in Durban over sixty years ago. Reckon that makes my family just as 'Afrikaner' as any Dutch rock-spider!"

"Ah, none of you Colonials know what it's like in the Imperial army such as I'm used to," O'Malley said, glad of a chance to tease his friend. "All spit and polish, maybe, but real soldiering just the same. Too bad this treasure-hunting lark will miss us the chance for another last go at the Boojers. If you'd been with the Paddies at Paardeberg, you'd understand why I still fancy evening up old scores yet."

The troopers sensed a story, and settled back with a smoke to hear the telling of it. Harry knew what was coming, as he'd been there himself at the time. Because O'Malley tended to ramble, spinning out any reminiscence, Harry leaped ahead in his mind, remembering how it had been that day.

When Canadian troops took Paardeberg Drift in February, 1900, their victory was considered a turning-point of the war. Lanyard became involved because he rode to Modder River with a message for General Otter just before the firing started. He found himself drafted on the spot as a replacement into an infantry platoon of the Royal Canadian Regiment. It was his first experience of combat, and he learned there is no time to be afraid during the frenzy of kill-or-be-killed.

Most of all, he was proud to have taken part when his fellow-countrymen fought so decisively. The struggle for Paardeberg lasted ten days, the longest, bloodiest set-piece battle of the war. There were units of the Shropshires, Gordon Highlanders, and Duke of Cornwall's Light Infantry in at the end, but it was an attack by Canadians that finally won the day.

After the guns fell silent, Harry took a curious stroll along what had been the firing-line. He had come across some Imperials leaning over their parados built of fallen comrades' bodies. Irish from the sound of them, calmly lighting pipes and placing bets on which of the fallen enemy out front were shamming or really dead.

Men from either side started to move through the casualties, giving aid to wounded. None were treated any differently, as Boer or Briton gave and received the same medical care. When Harry saw this compassion to friend and foe after battle, it made him wonder what had been the point of the carnage in the first place.

The impartial treatment must have reassured one man who had been lying doggo among the corpses. He stood up and waved, a big man in corduroys with not a scratch on him. He threw aside his bandolier and strolled towards the soldiers. When he got close, he held out a hand to catch the light drizzle of rain. He called in a cheerful brogue. "A soft day, lads!"

O'Malley said, "Joseph and Mary, since when did a Boer get to talk like my own da?"

"By being born to it, as yourself. Speaking of which, would you have spare fag handy for a Tipperary man?"

"You're surely not dressed like one."

"Ah, there's over three hundred of us Irish volunteers fighting for the Boers against bloody England."

"Is that a fact, now? To think I'm among another twenty-eight thousand Irishmen in Kitchener's mob, here just for our own amusement and the grand pay."

"Lucky I am to be giving up to you lot, then, and not some Protty sods with a grudge against honest Micks."

"Fortunate, indeed." O'Malley nodded at the khaki bodies. "You didn't happen to have a hand in that, of course?"

"Not at all. I'd just arrived, and hid without firing a shot."

"In that case, here's a Woodbine, and we'll be winking our eye as you leave. We'd never take such as him a prisoner, would we, fellers?"

There was a happy chorus of, "The devil we would, Pat!", and they sent him off running to freedom. He got about ten yards when somebody snarled, "Fokkun bahstud!" Rifles crashed, and he fell riddled among the dead Irish soldiers.

O'Malley was saying now, "We played football with his dirty head, just to be sure."

It was a grim tale, and Harry sensed the cheerfulness leaving his men. To lift their mood again, he said quickly, "Hey, Ned, remember that crazy night when we all first met down in Cape Town?"

"Do I?" Sergeant Coveyduck was quick on the uptake, and boomed an extra-loud laugh. "A hundred of us drongos on demob leave from the army, Aussies, and Kiwis and Canucks, boozing in the Grand Hotel Long Bar, pissed as newts, and you come riding up the stairs on that jeezly great horse of yours!"

"Hell, I wanted to make a good first impression on old Gat," Harry chuckled, drawing in the newer men. "Holding court in the Millionaire Suite upstairs, signing us on for his Scouts. He made everybody feel so good about joining, we shot every bottle off the bar."

"Must have scared six different colours of shit out of those poor wog waiters!" There was general laughter around the fire. "But you set an example, Harry, passing your hat for us to pay for damages."

Lanyard caught Scayles' warning glance, and left the chaffering troopers so as to join him. Without pointing, the policeman said, "Down among those white rocks. There's some old nosey-Parker with a spy-glass." He passed his binoculars, Zeiss. MPs always did themselves well with captured equipment.

The bright lenses pulled the mounted observer in close, a

white-bearded man with a woman's shawl around his shoulders. He was resting an elbow on the butt of his scabbarded rifle, steadying a telescope, looking into Harry's eyes. After a moment, the watcher raised his arm in casual salute and rode out of sight among the boulders.

"Too close for comfort. He could bring some company to hit us at dawn," Harry said. "Order the men to turn in early, Glen. We'll rouse 'em at midnight for a moonlight flit."

CHAPTER TWELVE

The second day back, Bethany was awake soon after dawn. She quickly dressed in jodhpur riding-britches and a dungaree shirt without attendance from Hetti, who was nowhere to be seen. Beth deliberately made more noise than usual while going downstairs, to rouse old Hiram. After a few quick bites of mealie-cake in the kitchen, she called up loudly, "Come on, Dada, we can't delay any longer!"

She took her slouch hat and went to the stables. "Simius, lazy-bones, are you up?"

Her turn of phrase caused unseemly giggling in the loft, and the young man's straw-spiked head peered down. "Right away, Baas-lady." He disappeared to whisper something, then came down the ladder quickly, buckling his pants.

"Saddle Swazi for me. Now. And tell Petta to rig the Baas's spyder. We leave within a half hour." Going out the doorway, she called without looking around, "And, Hetti, get yourself down here back to work, before I take a switch to your behind!"

Hiram was scowling in the kitchen, with cook and Marthe hovering disapprovingly over his cold breakfast. "I wanted time to sleep on it, but I've barely had time for forty winks since."

"You say that every night, but we're still no further forward. And you insisted I spend all yesterday riding to look for strayed cattle. Let's admit, they've been rustled by bandits like the rest, and never be will be found."

"Sure they will. Got Vincennes' mark on every one." Hiram branded his animals with a hot iron, American-style.

"Oh, they're gone forever now, and you know it!" Afrikaner farmers seldom bothered to identify their livestock. Buyers would not even look for signs of previous ownership. "Do hurry, Dada! Let's talk outside." She carried his plate to the garden-table, away from eavesdroppers.

Hiram smoothed the gray trunk of a mimosa tree, looking around at the lush tangle of fruit trees and flower bushes. Unpicked ripe oranges, figs, quinces, and aloes bent the branches low. He sighed, "She planted all these herself, before you were born. Her favorite place."

"Mine, too, Dada."

Misty memory came, of standing on tip-toe beside this bench, reaching to brush the hair of soft-voiced Mama. Another image flashed, that last night with Harry here, blossoms fragrant as musk in the night. Thoughts of his urgent kisses, his fingers gently opening her, brought a sudden rush of inner warmth, unbidden moisture. She squirmed, angry at herself.

"It's today we have to think about!"

He gave a tight, fond, smile. "Like her in every way, you are. If your Mama was here, I fancy she'd tell me to cut the cackle and stir my stumps, both at the same time." He laughed shortly, "And it sure would make a great gift for old Kruger to crow about in Hilversum, I'll admit."

"So you are all for it?" He nodded wearily. "Oh, don't look so grumpy. I know full well you're dying to find it for Oom Paul's sake!"

"No argument there. The man was our rock. Elected president four times, and held the Transvaal together for twenty years. To think, one of Kruger's ancestors was a coloured woman. What a winding path to greatness, from slave to president in a few generations!"

"He'd have been a sight greater if he hadn't run off and left his poor wife dependent on charity from the British!"

"Come on, daughter, he's seventy-five years of age, so let's have some respect for the man. Gezina was too sick to travel with him, and she passed away soon after. The only reason he went, was to try and get some European support for the Volk's cause, especially Germany. But after all Kaiser Bill's big talk of help, he wouldn't even allow Paul come see him when he got there."

"Isn't it always the same? Nobody ever helps Afrikaners but the Lord and ourselves!"

"Uh, listen daughter, I'd gladly help you search, but I've a farm to run, with bad crops, shrinking herds, and due-notes coming in left and right."

"It's true then, about Nikki?"

"Eh? What's he said?"

"That you owe him so much money, he could throw us off Vincennes." She blushed faintly, "He told me the other night."

Hiram growled, "Marthe said there was some ruckus upstairs, broken bowls and such." He touched her face gently with his dirt-grained hand, breathing tightly. "Why, the Russky snake-in-the grass, coming to your room! I'll kill him if he so much as—!"

"Nothing like that, Dada. I had a tantrum after he'd left, about the debt, that's all."

He searched her expression for a long moment, then shrugged. "Anyway, he snuck off someplace two nights ago, didn't he? Took one of my last horses without so much as a by-your-leave."

Small wonder he sneaked away, she thought. That terrible evening, when he saw she intended to resist, Nikolai had staggered from her room. Not knowing if she would arouse Hiram and the entire farm population to lynch him, he had fled the place within minutes.

Hiram went on, "Off after the gold for himself, I'd guess. But, be honest Beth, you and me wouldn't even know where to begin looking."

"We start by involving folk in the dorp. Two years ago, hidden treasure was all the villagers could talk about. Some even said they were at the rail-siding when it was unloaded. They can help us search any promising spots."

"Sit down, girl, for God's sake. Pacing like a panther won't move us any far forrad." She flopped onto the bench opposite, and reluctantly let Hiram have his say. "What makes you think they'll be so all-fired keen to get involved against the Limeys these days, anyway? There's so many who opted out of the war living in the village now, the commandos call it 'Handsupdorp'. Those folks know this war's darn near over, and sure won't take any side at this stage."

She huffed and made to argue. Hiram waggled a finger. "Let me finish. Two years is ample time for any gold to have been dug up long since. We know nobody ever did, so odds are, it just ain't there."

"If you're so sure, why would the British offer Harry a pardon if he'd lead a patrol here to find it?"

"Him coming back? That Canuck tin-soldier had me bamboozled for a while as being a decent feller, but now he better not set foot on my land again!" Blenkarn half-stood up in anger, then bent sideways with pain. He held on to the table, staring into her intense face. "Say, is that the real flea in your ear? To best Harry for letting you down?"

"He let us all down, but that's not the point. We might be able to help finance a delay, to fight on! President Burger could bargain for a better peace settlement."

"Surrender, you mean!" Marthe stepped from behind a tree where she'd been listening. "If I was a man, there'd be no backing down short of our every demand being met."

Beth was impatient with just talking. "Well, I'm off to see Neave right now. She'll get word to General Botha to send help. He'll listen to a baroness."

"Baroness, my foot!" Marthe snorted. "That chit of an uitlander girl would still be emptying bed-pans if she hadn't married so well."

Petta came running, "Kakies heading this way up the road, Baas!" He glanced at Beth. "Mister Lanyard's bringing them."

"Why that two-faced, no-good . . . !" Hiram shambled towards his front door like an injured crab.

"Simius!" Beth shouted, and ran for the stables, realizing she had to get away while there was time. If she could reach Spitsdorp, maybe they could be roused to form some kind of resistance. At that moment, she did not care about the danger of fighting British soldiers, or what might happen to Vincennes afterwards as a result. What mattered first was to bring riflemen to drive away the British patrol. Anything to gain time to unearth the gold for liberty's cause.

The stable-boy had the bridle over Swazi's head, but was just starting to saddle him. "Oh, give me a hand up!" He hastily dropped the leathers and cupped his hands so she could vault onto the big black gelding, bareback. She slashed her sjambok and the stung horse jumped forward into a gallop. Staring dark faces blurred in the yard, and Hiram's call to her was lost in the clatter of hooves.

She reined hard left at the gates, kneeing Swazi to race ever faster along the track to the Spitsdorp road. Her face was set in a mix of fury and anxiety, blonde hair streaming straight back with the speed. There was no time to avoid the kakie who suddenly rode out of cover beside the track. Their horses' collided, Beth shot forward over Swazi's head, and she would have fallen badly if the soldier had not grabbed her by the arm.

He said in Afrikaans, "Careful, pretty lady!"

She had time to notice he was very good-looking, with thick black lashes, large grey eyes, and the head of a Greek god. As well, his voice was richly masculine, speaking almost pure Dutch. One of those joiner turn-coats. It made her hate him instantly.

"Take your hands off me, traitor!"

He shrugged and elaborately let go. She began to slip again, and it was maddening how he saved her once more. Beth settled herself, and pulled away from his steadying hand.

One of the kakies with him was a stern-faced officer, while four ordinary soldiers sat grinning like apes. She raged at the lieutenant, "How dare you trespass on our property!" That only set the troopers snickering, and she raised her sjambok to lash the nearest one. The smirks remained, but they backed out of reach in a ring, admiring her flushed beauty.

"That'll do, Miss." Scayles was the only one not smiling. "You will go back with us now. Either under your own steam or across my saddle. Take your pick."

She would have fought them, but deKrieger said in Afrikaans, "Best play along. None of these idiots intend you any harm." He nudged his mount close to take her reins, and she was glad to see Swazi nip at the army pony. When he switched to English, he sounded disappointingly shrill, "Lieutenant Lanyard just wants a word, Miss."

"And I know the very word to suit him!"

Fear squeezed her heart when she saw all the soldiers with rifles in the yard, staring down at Hiram. Christmas stood loyally by his side, two old hunters facing the British lion. Her father looked frailer somehow, but all the more brave, cradling his lever-action Winchester '73, finger through the trigger-guard. Behind him, rifle muzzles stuck out of every loop-hole along the big house's front wall.

She looked up boldly, trying to hide how frantic she felt, and found Harry looking at her. "Hello, Beth."

"So, they let you weasel out of it, Judas!"

"Hey, now." She could not believe how he could smile at her so calmly.

"Yeah, daughter, looks like the usual Limey whitewash sprung him." Blenkarn did not take his gaze off the soldiers while nodding to the steady barrels behind him. "I give the word, you're all dead men. And if you n'the rest of your sorry-assed Brits ain't out of here in ten seconds, I'll make my call."

Lanyard nodded to Scayles, who jabbed a finger at six troopers in the rear rank and led them away noisily through the gates. Harry said, "We're here to search the ranch for weapons and confiscate them. As much for your people's sake as mine. I'm under orders to recover bullion that rightfully belongs to Transvaal bank depositors. When we find it, we will leave. Now, stand aside, please."

Blenkarn levered his Winchester to put a round up the spout. Ned pointed his Webley, the one Harry had given him. The front rank of troopers aimed their rifles, vectoring the rancher.

"Lower your weapon, Hiram," Harry ordered. "You men as well."

Beth cried, "You're such cowards, to pick on a lone man outside his own home."

"That's right, he is, alone. Come on, Hiram, nobody's inside backing you up. Those barrels haven't moved an inch since we got here."

As he spoke, there was a gabble of Bantu voices inside, and the rifle muzzles began to be pulled backwards, one after the other. The front doors crashed open, and Lt. Scayles strode out, a huddle of frightened blacks behind him in the hallway.

"Typical! Nobody thought to lock the back door. All clear, sir. No snipers upstairs, just natives inside, and all rifles secured."

"Good going." Harry turned to his men. "Make a thorough search of the whole property. Scoop every weapon. But no sticky fingers otherwise, mind."

He said to Blenkarn, "Now, hand your gun to my sergeant, if you please."

Troops went back inside, and Hiram passed his Winchester to Ned. "You take this, and we're left plumb defenceless." Beth cringed at the faint despair in Hiram's voice, "Thieves and rustlers are bleeding me dry as it is. With nary a gun, we're as good as finished. Cut us some slack, for God's sake!"

Lanyard rubbed his chin, and glanced at Scayles for any comment. All he got back was a non-committal stare. "Okay, hang on to your own rifle for now. But strictly for personal protection. I warn you not to use it to hamper my men."

The Australian levered the breech, trying to eject a round, then handed the gun back with a grin. "Took some guts that, old timer. Waving an empty rifle at us."

Hiram stared. Obviously, he had neglected to load it. The troopers hooted with laughter, amused as schoolboys, and even Hiram smiled ruefully.

"You're all mad!" Bethany burst out. She charged into the house, pushing through the searchers, calling upstairs, "Don't you dare touch my things 'til I get there!"

Marthe told Harry he hadn't the sense he was born with, took a worried look at Hiram, and ran inside after his daughter.

Lanyard nodded at the guest cottage. "Nikki hiding in there?"

Hiram shrugged, "Search me." He scowled at his own words, and went on, "Which you are. The guy vamoosed night before yesterday. Didn't say where."

"If you do come across him, he's to report to me. We'll be at the village for a bit."

Field-hands and their kin hurried into the yard, as much awed by actually using Baas Blenkarn's front door as by the presence of armed soldiers. Coveyduck sent his men fanning out to search the barns, servant-quarters, and tobacco sheds. When they were done, it was obvious the farm hid nothing more dangerous than a few bill-hooks and scythes. Nobody had looked behind the manger.

Searching the great house was hurried along by the constant tirade of complaint by Marthe, who followed troopers from room to room. She even boxed Jiggy's ears when she caught him pawing through her underwear drawer. When Scayles carried out a light shotgun, Harry asked for it back.

He found Beth in the garden, talking with her tearful maid. "Guess you better hang on to this little .410 at least.

There's talk of bandits about."

"Yes, and some of them are here already!"

"Come on, Beth. My men're just doing their job." He glanced at the black girl, who kept up her noisy sobbing. "Can't we talk alone for a minute?"

"We've nothing to discuss. Far as I'm concerned right now, Hetti's problem's greater than the whole British army's."

"And so is ours. Listen, this war's going to be over any day soon. You said we could have a chance then."

"Without an honorable settlement, it will never be over for us Boers! And you are standing between us and it."

"D'you think all these politicians and generals on either side care a damn about ordinary people like you and me? We have to make our own happiness, war or not."

"Perhaps we could have, afterwards. If you hadn't turned out to be a murderer!"

"Which I'm not." At that moment, Hetti sobbed even louder, spoiling the effect of his words. He raised his voice, "You're not even interested in hearing the truth of what I say."

He gripped her shoulders, but she wrenched away. "Get off me! There's blood of innocents on your hands."

"I love you, Beth. Always will. Doesn't that mean anything?"

Colour flooded Beth's cheeks, and she made to reply, then was distracted by the maid vomiting lavishly across the picnic table. She held the girl's forehead, and irritably waved Harry away.

There was some sort of commotion in the farm-yard, and he found it centred on Marthe Keller, fiercely caning a young black man about the shoulders. He cowered and yelped while she laid into him, screaming "Filthy kerl!" Some troopers watched amusedly, and Harry asked Jiggy what was going on.

"Old story, sir. That young buck put a servant-girl in

t'family way. He'd just told her he don't intend to marry her or pay for t'kid's upkeep. So t'Boer lady's busy changing his mind like."

"I think I just met the lucky bride."

The search of Vincennes' buildings was finished by ten hundred hours. All the weapons found were those nine rifles Hiram had stuck through loop-holes. They were brand-new Mausers, still with packing grease on, and obviously being stored for commandos. Under martial law, the guns were just cause to torch Farm Vincennes, but Harry decided to turn a blind eye.

He had hot words with Lt. Scayles about the decision, and also overheard grumblings about his favoritism by some of the men, but he insisted no destruction would occur. More important even than a past liking for the Blenkarns, his reasoning was that a farm-burning would discourage any possible co-operation by local villagers. The MP sulkily agreed in the end, but noted all serial numbers of the rifles before Ned field-stripped them. Coveyduck made sure nobody saw when he plopped the bolts down the outdoor privy hole.

Orders were being given for the troop to mount when Jiggy Mendip came to Harry about having learned something interesting. He led the way inside the barn, where the African expectant father stood, rubbing sore shoulders.

"Simius remembers working near the trail one day a wagon from Kruger's train came by."

"Sure it was only the one?"

Jiggy and the stable-boy jabbered back and forth some more. "Positive, sir. He'd been sworn by t'Blenkarns never to say owt about it, either. He's madder'n heck about being thrashed, so I'm inclined to believe him."

"Where'd it go? He remember what direction?"

"West, sir. Some stone-quarry or other up there's his best bet."

Harry gave Simius a sovereign for now, and told him

there'd be a lot more if what he said proved correct. This seemed the best lead yet, but time would tell whether it was based on anything more than idle malice as result of Marthe's caning. Simius grinned widely, bit the soft gold coin, and blurted something else.

"A bonus, sir. He helped that Russky bloke saddle up t'other night. It turns out Simius told him about the lorry, too. Says t'Russian gave him nowt but a shilling for his pains."

There was all the more need for urgency now, and within minutes the patrol moved off behind their officers. When Harry looked back, Bethany leaned out the window to shake her fist. Last man to leave was that disgusting *verraaier*, who had the gall to wave his plumed hat in courtly farewell.

CHAPTER THIRTEEN

From a distance, Spitsdorp seemed a hopeless-looking little place, sun-baked and deserted. Scarce more than a hundred or so corrugated iron or wattle-daub huts along straggling alleys, with a few better houses gracing the single main street. A white-walled church gleamed among deep green bushes, its steeple crowned with a large crucifix prodding above tall gum trees. The only sounds came from the water-pump windmill screeching atop a skeleton tower, and the ringing of a blacksmith's hammer somewhere.

Harry had been here a couple of years ago, but couldn't remember much about it now. Even at eleven o'clock on a Sunday morning, there were fewer than a dozen villagers to be seen at first. As the patrol came closer, the church doors opened and people came out from morning services. They dallied near the village centre, women lifting brims of their special go-to-kirk kappies of flowered linen to see better as the soldiers approached. Men stared, too, a fair number of young Boers of military age among them. Since the time of General Cronje's surrender, Tommies rarely came through Spitsdorp anymore.

"Troop, ride-at, atten-shun!" Lanyard ordered. His men closed horse ranks and sat straighter in saddles, despite the weariness of their long night ride.

"Come on lads," Coveyduck urged. "Bags of swank, now."

They cantered into town looking their best, backs rigid, rifles canted on hips, ostrich feathers nodding on their bush-hats. The troopers knew the importance of making a strong first impression on these possibly hostile civilians. They were joined by Lt. Scayles' detachment riding in smartly from the opposite end of town as a precaution.

Seen closer up, the village was not quite so run-down as

it first seemed. The dusty street was clean enough, lined by hitching-rails outside a score of shop fronts. Folk looked decently dressed, and there were well-fed horses about. Lanyard wondered idly what was the source of money coming into the little place. Ragged black servants were everywhere, big-eyed with interest, but careful not to call friendly greetings. Despite their caution, though, some broke into delighted laughter when Jiggy called bawdy remarks in Sotho.

Harry ordered dismount, and the troopers swung down stiffly with many a saddle-sore groan. Boer females moved quickly aside, spreading away from soldiers like stones rippling a pond.

"Calm down, girls. We won't eat you," Haywood said.

"Speak for yourself, mate." Jiggy laughed. He called to a group of glum-faced young women in Sunday clothes. "How are you, darlings? Looks like you needs a bit of cheering up."

Menfolk growled angrily, and edged themselves in front of their women. "Private Mendip, behave yourself!" Harry snapped, "We've enough grief as it is."

The two officers stayed mounted, weighing up the place carefully for advantages or dangers. Troopers looped reins over their arms, easing cinches, and chatted about getting some grub. The Griquas rode in last with the mules and remounts, and began tethering them to the last unused hitching rails, in front of the church.

Harry noticed a platform ringing the steeple, with a small access door. He told Jiggy to ask to set up an O.P. there. The signaler rested the helio across his shoulder and ambled along the graveyard path. He had to weave between parishioners who lingered and did not make way for him.

The church doors banged wide and a scrawny-looking man in a black suit charged out, roaring. He barged into Jiggy, almost sending the tripod flying, and ran to the two Griquas. He flailed his hat at their faces, screaming outrage in Afrikaans.

The hammering stopped in the smithy, faces craned from doorways, and parishioners gathered to take in the commotion. Piet trotted over, trying to calm things down.

"Sacrilege!" The preacher shouted in English, with an incredibly loud, booming voice. "Get these cursed sons of Ham away from my church this instant!"

Bertil declared proudly, *"'n Griqua is nie 'n swart man, en hy is nie 'n coloured!"*

For him to deny he was neither black nor a Coloured infuriated some villagers. A burly man ran from the smithy and started pulling Bertil's coat off. When Rao tried to interfere, the Boer felled him with one punch to the jaw. Several burghers laughed and clapped, but fell quiet when Canadians swore and leveled their rifles at the blacksmith. The cheerful Griquas' skill with horses had made them popular already, and no Boer was going to get away with abusing them.

"Hold!" Lanyard called. It was only the angry troopers' good fire-discipline that saved the smith from being ventilated.

Ned planted himself between the Griquas and their attacker. The two big men squared off like sparring gorillas. Coveyduck was an imposing size, and he wore Harry's Webley on his left hip in a cut-away holster, butt-forward for a fast cross-draw. Still, the massive bare-chested smith showed no sign of backing down.

Scayles led three men with rifles at the high port to press the Boer into his own doorway. He stood there scowling and talking loudly to sympathetic villagers. Ned helped Rao to his feet and told the Griquas to tether the mules further off under the trees.

Harry kneed his pony forward. "What's his trouble?"

"Seems the blacksmith took exception to Bertil wearing an old ZARP uniform coat," Piet explained. ZARPs were Zuid Afrikan Republic Police, who had become some of

Kruger's best troops early on.

"No need for an upset, Padre," Harry said.

"Predikant!" The minister corrected, and slapped his low-crowned hat on, dead straight. "I am Predikant Emanuel Carolus, spiritual leader of this independent Boer community!"

"And I'm Lieutenant Lanyard, military leader of this British army patrol. So let's both just talk things over sensibly." He dismounted, raised his eyebrows questioningly, and when the minister nodded permission, Harry looped reins over the rail.

"One of my men needs to use your steeple for signaling."

"Out of the question!" But the officer's courtesy seemed to calm Carolus down, and he even explained himself. "We consider each church to be the very body of Christ, and cannot allow its use for warfare in any fashion."

"I understand that, Predikant. But I have to say with all respect, I've uncovered too many Mausers hidden in churches just like yours. And I insist my man goes up there."

Carolus ignored the come-back, and gestured resignedly at the troopers. "So many armed men give me no choice. Still, I formally protest against you putting my flock in danger. To use the steeple for military purposes could draw reprisals against our village."

"We're here to prevent just that," Harry said. He nodded for Scayles to carry on, and led Jiggy into the church. Behind him, Carolus boomed, "I expect full compensation for any damage your soldiers cause, mind!"

They climbed up a zigzag of ladders inside the steeple, sneezing from the dust. It was hard going for Jiggy, one handed. Half-way up, he lost hold of the tripod and Harry just managed to catch it. When Jiggy flung back the trapdoor, their nostrils crinkled at a feral smell. "What a pong!" Dried guano crunched under their boots, and they peered around the chamber lit by fingers of sunlight through vent holes.

"Bats, sir." Jiggy pointed upwards. Hundreds of leathery little pods hung down from the steeple-beams, quivering and rustling. "Hopes they aren't vampires."

"Or carry rabies. Relax, they're harmless otherwise."

They had to prise nails out to open the little door to the platform. The narrow walkway had an ornamental fence less than a foot high, and they were careful to stay well back. The steeple gave a panoramic view of the surrounding territory, with crystal-clear visibility in every direction.

A lot of it was familiar to Harry, from early last year when he patrolled the ground and rode in to visit Bethany. His binoculars picked out laborers working the tobacco-fields around Farm Vincennes, and he lingered for a moment hoping he'd see her as well. Knowing Beth, though, she was just as likely to be off riding elsewhere, seeking the hidden trove.

Other smaller farmhouses showed, many with white tablecloths flapping to advertise their neutrality. Far to the south, brass-work gleamed on a tiny train moving along the repaired Delagoa Bay Railway. Beyond, Lanyard could see the wrinkled layers of jungle and ravines forming what settlers called the Valley Of Death because of the deadly fever there.

The open veld undulated away forever ahead, blue koppies sticking up like islands, and only the occasional small mimosa tree to give shade in the enormous landscape. Nearby, to the northwest, the Devil's Knuckles rose in two smooth rock domes. In the other direction, Spits Kop mountain bared rocky teeth that gave the village its name.

"Now, this is what I call a real observation post, sir."

"And perfect for signals." Harry checked his Ingram for the time. "Close to the morning sked. Get a move on, Jiggy."

Minutes after Harry's SitRep was sent, other flashes winked from distant hills in the south. One helio was at the Field Intelligence unit near Machadodorp, that signaled,

"RECEIVED. STAND BY." The other was from the same Boer comedian as yesterday. This time, he flashed, "GOOD TO SEE YOU ARE IN CHURCH TODAY TOMMY."

"They know where we are again, sir." Jiggy broke off when the army helio began sending, and he jotted down words rapidly. "In clear, sir. Addressed to Mister Scayles."

Harry grunted, focusing on a billow of dust rising between hills to the southwest. An army mounted column from the look of it, big enough to include a long supply train. Most British cavalcades out in this foodless country were as much escorts for supply-wagons as they were combat formations. Farther west, a smaller dust-cloud indicated the slow advance of infantry, an hour or so behind.

Ned called up, standing in the middle of a large crowd of civilians, so Harry had only time for one last long sweep before he went down. Other movement caught his attention, tiny specks of horses riding fast from the west, in and out of sight as they crossed the rolling land. They were a scattered bunch, not in military straight column formation. It could be a wing of those National Scouts, but somehow he didn't think so. They were too far to make out numbers, but he guessed at least fifty. He swung his glasses along the route they were headed, aimed straight to converge with the army column before long.

"Hell, there's an attack shaping up over there!"

Mendip took one look and swivelled his helio mirror towards the column. Harry dictated a short signal, LARGE PARTY OF ENEMY RIDING FROM WEST ETA YOUR CONVOY TWO HOURS. "Keep sending until they acknowledge!"

Harry stuffed the message for Scayles into his pocket and hurried down the ladders. A bunch of serious-looking village men in sober clothes stood waiting for him in the street. Their leader had a big gut and pompous way about him, and looked like a shop-keeper. He articulated English well, if in a throaty accent that was hard to follow. He introduced himself as Burgemeester Kleinhaus, chairman of the village committee, which Harry presumed meant mayor. It was confirmed when the man's next sentence sounded like a platform speech.

"I must inform you we intend to send a civic letter of complaint direct to Lord Milner detailing the unconscionable way your troops have invaded our peaceable community without explanation in any shape, manner, or form."

"Yeah, well, we were kind of side-tracked, first off." Harry nodded towards the frowning predikant.

Lanyard explained matter-of-factly what the patrol's mission was. "It's the British government's intention to return the gold to the banks it was stolen from, to help re-build the Transvaal's economy. I'm authorized to pay a substantial reward to anyone able to help us recover the money, even just useful information. And we offer good daily wages to local civilians who'll join our search."

Most of the town committee laughed mockingly and nudged each other. With wild-goose-chases like this, no wonder it was taking Kitchener so long to get the war finished. Their smiles faded when they heard the lieutenant's shocking next words.

"Gentlemen, please inform your people I require all firearms in this town to be turned over to my men by sundown today." Kleinhaus started to shake his head angrily, but Harry went on. "This is to prevent any untoward incidents, for your own protection as well as ours. If it's done quick enough, I can promise we'll be out of here tonight."

The burghers shouted all at once, red-faced with indignation. Harry held up his hand, "Receipts will be issued for every weapon turned in. They'll be held only temporarily, locked up safely. We'll return all guns to their owners after our job's completed."

"Your orders are impossible," Kleinhaus blustered. "Since the surrender at Pretoria, we have kept Spitsdorp out of any hostilities. We wish to remain only neutral, supporting neither side. But, now d'you realize what you're asking? To give up our guns, while you ride away and leave us to the mercy of commandos or every bandit within a hundred miles!"

"The predikant may keep the key in case there's a genuine emergency requiring firearms. I am prepared to accept his judgement on that. But if there's any threat to your village, my men will protect you. You have my word."

"Your word!" In Afrikaans, the blacksmith shouted, "What's worth the word of a bunch of English skelms like you? Nothing more than bandits yourselves, who'd steal pennies from a dead Boer's eyes!"

Lanyard didn't understand much of the Afrikaans, other than 'skelm'. Beth had called him the same thing. He made his voice hard, "Mister Kleinhaus, your people can either co-operate or face being arrested."

He sought out Carolus' blazing stare. "I'm sure you will voice your support, Predikant. An announcement at afternoon services today would be a big help as well. We all want to avoid any serious confrontation." He raised his voice. "Lieutenant Scayles, soon's the men have eaten, detail them to go house-to-house for surrender of weapons. Peaceable as they can, though, with rifles slung. Make spot-check searches as well, and arrest anybody who holds out on us."

He turned back to the committee, "Meanwhile, I'm sure you gentlemen will start spreading the word. Everyone's to bring their weapons voluntarily to Sergeant Coveyduck here in the village square. Good morning."

Harry walked away from their grumbling, joined his men, and saw that the Griquas had tended his pony already. He took a few minutes in the shade for a bite to eat while he told Scayles about spotting a commando heading towards the distant army formation.

"The column's out of view now, and too far off for us to

lend a hand. Jiggy says he didn't get any acknowledgment of my warning, either, so they could be caught flat-footed."

"Dozy Cuthberts, not keeping a signals watch." Scayles pulled out the message from Provost HQ. "Speaking of which, look at what you brought me."

Harry chewed the last of his bully-beef, then casually unfolded the flimsy. A name jumped off the paper, and he read the message through twice. BELFAST POLICE IDENTIFY ASSAILANT OF LT L AS JOSS KOLBECK AKA COCKEYE STOP TWO PREVIOUS CONVICTIONS GBH STOP NAME OSSEBOOM NOT KNOWN HERE ENDS.

He shook his head and handed the paper back, "What do you make of it?"

"It looks like that bird who tried to kill you was just some street thug. He'd been nicked twice before for grievous bodily harm. Anyway, not your Osseboom chap. Or my master-spy, either. Pity." Scayles wrote a note in his book and folded the message inside. "When I told the civvie 'tecs, they thought that vrou's story sounded queer. But she seemed pretty convincing to you at the time, I gather."

"She still does, somehow."

"Well, the Belfast bobbies'll keep their eye peeled. If this Ossie bird does turn up on their turf, they'll give him a royal grilling, believe you me. Probably just some Boer blowhard, though. Anyway, we've got bigger things than him to worry about just now."

"That's for damn sure."

Harry agreed when Scayles suggested he go through the village with Piet van Praage as interpreter to canvas for any information about the Kruger cache. The MP began to assign troopers into search teams before he went off to play detective.

Some giggling along the street drew Harry's attention to two rawboned young women enjoying the flirtations of Haywood and Mendip. Jiggy did not let lack of a common language slow down his approaches. Posed hip-up on a hitching-rail, he used comical grimaces and a playful tone of voice to amuse the girls.

"See," Jiggy grinned. "Just get 'em laughing, and you're halfway inside any bint's knickers."

Haywood did not seem too keen. "Nah, this pair of scrawny dames ain't worth the effort."

"Garn! You doesn't look at t'mantlepiece when you're poking t'fire!"

"Mendip, get over here!" Harry tried to keep his face stern, and the man's incorrigible randiness gave him an idea. "I want you to make yourself useful. Get acquainted with some village ladies, and listen for any gossip about suspicious lorry-shipments."

"Right away, sir." Already Jiggy had spotted a group of prettier young house-vrouws outside a nearby shop. He saluted smartly, "I'll start make making probing enquiries, sir, if it takes all night. Very probing, indeed!"

Harry shook his head, amused, then started door-knocking for guns. He approached the more prosperous-looking houses, where his rank would be persuasive with wealthy residents. Now and again he had to insist forcefully, but the process moved along better than expected. Villagers wanted no trouble with soldiers this late in the war. Cameron drove along to load collected guns aboard a hired cart, while Scayles was working the houses opposite.

The MP noticed two roughly-dressed men squatting on their hunkers against the wall of a rooming-house. Their horses were hitched at the rail near a spyder-cart. What drew his attention was that both men carried a revolver on their hip. He drew his notebook and demanded they account for themselves, intending to confiscate the guns.

It turned out he had to let them keep their pistols, as they were not Spitsdorp residents. The tall skinny one wearing a battered bowler hat and filthy dress shirt was a uitlander. He called himself Maddocks and claimed to be a gold prospector. His whining gutter-snipe way of talking made Scayles wonder if he was a deserter.

"Just an 'armless bit of fun, squire, watching all the Boer bits of crumpet in their best frocks. But if it bothers you, we'll be on our way in 'alf a mo'," Scayles' cop instinct caught something false in the man's chirpy manner. His hands looked too soft to have handled a miner's shovel.

The other, with a scraggly black beard and torn overalls, was another suspicious-looking down-and-outer, one of those bywoner drifters. He admitted to the name of Zoller, and held a permanent scowl on his face. "We have a right to carry weapons as protection against blackies, and go where we please, no?"

"Unless I say otherwise."

"We are not soldiers, so you have no authority over us, I think." Zoller spat a gob in the dust near Scayles' gleaming boot.

"Step over the line, and we'll soon see about authority."

"No need to get shirty, now." Maddocks' hard eyes belied his lop-sided grin. "You must be wore out today. What with guarding money-bags and rounding up guns and everyfink." He turned to Zoller, and said meaningly. "Rather than be in anybody's way, we'd best be getting along."

They swung into the saddle without another word, and Scayles stood hands on hips, watching them out of sight. He glanced at the waiting spyder, its black driver dozing over the reins.

Harry was carrying a Guedes hunting rifle to the cart, when Scayles waved from across the street. He was standing beside a two-wheeler at the boardinghouse. An expensive leather suitcase was on the seat. Scayles slapped the "V" brand on the animal's haunch. "Seems we've found your dodgy Russian again."

The landlady led the way through to where Feliks Nikolai sat sipping tea on the back veranda. When he saw them, he froze, cup to lips, but quickly recovered. "What a pleasant surprise. Prisoner and escort out for some exercise. But perhaps events have changed since we last met?"

"Shut up and stand up!" Scayles roughly pushed his hands inside the man's jacket, patting up and down.

"Why, Lieutenant, I didn't think you cared!" Nikki mimed effeminacy. "*La vice Anglais*, so early in the day."

Scayles found a bank-bag heavy with sovereigns. "Who'd you rob this time, Sunshine?" The Russian did not reply, so Scayles reluctantly gave back the money, and pushed him into his seat.

Nikki crossed an ankle over his knee and cradled it there. "You're looking surprisingly well, Harry."

Guessing because of the bank-bag, Harry snapped, "Which is more than your pal Cockeye could say!"

Nikolai shrugged in a pantomime of bewilderment. Scayles growled, "Is that fancy gun hid in your luggage?"

"My word as an officer of the Imperial Guard, it is not." Harry noticed a badly inflamed sore on Nikki's cheek, oozing from what might have been an insect-bite or something.

"Very convincing, I don't think." Scayles tapped his handcuff case. "Right off, I could put you in irons for theft of that horse outside. Under martial law, a hanging offence."

"The nag's not stolen, merely borrowed. Besides, Hiram's my business partner now. He would never press charges."

"We're here to recover officially what you're after illegally," Harry said. "I'm warning you, drop the hankering for gold, and get out of my sight for good! All the way back to Moscow, preferably."

"But Harry, this is even better! You, me, and now a professional Sherlock Holmes with us on the search." He bowed mockingly to Scayles. "We just share the boodle three ways instead of two, and none's the wiser."

"Except for my entire platoon."

"Ah, brought that many with you? So, discreet sharing's

out of the question now, obviously." Nikki slowly lowered his boot, pressing both heels together.

Scayles said, "If any cronies of yours get involved, I'll run them in, too. Who else've you discussed it with?"

"Only our lovely Bethany Beatrix." Nikolai smiled lazily at the Canadian. "She sounded quite keen to go treasure-hunting, last time we spoke. Late the other night. In her bedroom." He smoothed his raven hair, "Aah, Harry, that kissable little beauty-spot, on her pretty left *mamelle!*"

Harry went white around the mouth. "If I didn't know you're such a Goddam liar, you'd be a dead man now. I should plug you anyway, for setting that shotgun artist on me."

"Probably the bastard did, but we've no evidence to go on." Scayles turned to go. "Let's not waste any more time with this piece of shyte."

"Hear me right, Nikolai," Harry grated. "You've been a Czarist agent and out on commando. That makes you an enemy of the Crown twice-over already. Next time you're caught within fifty miles of this town, I'll shoot you myself on the spot! Now get out of Spitsdorp!"

They strode away, until Scayles paused in the vestibule. "Crafty sod. Notice he avoided replying about accomplices by casting aspersions on your lady-friend? Knowing how touchy you are about her." Scayles fingered the scab on his nose. "Which reminds me, when this hare-brained treasure-hunt is over, you and I have something to settle ourselves. A pleasure deferred for now, though." He stamped towards the stairs. "I'll toss his room, just on the off chance."

Nikolai waited a few minutes, then adjusted a trouser-cuff over the Nagant tucked in his boot. He went out to the cart, and paused to hit his right bicep, jabbing an obscene fist towards Harry's retreating back. He snapped an order, and the driver whipped the horse at a gallop out of town. Maddocks would not have gone far.

For the next half hour, Lanyard continued to canvass

homes for weapons. Occasionally, he caught glimpses of troopers moving through poorer side-streets, loading an average of one gun from every third dwelling. If these were Boer farmers out on the veld, the ratio of rifles to homes would be the other way around.

"Yoo-hoo, captain!" A young woman called from her garden gate, smiling under a frilly parasol. "I rather hoped you'd come in my direction." Her Irish speech gave words the lilt of a flute.

He touched his brim and asked if his men had called there. "Indeed, that dishy Trooper Lascelles has been already. My, with his looks and posh voice, he should be an officer, that one. But you seem so sad, yourself, I wanted to say a cheerful word."

She was uncommonly pretty, with jewel eyes that matched her lavender dress. "I am the Baroness Neave von Gliewitz. And you?"

Harry gave his name, but made to move on, attractive though she was. He needed to get the disarming finished. She sensed his haste and said breathily, "My dear husband the Baron was a soldier. We came so he could train gunners for the Free State." She sighed, "He died last year at Bloemfontein. Of the plague, not battle, but taken from me nonetheless."

"Sorry to hear, ma'am."

"Baroness. He was so headstrong. So manly. But I can hold no hard feelings about this war." She tilted her head and smiled to take the sting out of the words, "I grew up coping with British soldiers, you see. In Ireland, of course."

"Well, I figured you don't exactly sound German, Baroness."

She laughed delightfully, as much for the benefit of two elderly vrouws who walked by, whispering about the foreigners. "Now look, my reputation sullied even more. That brazen Catholic hussy, consorting with a kakie." Her smile faded, "My own family back home disowned me for marrying dear Horst, a Protestant. And now here I am with my True Faith among pious Calvinists, beyond the pale again."

"Maybe you could just go Dutch."

She rewarded him with another silvery laugh. "You've no idea the effect your young men are having on the village ladies today. We've never seen so many roguish smiles at one time."

Harry doubted the attraction. Most Boer women considered it their patriotic duty to act coldly towards Tommies. "Well, the boys won't have much time to get into mischief. Now, if you'll excuse me." He tipped his hat and half-turned away.

"Oh, surely not leaving already. It's so seldom I get to chat with a gallant officer."

It always took Harry by surprise if a woman bothered to flirt with him. He had few delusions about his plain looks. There had been nothing coy about Beth though, just a straightforward acceptance of him from the start. Well, that one big chance of romance was not liable to be repeated. The thought made him sound harsher than he intended. "I have to be going, ma'am. Good day to you."

Baroness von Gliewitz barely had time to pout, when the crack of a rifle made her jump. Harry drew his Colt and started to run along the street. Scayles was ahead of him, elbows pumping like a rugby centre-forward. They found some angry troopers in a front garden, shaking and hitting a spindly old man. There was the welt of a fist on his chalky face, and Terry Bramah was jabbing a Mauser into the man's ribs.

"Let's string the old bastard up, Harry," Fontaine shouted. "He just shot poor Barney Wignall!"

Their friend lay spread-eagled in a rosebush, making croaking sounds, his tunic stained over the heart. His rifle was still slung across his back. Harry knelt to check, but it was obvious the ex-cowboy from Kamloops was near death.

He started to open the jacket, when someone knelt hurriedly, pushing him aside.

"Quickly now!" Baroness von Gliewitz ripped the tunic wide, buttons flying. Pale pink bubbles swelled and burst with sputters of air. "Not good, I'm afraid."

"Better let us handle him," Harry said impatiently. This was no time for some well-meaning lady of the manor.

"Hardly. I'm Berlin trained, and've nursed half of Bloemfontein, too!" She ripped the field-dressing pad from where it was lightly stitched inside Wignall's tunic, and pressed it to his wound. "Hold that tight a moment." She dipped in her skirt to tear the hem off her petticoat for a bandage.

Wignall sounded a phlegmy rattle. "He's gone, I'm afraid," she sighed. Troopers swore, and Bill Fletcher thumped the old man.

Harry struggled to sound impassive, "Thanks for the effort, though."

She nodded and sank back on her heels. "Not much chance to do anything with a sucking wound like that." She sounded both sad and matter-of-fact.

Harry unbuttoned the breast pocket to take Wignall's service-book for the Graves Registration people. Its pages were sticking together already. He'd have to write one of those next-of-kin letters he always dreaded.

"Somebody escort the baroness home, please."

A man took her elbow, and she looked into deKrieger's face. Her cheeks drained of colour and she started to speak. The trooper interrupted quickly, guttural sounds, and she replied in the same tongue. Nobody else could understand what they were saying.

"Yes, thank you." Her words were directed at Harry, but she never took her gaze away from deKrieger. "I'm sorry we couldn't save your man. But I would like to rest now, if you don't mind." Neave took the soldier's arm and the pair walked off. After a few steps, she halted abruptly, staring up at something he said. Her shoulders shook and she dabbed her eyes with a hankie. He patted her shoulder and led her away.

The killer kept whimpering, his reedy voice rising and falling with a mix of curses and prayers in Afrikaans. Piet shouted at him to *"Hou jou bek!"*, but the man would not. Bramah grabbed him by his nanny-goat beard, "I'll shut your mouth, shithead, for good!"

"Fair play, and all that, chaps," Lascelles drawled. "The old boy's obviously mad as a hatter."

"Who're you to be sticking up for a murdering Boer?"

"Pipe down the pair of you!" Scayles interrupted, "How'd this happen?"

They all spoke in a rush, but gradually it became clear that Wignall, aggressive as ever, had gone up against a man with the drop on him. A frightened woman next door explained. The oldster had stepped outside with his gun, and ordered the kakie to get off the property. She said, "The Tommy said he'd never turn tail from any Boojer, and Mister Muller shot him."

"Christ, I wish we had one of Gat's old machine-guns along," Bramah was maroon-faced, jowls wobbling with rage. "We could clean out this whole friggin burg!" His mates growled agreement, and shouted the glum news when more troopers ran up.

"Take it easy, men!" Harry yelled above their rowing. "I'm upset as anybody about Barney, but we can't punish all the village because of one crazy galoot. We're still soldiers. Anybody gets out of line with civilians will answer to me!"

That drew some hollering protests, and Schammerhorn drawled to nobody in particular, "Guess this comes from ordering troopers to keep their guns out of reach."

Bramah sneered, "Yeah, and we know whose half-assed idea that was!"

Lanyard snapped, "Don't push your luck, Private!"

He shook his head at Scayles to not intervene. Unlike the

strictly disciplined Imperials, Colonial troops were used to speaking their mind, and it usually went no further than that. But if this lot were confronted in the heat of their anger, a protest could escalate to something far more serious. Mutiny in time of war was a capital military offence, liable to summary field court-martial and a firing-squad more often than not.

It took all Harry's force of will to calm the troopers down from wreaking random vengeance. He busied them by detailing some to gently lay Wignall on the cartload of rifles and trundle him away to the church. When the others sullenly went back to confiscating weapons, Harry knew any Boer gun-owner who argued at the door would risk a beating.

Scayles clamped handcuffs on Muller, and said flatly, "My prisoner. We take him back alive, to stand proper trial."

"Shit, Harry." Bramah glared resentment at his friend of years, as if seeing a stranger. "Those officer pips sure made you go soft on us!"

CHAPTER FOURTEEN

As soon as breakfast was over, Dirk could not wait to sneak out of camp. He had to get away from the place, with its hymns and dust, and the stench of rotting meat. When animals were butchered for food, the skins and offal would be just left where they lay in the sun, attracting swarms of flies. Other than meat from wild game, supplies were growing short, clothes were in rags, and another few commandos had deserted overnight. *"Bangsiekte"*, Ox called it, fear-sickness.

Dirk decided to do something more exciting today than sit listening to the latest rumours of surrender. He saddled up, slid his Plezier into its leather bucket, and rode off to find something to shoot. He headed onto the open veld, eyes roving for signs of game movement.

Dirk felt a heart-racing sense of his own youth and wild freedom. Six months of hard living outdoors had built his muscles and added at least four inches to his height. He glowed with a sort of fervour, a feeling of being master of himself and few possessions. He had all he needed to go anywhere; a good rifle and bandolier, the water-bottle hanging on his shoulder, haversack and blanket strapped to the saddle of his strong pony.

The takhaars were forever warning him not to rove far alone, nor shoot his rifle at game without first checking that no army patrol was nearby to hear it. Now, it was good to escape from their old-woman nagging. He let his horse take the lead, ambling up and down the rolling veld.

Out here, the world seemed a circle of rest, from skyline to skyline. Once the encampment was hidden, there was no sign of war. The coming winter showed in the yellowing grass, where cobwebs lay like threads of silver. This feral life had sharpened his senses of hearing and seeing, of observing things, noting signs and drawing conclusions from them. He never ceased scanning earth and sky, alert for animal spoor, the flight of startled birds, or hoof-beats.

He caught a flicker out of the corner of his eye, a shift in the rays of sunlight that slanted through a screen of bushes. Something skulking into cover behind a big ant-hill. Hoping it was a fat impala, he unsheathed his rifle, and reined in a wide circle behind the pillar of earth.

Dirk's horse made no sound on the dew-wet grass, so the man he came across did not hear him coming. He was a tall fellow, lath-thin, craning to look in the direction of the commando camp. Dirk could see he was an enemy, because he was clean-shaven and standing at the left of his horse's head. All commandos grew bushy beards, and made a practice to stand on the right side of horses when dismounted, so as to be easily recognized by their own from a distance.

"Hends op!" Dirk enjoyed shouting those particular words at this obvious defector.

The stranger raised his arms high, looking disgusted at being caught by a mere boy. *"Ag, nie!"*

His pony was so short, the man's long folded legs stuck up like a locust's. Dirk disarmed him of a rifle and pistol, and kept the Webley pointed while they rode back. He tried to answer gruffly when his prisoner forced some friendly conversation, sensing it was intended to put him off guard.

"Never mind the weather we're having, better think what you'll have to say for yourself with my veld-cornet!"

"Why bother to take me in? I'm just wandering. Looking for my family." The joiner told his sad tale simply, and Dirk found himself responding sympathetically after a while. That changed when the man pleaded, "Look, young'un, why don't you let me go? Otherwise, you know what's going to happen to me."

Dirk's temper flared, "It's your own God-damn fault if they tan your hide raw with a sjambok!"

Using the Lord's name outside a prayer made it a serious Boer oath, and the man was so shocked he did not speak again. He slumped in the saddle while Dirk rode behind, not hiding his pride at bringing a prisoner into camp single-handed. They met him with laughter and hand-claps, calling, "What've you brought for the pot this time, penkop?"

Cornet Vilberg knew in a glance what the stranger probably was before Dirk handed over his belongings. "You got a proper name, man?" He received only a scowl and silence for answer.

"All he'll say is, he's called Henk," Dirk reported. "From down Piet Retief way, and claims he's only searching for his womenfolk."

"You're a long way from home, Henk What-ever's-your name. So your family loved-ones 've disappeared, eh? That your story, eh, my slim beardless friend caught with English money in your pocket?"

Vilberg hefted the Webley. "Well, I think you're a bastard National Scout, one of those traitors to every decent Boer! Is the rest of your wing skulking nearby? You'll tell us where your cursed cohorts are, if you don't want to die!"

The prisoner shrugged, "Do what you like. What difference will it make? My wife and little girl are probably dead by now in some camp, because of such as you." He spat at Vilberg's boots, *"Bitterenders? Hah—poephols!"*

The cornet's face went very red at hearing his men called arseholes. He jabbed the revolver into the traitor's chest and pushed him towards the stream-bank.

Commandos stood in a group to discuss the obvious fate for this hireling of the British. To them, nothing was lower than the National Scouts. They were Afrikaner levies who signed an oath of allegiance to King Edward, and accepted a certificate of engagement binding each to serve His Majesty under arms for six months. They took five English shillings a day, to scout and loot and fight their own kin.

Now, this one who was delivered into their hands must

reap another kind of payment. Vilberg asked Advokaat Boergaard for a legal opinion on the situation. *"Ach, wat,"* Gabriel sighed, "I don't have the martial law books to consult, but I recall they're clear enough when it comes to treason. Myself, though, I'd feel better if there was a proper formal hearing. But it's up to you." That was no particular help, so Vilberg asked his commandos individually for their verdict.

Burghers cheered when Ox shouted, *"Maak dood die verdomde spion!"* Only a thoughtful few did not agree they should kill the damned spy.

Dirk shouted, "No, Cornet, please! He is my prisoner. When I brought him in, I thought he'd only get a good whipping!"

Nobody paid attention to the boy, all ears being tuned to Vilberg's words, "We are witnesses this man is a spy in the service of the invaders. He's acted traitorously against the Transvaal Republic and the Orange Free State. Though we have no courtrooms to try this case, the evidence of guilt is clear. So, Mister Henk, by authority of our War Laws, you are sentenced to die."

It was not a duty Vilberg could shirk by including others in the act, like the enemy, who ordered Tommies to be firing-squads against comrades. Carrying out the sentence personally went with his rank and responsibility.

Most of his men formed a curious crowd to watch justice being done. Ox shouted, "If the Almighty lets you into Heaven, you pig, seek my poor wife and kids and beg their forgiveness!" Others would not look, but turned their backs to read the Testament instead. Oom Languedoc made the youngest penkops walk out of view, and led the boys in singing a psalm.

The condemned enemy scout met Vilberg's gaze calmly. He had not lied to save his life, or betrayed the whereabouts of his comrades, you could credit him that. The cornet said, "If you choose to die nameless, so be it. Now, it's time to meet your Maker, traitor."

He kicked the prisoner to his bony knees on the bank. He began to speak loudly to God, making his Peace, man to man. Cornet Vilberg waited to shoot him in the back of the head at the right moment, so Henk died with the Lord's name on his lips.

Without warning, Dirk Blenkarn started to cry, though he had not intended to. His sobs were more shocking than the pistol-shot, and his companions did not know where to look. Wim came and put an arm around the boy's shoulder, but most others turned away in embarrassment.

The executed spy was buried without much dignity where he fell. A few solemn-faced burghers came to pause by the mound of earth and read aloud from the Bible. Certain younger men laughed at such sentiments, and even hooted insults. "Let him rot there, it'll be good for the crops!"

The same pack turned their scorn on Dirk as well, all respect for his previous bravery lost through his unbidden tears over a traitor. Boschie Petersen jeered, "Hey, Moffie! After this, we'll have to leave you home in a pinafore!"

Being called such a name made Dirk sick with shame. A moffie was a castrated sheep, but it also meant a sissie-boy, who did lewd things with other males. Unspeakable acts that he could not quite imagine but which were forbidden by the Old Testament and reviled in the Boer creed. Dirk bent his head over his Mauser, cleaning and polishing it endlessly to avoid looking at the friends he had dismayed with a moment's softness.

"Never mind their *pappe-kak*, lad." Ox pushed a mug of coffee into his hand. "Soft shits, themselves. None've shot as many rednecks as you. Next one that calls you that, spit in his eye like you always did. Come on, Wim, give the boy a stomach-bomb."

Hartsma passed Dirk a fried dumpling, and winked. "Happens, the first time you see a dead man up close. Even worse with somebody you've got to know. Different from when you shoot soldiers at a distance and they just seem to fall down. Nothing to be ashamed of, weeping."

Ox boomed, "Yes, you'll soon get over it, kid!" and pounded him on the ribs as if he was a favorite hound. He passed a slice of fatty meat skewered on a fence-wire fork. "Now braii this and get it inside you."

Usually Dirk hated cooking over the acrid stink of dried cattle-dung they burned for fuel. Now though, it seemed a warm focus of manly conversation. He felt the joy of comradeship and acceptance again, and laughed loudly at even the thinnest jokes.

Vilberg felt isolated from the yarning men around their fires. Though the execution verdict had been all but unanimous, Vilberg noticed few of his commandos had come near him since. As well, he overheard burghers saying they were ripe for some *huis-toe,* and wondered how many would sneak away home at nightfall. He was worrying about that when the old verkenner wearing a woman's shawl rode in with new orders for the Crocodile Commando.

Headquarters wanted them to finish off the job of destroying that British patrol they missed at the train. Quick results were expected, as Spitsdorp was only half a day's ride away. This time, there was no mention of the disposition of any survivors.

The old scout added, "I came across a supply-column of kakies fording the river near Machadodorp this morning. Heading this direction. It'd make a fine extra target for you along the way."

Vilberg asked a few questions, weighing up the prospects for success with both attacks. After he thought things over, he called Ox to his tent, and told him he had a special job that'd require having to shave. Then the cornet gathered his men for a battle-discussion, so everyone knew what was involved. The news of some more action was greeted with approval, especially as both attacks sounded easy and there might be some fresh supplies to loot.

When Dirk heard Vilberg's command to break camp, he felt stimulated by a hot desire for the chance to prove himself in action once more. He was saddling up when young Saul ter Hoven sneered, "You don't have to come along, little Moffie. This is man's work." So Dirk shouted back, *"Gaan trek draad!"* Go masturbate. Saul charged over and Dirk punched him hard, then sat on his chest to hit him some more.

"That's enough dirty language from the pair of you!" Corporal Schippers yanked the boys apart, cuffing their ears. "Save your breath for the kakies."

Within a half hour, the commandos moved off singing psalms lustily, leaving their native servants to load the few vehicles and follow later. The commando group rode at a steady trot, in no particular formation. Vilberg took the lead, holding his black umbrella against the noon sun, letting the old scout show the way.

The route was over dry ground, that threw up a great cloud of dust, so they could not see ahead, and it was as well they had a guide. Vilberg became anxious in case they missed the interception-point with the target, and ordered a fast gallop.

It almost caused disaster for Dirk, when his pony caught a hoof in a meerkat hole, snapped a leg, and threw its rider. The penkop fell heavily, hidden in the haze. Sand-mist roiled as he ran this way and that, dodging heavy horses that boomed out of nowhere, burghers yelling to get out of the way, then disappearing as quickly.

Hooves thumped beside him, Ox looming down, pointing his rifle. "Grab your stuff, boy!"

In one continuous movement, the big Fleming fired once into the forehead of the kicking pony and scooped up Dirk by the collar as if he weighed no more than a puppy. They charged onwards inside the dust-cloud, invisible hoof-beats all around, and the boy laughed aloud in crazy exultation of this mad ride towards the enemy.

CHAPTER FIFTEEN

Vilberg did not waste time devising any fancy strategy of attack when he came in sight of the British column. He counted about fifteen horse-dawn carts, with maybe a hundred soldiers. Some clung asleep on the cargo, others plodded along behind in uneven column of fours, unready with rifles slung or held by the muzzle across a shoulder.

As was expected of him, the veld-cornet fired the first shot, knocking a black driver from his seat. Whooping commandos charged forward in a wide line to hit the length of the wagon-train. They fired from the saddle as they charged, bowling kakies over like skittles before they even knew of danger. There was not much return fire at first, as soldiers tried to rub grit from their eyes, unable to make out the attackers.

The green English soldiers were poor marksmen, but remained steady under fire and did their best. In battle for the first time, most fought in desperate silence, but some had a careless gaiety about them. To cope, a few Tommies mocked death itself, actually shouting jokes to each other. "Eeh, Albert, you think these Boojer's are mad at us about summat?" Another called, "Go on, mate, stand up and catch a Blighty-one!"

Dirk threw himself off, kneeling to shoot at a British uniform dimly-seen in the swirl. His first bullet creased the head of the noisy Tommy, who laughed shakily, "Cor, mates, I just 'ad a free 'air-cut!" Dirk shut the clown up with his next round.

Cape ponies galloped close by but somehow failed to crush him, and he worked his breech-bolt like a mechanical toy. Rifles banged, bullets zipped and ricocheted, officers yelled orders, soldiers screamed in pain, Boers shouted taunts, and whinnying maimed horses added to the chaos of slaughter. A pom-pom barked a few rounds, then fell silent along with its crew.

There was no sense of time, just the hideous bedlam that went on and on. Dirk's shoulder began to hurt from his rifle's steady kick. After ten chaotic minutes that seemed like eternity, he realized the musketry had died down. Triumphant Taal shouts of "Hallelujah!" went up. He was among the last ones still shooting when he finally heard Vilberg repeating, "Stop firing, men!" The cornet's calm voice carried strongly, "That should do for now."

Burghers moved in among the wagons, calling for soldiers to come out, weapons first, no tricks. English voices replied, "Easy on, Johnny! We're packing it in." Rifles pitched onto the ground, and the defeated troops came from cover.

Three of the vehicles turned out to be ambulance carts, choked with a score of soldiers suffering from enteric. Dirk took a cautious glance inside, fearful of contamination by getting too close. The victims squirmed in their own filth, skins flecked by the tell-tale flat spots of typhoid. They moaned with pain, knees clamped up against chests, or else lay gray-faced and unconscious.

Veld-Cornet Vilberg ordered three of the Army Service Corps drivers to take their sick comrades away to whatever field hospital they could reach. He put three of his most seriously wounded burghers aboard an ambulance as well. Even though it meant them being "Ceyloned" to some overseas prisoner-of-war camp, at least their lives could be saved by military doctors. The one redeeming feature of this cruel war of farm-burnings and civilian camps was that the English soldiers were unfailingly humane after combat. That was so well known, there was no hesitation in turning over an ill or wounded Boer to the mercy of the troops, in the sure knowledge he would be as carefully nursed as their own. Commandos returned the compliment by their decent treatment of wounded military prisoners.

There was no question of quarter for the uniformed natives with the column. Ox and others of like mind found ten black Auxiliaries and just shot them dead where they stood. Many Tommies lay still, hanging over wagon sides or sprawled on the ground. Wounded soldiers flopped and squirmed, calling. "Christ, it hurts!" "Give us a hand, Tosh." "Oh, sodding 'ell, they've done for poor old Nobby Clark!"

A gray-haired British colonel writhed in pain, yelling obscenely at top of his voice. His frantic batman began to rip off the officer's tunic, and was cursed for his trouble, "You fecking imbecile, it's my bally leg!"

With offended dignity, the private said, "Beg parding, sir. From your langwidge, h'I concluded you was 'it in the habdomen!"

Nervous laughter sounded over the moans of wounded, as survivors tried to cope with the shock. One called, "Sarge, d'you think I could put in for my discharge today?" As the shambles calmed, Dirk saw soldiers with their hands in the air being disarmed by commandos. "Good fight, Tommy", some Boers said in English, and shook hands with their astonished prisoners. They let the army farriers keep their revolvers, which soon cracked repeatedly to silence wounded horses.

"Hey, we won, Wim!" Dirk shouted as his friend rushed past through the haze.

"Not yet, kid." Hartsma jerked his head to follow towards scattered rifle shots.

As Dirk ran, he slapped at his bandolier. Only one clip left. He jammed his last five Mauser bullets into the magazine, slammed the bolt home, and heard the charger clip tinkle away with a final sound. After this, he'd have to make do with one of those Lee-Metfords.

A few British were still holding out amid a tumble of rocks. Boers ringed them, shouting "Give up, rooineks!", between firing back whenever they saw movement. The boulders gave enough cover for a soldier's body, but arms and legs showed here and there, easy targets for marksmen. Each time a rifle cracked, there would be another answering cry of pain, adding to the constant moans of agony.

Ox shouted, "Now stick your other foot out for me, Kakie!" He was on one knee for steady aim, a pitiless avenger with bushy yellow hair and beard like a haystack, firing at the slightest movement. Each round was for memory of his wife and three sons, dead a year past in one of Kitchener's camps. He shot carefully, inflicting terrible wounds with his soft-point slugs, drawing new screams.

He glanced sideways in welcome. "The Brits must really want those rocks, eh, Dirk?"

The sixteen-year-old wriggled into a comfortable firing position, resting his rifle on one knee. He wanted to put each of his few rounds to good use. When a khaki sleeve showed, he squeezed off once, and heard a yelp.

Somewhere nearby, Boschie jeered, "Baaah-baaah! Good shot, for a moffie cry-baby!"

A red mist of rage filled Dirk's brain. He rolled sideways, pointing his gun, seeking out Boschie to kill. Ox laughed like a mad baboon. "Tend to business, boy! Concentrate on scoring British bulls-eyes." He snapped off another shot, "Ach, I think I got their officer that time."

Maddened, Dirk turned back to the trapped soldiers. He squinted through the peep-sight at a careless boot showing and sent a 7mm. into it. He fired at other targets, but over-fast to take effect. Only two Mauser rounds left.

A loud English voice brayed, "All right, you win, you bastards!" Cautiously, a hand rose over a rock, waving. Dirk drilled a perfect snap-shot through the hand before he noticed it held a white handkerchief. Ox grinned and winked.

"Cease firing!" Cornet Vilberg shouted angrily, "Let him come out unharmed!"

There was an unsteady clatter of hooves and a shabby horse staggered out, drooping with the weight of the limping officer. He held himself erect with his elbow looped through a pistol-belt on the saddle. One of his boots was a mess of blood, bone, and leather, and a stained handkerchief still fluttered from his shattered hand. He wore a Wolseley sun-helmet bearing a scarlet diamond patch. Dirk stared hard at it, reminded of Herzog's burning farmhouse.

"We're surrendering, I said!" The captain had a rough Staffordshire accent, and sounded more outraged than afraid. "My poor lads have had enough. For God's sake, let them be." He staggered, and grabbed the belt to stop himself falling.

The sudden move startled Dirk, and he jerked the trigger in reflex. His last round punched into the officer's head, brain-matter splashing the weary horse.

"Dirty rotters!" Wounded soldiers crawled out of the rocks, hands held up but raging still at the damnable thing done to their captain. Boers hurried over and disarmed them before any tried to pay back with the same coin.

"Who in hell fired that shot?" Veld-Cornet Vilberg was livid with rage. "Own up to me now!"

"I did, Laurens." Dirk Blenkarn tried to sound defiant, resolved he was not going to lose control of himself this time. "I thought he was—-."

"You thought! After I had called cease-fire!" Vilberg waved his sjambok in Dirk's face, somehow stopping himself from flogging the lad senseless. His commandos were watching, curious how their cornet would handle this. He wondered, could any one of them ever obey a simple order?

"Curse you for a young fool! After your exhibition, we never should have let you come along."

"Ah, leave him be," Ox said. "That redneck could have been going for a gun."

"The state he was in?" Vilberg scoffed. He abruptly focused on van Antwerp. "And you're another one! Didn't I order you to Spitsdorp?"

"I didn't want to miss this sport, man."

"Don't argue with me. Get yourself there, now! And don't mess things up before I arrive!" He gave a final contemptuous look at Dirk, and hurried back to his unruly men.

"Lucky you. I can't take these with me." Ox lifted off his bandolier and hung it over Dirk's shoulder. "Six clips, so your Plezier's still in business." Tips of five bullets grinned from each pouch like blunt lead teeth.

Ox thumped the boy's back, "So long, penkop. Keep your pecker up." He lumbered off towards some interesting sounds of looting.

A shadow passed across the ground, and Dirk looked up to see aasvogels hovering already. The vultures' amazing sense of smell had drawn them from miles away to the feast. From look of it, the officer's horse could be next on the menu. The poor beast stood droop-headed, ungroomed hair like a burst sofa, its ribs showing, and a loose fold of skin hanging from its starved belly. It had been in the wars before, with a perforated ear and a long stripe from an old wound along its flank.

Dirk took the dangling reins. "Come and get some scoff, girl." It would be something to do. On the way, he noticed Wim sitting alone, rifle between his knees, tamping his pipe with captured English tobacco. Dirk went to sit beside him, and asked how many men they had lost.

"Four burghers killed, and as many wounded. Nineteen dead kakies." Wim gave a look. "One more than need've been."

Dirk began to stammer how it happened, but Hartsma interrupted silently by raising a hand. He rested his pipe on a rock, thinking carefully what to say.

"Heed, boy." Strong fingers clamped Dirk's arm. "What you did shames us all." His hand felt like steel, and he squeezed to hurt. "Next time you kill a man who wants to surrender, the cornet won't just take his sjambok to you. You'll be lucky he doesn't stake you over an anthill for a couple of days before packing your remains off home."

Dirk stilled the hot words that came to his throat, knowing there was no way he could ever explain. Wim let go, and pulled at his pipe. Smoke coiled through his beard, eddying with his words, "It's best you go home now, anyway. Man or boy has just so much courage in him. Each of us fights on as best he can, but sooner or later something tells us our well's run dry."

He stared hard into the boy's eyes, willing him to understand. "So, leave now. You might never get over this wicked act. But at least you'll save yourself from worse."

"Desert? Never!" Dirk stood rigid with fury. "I can't believe you'd want me to slink away like some hyena!"

"It's my best advice, lad." Wim put a hand on the penkop's shoulder. Dirk shrugged him off.

"Well, I'll be soon taking it myself. *Huis-toe.*" Going home. Hartsma shook his head sadly, and walked away.

After that odd handshaking business was over, the British ignored their captors, intent on identifying who was dead and looking after wounded comrades. A few Boers offered help with bandages, but most started enjoying the fruits of victory. The carts were filled with impossible luxuries; hundreds of cases of tinned meat and butter, fresh bread, bales of blankets, saddlery, boxes of ammunition, and crates of enough liquor to supply every officers mess in South Africa.

Vilberg wondered at the stupidity of a score of men's lives being lost while transporting all these bottles of champagne, whiskey, and gin. Before long, he was more concerned about the cargo's effect on his own men. Booze of any kind was rare in Boer camps, and drunkenness never seen while out on commando. Today, though, a sort of madness grew. A few of the young men knocked the necks off champagne bottles, drank the fizz, and hooted as they sprayed each other with foam.

"Apple-piss, for women!" Ox threw a three-guinea magnum of Mumm's aside and unscrewed a bottle of

Plymouth Gin instead. He guzzled a long pull. "Geneva, now, that's more like it!"

Others broke open cases of liquor, "Help yourself, man!", they called. Dirk did not fancy the taste of gin at first, but soon started to enjoy the careless rapture it gave, making things seem not so bad after all. Half the Boers became gloriously drunk, giddy with laughter or turning nasty, depending on how booze affected each.

Laurens Vilberg shouted at them to stop being idiots, but they just shoved him away, giggling or cursing. In the end, he had to lay about with his whip to get them to work sorting more useful supplies. "Take whatever we can carry, and destroy the rest."

The sweets-starved burghers opened jars of marmalade and jam, gobbling mouthfuls. They ripped into blue paper bags of Tate & Lyle sugar, pouring the grains down their throats until the unaccustomed treat made them vomit. Penkops threw flourbags at each other, ya-hooing as they splashed powder on themselves and the kakie corpses underfoot. Each looter grabbed whatever took his fancy; horses, food, blankets, rifles, and ammunition being the favorites. Any supplies they could not carry was thrown onto a huge pile along with broken carts and surplus ammunition.

Despite the chaos, the cornet and Corporal Schippers managed to restore order among the commandos before long. What brought many to their senses was the hurried ceremony to properly bury their dead. Vilberg read from the Testament over the four sad mounds, and the Boers sang hymns devoutly, slurred or sober.

"Hook up that pom-pom the British kindly brought us, Swarte," the cornet said. "It might come in handy for street-cleaning."

Schippers looked pleased, "And there's enough belts with it to last a month of Sundays." He gestured at the British busily digging graves. "Too many prisoners to take with us. Strip them as usual?"

"Yes, then send them home with a boot up the arse." Vilberg scratched lice inside his ragged coat. "See if you can get a nice tunic to fit me."

He went and smashed bottles on the debris, splashing whiskey as fire-lighter. "Put a match to the lot."

He told the drunks and youngsters to stay behind to finish burning the British supplies, and catch up with the main party at rendezvous tonight. Ox shouted a raucous adieu to Dirk, but Vilberg deliberately looked through the youth as he rode by. That shawled old scout was at his side when he led the cavalcade away, headed north. The sun was dropping down the sky, throwing shadows from the low grave mounds.

The bonfire caught well, fueled by alcohol, and black smoke billowed up, visible for miles. The major of Highlanders who was leading support infantry along the next valley guessed right off what that meant. He was able to confirm it by trotting up a rise of land. Young officers clumped around him below the skyline, staring through field-glasses, but when he spoke, the major addressed his battle-wise senior n.c.o.

"Looks like our supply train's copped it, Sar'nt Major, wouldn't you say?"

"Seems likely, sir. Shall I send skirmishers to confirm?"

"Yes, would you. Quietly, mind. Don't want to flush the game just yet."

The CO gave command to break column of march and disperse the men in open order towards the smoke. Word came back quickly from the RSM, confirming the column appeared to have been destroyed, but that the Boers were occupied with burning supplies. No enemy lookouts could be seen.

The major clapped his hands together, pleased as Punch. He said to his platoon officers, "Well, gentlemen, we're going to get a crack at the Johnnies in a fair fight for once."

A youthful second-lieutenant laughed, "No hit-and-run

for these blighters this time, sir."

"Sar'nt Major, you were at Modder River, I believe."

"I was, sir." The RSM twitched his handle-bar mustache. "More'n a few of us here had our legs burned that day."

This was a Regular battalion, its men veterans of a half-dozen battles. Including the Modder River shambles, where hundreds of Highlanders were massacred one hot afternoon two years ago. The Scots had been mown down by Boers hidden in trenches along the riverbank. The survivors lay under constant rifle-fire for hours, kilts rucked up, the backs of their bare knees cooked raw by the blazing sun.

"Well, it's your turn today, Sarn't Major. Have the men fix bayonets."

"Sah!" A ghost of a smile curved the n.c.o.'s slit of a mouth. He strode away purposefully, and wished the bag-piper hadn't stepped on a boomslang last week and died. The skirl of pipes could have helped stir the men for the work ahead. That puny bugler-boy, Willie, would have to make do.

His low-voiced order brought the *wheep* of steel blades unsheathed from scabbards, and the click of boss-catches on muzzles. Ordered to strict silence, the Highlanders spread in a long tartan row along the ridge that overlooked the burning wagons. They nudged each other wordlessly, scowling towards the score of fresh earth mounds.

Orders were whispered, "Safeties off, check magazines. Range one hundred." They flipped up rear sights, slid peep-holes to the 100 yards mark, and cranked a round up the spout. Flinty eyes picked targets, cuddling rifle-butts, waiting for the CO's word.

A few terse instructions from the major sent officers running to take their places along the line. An undersized soldier hopped up the slope, bugle slung on his hip. He arrived breathless, and made a child-like salute. "Never do that in action, Bugler," the craggy-faced major sighed. "Snipers, you know."

His glasses picked out a line of barefoot men in long underwear straggling away. Quite clearly, he heard Boers laugh and call in English, pointing south. "You'll be home for supper tomorrow, Tommy!"

"Come on, come on!" The major breathed, willing the released prisoners to move more safely apart. There were Red Cross orderlies among the wounded down there as well, but he couldn't delay any longer. 'Just hope they all had the sense to put their heads down.

"When I say 'Charge', blow loud as you can, Private." He drew his revolver and shouted, *"Open faaaah!"*

Ninety-odd rifles crackled along the ridge. The veterans emptied magazines in seconds, shooting so rapidly it sounded like a child's stick dragging along iron railings. Boers leaped and twisted and moaned as cupro-nickle bullets raked them at 2000 feet per second. Still muzzy from gin, Dirk could not take it all in for a moment. He hid behind the spavined horse that stood shivering amid the metal sleet. He heard his name called, turned, and saw Wim arc backward onto the bonfire. He pulled his friend out, smoldering, but saw Hartsma was dead. The staring eyes seemed to repeat, "Time to go home."

A wavering bugle call sounded from the ridge. Sunset glinted on the brass held by a tiny figure standing up there in the open. A couple of Boers took the time to shoot at him. Terrifying men in checkered red skirts came charging down the hill, screeching Gaelic oaths, holding bayonets rigidly ahead. Dirk gaped at them, then jack-knifed forward to retch a gout of gin and green bile.

Roaring prayers, Oom Languedoc stood firing with deliberate aimed slowness, straddling the body of his grandson. He killed a Scotsman who got within ten feet, then threw aside his rifle. "I surrender!" But he'd left that too late, and was skewered, hands in the air regardless.

Dirk lay under a cart, helpless as white-gaitered boots thumped past. "Gi'e 'em stick, boys!" A last despairing volley of shots, then there were just the thuds and rips and screams as burghers fought hand-to-hand with rifle-butts against stabbing blades.

Dirk crawled out, and staggered to the trembling horse. He threw himself on its back, feeling the animal twitch in pain from saddle-sores. "Gee-haw, girl!" Dirk shouted in English, "Giddy-up!" He slammed his boots into its wash-board ribs.

Lt. Colonel Auckland's painful leg-wound had maybe crippled him for life, and he raged loudly to the Highland major about how many of his soldiers had been killed. The major was glad when his RSM approached to ask a question, trickily timed though it was under the circumstances.

"The prisoners, sir. Twelve are disguised in our uniforms. Should I have them dealt with?"

"Ummm." The major avoided the colonel's eye, and took in the British graves and moaning wounded. Still, his men had evened the score well enough this evening. He wavered a moment, then decided, "Oh, doesn't seem worth bothering to shoot them, this late in the war. Just pack the lot off as PWs."

"Yessah." The RSM allowed himself a bleak smile. "Now maybe they'll stop making all that unholy row, praying."

Dirk's sick horse had managed to hobble no further than the rocks where its master had been killed. It stopped in its tracks, head down, scarce able to walk, much less run. Half-sobbing, he kicked its heaving sides, flailing with his hat, clucking his tongue. *"Trek, trek!"*

Jeering laughter sounded, "Hey, jockey, ye'll no win the Grand National that way." Soldiers ringed him, spattered with gore, lowering their reddened blades in amusement at the antics of his frantic horsemanship.

"Hurrying home to yer mother, the now? And on an officer's mount at that." They pulled him off, grabbing his rifle, about to just hoik him back among the few Boer prisoners. The ones lucky enough to lay down arms in time before they were within bayonet-reach.

"What in Christ's name's these!" A hairy paw grabbed Dirk's bandolier, ripping out a clip of soft-nosed bullets. "Dum-dums!" He roared, and punched Dirk in the face.

"And look here." Another soldier was waving the Plezier. "Over a dozen notches! The murdering little scut's been keeping score!"

They would have stabbed him on the spot, if the hairy one hadn't shouted, "Hold awa'. It's about time we got wee Willy blooded."

The others howled like wolves, "That's the ticket!" Their call went up, "Where's yon pawky bugler?"

Somebody fetched him, and a reeking-bladed rifle was pressed into his small hands. "The Boojers put a hole in your trumpet, Willy. Now's chance to get your own back."

The two youths eyed each other with mutual dread. Dirk had killed his share of grown men, and wondered how his nemesis could possibly be this spotty-faced kakie even younger than he was.

The boy-soldier said, "Ah don't fancy it."

"High time you got used, Willy."

"Ah'm a-feared,"

"Just remember what they taught ye, 'Bash the Boer in the belly with ye'r baynit!'"

"Go on, do it, lad!"

Opening his jaws wide as if he could not breathe, the bugler slowly pushed the sharp point into Dirk's stomach. It did not hurt as much as expected, really. He was no moffie.

"Ach, wavery knees! This time, stick him hard!"

Eighteen inches of Sheffield steel jabbed, cold as ice, hot as fire. Irkie Blenkarn screamed like a stuck pig.

CHAPTER SIXTEEN

Predikant Carolus had acted unexpectedly decent about helping with the funeral of a British soldier. He provided a plot in the church cemetery, arranged for a grave to be dug at reasonable rates, and offered to preside over the burial service early on Monday morning. The entire troop were up for it at dawn, rolling out of their blankets, stiff from lying on frosty ground and bursting for a piss. They got breakfasts ready without their usual joshing remarks, and shaved in downcast silence.

The British army put great score on the discipline of its men taking a shave every morning, even while living rough in the field. To encourage the daily ritual, each soldier was issued a small steel mirror as part of his equipment. Tommies carried it in their left pocket, over the heart, in superstitious hope it would stop a bullet.

Harry preferred to use the heliograph as his shaving mirror. Rank has it privileges. He was scraping foam and bristles, thinking over details of the day ahead, when he saw the reflection of Lascelles behind him. "Got a moment, sir?"

"Sure, what's on your mind?"

"Bit awkward, really. About Wignall. Well, he was Catholic you see. A few of us are too, and we're just wondering about the service."

"I'll tell the predikant. He'll know how handle the RC part properly."

"Thanks awfully, sir."

Harry smiled faintly to the mirror as the tall man walked away; a tough private soldier who spoke like Little Lord Fauntleroy. The phrase tweaked some memory or other, and for some reason he thought of the Belfast concentration camp.

Then the loud blast of an explosion startled him, and he

nicked his chin. Shell-shock hadn't cured itself yet. The noise grew and swelled into a shuddering thunderclap that pulsed through the warm air, rattled windows in the village, and echoed back from the mountains.

Every soldier was grabbing a weapon, shouting questions to the sentries, "See where they're at?" Harry went to the edge of the trees to look around, but nothing untoward showed, and hills shut off his view further west. He sent McKay at the double to ask what the OP had spotted.

Some young villagers stood pointing at the soldiers who milled about, waving guns. "Better look out, rooineks," one boy laughed. "The Krokodilles are coming to get you!"

There were no more explosions, just the rolling faint murmurs still rebounding far away. "All clear, men!" Harry called. "Not artillery. Just quarrying, I expect. Stand down!"

"You heard what Harry said," Ned bellowed. "Now hurry up to get fell in."

"Wonder what that din was about." Scayles managed to convey amused superiority at Harry's undershirt and half-lathered face. The MP was immaculate already, wearing brown kid gloves as an added touch of formality for church parade.

"Some sort of civvy blasting in the foothills, most like," Harry made a last swipe with the razor. "I bet the locals know exactly what it is."

Before putting his boots on, he tapped the toes hard to dislodge any crawlies. This time, he was rewarded by a purple Emperor scorpion falling out; four inches long, its poisonous stinger able to fell any grown man in agony. He stomped it to death, brittle as a lobster, then finished dressing. McKay arrived back from the OP and confirmed there was no sign of enemy activity.

Scayles said, "The villagers aren't very forthcoming about Kruger's loot. Since you mentioned a reward, they seem more interested in how many sovereigns we brought on my mule than offering info. Too scared of reprisals against informers, I suspect." The MP hefted two leather satchels. "Carrying our funds around makes me feel like a beast of burden, myself. Maybe I'll just lock it inside with Muller."

"Want us to take it along?"

"What if you got ambushed? I'd have the hell of a job explaining the loss of a thousand pounds to the Provost Marshal."

"Be kind of difficult for me to explain the loss of eighteen men, too." Lanyard knew sarcasm was lost on this army cop. "Jiggy had no better luck collecting gen. However hard he tried to, uh, push for it last night."

"Eh? Well, Mendip's begged off his OP job to attend the funeral. I've put Parkin and Fletcher up there instead."

"Signal sked's not due 'til eleven today, anyway. He never saw more of that column, so we've no guess whether they got hit."

"Rumours about commandos headed this way have the locals all in a tizzy," Scayles said. "Especially as near every able-bodied man in the village cleared off to work last night. They won't be back before next weekend. Turns out they all have good jobs building the new railway."

"So that's how they're well-heeled." Harry buckled on his cartridge-belt. "How's your prisoner doing?"

"Bloody man's a problem. Private van Praage'll keep an eye on him while I'm completing inquiries, but we can't keep him chained in that shed forever."

"The Burgemeester'll have to be responsible then, 'til we take him back. Muller's so far gone mentally, he'll never stand trial anyway."

"Gets under my skin, that, a murderer going scot-free. Besides him probably hiding something useful inside that mad brain. Private van Praage says Muller used to own a cartage service that hauled freight from Machadodorp."

"I heard. But Piet can't get anything else out of him about it."

Coveyduck had the men ready, fallen in by column of

four, and Harry took his place at the front with Scayles. They marched away from camp, rifles reversed in the crook of elbows, military funeral style.

When they reached the church, there was a small crowd of Boers waiting, out of religious respect for a man who was being buried in their community. Kleinhaus was there with all the elders, and the blacksmith wore a suit. Baroness von Gliewitz was soberly dressed in black, standing apart among the women. She held herself modestly to the rear, but drew glances from every man on parade. Scayles could not take his stare off her.

Six troopers carried Wignall out of the church, rolled in a blanket for his coffin. A small Union Jack lay on his chest, borrowed from Mendip's signals kit. Several Boer women began to weep, and a few troopers wiped suspiciously damp eyes. His comrades lowered him gently into the earth. Following which, the predikant led his congregation in singing Psalm 130.

> "Uit diep-tes, gans verlore,
> Van red-ding ver van-daan . . ."

Most of the soldiers could not understand the words, a cry for mercy in Heaven, but appreciated their intent. Predikant Carolus said a very long, very sincere, Dutch Reformed Church service in Afrikaans. Despite his opinion that the Catholic church was *Roomse Gevaar,* "the Roman peril", he included proper acknowledgment of Wignall's faith. DeKrieger and the baroness crossed themselves, murmuring devoutly, while O'Malley, Lascelles, and two other troopers followed suit.

"Firing party, shun!" Harry commanded. "Aim!" Three Enfields pointed into the blue, over the open grave. He and Scayles snapped up open-palm salutes, fingertips one inch above the right eyebrow. "Single volley, fire!" The rifles cracked, and wisps of cordite smoke trailed a smell like burning wool.

Right after the ceremony, every member of the kirksraad insisted on gravely shaking Harry's hand. The church councillors were for the most part older men, but their grips were bone-hard, and he noticed some villagers expressing condolences to soldiers about their comrade. Amidst it all, some troopers were actually standing in line to speak with the blonde baroness.

O'Malley reached her first, shy for once, but she put him at ease and they shared a quiet Irish laugh. Then it was Lascelles' turn, chatting easily, hands on hips, very much the fellow aristocrat. He did not get far with her, as she was already smiling at deKrieger, fluttering her lashes at him to join her. Scayles hovered, but she did not so much as glance his way, busy smiling up at the striking-looking Afrikaner. When Harry went over, he heard their guttural conversation without understanding it.

"Good morning, Lieutenant" she said, while her gaze followed deKrieger's back after the man bowed and walked away. She gave her condolences about Wignall, but the excitement in her face said clearly how much she was stimulated by deKrieger. Harry followed her gaze. "You two get along well, in any language."

"Indeed, he speaks better German than I do. A graduate of Heidelburg that he is. And Cambridge, too." She smiled fondly. "A lovely educated fellow, but when he speaks English, well, oh dear me!"

Harry recalled that Lascelles was an Oxford man. Funny the pair did not pal up together like any Oxbridgers in the ranks usually did. He said it was good of her to come, and then would have moved on to thank Predikant Carolus. She touched his arm, and smiled teasingly. "Wagging tongues say you and I share a mutual friend. I recall Bethany told me she'd had a soldier sweetheart, but I'd no idea it was you."

"That's sort of changed, long since."

Baroness von Gliewitz dimpled, "Oh, never say die,

when a lady-love's involved." He tapped his hat-brim and hurried away to saddle up.

Getting the ceremony over seemed to end the depression that had gripped the troop. They made their usual jokes while breaking camp in a hurry, ready to ride within half an hour. Everybody roared with mirth when a mule farted and Schammerhorn said, "We hear you, Mister Lanyard."

Usually, Harry would have joined the laughter himself, but today he knew it was a signal he'd lost some of the men's respect. They blamed him for Wignall's death and resented he did not summarily execute Muller for it. Leadership command was always hard to maintain with Colonials, but the Spitsdorp shooting made his mission even more difficult now.

"Gather round," he ordered. They shuffled grudgingly in a circle, some of them lounging with lighted fags in their mouths until Ned bawled to put them out. "We've had a tip that what we're looking for may not be on Blenkarn's farm, after all. So today we have to quarter the ground along both sides of the road."

Harry drew in the dust with a stick. "We're here. The Vincennes property runs like this, from the river to the Knuckles over here. Bullion can't have been carried far from any road, and there's only two of them." He scratched a Y, "West through the mountains to Lydenburg, and east towards Pretorius Kap. Our latest hint says it was headed west, so that's the direction where we'll start."

"Split into parties of three, and search country bordering the Lydenburg trail. Look for old lorry tracks, disturbed soil, rock piles, caves. Any sign of hiding what we're looking for. I'll be riding straight for the north end. Sergeant Coveyduck is in charge south of the road. Any questions?"

There were none, another sign he had lost their enthusiasm for the patrol. "Fine. Fire three shots if you spot anything promising. Jiggy, you're with me. The rest of you, move out." As they headed for the ponies, he called a last reminder, "Boers are around, but avoid trouble if you can, and tend to business."

"Hear what our pansy officer says, fellers?" Bramah sneered. "You see any Boojers, try not to mess your drawers."

"Sergeant Coveyduck!" Harry shouted. "Put that man on a charge!"

"About bloody time," Scayles said.

Villagers watched silently while they rode away, but the troopers all got a wave as they passed the von Gliewitz house. The baroness even blew a kiss to deKrieger, which drew whistles and cat-calls. "You've clicked, no mistake, Sith-o!"

"Lucky dog, and you a married man!"

They were not far along the trail before Harry veered off with Jiggy to take a short-cut towards the Devil's Knuckles. It was rough going, shale making hooves slip, and the two soldiers continually weaved left and right around rocky outcrops. Harry's first objective was to reach the quarry he'd heard about, and make some enquiries. Though he could not see far ahead, another explosion told him they were nearing the place.

He squinted at the sun. "Close to eleven. Best find a signal look-out."

"That'd do, sir." Mendip pointed at a rocky hummock topped by thorn-bushes.

They scrambled up and found it gave a good overview towards where the Intelligence Corpsmen would be watching for their SitRep. While Jiggy assembled the helio, Harry used his binoculars in every direction. He caught sight of some of his troopers moving slowly about half a mile away, heads down while they searched.

"Ready, sir." Jiggy sent the daily situation report on their progress and location. Response came flashing back immediately, without any pause for decrypting Harry's message. PEACE NEGOTIATIONS STALLED BY RUMOURS OF NEW BOER FUNDING. STOP. IMPERATIVE TO COMPLETE YOUR MISSION SUCCESSFULLY SOONEST. STOP. STAND BY FOR MESSAGE.

"Are we in trouble, sir?" Jiggy sounded so like a worried schoolboy, Harry laughed ironically. "Well, we're certainly under the gun." He pulled off his hat, letting the sun dry his sweaty hair.

Another helio flickered, from the Provost Police this time. It was sent in clear, addressed to Scayles, and Harry felt impatient as Jiggy transcribed the message. "By gum! 'Might have known there was summat dodgy about yon soft lah-de-dah!'"

"Never mind that, look!" HQ had started flickering again.

"Long one." Jiggy calmly watched the signal coming in, jotted down blocks of letters, lips moving as he mentally began to decode while he wrote. He flashed an acknowledgment, then completed scribbling a translation of the message.

ENEMY VERY ACTIVE EASTERLY YOUR POSITION. STOP. COL AUKLAND'S COLUMN AMBUSHED THIRTY MILES NORTH OF RLWY LINE YESTERDAY. STOP. STRONG COMMANDO PRESENCE INDICATED IN YOUR SECTOR. STOP. SPEED UP SEARCH EFFORTS. STOP. MORE POSITIVE SITREP EXPECTED FROM YOUR END TOMORROW. STOP. GOOD HUNTING. SMITH.

"And tally-ho to you too, old boy," Harry said. Faulkner had told him the patrol's success was imperative, and now he "expected" positive results quickly. Lanyard wished he could feel as optimistic.

Jiggy kept a watchful eyes-front though binoculars, but Harry figured he was more on the lookout for comical insults from that Boer signaler. Lanyard scanned the police message and groaned. So much for Scayles and his positive vetting. Another petty admin detail to sort out.

He rubbed his sun-strained eyes, peering through the glaring haze. From skyline to veld, the African day seemed at peace. Distant cattle grazed, and only a sheepdog barking at its flock somewhere in the valley broke the silence. He lifted his hand to acknowledge one of his distant troopers who waved before turning off the trail again. There was time for another cig. He scraped a match, cupping it in both hands, bending his head to catch the flame.

Bee-yowww! Ockata-ockata-ockata! A bullet ricocheted off the rock inches from Harry's face, and went tumbling away into the distance.

The two soldiers threw themselves arse over tea-kettle into cover. Jiggy's boot caught the tripod, its mirror smashing to bits against a rock. They wriggled lower, easing safety-catches off, not raising their heads for a look yet. Each lay with mouth half-open to help catch any sound of the sniper.

The men stayed so quiet that a family of meerkats ventured out again. One of the little ferret-like creatures sat upright, front paws dangling, bright eyes looking curiously at Jiggy. It flicked back underground when Harry moved after a minute or so. He put his hat on his rifle end and let the crown peep temptingly over the rock. No bullet greeted it. Either the shooter had gone, or he was crafty enough to hold fire until his targets showed more of themselves.

Harry fired three rapid shots into the sky. They were answered by others, and Harry knew his troopers were closing in. He took a quick peep and was surprised to see a bare-headed man in khaki running beside a horse among some rocks. Harry snapped his rifle up, froze on the trigger uncertainly, then the man went out of view.

When his sergeant arrived with six men, Harry was scouring the surrounding rock-faces through binoculars. Moments later, Baxter hurried in, followed by deKrieger and

Lascelles. Harry warned, "Sniper near, don't bunch up!"

He quickly told Coveyduck about the shooting, and chopped his hand towards the rock tangle where the runner had gone. "Somewhere in there. Wearing our uniform, so I muffed my chance."

"Is good you did, man," Baxter spoke up. "That was me." He explained he was close by when he heard the single shot, and had gone stalking immediately, but found nobody.

"You damn fool, not wearing your hat!" Harry shouted. "A situation like this's why I handed out the doggone feathers in the first place. I could have blown your stupid head off!" Baxter took the bollocking without a word, and deKrieger ribbed him in Afrikaans.

The last of his men rode in. "Close shave, Harry." It was the nearest Bramah could come to showing regret for his recent lippyness. "Maybe you'll let us shoot this one."

"We have to find him before that, Terry."

They made as thorough a search as they could, but turned up no hidden rifleman. The only trace was a spent .303 cartridge-case Harry found lying among the bushes. He bounced it in his palm to show Ned.

"Yeah, the Boojers're all using our stuff now." Coveyduck frowned at the surroundings, "Shagged if I know how he got so close to you without any of us seeing him, though. There's not room for a flea to hide up here, yet he's hopped it out of sight."

The two veterans exchanged glances, coming to the same possibility. Harry nodded slowly, "One of our people?"

Without a word, Sgt. Coveyduck grabbed Baxter's rifle and sniffed the muzzle. He grunted and returned the weapon. "Not been fired today. Lucky for you." Baxter just stared, slack-jawed at having been suspected. Harry thought a fouled gun would prove nothing in any case, as several men had loosed off signal shots. Probably a Boer sniper after all.

"Looks like he's clean away." The Australian scratched his head, peering at the bald rocks. "But where did the slippery bastard get to?"

There was nothing to be gained by continuing the hunt, so Harry called it off. He did not have to tell his men to watch themselves when he sent everybody back to what they were doing before. Everyone carried on, but felt a tingle between the shoulder-blades.

"I'm right sorry about our helio, sir." Jiggy apologized every few minutes while they rode on towards the nearest Knuckle. Harry told him to forget it, accidents happen under fire. Besides, he was sick of sending nil reports.

The trail entered a quarry carved into the Knuckle's base, where heat was trapped like a cauldron. A noisy donkey-engine hiccoughed naphtha fumes through its exhaust pipe. Men scraped and shoveled rocks into the stone-crushing machine. Horses whinnied and drivers shouted curses, cruel whips lashing the beasts to strain harder at pulling loads of rock chips. The place had been worked for some time, judging by the litter of garbage, derelict carts, and broken machinery.

"Hey, you guys lost?" A bulky man wearing a corduroy Norfolk jacket despite the warmth stood in the doorway of a corrugated iron shack. His high laced boots were planted wide, and he seemed distracted by the work at hand.

"Not really. You hear tell of Boer wagons coming up here a good while back?"

"Only that junk-pile there, already dumped before I came. Hey, you from the States?"

"Nope, Canada."

"That's close enough. Say, this calls for a celebration! Come on in out of the sun."

In fact, it felt twice as hot inside the tin hut. Spots of rusty condensation dripped like blood on papers, dirty glasses, and surveying instruments that littered the desk.

"I'll just water the horses, shall I, sir?" Jiggy went back outside for fresh air.

"I'm Arne Akesson, head rock-breaker around these parts. From Stockholm by way of Minneapolis." His

Scandinavian tones were overlaid with an exaggerated American accent. The Swede rummaged in a sawdust-chest for a frosted bottle. "Join me for a shot of aquavit, Lootenant, fresh out of the ice-box?"

Harry said that would be fine, and noticed how the bottle rattled against glass as the drinks were poured. Akesson caught the look, and shrugged. "I know. Maybe getting too fond of this stuff. But what else's a guy got to do, stuck here on my lonesome, back of beyond?" He toasted, "*Skoal!*"

The chilled liquor went down smooth, welcome after a dry morning's ride. "So, what brings a couple of army doughboys to this hole in the wall?."

It took only a few moments to explain their mission. Harry had repeated it so often, he felt like a phonograph record. "Sure you never heard about any gold?"

"One for the road? No? Well, just as well, I guess." Akesson put the bottle away reluctantly. "Hell, I heard nothing else when I first came here, two years ago. These dumb Dutch quarriers used to blast open every cranny in sight, every spare minute. Figured to get rich quick, the lunk-heads."

"Any do that lately?"

"Nah. Bozos gave up long ago. But only after I went over every inch of the place myself, including the thorn thicket. I told that nosy Polack reporter the same thing the other day."

"Reporter?"

"Yah, sashayed in here with a quart of vodka, claiming to be a foreign correspondent for some Warsaw rag." The Swede chewed his lip like a jube-jube. "Guy kind of rubbed me the wrong way."

"If it's who I think, he does that to people. And he's no Pole."

"You come across him? Said he was researching a hidden-treasure story, but kept asking if I could suggest places to search. I told him to stop wasting my time. Guess that's why he took the rest of his bottle with him."

"Mind if we just look around, anyway?"

"Nope, just don't expect to find anything. I better show you, for safety's sake." Akesson frowned at the clock. "Let's make it snappy, though." Harry was amused at the implication he was to blame for the socializing.

Akesson led the way through the clangorous work area, past shouting workmen and grating shovels. "Hey, soldier!" he yelled. "Get that Goddam cigarette the hell away from there!".

Mendip sat smoking on a big rusted tank, his heels drumming a hollow rhythm in time to "There is a happy land." He was shaded by a wooden shed plastered with red signs warning of explosives inside. Harry made an angry gesture for him to butt it out.

The donkey-engine cut off in mid-stroke, and cogs made screeching noises. A foreman hurried up, scowling at Harry while shouting in Afrikaans to the engineer over the racket. From his hostile attitude, he probably was from Spitsdorp.

"Crusher problem. Have to leave you guys to it," Akesson called. "Drop back some time when we're not so busy." He went off with the foreman.

Jiggy idly kicked scaling off the ring of big bolts on the tank until Lanyard waved for him to come over. He hastily slid off, rust scraping against his britches, and joined Harry among the derelict vehicles dumped every-which-way. There was a big trek-wagon with its hoops still covered with tattered canvas, some ammunition carts bearing the British War Department broad arrow, and even a converted Hackney cab. Harry kept thinking about how Nikki had been here first, but glanced inside each vehicle-wreck anyway.

"Look, sir!" Mendip gasped excitedly, pointing at the high wagon's side. Viewed at an angle, Harry could see stenciled words showing through a faded overcoat of paint. AAN GOD EN DE MAUSER.

He jumped on the spokes to climb up, and saw three

metal canisters, labeled 'Naphtha—highly inflammable'. There was nothing else stored there in the shallow cargo-well. A wasted sovereign after all. But maybe Simius could use it towards his wedding.

"Let's go, Jiggy. Time to round up for camp."

CHAPTER SEVENTEEN

Petta told her that the kakies had left Spitsdorp yesterday, and were searching to the north. He also brought word a commando had destroyed a British column, not thirty miles away. So there was no need to contact the Boer authorities with what she knew. Praise be, Bethany thought, President Burger must have sent men up here for the gold. If nothing else, the Boer force would neutralize Harry Lanyard's patrol. She left word for Swazi to be saddled, ready for her to ride out at noon. She could meet up with the commando and volunteer as a local guide.

Beth's first satisfaction at news of the commando's coming quickly faded, and she felt an aching sadness over Harry's possible death. The war may have warped him into an indiscriminate killer, but she always recalled the man he had once been, a tender lover.

She shook off the image. "Grow up, girl," as Marthe would put it. "There's work to be done." She pulled her kappie tight, low against the morning sun, and followed Petta to the cattle kraal. Her father stood watching, part of trying to be everywhere on Vincennes these days. Since he no longer had a white foreman, he thought it necessary to supervise his workers himself. They pretended he made a difference, while carrying out their chores with the skill of long habit.

A whip cracked in the yard, and the field-hand shouted, "Move Englishman!" He whipped the lumbering ox into line beside its twin, "Hoy-hoy, Milner!" The lash thwacked their hides, making a sport of whipping animals dubbed with hated names. Each day on the farm started with bringing out oxen to yoke them up to the ploughs. There was no real need for the lash, as the lumbering ochre beasts ambled forward at sound of their own names. A dozen others followed, the keelvel wattle below their throats swaying as they moved out of the kraal.

Ploughs awaited them, blades newly honed, leaning with the furrow wheel larger than the other. Milner backed into his place, where chains and yokes lay ready on the grass. Englishman lingered, and had to be whipped in, until he stood tail to the plough, ready to be yoked as a pair.

Petta's field-hands worked swiftly with each team, lifting the wooden yoke across the necks of the lead oxen so it lay easily in front of their humps. Leather riems were tied to the horns of each, until four pairs of oxen were inspanned ready for work. So much muscle power was needed to pull each plow because the earth was brick-hard from summer heat.

Petta flailed his long whip, *"Kom-kom-kom!"* Slack trek-chains tightened, the massive heads were lowered, horns clicking, and the ploughs moved off, scraping behind the giant oxen.

"We'll get the furrows done, but there's no sign of seed delivered yet." Hiram's face looked more worn with worry each day.

"Oh, the bank must come through for us in the end."

"Not any more. That's why I had to let Nikki talk me into signing, a loan to tide me over."

"Troei-troei!" A ploughman shouted, and the blade scraped deep along the hard earth.

"What about our friends? All those you helped in the past? Perhaps some of them could rally round in turn."

"Half are dead, the rest gone away. And our new neighbors would be a *snoep* lot about lending any money."

"You must ask, though!" Beth's voice was unusually sharp. He looked at her sadly, feeling the reversal of roles; an aging father, a daughter made shrewish with anxiety.

Beth would have said more, but she saw a horse moving slowly over the rise. At first, she thought it was riderless, then saw someone was lying flat along the horse's back.

"What's that?"

Hiram peered, his distance sight not being what it was. She shaded her eyes from the glare. "Does he think we can't see him trespassing?"

"*Trek-trek!*" The oxen moved forward in a row, thin dust rising, whips cracking. The lone horse came ahead slowly, heading straight towards the plowing. A pale face lifted for a moment, but flopped back against the mane.

"Some consarned fool needing to be sent packing off my land," Hiram growled.

"No." Beth's voice was faint. "It looks like. *It is!*" She ran, skirts held high, ankles twisting painfully in the ruts, screaming. "Irkie! Irkie!"

The field hands had no permission to stop working, but halted anyway, staring at the Baas go limping across the field. Beth called his son's name with such distress that he was afraid of what she had found.

Runnels of dried blood streamed the horse's flanks. It stood there, head low, spraddle-legged, knees locked. A thick cake of gore was pasted between the boy's belly and the horse's bare back. He clung doubled over, as if frozen, one dirty hand coiled in the mane. His face was scrunched with pain, only his flickering eyelids told there was any breath of life still in him.

Christmas appeared from nowhere, the first one to help Beth lift the kleinbaas down. "Easy, oh, take care!"

Other fieldhands came, carrying him in a gentle litter of linked arms to the farm. Petta stopped chopping firewood, thumped his hatchet in the block, and hurried to lead Swazi out of the way. The men could not avoid jerking while they backed to the steps, and Dirk gave a ragged scream.

"Down a minute!" Beth ordered.

Servants crowded around, soft voices wailing at the boy's condition. Dogs barked excitedly to him, wagging tails in recognition, backing off from the smell of wounds. The bearers lowered Dirk to the ground, and his sister knelt.

She was peeling away the soggy flap of his shirt when

Hiram caught up. Two dark-edged cuts seeped through the crusted blood. Marthe ran down the steps, pushing field-hands aside. "Irkie, what have the devils done to you!"

Simius took a look, holding the spent horse shivering beside him. Distracted, Hiram waved it away. "Ah, that beast's so knackered, it'll need be put down."

"No! She remembered her way here, and carried Dirk home." Beth fondled it's mangled ear, then had Simius lead the mare into the stable. She knelt to press her ear to her brother's heartbeat.

Gunshots cracked, four-five-six times. Horsemen came galloping into the yard, whooping and hollering, pistols shooting in the air, yelling like madmen. The servants scattered, running for the fields, crying in fear at this sudden onslaught of new violence. The Blenkarns gaped, slack-faced with shock, looking dazedly from Dirk's contorted face to these crazed invaders.

"Don't bother to get up, Beth, my dear." Feliks Nikolai sneered. He seemed to be holding a long wink at her, one eye swollen closed.

His wild-looking companions hooted, and a black-bearded one sniggered in Taal, "Right, that young heifer'll suit me just fine on her knees!"

The others chorused, *"Lekkerrrr!"*

Nikki had six thugs with him, off-scourings hastily recruited in the shebeens and knocking-shops around Leydenburg. They were scruffy-looking renegades, of mixed nationalities, wearing mining overalls, or frock coats, or bits of uniform. One raised his dented bowler hat to Beth. "A proper prick-teaser like Nikki said you was, girlie, and that's a blooming fact."

"Watch your dirty mouth!" Blenkarn shouted, but they just laughed at him.

The two women refused to be distracted by these louts, and turned back to tending Dirk. He breathed shallowly, his bluish tongue dry as pumice.

"We must get him out of the sun." Marthe said. She and Beth tried to lift the youngster, struggling with his dead weight.

"Somebody give us a hand!" Marthe did not care who was waving guns, this was more important.

"Did we come at an inconvenient time?" Nikolai sneered, touching his own face. "People seem inclined to get hurt around you, Beth." His entire cheek bulged tightly, scarlet with infection. He rapped an order, "Put those horses out of sight for now." A couple of men led them behind the outbuildings.

"Fetch Simius to help!" Beth gasped, raising Dirk's shoulders. Hetti ran around the leering men, peeping back fearfully as she dashed across the yard.

Nikki saw the opportunity he was looking for. He nodded after the young girl and wiggled his eyebrows at Maddocks. "You've got time, if inclined for some fun."

Catching his drift, Maddocks and three others strolled after her, grinning slyly. At the stable door, Zoller crowed like a rooster before they swaggered inside. Simius came out of a stall, his arms wide, shielding Hetti. A bandit just cracked him across the skull with a rifle-stock, and they pulled the screaming maid out of sight.

Spitting her indignation, Marthe grabbed a broom and charged in after them. "Stop this filthy nonsense now!" She'd soon sweep out the whole disgusting pack of them. There was the sound of a hard slap, lewd laughter. Maddocks voice carried evilly, "Come for a looking-after too, old girl? Well, here's my *slang* to put a smile on your face."

She wailed desperately, then was muffled. Hiram started to lunge to her aid. "Don't!" Nikolai aimed the Nagant warningly, straight at Blenkarn's head. "Boys will be boys." He told the remaining couple of his gang to go catch a few chickens to eat on the trail. Then Nikki had the yard to himself.

He grabbed Swazi's reins and urged in a low voice to Beth, "Get on, now!" Stiff-armed, he pointed the shiny pistol at Hiram to keep his distance. The rancher was white with shame at being prevented from helping the women.

It was more than Christmas could bear, and he came at a run from the servant quarters, both hands gripping his assegai to protect the Baas one more time. Nikki moved the Nagant slightly, firing into the old lion-hunter's chest. He fell forward, still gripping his spear as it stabbed the earth.

"Stupid mujik." Nikolai watched Hiram collapse weakly to sit beside his dead friend.

Bandits hefting guns crowded the stable doorway, a couple with their pants half down. The Russian snapped, "Everything's under control!"

"Taking turns with this tasty dark meat," Zoller's voice grunted. "Won't be long."

"Finish what you're doing. No hurry." Nikolai glanced at his watch. Maddocks strutted over, red flannel drawers yawning. His quick glance took in Swazi's reins being held by the Russian. He shifted the grip on his rifle, casually pointed in Nikki's direction.

"What d'you say we rest this heavy boodle over here, squire?" Before Nikki could react, Maddocks pulled the money-bags off and draped them on the hitch-rail. "Handier there for divvying up, you might say." He nodded easily, but did not turn his back until he was safely indoors. "Here I am again, darlin'. Think I'd leave you half-way?" The others yelped for him to finish with Marthe so they could have some.

Hiram groaned, rocking back and forth, cursing the hopelessness of making a grab for the guns leaning behind the stoep rail. "Right, be sensible," Nikki said. He turned his pistol back on Beth. "For the last time, get mounted. Now!"

She was frantic with worry about Dirk and the women. "Have some pity! Please at least let us take care of my brother!" Bethany despised hearing her own half-sobs, mind still reeling from shock. Hiram rejoined her. He could not think about Christmas for now.

She dabbed ineffectually at Dirk's wounds. "What madness is all this, Nikki? There's no gold here."

"Ah, but there is." He nodded at the saddle-bags. "A small start, anyway. And I think I know where the rest is now." He noticed the hatchet, jerked it free, and slid it in his belt. "Now move, you stupid little cow! I need you along for insurance, in case Lanyard's patrol catches up."

"They just did. You're under arrest, Nikolai!"

Scayles spoke matter-of-factly. He rode alone into the farmyard at a walk, confident, not even with his gun drawn. He saw just the Russian there, with the Blenkarns bent over someone on the ground and a negro's body nearby. His shoulder throbbed like the devil, but it no longer mattered, now he'd made this unexpectedly easy pinch.

Scayles was puzzled at the man's bravado when Nikki just laughed. Then the Russian called, "What d'you make of this, gentlemen?" He glanced mockingly around the yard, and his bandits stepped out, pointing weapons.

"No, don't fire, he's mine!" Nikki shouted.

Impassive but furious, Lt. Scayles let himself be pummeled in the saddle. He was hardly aware of the blows, or the spittle and curses. Everything was dulled by the sure knowledge he was facing a nasty death very soon.

He looked into the farm girl's drawn face. Foolishly, he said, "Sorry. Made a muck of it, I'm afraid."

"Oh, pip-pip, old fruit!" Maddocks jeered. "You've fair bolloxed up the boys' soiree with their black and white hair pie, too. Lucky I've finished, or I'd be right annoyed at you, myself." He bashed the copper's face once or twice, just for luck.

Bethany heard distant hoof-beats, and felt a lift of hope. Then she realized they were fading away rapidly along the main trail.

Piet van Praage barely glanced left as he passed the end

of the track to Vincennes. He wondered what Lt. Scayles thought he was up to, going in there alone. Still, he'd given clear enough orders. Go and bring Harry and as many of the patrol they could round up. Piet lashed his pony hard, but knowing there was no chance of anyone getting back in time.

That rooinek officer had more guts than sense, tackling them single-handed. Wounded, as he was. He seemed less brave than almost crazed, though. Obsessed with recovering the informant money they took from him, even though nobody could blame him for losing it.

The gang had ridden into Spitsdorp right after breakfast-time. Seven of them, bold as brass. They waved weapons around, but not nervously, already knowing every burgher's weapon was safely chained out of reach in the church basement. From the purposeful way they acted, they obviously knew where Scayles had locked the money-bags, too.

The MP had been sitting drinking tea with Neave von Gliewitz on her veranda when the bandits rode by. Feliks Nikolai was at their head, with one fist on his hip like some Muscovite conqueror of the steppes. None of them noticed Scayles, but he saw from their guns out what they were up to. He let them get past, put his hat on with an air of calm, and suggested the baroness take cover with her maid in the cellar.

"That I will not. Unless you stay with us."

"'Can't be done. You understand."

"I only understand you're about to commit suicide. Duty's all very well, but you're alone, and there's over half a dozen of them! It's only commonsense to just bide your time here."

However, he was like men she'd known in Ireland, readier to die for a cause than live to fight another day. She watched his broad back striding off, an English policeman she did not particularly like, but due a bit of honour for this moment, just the same. Last she saw of him, Scayles had his pistol out, held against his leg.

Burghers in the street thought the bandits looked like a pack of *mamparas,* idiots who couldn't have tried a daylight raid on their own. But that mad Russian was in charge, and controlled them as if leading trained Cossacks. He called Kleinhaus from his store, and demanded the key to the lock-up shed. The Burgemeester denied having it, maybe playing for time until the predikant released the weapons so villagers could fight back.

Carolus did that exactly, within minutes of seeing the bandits arrive. He unlocked the long chain, rattling it free through the trigger-guards of weapons those fool kakies had torn from the hands of honest Boers. Solemn word or not that the guns would stay secured, armed robbers in his village street could be judged an emergency in any language.

The Burgemeester's delay was a mistake. The Russian just snarled impatiently and pistol-whipped Kleinhaus unconscious. He trotted ahead of his gang to the shed where old Muller was being held. Nikolai fired three times, trying to shoot the lock off. The blacksmith came running from next door, waving a hammer. He was an ungodly man, who even worked on the Sabbath, but very courageous. They shot him dead, and went back to splintering the door open.

Scayles was spotted before he reached them, and Zoller put a slug through his shoulder that knocked him flat. He looked dead, and was smart enough to lie still. The firing brought van Praage, but there was no good him opening up on them with his rifle, as civilians began running all over. Crossfire would have caused a massacre of bystanders. He ducked into the trees unseen, close by as he dared. He heard Muller's quavering voice raised inside, clear as could be. He maundered something about the gold rightfully needing to be returned to Oom Paul's wagon.

There was a single shot and the Russian came out lugging those heavy saddlebags Scayles kept the expense money in. He shook them in the air, laughing. "The old bastard was praying over it, all piled in little stacks!"

The bandits mounted up, ya-hooing over pulling off the easy holdup. As they left, they loosed a few final shots to send villagers ducking back with their empty rifles into the church. It had taken Nikolai's scratched-together gang less than ten minutes to kill a nonbeliever and a lunatic, maim two other men, and steal the best part of a thousand sovereigns.

Scayles had not even wanted van Praage to waste time patching his shoulder. He acted half-demented, mad keen to start chasing the bandits. He could not raise any interest among the villagers to help him go after them. The Boers shrugged, the stolen money belonged to the British. It simply proved how foolish that young officer had been, to disarm them and leave Spitsdorp helpless. Meanwhile, there was proper mourning to be observed, two neigbours to be buried because of army misjudgement. Few villagers had paid attention when the two soldiers rode away in pursuit.

Van Praage would be bringing Lanyard's patrol to the farm before long, but Scayles had no illusions it could ever help him now. Nikolai was seething with spite. His earlier plan to get away alone with the money was ruined. Instead, perhaps some delicious revenge on the MP could pay off double, as a distraction as well to help him abscond.

He jeered at Scayles, "So, remember threatening me about what happens to horse-thieves? Well, now you've committed a hanging offence yourself—getting captured!" He shouted, "String this British bobby up!"

The bandits cackled. They liked this Russian's style, slippery as he was. Zoller found a coil of rope and threw it over the hoist-bar. When the gangsters edged forward for a good look, Nikolai side-stepped his horse, positioned to make a run for it during the distraction. He'd have to leave the girl.

They put a noose round Lieutenant Scayles' neck, and

fastened the rope taut, so he was stretched high in the saddle. The hemp bit in below his jaw. "The army'll get you for this," was all he could gasp.

"Very original, Englishman." Nikki wound reins in his hand, ready to gallop. "Chin-chin, cheerio, and all that!"

He slapped the rump of Scayles' big horse, "Hey-up!" It jumped forward, trotting away, and Scayles was yanked out of the saddle. Dangling, he started to spin like a kitten in a sack. He made terrible gagging noises, clenching the thrumming rope with one hand, trying to pull against his own weight.

Harry Lanyard fired twice at the group, killing one, wounding another. He raged at himself, figuring he had wasted too much time talking with Piet when they met on the road and sent him back for the others. Now, he'd arrived just seconds too late for Scayles. He caught a blurred glimpse of Nikolai lashing his horse away out of sight around the outbuildings. The others scattered for cover.

Bethany jumped onto the stoep, grabbed her .410 shotgun, and flipped the Winchester to Hiram. She fired both barrels towards the bandits, a wide blast of pellets. Hiram levered a round and fired in one smooth motion. He drilled the nearest bandit through the heart.

Three bastards down, Harry thought. He rode straight across the yard, ignoring the buzz of bullets past his head. He hauled his pony underneath Scayles' agonized jack-knifing body, spraddling the man on the animal's back to loosen the strain. Trouble was, the pony was much shorter than the tall stallion they hanged him from. There was not nearly enough height to ease off the rope. Harry had no knife, so he could only push Scayles' boot through a stirrup to stretch up and save himself as best he could.

Harry called something encouraging, but had to leave him there for now. He loosed off a couple more rounds towards the stable where shots were coming from.

He shouted, "Get inside, honey!" Beth ducked out of

view.

Hiram stood flat-footed, levering and firing fast, emptying the Winchester. Maddocks was flopping about, howling from where Beth's shotgun had torn him. He pleaded, "Help me, squire!"

"Glad to oblige", Hiram gritted, and blew that stupid derby hat clear across the yard. Beth ran back outside with more cartridges just as it happened. She fed her gun, and fired both rounds at the two bandits still standing. Peppered, they rode away, racing for the veld.

Harry jinked and dodged towards the stable doorway. He dropped the rifle, pulled his Colt, and went inside at a roll. The two women lay staring at him mutely, arranging ripped skirts, eyes empty. Hetti whimpered, cradling Simius. Marthe pointed upwards and was about to speak. He motioned for them to stay silent. "Okay, you in the loft, give up!" he called, "You're the only one left."

At sound of his voice, a horse whickered feebly from one of the stalls. Lanyard moved as quietly as he could across the crackling straw. Something was pitched noisily into a far corner to distract him, and he whirled that way, gun raised.

"Harry, behind you!" Beth screamed from the doorway, and threw her empty .410 at Zoller as he rose to aim over a bale. Harry shot him twice in the beard, gave her a look, thanks, then ran outside.

Scayles was strangling slowly, the pony having flinched away from the last shots. Harry lifted the man's weight, pressed his gun muzzle against the rope, and shot it through.

Scayles clawed the noose open and sucked air, rubbing at a deep weal in his throat. Wounded shoulder and all, he threw both massive arms around Harry and gasped, "You little shit, I said we'd settle things behind the barn one day!" His eyes were wild. The bear hug tightened, and Harry tensed to free himself with a head butt.

Scayles wheezed with laughter, "Well, we just did! I'd

say we're even, wouldn't you?" He pounded Harry between the shoulders, fit to knock his breath out.

Beth watched the pair of them, dazedly. The laughing policeman saved from a lynching, Harry trying to smile. She recalled his ruthless lack of hesitation moments ago, his instinctive shoot-to-kill in a blink. That did not seem so bad a thing when she looked sadly at the body of Christmas lying there.

She called, "Tannie's safe, Dada!" From bullets, anyway, if not from degradation. She went to hold her aunt. Marthe shrugged off Beth's attempt at comfort and walked outside. Her blanched face was set with as much dignity as she could manage. Blenkarn wee-wawed across the yard, that tarnation limp taking him forever to reach her. She stepped around him, avoiding his eyes. All she could say was, "We must tend to Irkie."

"I'll do that. Look after yourself first." Beth whispered, "In my bathroom." Marthe went upstairs, hurrying for the rubber douche to sluice Maddocks out.

Hiram said, "Guess we're beholden to you, Harry. Put 'er there."

"You did pretty well yourselves."

Bethany watched the stilted male performance incredulously. Her father said, "Ain't you going to shake his hand, too, daughter?"

"I certainly am not!" She threw her arms around Harry's neck, kissing his face repeatedly. "*Geliefdie!* You darling man! The Good Lord must have brought you back this day!" His face lit up, and he gripped her tight, both kissing hungrily. Their eyes were so closed in rapture, they did not see the patrol come in. The troopers arrived from all sides, on foot, silent as ghosts, weapons up. They looked disappointed about missing a part in the retribution.

"Good on you, Harry! I might have known," Ned Coveyduck said. "Us all worried sick, and here you are, snogging a pretty sheila! Good to see you again, Beth." He waved around the bandit-littered barnyard. "You two've been busy otherwise, as well, from the look of it."

He noticed the blood splotch high on Scayles' chest. "You too, Glen. Piet thought you'd be a goner for sure, charging ahead on your lonesome." Off-handedly, the Australian added, "Glad you made it okay. Sir." He hoisted the saddlebags onto the MP's recovered horse. "When word gets back to the army cop-shop, they'll give you a leather medal."

DeKrieger hurried to join the Blenkarns, and his anxious expression changed to a wide smile at seeing they were safe. "Oh, good egg!"

"Their kid's in a pretty bad way," Harry said. "Wounded a couple of days ago I'd say. Stab wounds."

"Blacks?" DeKrieger asked.

Beth snapped, "No, more probably some of your traitor friends!" Her gratitude today still did not extend to joiners. DeKrieger started to say something more, but thought better of it. He and Lascelles gently lifted the boy into the cart Petta brought. She rolled a blanket to pillow her brother's head. "We must get him to Spitsdorp. I know a trained nurse there."

"We're acquainted with Neave, already." Harry passed her Swazi's reins, and she swung into the saddle.

Lanyard wanted to get Dirk to town as quickly as possible. "You better come, too, Hiram. Nikki's gang might be back."

"That Russki side-winder won't stop running before sundown. But it'd be a real pleasure if he did show up." Blenkarn patted his Winchester. "Sorry, Beth, I need to stay and look after things, get the plowing finished. After Marthe and me lay Christmas to rest." He flicked a glance at the sprawled bandits. "Not to mention dispose of some garbage."

"Dirk must be looked after right away, Dada. Will you be all right?"

"Never mind me. You'll get the best done for him if anyone can." The old rancher stroked his son's forehead. Dirk's lids flickered. He made out the blur of uniforms, and gave a faint whimper.

"It's okay, son. You're safe at home, now."

"Home?" The word seemed to ease the boy. He smiled, and dozed into exhausted sleep.

Harry motioned for the men to move off. "Take the point, Ned." Sergeant Coveyduck shouted, "Right boys, column advance!" The lieutenants waited by the gates until the last of their men rode out. Marthe came onto the stoep, changed into a shapeless gray dress. She and Blenkarn stood watching the soldiers carry Dirk away. After a moment, she let Hiram take her hand.

The two officers leaned to share a match. Scayles gave Harry a sardonic glance above the flame. "Good egg?"

CHAPTER EIGHTEEN

Many a Spitsdorper stood glaring his or her displeasure when the kakies arrived back. Some looked down in the mouth at seeing the policeman had survived his wound and recovered those army money-bags. A few hot-heads even wanted to fetch their rifles to show the village's resentment, but got an earful of wives' loud opinions about such foolishness.

Word was sent to Burgemeester Kleinhaus, and he came out, head bandaged like a turban, to add his warning. Now villagers had their *roers* back, they would keep them. But he made clear the weapons should be used only if ever necessary to defend their homes, and that it was wisest to co-operate with the British. A big newcomer who had walked in late that morning stood among the crowd, listening with a scowl.

The vrouws were more interested to note the soldiers halted outside that shameless Papist woman's house. Bold as always, she came sashaying down the path, smiling at the whistling men. "I'm glad to see things have gone well, Mister Lanyard. But what brings you all back to my front door?" She gave a little wave to Scayles, turned up again like a bad penny. But her gaze roved the column, seeking only one face.

"Wie geht's, Deneys?" she called, trying to sound casual, greeting an acquaintance, nothing more.

He flourished his hat and forced a loud laugh. *"Schoen danke, mein gnadige Baronin!"* Nobody seemed to have noticed her slip of the tongue.

Beth waved anxiously from the rear. "Neave, come quickly, do!"

One look at Dirk lying there, and the titled Irishwoman became a ward nurse once more. She barked orders to her maids for hot water and a bed turned down, and bossed the boy's litter-bearers every step into her house.

They left Scayles to get patched up as well, and Harry led the way to the encampment. Soon the two Griquas reappeared, leading back the remount herd they had saved from the bandits. Giggling with relief, the blacks hurried to groom and feed the ponies. With sentries posted and lookouts up the steeple, troopers settled into their favorite routine of making a meal.

"Soon's they eat and have a kit-check, get some rifle pits dug," Harry told Ned. "Looks like we'll be here a couple of nights longer, so let's not be caught flat-footed."

Harry took van Praage along to interpret his enquiries about the Burgemeester's condition. Polite use of the knocker drew no response, though he saw a lace curtain twitch. There was more response when Piet hammered on the door with his fist and shouted, "*Maak op!*" The door opened a crack, and the wife glowered at him.

She explained that Mayor Kleinhaus was resting and could not come down, but she thanked the Englishman politely for his concern. Then she slammed the door in Piet's face, obviously resentful at having to talk through a joiner.

As they walked to the church, Harry said, "It must be hard, being treated like that."

"And harder still ever afterwards, I think." Van Praage nodded sombrely, his stare far away. "The war may be over soon, but many like her will always hate us who rode with the British. Marked as traitors as long as we live, and our kid's kids as well, forever more." Piet paused while some local women passed, trying to overhear while giving him looks that could kill.

He went on, "Funny in a way. When Kruger started this war, making that pre-emptive attack, he expected every Boer in Cape Province and Natal to join him as well. Instead, now there's more of us Afrikaners in British service than with the commandos."

"Well, maybe that'll help you later."

"Don't you believe it. I know my people. In a few years, the truth'll be forgotten. Nobody will remember this was a civil war, too, Boer against Boer. In future, every single Afrikaner family will hand down a story about how their grand-papa was out on commando."

"Let's hope your sharing the same language will draw you back together. By the way, meant to ask, what's a 'soetpiel'?"

"Where'd you hear that one?" Van Praage gave a sly look of amusement. "It means 'salt-prick'. What Afrikaners call somebody who talks as if he stands with one leg in England and the other in South Africa, with his prick between hanging in the ocean. Why d'you ask?"

"Oh, just I heard somebody called that once."

It certainly was not a topic to continue in front of the predikant. Carolus glanced over the shoulder of a burly man he was talking with, watching them come up the path. The stranger turned toward the crunch of boots, and set his jaw at sight of kakies. He quickly shook hands with Carolus, and lumbered past the soldiers, face expressionless. Harry took in the worn clothing, hacked-off flaxen hair, and untanned cheeks where a beard had been. Another one who'd decided to quit the war.

Carolus called after him, "Remember, friend, there's church supper available for any in need." He turned to Lanyard, "Before you start lecturing me, Lieutenant, I had no choice. My conscience is clear."

"I'm sure it is, Padre. No, it's not about you releasing the guns. Guess that's over and done with. I just want to know if there's anything we can do to help. Because of the raid, I mean."

"Well, for a start, you could take your men and leave." Then Carolus made a little erasing gesture. "Pardon, it is not Christian to be rude. But your continued presence is a danger to us."

"Maybe not for long. A surrender, uh, peace treaty could

be signed any day now."

"Surely all the more reason for you to go."

"We were sent here to do something. I've not received any orders to the contrary."

"But how would you know? Your signaling machine is broken." The predikant allowed himself a little unpriestly satisfaction. "Now, I have work among my flock. They are upset over the woes you brought on us. Good afternoon to you."

When they got back for some grub, Lt. Glendon Scayles was polishing his boots, one-handed, his left arm in a white sling. "Damned good medic, the Baroness, besides being stunning. Too bad she's so taken with that ranker."

Harry was amused how Scayles was annoyed at being edged out by a mere private. "Think Sith-o's got to first base with her already?"

"Eh? Oh, baseball. Well, that's certainly not the game he's playing. They clicked in a hurry, I must say."

Jiggy handed the officers a tin plate of stew each. It embarrassed Harry, considering he'd given Scayles a bollocking about making his own meals. The English officer accepted his plate with a lordly nod.

Harry looked at the ground carefully before he sat. He never fancied getting bitten in the behind by one of those foot-long poison centipedes that squirmed around here. "Relax, deKrieger's not such a fast worker, really. I'd bet they knew each other before."

"Really? Interesting. I said there was something fishy about these chaps."

"Yeah, well your positive vetting has revealed one deep, dark secret at least." Harry handed over the crumpled signal form from yesterday.

"Hah!" Scayles slapped the paper. "Suspected to bear a false identity!" He scrambled to his feet. "We must bring him in for a spot of grilling."

"Finish your lunch, first. The army's full of guys who

enlisted under another name."

Scayles would have none of that. He sent Private Rimmer to fetch the defaulter at the double from his sentry post.

"But don't you see?" The MP was too agitated to eat his stew, so Harry reached for it while Scayles fumed. "This one in particular. Well-spoken officer type. It could be our under-cover enemy agent. What better way to hide, than as one of our own rankers?"

"If it is him, he must be awful good at language skill."

"And at hiding behind rocks! It was probably him who took a shot at you!"

Harry wiped his plate clean with bread. "Could be." He asked Coveyduck to bring the nominal roll. They glanced through it before Rimmer arrived back with their man.

"You sent for me, sir?" Lascelles looked mildly curious. Scayles started fiddling with his revolver-butt.

"Provost HQ's sent a report about you," Harry said. "What's your full name, soldier?"

"Why, Lascelles, sir." He blushed and stammered. "Charles Courtney Lascelles."

Scayles pointed with the clip-board, "Let's see your Description Card!" The trooper lifted the corner of his jacket to show the calico Form B 2067 sewn there, listing his particulars. Scayles read it, still un-convinced. "We want your real name! Out with it, man!"

"I see, sir. Awkward. Bound to come out, I suppose." He drew himself up, well over six feet, licking his dark mustache. "Actually, it is my real one. Honor bright. In a way. Well, my mater's family name. Lascelles sounds much better for a trooper. Rather than pater's, I mean."

"It being? Come on, make a clean breast!"

"It's, er, Margery, sir. Been the bane of my life since kindergarten."

Harry shook his head slowly, feeling the grin spread across his face. What was funnier was seeing Scayles's reaction. The MP blinked, his hard copper's expression slowly melting into reluctant amusement. "You mean to tell me that's all your bloody mystery's about?"

"Easy for you to say, sir. Just try having a last name like Margery in a boy's school! Got me ragged unmercifully. Sure to be worse still in the army, called that. I'd be most awfully grateful if the chaps didn't hear."

"Our lips are sealed, Private Lascelles." Harry said. "Dismissed." Coveyduck was still chuckling when he led the trooper off to see he got a strong cup of coffee.

Harry said, "Forget it, Glen. Your spy'll have a genuine Boer moniker."

"God knows you hired plenty of them." He flipped the names list back and forth. "Piet, Jan, Adriaan."

"Not to mention Deneys," Harry joked. "Better known as Sith-o."

"DeKrieger? It says Jan here."

"Well, Neave called him Deneys today."

"There's no middle initial shown." Scayles groaned, "Here we go again. The Constabulary've got the right approach. Every man Jack of them must carry an identity card with his own thumb-print on it."

"What's that in aid of?"

"Fool-proof ID. Scotland Yard's found that no two men in the world have the same fingerprints."

It sounded a pretty far-fetched theory to Harry, but he said nothing. The South African Constabulary was a hard-headed outfit, with over 1200 Canadians in it, so maybe there really was something to the idea.

Scayles massaged his raw neck, then noticed his empty plate. "Bit much, Lanyard, scoffing a fellow-officer's grub!"

As was routine following a patrol, Sergeant Coveyduck ordered a full kit-inspection. They bitched about it loudly. "Come on, Ned, we ain't the friggin' Lord Kitchener's Bodyguard. Why all this sock-counting crap?"

"Never mind your back-talk, Bramah!" Coveyduck

roared. "Off parade's off parade, and we're all mates. But on parade's on parade, when I'm Sergeant to you. Which is now, and I just gave an order, so move your fat fanny!"

Harry approvingly left him to it, knowing if equipment was left neglected, it would soon become unserviceable out here. Saddles and tack were gone over, leather-soap applied, every loose stitch or bent buckle to be repaired. Boots came in for particular scrutiny, and spare clothing was laid out on each man's waterproof cape.

"And for Christ's sake, Mendip, clean that rust off your trousers!" the sergeant bawled. "You look like a red-arsed baboon in heat. Which isn't so far off the truth, come to think of it!"

Arms inspection would be next, and Harry took time to clean his Colt before making his circuit of the guard piquets. It was Scayles' turn to be orderly officer, but he still looked green about the gills from his wound, and could do with some rest. He was told to take a snooze in the shade.

"You got time to take defaulters' parade, Harry?" Coveyduck looked almost harassed. "These charge-sheets are piling up."

"How come?"

"Discip around here's a fair cow. There's Bramah, conduct prejudicial to good order and discipline. Scayles has charged three others, and I put Jiggy on a fizzer myself, just now."

"Okay, let's get it over with."

The sergeant marched the crimed troopers up, barking, "'Eft-'Ight! Halt. Hats off. Attention!" He saluted, "Defaulters on parade, for commanding officer's hearing and punishment, sir!"

The offence was cut and dried with Bramah, and the man even apologized for having spoken out of turn. Harry gave him three days extra duties. Schammerhorn, McKay, and his crony O'Malley were ordered forward together, each on the same charge of 'Dumb insolence'. Scayles' wording was similar on each charge-chit, "Showing contempt for a lawful order, in that he did move deliberately slowly and pull his face."

"What's all this about?"

"Chicken-shit, if you ask me, Lootenant," Schammerhorn drawled. "What kinda charge is 'dumb insolence'? Some crazy British army, if you can get crimed for just giving dirty looks to a stuffed shirt."

"Well, you can, and keep that in mind from now on," Harry said. "Mister Scayles is inclined to be strict, but he's a brave officer. I'm not about to wake him up to testify, though, so I'll dismiss the charges this time. Now you can all go dig some foxholes to smarten you up!"

Coveyduck told them to salute before being dismissed, "And I want to see those shovels fly!" Next, he brought Jiggy forward. Harry snapped, "Goddam it, can't you stay out of trouble for five minutes?"

Ned handed over two yellow cardboard tubes. "I found these in Private Mendip's kit. He is charged with unlawful possession of explosives, and theft of civilian property."

Harry looked at the evidence, two sticks of Swedish dynamite marked 'Nobel Vinterviken', with fuses taped down the side. "You mean you've actually been riding around with these in your pocket?"

"Yessir. Just a couple of souvenirs, like."

"Pinched from the quarry, no doubt. That's bad enough, but you could have blown us all to Kingdom Come!"

"Not if you don't light 'em, sir."

"Or get a bullet through them! That's acting like every kind of fool. Give the sergeant your pay-book to be written up. An official reprimand, seven days extra duties, and docked three week's pay. Now, get out of my sight!"

When the men were beyond earshot, Harry said, "You handle the men well, Ned. It's something you could make a career of back home."

"'Admit it's crossed my mind lately. Now we're a Dominion, Aussie's going to need our own army."

"Sure, I could write a letter of recommendation. Might not do you any harm."

"Thanks, cobber, that should do the trick. Too bloody bad there was no officer your senior in rank to witness what you did at the farm. You deserve being put in for a gong."

"That'll be the day. Scayles's got some kind of medal commendation due from me, though, for tackling that gang alone. If I ever get time for the paperwork." Harry span the oiled cylinder of his Colt and checked the firing-pin. "I'll take a look around, before our band of merry men stir up any more headaches."

On the way into town, he ordered Mendip back up the steeple as extra duty. Jiggy was eager to go, "I'll keep a lookout, sir, but with no helio, I aren't doing much good." He fairly babbled his eagerness to make amends. "HQ keeps trying to contact us. Maybe using Morse-lamps tonight, too. Even that cheeky Boer's flashing to ask if t'cat's got our tongue. I'm right sorry I upset t'apple-cart, sir."

"Don't keep apologizing. If it'd make you feel any better, I'd send you back to HQ with a written SitRep. But we've nothing to report, so what's the point? For now, keep a permanent signals watch, in case."

After inspecting each sentry-post in turn, Harry took a stroll along the main street. He reached Kleinhaus' store just as a postman was about to ride off with the week's sack of mail to Nelspruit station. It reminded him to send his letter home to BC. Soon afterwards, he found himself going up the path to Baroness von Gliewitz's house.

"Thought I'd just see how Dirk's coming along."

"Indeed." She tilted her head impishly. "That would be your only reason to call, I'm sure."

"What's his chances?"

"He's coming along famously. The worst wound went in deep above his pelvic bone, but missed any vital organs. No infection, praise be, thanks to that healthy outdoors life he's been leading. Whatever it was." She twinkled a conspiratorial smile. "We got some barley broth into him, which is a good sign. He needs rest mostly, though, time to heal. You just might be interested to know his sister happens to be in there, too, gorgeous as ever."

He went along the corridor to a back bedroom where Bethany sat beside Dirk's bed. She smiled and put a finger to her lips, it was not all that necessary. The boy was sleeping deeply, sedated from the vial of laudanum on the side-table.

"He looks well in baron's silk pajamas."

She smiled wanly, and put aside her Bible. "Lord be praised he's young and strong. Neave patched him up, and thinks he'll pull through quickly now." She busied herself at clearing up bowls and glasses. "I don't know what we'd have done without her." Beth's voice caught, "Or you."

He put his arms around her, just holding for a minute. There was a brightly coloured print of the Virgin Mary above the headboard. It disturbed him for some reason. Beth stirred, balancing glassware to free one hand. She drew his face down and gave him a soft kiss. "If you had not come when you did, we might have lost him."

There was a tap on the door, and they stepped apart. A maid came in, curtseyed, and said the Baroness had sent her to watch over the klein-baas. They found the house bustling with servant-girls. Places were being set at the dining-table and the kitchen clattered with preparations. Neave announced there were too many long faces about and she intended to cheer everybody up. She invited Harry to come for dinner, and to bring Lt. Scayles, as there must be a gentleman for each lady at table.

When Harry said he couldn't take his ease while the men roughed it, Beth shushed him happily. "They should have an evening off, too, if you'll allow. Pa's sent a side of beef for them, already."

"Wonderful!" Neave clapped her hands. "All your boys

can enjoy a braai in my orchard."

His news of a barbecue bucked up the men no-end. They finished repairing equipment in record time, so as to get at butchering the meat for steaks and spare-ribs. Scayles showed his pleasure by changing from his bloody tunic into a fresh spare. The defaulters on fatigue duties hurried to complete shovelling out foxholes so they would not miss the party. A few other men volunteered to pitch in and help.

"Digging for Oom Paul's treasure-chest, man?" A rough-looking civilian was watching Adriaan Baxter swing a spade to finish his rifle-pit. He growled in Taal, "Why not get one of your blackies to do it?"

"Their job is looking after our horses."

The stranger scowled, picking scabs off his razor-nicks. "Ag, a kaffir's job's whatever his boss says it is!"

"About finished now, anyway." Baxter struck the blade into soil, and sat down with a grunt. He started to stuff his pipe with dark tobacco. The newcomer took out his own meerschaum and blew through it meaningly. Without a word, Baxter passed his pouch. They rubbed dark plug into flakes, tamped their bowls, and lit up in thoughtful silence.

The stranger blew smoke through his nostrils. "That's the first good puff I've had in ages."

Baxter could smell the strong odor of horse sweat and wood-smoke on the man's clothing. "You've had a long spell on the veld, I'd say."

"True. There's more to life than baccy and a soft bed." He stood noting each position where other troopers dug trenches. "You're staying a while yet?"

"Our officer says we don't leave until he finds the gold."

"Meaning you'll be here forever then, eh, man?" Ox van Antwerp nodded his thanks for the pipeful, and walked off slowly to see whatever else he could spot about the town's defences before reporting to Vilberg.

CHAPTER NINETEEN

After checking the roster to see when they must each take a stint later on sentry-go, troopers started heading for the orchard. There was a relaxation in the balmy autumn evening they had not felt in weeks. They strolled along, chatting in groups, trailing cigarette smoke in the dusty street. Ox caught its foreign whiff in his throat as the two rooinek officers passed by, and spat loudly.

Harry always felt slightly shabby alongside Scayles, and tonight the MP fairly squeaked with smartness. For all that, Jiggy helped save the day. "Here you are, sir. Can't have you calling on t'ladies without a posy." Mendip presented him with a bunch of pink and crimson frangipani. "Some for you too, Mister Scayles. I always find the trick's to get girls all soft-hearted early on in t'evening, like."

"You're a hopeless romantic at heart, Jiggy. Even if you did steal these out of somebody's garden."

"Enjoy yourself, Harry." Mendip saluted. "Now, I'll be off up t' tower. Before I put some local girl up t'stump, instead." He snickered at the double-entendre.

Harry returned the salute. "Come and join the barbecue, soon as it's sundown."

A maid took their hats, and they hung their gun-belts on the hallstand. Neave and Bethany made a great fuss over the flowers, arranging them in special vases with such delight that Harry realized he had been away from civilized company too long. He made a note to ask Jiggy in private for some more courting advice.

The young women had done wonders with their appearance for the occasion. Her rich golden hair coiffed high, Bethany was radiant in a borrowed blue satin dress that fitted her trim body snugly, thanks to frantic last-minute bastings by a maid. The Baroness was spectacular in green silk chiffon, a Berlin evening-gown with cross-over bodice.

Tres decollete. No stays or drawers of course, on such an excitingly relaxed night in her own home. Scayles hardly know where to look. Meaning he did, but tried not to.

"Something to cool you down, gentlemen?" Neave said demurely. "There's cold lemonade, whiskey too, if you prefer. Though not the best Irish variety, I'm ashamed to say."

Scayles grabbed the double Haig & Haig she served, and knocked it back quickly. "That's the ticket!" Neave topped him up again without a word of caution about drinking alcohol after being wounded. Harry went for a good splash of gin and lime.

Her glamorous friend made Beth wonder how she would be able to compete for Harry's attention tonight. She felt a stab of jealousy when Harry quickly ran his gaze over the Irishwoman's lush body. Then he looked back at her and grinned. Beth's worry eased quickly from the way he stood close and watched her every move. The satin lovingly encased her high breasts, and he found himself wondering if one was decorated with a freckle. But if so, how did Nikki know? Harry pushed the thought away.

"Like old times, Beth." He raised his glass, the strain gone from his face, smiling like a boy. "Our last dinner together was exactly eighteen months ago. Remember?" She almost corrected him, but mimed an air-kiss instead. It had been nineteen months.

Scayles was talking, "Your late husband?" A fiercely-mustached portrait commanded from its place of honour over the fireplace. Baron Major von Gliewitz looked to have been a good deal older than her.

"Yes, I had it taken of dear Horst just before we came out here. To Bloemfontein, I mean."

"Prussian Artillery?" Scayles knew every uniform.

"Yes, he was proud to be of a very old Brandenburger family."

"How did you two meet?" From anyone else, it would be

polite interest, but she sensed him opening some invisible dossier on her.

"He was under my care at the Rheinischer Hospital, in Berlin. Horst had been invalided home from Windhoek with serious fever. Glad of it, he said, as that wasn't his style of soldiering."

"No wonder, considering what the Gerries are up to there," Scayles commented.

He would have said more, but Harry silenced him with a look. The entire Herero nation was being systematically exterminated by Kaiser Wilhelm's troops in German South-West Africa, just across the frontier from Cape Colony. There was no point discussing it and spoiling the ladies' evening.

"He was rather fond of you, obviously." The police officer took everything in. This fine bungalow, three maids, the cook and a garden-boy somewhere, latest gadgets like the His Masters Voice gramophone with its gold-edged horn. The baron had left his widow pretty well-fixed.

She seated her guests in overstuffed chairs, red plush prickly from rare use. "He was a fine man," Neave said levelly. "We bought this little place towards his retirement. Thank goodness, as I couldn't afford the cost of living in the Orange Free State now. There's not been much free of anything there since the war." The word hung in the room, despite her smile, intruding a sudden self-consciousness of their opposing alliances.

Harry said, casually, "That where you know Deneys from?"

She paused bent over the drinks tray, taking her time before speaking. "That's right", she replied in the same light tone. "His wife, Fanny, was my closest friend. When I came across him here and he told me she'd died, I was devastated entirely. Lost a baby on the way, too, the dear man." Harry stared at her, then put his drink down unfinished. He needed to keep a clear head tonight.

Neave prattled on, "Do y'know, this is the first time I've entertained since moving here. Any gentlemen, that is." She smiled at her friend, "Bethany's visited me often."

"Not often enough lately. There's been so much to do at the farm. Since every last one of our bywoners left to join the, er, went away."

"Maybe they'll all be back soon," Harry said. "The whole deal could be signed and sealed within a couple of weeks."

"Who's deal would that be?" Beth could not stop the tartness in her tone. Scayles bristled with resentment at her for a moment, but was soothed by a glimpse of the Baroness' creamy valley.

"Everybody's. President Burger, DeWet, Kitchener, Lord Milner." Harry spoke mildly to defuse things. "They're talking over armistice terms 'til both sides are happy." He realized Beth and he still had some fence-mending to do.

"Oh, come on the pair of you! Not one word more of politics in this house tonight." Neave poured Scayles another drink and gestured towards the growing ruckus out back. "Your boys are setting us the right example, Lieutenant. As if they haven't a care in the world."

"Just call me Harry. Yeah, I don't know how they do it."

"Sit down and make yourselves comfortable, do." She stayed on her feet herself, continually bustling about, freshening drinks, darting in and out the kitchen to supervise cook. Beth noticed her friend often walked by the rear windows, shoulders well back, with proudly borne bosoms. Giving the lusty soldier-boys a treat? Or just one of them, perhaps?

She pressed more drinks on the officers. Harry said he was fine for now, and mentally cursed Scayles for saying he wouldn't say no to another. Beth was still nursing her glass of sherry.

"Not drinking yourself, Baroness?" Scayles was glassy-eyed already.

"Gracious me, no. Wine makes my nose go shiny. But maybe I will take a wee nip of the green fairy."

Neave brought out a bottle of absinthe and rolled it in her palms for all to see. "All the rage at the Adlon in Berlin. Anyone join me?"

They said no thanks, but curiously watched her decadent Continental ceremony. She poured two fingers of cloudy liquor into a parfait glass, then rested a sugar-loaf on a perforated spoon across the rim. "Sweetens the horrid wormwood a bit." She dribbled cold water onto it, dissolving to drip into the absinthe, which turned a pale opalescent green.

The baroness sipped, "Aaaah!" She shuddered deliciously, with such jiggling effect that Scayles choked on his Scotch. "Lovely! No wonder it's been banned in France. Too good for them, Horst always used to say."

She kept the absinthe within reach, determined to enjoy a giddy evening. She wound up the gramophone, and put on a record that played London cabaret songs. She excused herself to check on cook. Beth went quickly down the hall to peep at Dirk.

Harry said,"Glen, it's him! DeKrieger!"

Scayles reacted dully, trying to concentrate through the whiskey fumes. "Wha'?"

"He's the guy who wants to bump me off. Probably your spy as well."

The MP breathed out sharply, took in some air. "How're you suddenly so sure?"

"Just now, it all came together. All the bits we knew about him? His wife died, lost a kid. That vrou in the camp said he swore by the Virgin he'd kill me. Well, that matches deKrieger's faith. And, him using different names, coming out with 'Good egg'."

"Granted. But other'n that, he doesn't sound remo'ly upper-clash, class."

"I always wondered about that phony 'Iffrikin' accent.

And how he doesn't know British army routine. Eating iron rations, wearing civvies off duty, and stuff. We've got to pull him in tonight!"

"What mischief are you two rogues planning, now?" Neave appeared beside them, maids with serving-carts in her wake.

"Guess it'll keep 'til later, won't it, Glen?"

"Firs' thing t'morrow."

Beth took her seat, beaming that Dirk was sleeping like a baby. Both women said short prayers of thanks at the table and the meal was served. One maid changed gramophone discs throughout, and got a sharp look from her mistress if she forgot to keep the motor wound. The recorded music added a touch of sophisticated modernity as Neave presided over dinner like a baroness to the manor born.

Two maids served delicious vichysoisse soup, and perfectly grilled trout with crushed lemon sauce. There was a choice of sliced beef with Yorkshire pudding. "Colorful ethnic food, specially for you, Mister Scayles," she laughed.

Bethany caught a hidden edge to her friend's coquettish way with the policeman. A veiled dislike mixed with the need to either distract him or gain his goodwill. Relationships were so complicated these days.

She let the evening wash over her, gay music, sweet-scented frangipani, candle-light, cutlery ringing on china, easy conversation and bursts of laughter. "This is so marvelous, Neave," she blurted. "To be here enjoying ourselves, when just a few hours ago . . . It was a near thing for everybody."

"You don't know the half of it, young lady," Scayles massaged his throat, and slurred, "When I was left there strung up, you won't believe what this crazy Canuck of yours said to me. He told me to 'Hang on'!"

They all exploded into laughter. Beth fairly wept with it, and realized how close she was to real tears after this day. "Harry, you didn't!"

"Well," Harry said, "I hated to leave him in suspense."

That sent them into more merriment, and when they recovered, Neave asked, "Speaking of which, I'm dying to know if you've found anything to go on about the treasure yet?"

"Not a sausage," Harry said. "Your neighbours either won't co-operate with us, or they really don't know a thing. We'll keep searching, but I'm wondering if we'll ever find a nickle."

"Just as well," Beth said, "For everybody's sake."

Harry smiled, hiding his puzzlement. "That's a switch, hon."

"Kuger's so-called missing millions've brought nothing but trouble and pain for us all. Boer and British alike. It'd be better you gave up looking."

"We can't, in case your, the other, side might find it."

Beth flushed, angry despite herself, "Oh, we couldn't have that happen, could we?"

Neave cut in, "Anyone for fruit preserves, now?" She chuckled tipsily, a gorgeous hostess offering ginger-cake with thick cream, or honey-syrup over green figs, and tangerines in brandy. "That's the County Galway in me. I'll never get used to saying dessert."

"We say *konfrits.*" Beth smiled at Harry, truce declared again.

"So you obviously preferred to stay on here, rather than go back to Ireland, Baroness?" Scayles asked. He probably interrogated his own mother after she had walked the dog. "Any particular reason?"

"A small difference of opinion, you might say."

"With the authorities?"

"Whisht, no." She despised his rudeness, the drink in him talking. "I'd long since given up on that sectarian nonsense you're hinting at. A pox on both their houses. It was a family matter, entirely. Disowning me for marrying the wrong religion, aristocracy or not."

"Still, it brought you happiness for a time," Beth said.

"It did too, my dear." Neave's glance strayed beyond the windows. "Led to the love of my life, you could say."

They went back to the drawing room, and Beth noticed the bottle's level was well down. Neave caught her glance, and laughed throatily. "Know what they say? Absinthe makes the heart grow fonder."

She dreamily cranked the gramophone, "Here's some ragtime to liven you two lovebirds up." The syncopated rhythms of Scott Joplin span into the room. "Roll the carpet back if you want to dance. I'll just take a look at our patient, and see to the clearing up. Won't be long."

Neave checked that Dirk was sleeping quietly, his temperature lower. Then she tripped to her boudoir, dabbed Volupte perfume behind her ears, on her throat, and deep in the swells of her cleavage. She slipped out the side door, and walked down the rear steps as if in a dream. He loomed in the garden, his bulk silhouetted against the bonfire's rosy glow.

"I felt you were watching me."

"I knew you'd come," he said.

It happened quite naturally then, the way she had often dreamed. He pulled her to him, almost roughly, and kissed her. She sucked on his mouth, letting him taste the heat and yearning inside her. Absinthe and desire made her reckless, melting for need of him. She gasped and pulled away.

"Deneys, darling, there's no time for this." Still, she pressed closer again. "They're talking about you. I'm sure Harry knows!"

They spoke in English. His deep voice was manly, cultured, none of that absurd play-acting now. She could hear a self-assured smile in the words. "From the look of Scayles, he won't be much good at coppering tonight."

"I got him as drunk as I could, but he might come round soon.. I know constables, tough as old boots. Besides Harry's formidable enough on his own. You must go!"

"Not 'til I finish some overdue business with Lanyard."

A loud cow-puncher's whoop sounded from the troopers. Deneys pulled her into the rose arbour, lifting her backwards onto the table. They kissed avidly, whispering whenever their lips could part.

"Dearest, oh, poor Fanny. If she'd lived, I'd never have told you."

"And I'd have never realized. But as soon as I set eyes on you again, beside that dead Tommy, I knew." He kissed her throat and trailed his lips, following her perfume down between silken warmth. Fontaine started to yodel, and ragtime tinkled inside the house. Neave thought it sounded a million miles away from this paradise.

"I learned them all," Beth was saying. "The Turkey Trot, Mississippi Rag, Heliotrope. The musicians are black, you know. So naturally Dada would never let me listen to jazz in the house." She swayed left and right, strutting the Cakewalk as if it was yesterday she'd last pranced it, instead of a good four years ago. "Let-me-see-you-do-the-ragtime-dance."

She slipped into his arms, "Come on, this one's specially for you, the Maple Leaf Rag." Harry tried to keep up with her, sliding in his clumsy ammunition-boots, happy just to see her move and laugh.

"He'd die if he ever knew what we got up to when I was at college in the States. Oh, nothing terrible, really, but we used to sneak every weekend into Terre Haute for dances at the Tea Garden. We smoked Turkish cigarettes, and some girls smooched with college-boys behind the potted palms." She laughed, carefree with memories. "Shocking for a strictly brought up Calvinist miss. At first, I thought American girls were awfully fast. I rather liked it after a bit."

"I bet you did, you brazen Boer hussy." He tried to steal a kiss. She flashed a glance at Scayles. He waved his glass sloppily, though his eyes were not so glazed now.

"Be off'n enjoy yourselves, kiddies. I'll hold the fort." He started to paw through the records. Harry led the way outside, letting the screen-door bang behind them.

It shocked Neave and Deneys apart for a moment. She gripped his hand, pausing it to stay between her thighs. He whispered, louder than he should, "Nobody can see us." She pulled her bodice wide, and her fire-tipped nipples stiffened in the chill air. She pressed his mouth to them. Only to quiet him, of course.

"How do they do that?" Beth asked. "Cowboys make that funny yodelling noise?"

"From listening to coyotes howl," Harry said. "Every night, while they're riding the range."

Beth's fond laughter hid the shuddering gasp Neave made when Deneys entered her. It was tremendously exciting, making love unseen just a few feet away from the couple on the veranda. Deneys stood gripping her haunches, pumping, pleasuring. She clamped her thighs around him so tight he could never ever leave.

"Uh-oh," Harry said. "Here comes Bronco's full repertoire." The Canadians had finished a big meal and brewed up more coffee. They threw logs on the bonfire and started to serenade the moon. Voices of some Boer neighbours also joined in the sing-song. Beth sighed and cuddled close as he held her, savouring the rumble in his chest while he hummed along with the men's chorus.

Troopers harmonized 'Darling Clementine', and 'Old Folks At Home', then rounded it off with their favorite, 'Red River Valley'. After the first few notes, Beth said, "I remember. Please, Harry, sing it for me." At first self-consciously, then with increased enjoyment, he joined in with a surprisingly fine tenor voice.

"From this valley they say you are going
We will miss your bright eyes and sweet
smile
For they say you are taking the sunshine
That has brightened our path for a while.
Come and sit by my side if you love me

Do not hasten to bid me adieu
But remember the Red River Valley
And the cowboy who loved you so true."

The troops trailed the last notes, making fun of their own sentimentality, "De-dah-dah-de-daaa!"

Harry laughed a bit awkwardly, but Beth stirred and kissed him. "That was lovely."

The words made Neave roll her eyes and sigh, giving Deneys a dazzling smile while he pulsed within her. He started again, such stamina he had, doing other secret things to peak her satisfaction. She moaned quietly, straining herself wider, exulting in this sweet wantonness.

Harry said, "I'm not complaining, but . . . ?"

"How come we're together again?" Beth finished for him. "This morning, I saw my own father kill a wounded man. How could I go on judging you for the same thing?"

"Truth to tell, it wasn't quite alike. That kid really did ask me to do it. He said . . ." Harry's voice faltered. His words un-nerved the writhing lovers close-by. Deneys stopped in mid-thrust to listen, his entire body trembling.

Harry went on, "It was weird, a Boer who talked like some English public-schoolboy. He'd been caught in his own shellfire, banged up pretty badly. An arm blown off, guts hanging out. No hope for him at all."

A match flared, and Neave tried to read the pale blur of Deneys' face. Uncontrollably at that moment, he spasmed, scalding jets that thrilled Neave even as she knew her lover had silently started to weep.

Harry blew out a long drag of smoke loudly. "He knew he was finished. He kept saying, 'Go on, old chap, do it for me. Be a sport.'"

Deneys bit harder into the woman's neck to stifle his groan. She tried to ignore the pain, and clamped him inside as comfort. She locked him there, drawing his essence, clenching, clenching.

"Can you imagine? Be a sport. I'll never forget him. I didn't have any gun, just a bayonet. I made it as quick as I could, but it's not easy to forgive myself. And hear-tell, there's somebody who never will."

Deneys withdrew from her roughly. Neave touched his face, wiping the tears. She kissed his eyes, and he nuzzled her hair, shaking less now.

"Oh, Harry." Beth said softly. "If you'd only told me."

"Been kind of hard to get a word in edgeways, sweetheart." He gave a short laugh to make light of it. "I think I need a drink after all."

The stoep door opened and closed on some Gilbert & Sullivan. Neave whispered, "I thought Kurt was still safe at Eton."

"He came back to fight. Only seventeen, and he gave up everything, even his young life."

"I can't bear you to be lost as well. You've got to get away! Take my horse. Now."

He did not speak for a long moment. "I'll be back, my darling."

He gave her a last embrace, and turned towards the little paddock. "I'd best saddle up."

"You'll need money. Wait!" Neave slipped in the side door.

Scayles was nodding along in time to 'The Very Model Of A Modern Major-General'. He sniggered foolishly as the ditty slowed to sound like warbling under molasses. "Crank her up again for me, there's a good chap."

Harry carried his gin over and began winding the motor. Beth heard light steps in the hall. She went there, calling, "Is Dirk alright?" She halted, looking shocked, and backed away.

Neave came in, holding her purse and Scayles' gun. The others stared, as much shocked by the obviousness of her appearance as by the weapon. Her mussed hair, dress gaping at the bodice, a raw bite-mark on her neck. She grasped her elbow with the other hand, supporting the Webley to threaten the officers.

"You sha'n't have him! He's leaving this instant, and no-one'll prevent it." Scayles growled and started towards her. "Stand still! If you imagine this is the first gun I've aimed at such as you, you've another think coming."

"You've opened yourself to very serious charges," Scayles said.

"I'm a Prussian citizen long since. I doubt you can cause me any repercussions."

Harry saw her determined half-crazed stare. It was more than absinthe driving the woman now. "Careful with that thing, Neave."

"Shut up, Harry, and put your hands behind your head, please. You too!" Scayles glowered down the barrel of his own gun and did what he was told.

Beth tried to make some sense of this. "Neave, what on earth's going on?" She felt no wiser a moment later when that turn-coat trooper barged in from the stoep.

Harry managed to sound sardonic, "Doctor Osseboom, I presume?"

"I've had a bone to pick with you for a long time, Lanyard." His change to beautifully spoken English shocked Beth.

"So they say." Harry wished he had nabbed the guy earlier while they had the jump on him.

The big soldier took the Webley, twirling it around his finger. He strode across the room, his face twisted, chest heaving. The record's libretto came to its end, scratching round and round in the abruptly quiet room.

"Oh, put your arms down!" Deneys changed gun-hands, and stuck out his open palm. He gripped Harry's, pumping firmly up and down. "What's done's done. I overheard, so I'm not sorry those wonky sights made me miss you the other day."

"Me either."

Cheerfully unaware, his troopers started a chorus of 'She'll Be Comin' Round The Mountain', so loud Jiggy heard them at the far end of the village. It was a sodding hard climb, up all these zigzag ladders with a lit oil-lamp. He almost changed his mind a couple of times, but it was his fault the helio got broke, and this would make up for it. The hike seemed even more worthwhile when he reached the trapdoor. He threw it back, hearing the loud rustling above him.

Jiggy sneezed loudly at the moldy bat-pong in his nostrils, and hurried to get the outside hatch open for some fresh air. Dusk was fading to night already, dozens of lights prickling from isolated farms across the darkened veld. Up here, you could make out every word sung by the lads, well along with their party. Bet the steaks would be all gone before he got this job done. Maybe Harry could find him a slice, when told how a message had gone through.

He looked south into the already darkened valley, towards the distant signals station. After all this climbing lark, there'd better be some keen squaddie with binocs on night-watch out there. The narrow railing was just wide enough to hold the lantern base. He turned the wick as high as it could go to reflect more light off the white steeple. His bush-hat should work fine as a shutter to flash Morse dit-dit-dahs.

Hello, what's this? Tiny searchlights started to come on, dozens of bluish rays stabbing the night sky. They flickered, waving back and forth. Not signals, just flashing any-old-how, as if some barmy idiot was twiddling switches. That set off the star-shells and rockets, going up all along the railway line as far as you could see. Distant silent explosions of scarlet, brilliant white, and vivid blue. Streaks of machine-gun tracer bullets appeared, like coloured chalks scrawling a huge blackboard.

"Bloody heck!" He shouted, "T'war's over! By gum, it is! Hip-hurray!" He skipped a little dance.

Then a stream of furry bodies poured through the open hatch, hundreds of leathern wings in a beating wave that pushed against the soldier. He threw up his arms, losing grip on the lantern. He spun, flailing, blinded, stepping back off the little platform. Private Samuel Mendip fell into the dark, not making a sound the whole way down.

CHAPTER TWENTY

Commandos strike at dawn. Any British soldiers who forgot that could end up dead in their beds. Lanyard had not slept much, and found it easy to arise before sun-up. Haze from smouldering camp-fires drifted over the sleeping men wrapped in blankets or greatcoats, crusted with hoar-frost, rifles by their side. He and Coveyduck moved through the camp awakening them with a quiet word. "Rise and shine, feller. Stand-To."

They hawked and cussed and rubbed gummy eyes, but took positions quickly, bored by the routine but alert for trouble as ever. Harry arranged for hot coffee to be taken around, first to the sentries. They all tried to ignore Lt. Scayles while he chivvied any trooper unlucky enough to get within earshot. He was in a foul mood, the combination of a bad hangover and failure to make an arrest.

"Been better if we'd just shot him soon as his name came up," he groused. Harry felt no need to ask who he meant. "The arrogant bastard's got clear away."

"Kind of wish he was on our side, myself."

"Well, he certainly isn't. Instead, he's riding around free as a bird, up to all kinds of murdering mischief again, no doubt. On that blasted woman's own horse!"

"Still lucky I talked you out of arresting her."

"Mm, suppose you're right at that. If I'd taken Lady Muck in charge, imagine the row it would have set off. All the way down from the Kaiser, ending with yours-truly, looking like Joe Soap. Kitchener would have had my balls for breakfast over that."

"Take it easy. Your lot will nail him for sure, now we know who he is."

"Fat lot of good that'll do me." The MP scowled his blackest. "My name's going to be mud around Provost H.Q. Be lucky if I get off with a severe reprimand."

"Ah, you'll be okay after my report on what else was

keeping you busy." Harry decided to keep it a surprise that he was putting Scayles in for at least a Mention In Despatches.

"Not bloody likely. Us coppers are never a band of brothers at the best of times."

They tensed when Rimmer's voice challenged loudly through the trees, "Who goes there?" There was a mumbled reply, and Rimmer said disgustedly, "Jesus, Mac, sneaking up like that could get your ass blown off!"

It was the predikant, too agitated to even notice the profanity. "It is bad news, I fear. That signaler of yours."

He led to where Jiggy lay broken amidst the tombstones. Harry knelt beside him, feeling the pulse in hope, but the body was stiff already. In a daze of disbelief, Harry took in the shattered lamp and looked up at the steeple. He angrily waved off some comforting words by Carolus, and lifted Jiggy in his arms. He was heavier than he looked, and Harry stumbled a few times on the way back to camp. Or maybe it was because he could not see very well.

Troopers rushed from their positions when they heard. "Screw it to hell, it's Jiggy! He's snuffed it!"

"Aw, shit, no."

Harry lowered the body beside a tree, and Ned draped a blanket over him. "Strewth, we'll miss the little bugger."

Scayles said, "Anything suspicious about it, you think?"

"No, perfectly normal. Just another Goddam ignorant insolent soldier getting himself killed for King and Country." Harry made his voice hard, but he didn't want the men to see his face.

"Steady on." Scayles grasped his shoulder awkwardly.

Harry brushed the faint rust from Mendip's uniform off his hands. It came to him then. Jiggy might have been closer to the gold than any of them. He started to say something to Scayles about it, when the loud whinnying of horses distracted him. Glad of the excuse to investigate, he left Scayles to write the casualty report.

The mounts put up such a racket, it was a moment before Harry caught the sounds Bertil was making. He was held at the throat by that crop-headed stranger they spotted yesterday. The man held the reins of a horse over his arm while he pistol-whipped the Griqua's face. Slowly, left and right, making a meal of it.

Harry ran through the herd, shouting, "Cut that out!"

The Boer turned, growling with pleasure at seeing this rooinek officer delivered ripe for the kill. He swung his revolver up, calmly taking aim. Harry cleared leather in a fast draw and shot the guy twice through the chest. Ox crashed backward like a felled oak.

In camp, Coveyduck yelled, "Back to your possies—move it!"

Scayles blew his whistle, "Watch your front! Prepare to fire! Remember to aim skewed a bit off to the right."

Ox was left lying among the stomping hooves. Bertil spat a couple of teeth and went to help Rao recover from his knock on the head. Harry told them to hobble the horses to prevent a stampede. He no sooner spoke, than rifle-shots sounded along the road into town. Just one first, followed by ragged firing from two directions.

The target was a lone man in khaki riding a dappled mare, coming so fast her legs stretched full out. Harry recognized Deneys Osseboom, who was shouting something in Afrikaans at the top of his voice. Whatever his words, even more shots buzzed around him. He bent to lie along the mane, rowelling the beast for top speed and never mind its pain. Then somebody figured out how to stop him. Bullets smacked puffs of dust off horsehide. She collapsed in mid-stride, rolling over, kicking and squealing. Osseboom jumped off before she went down, landing flat on his feet and running for cover.

"Over here!" Harry shouted.

Laurens Vilberg was spitting with rage that some trigger-happy fool had sprung the trap too soon. Just for the premature urge to shoot one kakie. The plan of attack could have worked perfectly. With van Antwerp's report on enemy defences, they knew exactly where to ride in after Stand-Down and surprise the soldiers at breakfast. That was ruined now, so nothing could be done but make the best of things.

Vilberg led the charge, his commandos riding in from all sides. Being able to shoot accurately from horseback was not much good this time, they found. There were no standing targets in sight, just a few ostrich feathers nodding above the rim of foxholes. Their officers could be heard yelling, "Fire at will!" Lee-Enfields cracked steadily, and emptied five saddles before the Boers covered forty yards.

"Back, back!" Vilberg ordered. "Take cover among the houses!" He had to act quickly to stop it turning into a rout, and was glad to see that crafty Swarte Schippers had placed himself to block the main street. His rifle was up, to discourage any Boers from continuing their retreat right out of town.

"Plenty of cover here!" the corporal yelled. "Hold them off 'til I bring the pom-pom. That'll soon finish them!"

"Don't shoot, it's me, boys!" Osseboom ran at a crouch across the road, Boer bullets snapping at his heels. Just in case any itchy-fingered Canadians had the same idea, he kept shouting, "The war's over, I tell you!"

He threw himself into Harry's rifle-pit. "Good Lord, is everybody deaf?"

"Maybe it's all this noise." Harry pulled Scayles' gun from Deneys' belt, and jabbed the muzzle to make him crouch down.

Schammerhorn shifted the chaw in his cheek to drawl at Osseboom, "Sure don't fancy your chances, fella, once our Redcap gets a-hold of you." He spat brown juice, and loosed off five rounds rapid towards the houses.

"Go easy on the ammo, Tex," Harry said. He thumbed ten more cartridges into his magazine. "You on the level, about an armistice?"

"I keep telling you, yes!" Osseboom jumped up in anger, ignoring bullets that spat dirt from the trench wall. "I met the postman coming up here, and raced straight back. He's bringing a copy of the official Cease-Fire telegram. I saw it myself. DeWet and the others signed the surrender at Vereeniging yesterday." He laughed hollowly, "Apparently, Kitchener shook hands and said we can all be friends now." A sniper clipped an inch off his feather, and he ducked back into the hole.

Tex said, "Be swell if you could convince your pals out there."

Boergaard was trying to do just that with his veld cornet, having caught what Osseboom shouted. He reasoned, "At least we should try to find out if he's telling the truth. Call pause 'til we know."

But Vilberg's blood was up, and in the middle of a battle he would take no notice of some mystery-man's lies. He said, "Let up on these kakies? After they took the lives of seven friends this morning? I cannot leave them un-avenged." He waved at commandos to take position in nearby houses. Villagers were abandoning their homes, a terrified pack running away down side-streets.

While they had the chance, Ino van Kettel and a couple of others made it their business to put paid to that collaborator who Ox had told them about last night. They pulled Burgemeester Kleinhaus out of bed, dragged him into the front garden and shot him dead in front of his screaming wife. If some of his cowardly neighbours saw, well and good. It would convince them what real bitterenders thought of all traitors.

The troopers heard the fusillade, and could not understand why Harry blew his whistle, ordering, "Hold your fire!" He called Glen over to discuss the developments.

Scayles' eyes bulged when he saw Osseboom in Harry's trench. He clamped hold of the man's arm, voice grating, "You're under close arrest! For murder, espionage, and impersonating a British officer."

He would have put his prisoner in irons if Harry had not snapped, "For Christ's sake, Glen, not now!" He explained the turn of events. Scayles' grim expression did not change. Even if true, the news of peace seemed strangely flat.

Troopers in pits close by strained to hear what Harry said, cautious in case of snipers. "Pass it along. Word's just come in that the Boers've surrendered, yesterday. I can't confirm it yet. But," he jerked a thumb at the man they knew as deKrieger. "He swears official notice might reach here any minute."

The scouts looked at each other uncertainly. Some were puzzled at word being brought by the prisoner in Lt. Scayles' grip. Last night, they heard Sith-o had deserted, but this seemed no time for playing MP. Any talk of peace sounded unreal, anyway, considering they were ducking enemy pot-shots at the moment.

Harry said, "Obviously, our local Johnnies haven't got the word yet. I'm going to try to parley first, maybe convince 'em the party's over. If I can't, then we'll have to flush 'em out, peace treaty regardless."

He pointed. "They've pulled back among those houses. Glen, take Fontaine, Cameron, and Parkin to get around behind. Then split up and start sniping. You others form two sections along each side of main-street. Ned's party, advance on the left. The rest of you, wait here. Piet and me'll try a chat with these characters first, but be ready for hell to break loose again any minute."

Scayles' group moved off, for a cut-and-dried job of street-fighting with no need for questions. 'Far as they were concerned, this war was not over until the Boojers finally got it through their square heads.

"Let me," Osseboom said. "No offence, Piet, but I might be able to handle negotiations better."

Van Praage made a faint sneer, but shrugged. Harry said, "Yeah, well, okay." He left his guns with Piet.

"Hurrah, they're surrendering!" Ino laughed, pointing at the white handkerchief being wig-wagged around a corner opposite. A voice speaking good Taal called, "The war's over! Don't fire, we want to talk."

Vilberg wavered. Maybe those lilly-livered politicians really had given up. Well, it would not do this particular bunch of kakies any good. The shouted rumour had already been discussed by his men, and worsened the war-sickness many were developing. Confirmed or not, word of a treaty-signing was enough to send almost a third of the commando straggling away already. He could tell even as steady a one as Boergaard was tempted to leave. Only his lawyerly reluctance to believe anything without proof kept him here.

The remaining men's blood was still up though, 24 stone-faced Afrikaners who had lost their women and children, and to whom peacetime would be meaningless ever after. They agreed there must be one last honourable whiff of cordite before they left this unfaithful village.

Still, Boergaard urged, "Come, Laurens. Let's just hear their story first. A parley'd gain Swarte some time, anyway."

He nodded at Schippers' crew wheeling the Nordenfeldt into position just out of sight of the street. The corporal quickly lifted an armful of ammunition belts out of the pannier, nodding urgently. They needed only a few minutes more to get fully ready.

Vilberg ordered, "Stop shooting for now!" A few more shots sputtered, then the commando rifles fell silent. He called, his voice almost casual, "Come ahead, Tommy, and spit out what you have to say. No tricks, mind!"

"Look who's talking," van Praage muttered. Despite the white flag, or maybe because of it, he was nervous of the Boer rifles still pointing towards Harry.

When the pair were halfway across the road. Harry said, "Okay, close enough. See if you can convince them."

"Despite this uniform, I am an Intelligence officer holding President Steyn's commission," Osseboom could be heard clearly in the silent street. "Believe me, there is no need for us to go on fighting now. All hostilities have ceased between the Boer Republics and Great Britain. The treaty was signed at Vereeniging by our leaders yesterday morning."

There was no response, just disbelieving silence. Deneys raised his voice louder to be sure all the concealed Boers could hear. "An official peace proclamation is being circulated. It's on its way here as I speak!"

Vilberg stepped out of cover, "More like, you speak for the English!"

"That I do not! But it's foolish for us to keep killing each other after peace has been settled."

Boergaard showed himself to demand, "Precisely what kind of settlement?"

"That we lay down our arms, on condition the two Republics become British Protectorates." The words stuck in Osseboom's throat, but the deal had been made and there was more than enough blood spilled in these streets already.

"We're to become Crown Colonies? Acknowledge King Edward as our lawful sovereign! Surrender our independence!" Boergaard paced back and forth in the roadway, his courtroom voice rising like some summary of indictment. "Let savages vote as equals to us? With Burger and Steyn and those craven generals like Botha, Smuts, and DeWet party to it! How could they agree to such shame, when we commandos are still ready to fight to the last man? After all the dead children, and lost farms, and devastation of everything the Volk hold dear!"

Bearded commandos leaned from cover, shaking weapons, yelling, "No surrender!"

"No, Listen, it's not all gone England's way!" Osseboom strained his voice to be heard. "We will remain the South African Republic and Orange Free State, and elect our own internal governments, as before. The Crown has agreed to pay us three million pounds, to pay off our pre-war debts and make resettlement loans to burghers."

Ino shouted, "Never mind sweet-talking us about bribes! They'll hand votes to Godless kaffirs, who'll overwhelm us before we know it!" That drove the burghers into a fury. The concept of British-imposed racial equality so outraged them, several aimed their rifles at the two kakies.

"No, Milner and Kitchener backed down on native rights." Deneys forced a meaningful smile. "Now, all the treaty says is that granting the franchise for blacks will be delayed until after it's been introduced for discussion in the Volksraad."

"Meaning never." Advokaat Boergaard caught the point, and tried to convey it to his fellow Boers. "No new equality law is likely to pass, considering we'll be self-governing!"

Things might have gone well at that moment, with the commandos perhaps talking over this fresh information. If it had not been for the three Spitsdorp villagers who trotted into the street, waving rifles. Before they could explain they wanted to join the commandos, they were mown down. Boschie and Ino snapped off the first nervous shots, and others joined in.

Harry and Deneys ran for cover, bent double against being included as targets. Troopers started giving covering fire, and the street blazed into a renewed gun-battle. The combatants were only the width of a street apart, and exposed soldiers got picked off almost immediately.

Cameron took a flesh-wound, but Phil Abbott got hit in the head and slumped loosely in that final way. Harry bent over him, saw there was nothing he could do, and caught Osseboom watching. "You better make yourself scarce, before one of the boys takes things out on you."

"I should get to Neave, anyway."

"Fine, make it snappy. Look after things there for me." He meant Beth, of course. Then the Nordenfeldt started quacking.

Schippers cuddled tight into the shoulder-pad, the fine

English gun juddering in time to his trigger-finger. A dozen explosive 37 mm. rounds hammered into walls and earth, showering troopers with debris and steel splinters. They howled and cursed, making themselves small or high-tailing it for better cover. The soldiers crouched around the side of a house, while the pom-pom spat shells in slow vicious bursts. Women and children could be heard screaming inside the rooms. Chunks of masonry and wood flew off close to trooper's heads. The quick-firer was gradually chewing away the corner where they hid with their heads down.

They counted the shots, old hands at this. The Boer gunner was using short belts. Spraying the whole twelve rounds at a time, a sign he had plenty of shells. When the gun stopped, Harry ordered, "Open up, before they re-load!"

They laid down all the answering fire they could, but soon had to stop when the pom-pom began again. McKay sprawled gray-faced near them, his rib-cage a mess. O'Malley crawled to his friend, and put a handkerchief over the wounds. "Oh, they've scragged you hard, Jock, but I'll pay the spalpeens back." He clipped on a bayonet, his face gone savage.

When the next fusillade paused, O'Malley snarled, "Twelve and yer out!" He charged from cover, roaring berserk threats, straight at the Nordenfeldt's crew. Schippers pulled his trigger and blew the Irishman to rags. They had loaded a 20-round belt this time.

"Oh, bad show!" Lascelles went up on one knee and fired cooly at the gun-emplacement. He was the only trooper still wearing his hat, cocked over one eye, squinting through smoke from a cigarette in the corner of his mouth. He patted his bandolier and shouted. "Out of ammo!"

Ned shared out what was left, and detailed Baxter and Haywood to go fetch more ammunition. "I'm going with them," Harry told Coveyduck to take over, and led the pair at a run to the encampment. They caught a gang of teenage villagers rifling baggage, and Baxter slapped a few ear-holes. The boys scooted off, laughing, one wearing Jiggy's hat. They had not found Harry's pack, and he opened it to grab what he needed. He hoisted two boxes of .303 and staggered after the others back to Ned's position.

Pom-pom-pom-pom!

His men were still pinned down by that one frigging automatic pom-pom. Most now bled from small wounds in face and body from the steel confetti of shrapnel from bursting one-pounders. Harry and Ned scooped paper packets of ammunition from the boxes and flipped them towards crouching troopers. "This is getting serious, mate." Coveyduck barely flinched while hot fragments hissed around him. "Scayles' lot tried out-flanking the bastards through the orchard, but they've got snipers covering there, too. Cameron's wounded."

"Yeah, well, I brought them a souvenir." Harry waggled one of the dynamite sticks.

He thumbed open a box of Vestas, shakily, spilling little wax matches all over. He scratched one alight, and held its flame against the fuse. It fizzled sparks, and he stepped into the alley. Bullets thrummed past his head, one tugging his tunic flap. He pitched the dynamite in a high sputtering arc towards the quick-firer. Boschie Petersen just laughed, reached out, snatched the stick in flight and threw it back. It went off in mid-air, knocking men prone, booming so loud it deadened everybody's hearing.

Deneys reeled from the shock-wave that cracked windows as far as Neave's home. It also startled a bearded young man out of cover behind a nearby hedge. Surprised at seeing the kakie running towards the big house, he raised his rifle, too late to fire. Bethany threw open the door and pulled Deneys inside.

They heard a shout, "Not so fast, you!"

For a moment, they gawped at Scayles waving angrily over the garden wall, ignoring gunfire. The man was duty-bound, police instincts stronger than soldiering. Deneys saw the heavy figure throw aside his arm-sling, vault the wall, and race towards the house. Saul ter Hoven snapped off two shots. Scayles went down hard, then scrambled to his feet, jogging lop-sided the rest of the way.

They dragged him inside, slammed the door, and bullets shattered glass panels around them. Deneys shoved the others to the floor. Neave crawled forward, her arms reaching for a quick hug. "Oh, Deneys, whatever possessed you to come back?"

"Somebody told me the war's over."

Bullets chipped and buzzed along the hallway. The pom-pom thumped slowly up the street, mixed with continuous rifle-shots like corks popping. She managed a smile, "Could whoever it was be after telling you fibs, darling?"

"Your precious Sith-o's the champion at that game!" Scayles winced and tenderly reached behind himself.

"Get out, rooineks!" Dirk's voice was hoarse, and he leaned in the corridor doorway to keep upright. His finger pointed at the two men in British uniform. "Leave now, so my comrades can deal with you!"

"Please, you must go back to bed!" Bethany took his arm, trying to steer him out of danger. He shook her off, weak on his feet but stubbornly refusing to obey. He scowled at Neave, tending one of the soldiers. She had noticed the blood Scayles was trailing, and motioned Deneys to drag him into the dining-room.

She tossed his belt aside. "Quick, pull these britches off him." Scayles made half-hearted attempts to resist being debagged. "Ah, spare me your blessed modesty. Nurses see more men's twiddley-bits than you've had hot dinners!" She hurried for her first-aid kit.

Dirk stood propped in the hallway and she had to step around. "You'll pull those stitches, if you're not careful. For Heaven's sake, lie down before you fall down!"

Beth pleaded again too, while she rushed for towels, but he would not move. His pale face streamed with sweat, near out of his head, never taking his gaze from the soldiers.

There was a good deal of blood from Scayles, but wiping showed only neat puncture wounds through each buttock. Neave said briskly, "Lucky again, Glendon, me bucko. This time, just a clean shot right where your brains are."

Boots clumped on the front stoep, and a young man's face showed through the broken glass. Dirk called, "Saul, Saul ter Hoven, it's me!" He found sudden strength enough to snatch Scayles' handgun and lurch unsteadily down the hallway. The MP struggled after him, bloody shirt-tails flapping. Hobbled by trousers around his ankles, he fell flat on his face.

Beth shouted, "No!" She pulled handcuffs from the belt-pouch, closed one link around her wrist, and stepped to Dirk's side. He was rattling the latch, "Coming, Saul!"

"Irkie, no!" He turned, snarling. Beth clamped the cuff on his wrist, ratcheting it tight. "Now commit suicide out there if you want, but you'll have to take me with you!" While her brother hesitated, hand on the lock, Deneys punched the damned boy cold before he got somebody killed.

A rifle smashed through the glass, it's iron snout pointing towards where Neave crouched over Scayles. Feeling no choice, Deneys snatched up the pistol and fired twice through the door. He aimed low, heard a cry of pain, "*Eina!*", and the rifle clattered from view. Both women stared at him, the hall filled with the sour smell of gunsmoke. He took a quick peek outside, and saw the youngster dragging a shattered ankle away.

Both sides stopped firing when Predikant Carolus walked into the street to where the shot village men lay. He calmly helped the two wounded ones stumble away to safety. Nothing could be done for the other, so they left his body in the gutter. The moment the predikant moved aside, firing started again.

The troopers were pinned down, enfiladed by Boer snipers who tried to drive them into the Nordenfeldt's maw. A man next to Harry reared back, flopping like a gutted fish. It was Schammerhorn. He pushed himself up on both elbows, tucking in his chin to look down at the damage. He dropped back, and Harry held his hand. Bloody tobacco juice dribbled through his lips. "Well, Lootenant, guess the joke's still on me." It was important to him, that; dying game.

A sniper must have got up on one of the rooftops. Another slug found its mark, ripping across the blubber of Bramah's belly. He yowled, trying to close the tear. Haywood craned to see, showing enough of himself to let Vilberg put a bullet through his collar-bone.

Baxter was chanting curses in Afrikaans, as he fired steadily from cover behind a wall. Van Praage crouched near-by, silent, eyes narrowed to spot targets before he placed slow aimed shots. What felt like a red-hot poker scored Harry's upper arm, spinning him around. He fell, and another bullet kicked dirt in his face. Somebody heavy jumped on top of him.

"You cop a bad one, sir?"

Lascelles covered Harry's body with his own, protecting against the next sniper's round. He got up on one knee and loosed off an answering shot. Then his entire body jerked, and he slumped weakly. He sounded honestly surprised. "My giddy aunt! The blighters've pipped me!"

Harry rolled over, yanking the man's tunic open. A small blue hole dimpled Lascelle's chest high up. "You'll live." He snatched the man's cigarette, and dragged him by the collar behind a garden hedge. "Don't move from here!"

Harry pulled the other stick of dynamite from his boot-top. He shouted to the troopers, "Cover me!" He wormed his way to the corner of the house.

Ned tried to reason with him, "No soap! They'll get you for sure!"

Harry snapped the fuse to half length and ran into the street. Lead thrummed past his head, so close he felt its heat.

Swarte saw him, and the yellow stick he was holding. He bunted the shoulder-pad hard to slew the cannon in that direction. He knew the Tommy was still beyond the pom-pom's arc, but loosed off some rounds anyway. Desperately, he yelled to the loaders, "Quick! Swing the whole carriage left!"

Harry touched his fag to the short fuze and threw it underhand towards the thudding Nordenfeldt. Boschie laughed, reached out, catching it easily on the fly. Then the dynamite exploded in his hand, and tore apart the gun-crew. Half-deafened troopers and commandos squinted at each other through dirty brown smoke, rifles lowered in numb hands.

A muffled shout came from the road, where the postman's cart came into view led by the old Boer scout. He trotted ahead, waving his shawl like a flag. In the other hand, he held up a piece of paper.

"Vrede! Vrede!"

Peace

CHAPTER TWENTY-ONE

The half-naked soldiers sat in camp, chatting-up cooties. They carefully scanned their shirts, grunting with satisfaction now and then. "Got you, little bastard!" A few lucky troopers had a stub of lighted candle to do the job faster. You just ran the flame along a seam, and the lice popped and fizzed a treat. Since leaving Belfast, the men had seldom washed more than a lick-and-a-promise. Their clothes stank, already starting to fall apart from hard wear. There wasn't a man among them not infested with gray-backs, and they welcomed the leisure to pull off their shirts and seek what they may find.

Usually this chore had been done with a good deal of joking and laughter. But not today. Some of the patrol's most cheery voices had been stilled forever. They rested now in what had been the foxholes, earth filled in already, marked with four wooden crosses. Even confirmation that the war was really over made things seem worse, if anything. It was bitter to face loss of such good comrades hours after there had been no longer any need for their waste.

To overcome their gloom, Harry had kept his men busy at clearing up after the carnage. The Boer villagers were a resilient lot, quick to start repairing the shattering effects of the raid. Still, they were pleased by how readily the soldiers acted to help. Troopers cleared rubble in search of residents trapped underneath, handed out all their medical kits, and carried casualties to either the church mortuary or the baroness's first-aid station.

Even she, Papist that she was, proved to be more admirable than ever given credit for. Folk who had snubbed her months past now found time for shame at the way Neave immediately threw open her home to everyone, treating injuries of burghers and Brits alike. She briskly organized the village women into teams, allocating tasks to suit needs, from boiling water to ripping bandages or cleansing wounds.

Harry found Bethany on the von Gliewitz's front steps. She was dressing the cut knee of a stoical small boy, while helping soothe his tearful infant brother. Her face lit with joy at seeing him, but looked anxiously at his bloody sleeve.

"My prayers have been answered," she said simply.

"Same here."

He watched her finish the bandage and return the boys to their grateful mother. Then, "You work well with kids. I'll keep that in mind."

She gave a harassed smile. "Let's look at that arm."

The iodine made him jump, but she worked deftly to cover the wound with a bandage-pad. "Missed the bone, but you'll have a nasty scar there. Pity." Her fingers lightly touched his bare chest. "Your skin's perfect."

"Now, now, not in front of the children!" Neave teased from the doorway. She wore a crisp dress with the sleeves rolled up and an air of pleased competence. "I'm utterly exhausted!"

Harry thanked her for the good work she was doing, but the Baroness waved dismissively. "Everybody's pitching in. That's often the pity of things, needing sorrow itself to bring out the best in people." She touched his arm. "God be thanked you survived. All my brave talk last night, threatening you. Truth be told, I never in my life held a gun before."

"Now that really scares me." Harry smiled, "It could have gone off accidentally." A passing family called greetings, and he waved to them. "Folks have offered to billet my men in homes overnight. For rent, mind you, but it sure indicates a change in attitude."

Petta drove up at the reins of the spyder, grinning widely at Beth, but carefully greeting the three whites by name in turn. Neave said, "Yonder postilion awaits, and has done long enough. Time for making your departure."

"I don't know if I should leave just yet."

"Stuff and nonsense! You've helped enough. Take the lad home to be with his father. Hiram'll be beside himself with worry, not able to come and see you both himself. You've done all you can here, and besides, we can fit three patients in his room."

She waved for young Blenkarn to come out, and said brightly. "Well, you're looking fighting fit already, I must say. Though praise-be there's no need for any more of that particular activity hereabouts."

He did not respond, busy taking in how this rooinek stood close to his sister. These last months, Dirk's eyes had changed oddly. Their chitinous surface seemed to reflect light in a glaze that hid all thoughts and feelings.

Harry nodded as casually as he could, "Good to see you made it back in one piece. Or close to it."

The boy just sulked, and when Harry reached to give a hand he was shrugged off.

Beth said, "Don't be silly, Dirk. Let me, at least."

He did his best to hide flinches of pain, but had to lean on her heavily while he struggled to get aboard. Beth gave Harry a veiled glance, and allowed Dirk to lean sideways. Harry moved fast to save him, and the boy mumbled grudging thanks.

The two women embraced, and Lanyard held Swazi's head while Beth mounted. She said with forced gaiety, "From that sorry mule, Petta, maybe we should put Swazi between the shafts, instead."

"Those rustlers came calling again last night, boss-lady. Took some more cows and the rest of the horses but the sick one."

That reminded her. "Be sure to come tomorrow, Harry. Early as you can. I know Pa wants to see you. Marthe, too. Besides, I have a nice surprise for you." She sensed Dirk's glowering resentment.

"Sounds good. I have to go to the quarry, first, though.

Tell you what, meet me at the trail around noon, and we'll take a nice ride up there."

She blew him a kiss and followed the spyder out of town. Dirk stared grimly into space, ignoring Spitsdorpers who waved greetings. Many called good wishes to Hiram and Marthe, which drew Beth to worrying how the older pair were coping, left alone after all they had been through. Petta confirmed that travelers had already brought word to Vincennes about the commando raid and the armistice. He drove the mule as carefully as possible, seeing the kleinbaas wince at each jog of the wheels.

Suddenly, Dirk snarled in English, "So. While I was away fighting for our freedom, you were home taking it deep from one of them."

"How dare you be so horrid!" Her face drained, white with anguish. "And where did you hear such language?"

"From real men on the veld, patriots who expected their womenfolk to remain true!"

"Harry came back only a few days ago. For which you should be grateful. There's a lot you don't know."

"My slutty sister's a *kakie-boetie!* That I know."

"And, is a kakie-lover somehow lower than a kakie-killer? I love him, yes, and whatever differences we may have over the war will be our own cross to bear. It's none of your business, nor anyone else's!"

"It's been my business for months, so don't expect me to just roll over on my back for them now—like you!"

"Oh, grow up, and stop being such a self-centred boy! Instead, give thanks for how lucky you really are. You have survived terrible dangers, and come home to a family who prayed for you every day and love you dearly."

Petta could not understand English, but grasped their anger. He was glad to distract them, "Here's home, kleinbaas."

As they turned into the gates, she warned, "There have been hard times at the farm too, lately. Try not to make things any worse." She faltered, "And that thing you said about Harry and me . . . We never did."

Hiram looked nowhere near as upset as Beth expected. In fact, he was sitting at ease on the front stoep, drinking a sun-downer of tea of all things. Marthe sprang out of her chair, eager to greet the home-comers, but waiting to let Blenkarn limp down the steps first.

"Dada, dear!" Bethany hugged him tight. He was clean-shaven, wearing a fresh shirt, and even sported a white collar with a string tie.

"Thank you, Tannie," Bethany whispered as she embraced Marthe. Dirk started to climb down on his own, and the women rushed to help, clucking concern.

"I'm alright." Despite what he had been through, he felt the constraint of domesticity smothering him once again.

"Aw, stop acting the tough guy," Hiram said, and stopped himself from ruffling his son's hair. Taking the youngster's lead, neither male smiled, just shook hands and nodded, and said things like it was mighty fine to see you and good to be home.

"Look how the boy's grown!" Marthe said, not hugging because of his wounds. "Must be all that lazing around eating antelope steaks for breakfast."

When the two walked ahead with an identical limping gait, Marthe nudged Bethany. She called, "How's your hip feeling, Dirk?"

"Sore, but the nurse said it won't be permanent."

"Her opinion sounds all very well," Marthe said, "But we must get a proper doctor to look at you before long."

They talked him into having a rest before dinner. While it was being prepared, Beth described the horrific events of the day at Spitsdorp. Hiram watched his daughter without interrupting as she spoke calmly of surviving battle and narrow escapes. She did not mention Dirk's outburst and the handcuffs. When she finished, he said wryly, "Here we were thinking we'd sent you away to safety."

"It's all over now. And with the armistice, such troubles are ended forever."

"Maybe, but now we're under the English, there'll be many a new problem. On top of still trying to hold onto our property."

"It's not going to be bad as you fear. Harry says–."

"Yeah, I'd guess Harry says a lot, his side being top-dog at the moment."

"No, it's official. There's to be big subsidies for farmers. Millions in war reparations funds for losses in stock and property, to help us get back on our feet."

"Naw, if there ever is any funding, it'll more benefit that Goddam–!" He flashed Marthe an apologetic look. "I mean, that blasted Russian swindler. He holds debt paper that good as grants him ownership of Vincennes, signed and sealed in a lame-brained moment of desperation by yours truly."

"That creature shouldn't be allowed to live long enough to claim any land more than six feet deep!" Marthe's face went mottled with rage.

"It's okay, lambie." Hiram leaned across, patting her hand. "We spot him around here, he gets turned over to that army cop for sure."

"Police, jail, whatever!" Marthe spluttered. "Even behind bars, he could still hire a lawyer and steal the property." Her pale blue eyes were moist, something Beth had never seen. "That devil's capable of arranging any sin. He's better dead!" Tannie rushed into the kitchen, raising her voice at cook.

Bethany joined her, glad of the clatter of pots and servants to cover what she needed to say. "Is it as well between you two as it seems, Tannie?"

"Hiram and I have agreed we'll never speak again of what happened in the barn." She straightened her back stiffly. "He's a fine man, your Pa."

"And all the better for you taking him in hand lately."

Almost defiantly, Marthe met the girl's gaze. "While

you were gone, we, we've come to a sort of arrangement. To wed. If you don't object."

"Object?" Beth squeezed Marthe happily, imagining her as a step-mother. "Why that would be the most wonderful thing!"

"No greater than you and Harry coming to your senses. He'll make a good husband, even if he is a rooinek. The sort who'll never let you down." She lifted the top from a huge meat pie, and added slyly, "Worth more than his weight in any gold."

"Oh, we've given up on that hidden treasure story. We must get on with life now. But it's going to be hard for him and me at times, I think," Beth sighed. "No Afrikaner can forget overnight all what's happened these last three years."

"Including you least of all," Marthe warned. "Any time you two have a lover's quarrel over the slightest thing, expect the past to be brought up as well."

"I think we'll be able to handle that. It's how friends and neighbors may react to my marrying a kakie that worries me. Not for myself, for Pa and you."

"Bugger them, bugger them all!" Marthe blurted in strongly accented English.

"Tannie, what would the predikant say!" Bethany laughed and threw her arms around Marthe. The servant girls giggled with her, without the slightest notion why, just to share her pleasure.

"I mean it. Hiram and me'll never heed any spite over having a Tommy son-in-law. Nor should you. But be prepared that from now on, this war'll be chewed over for ages. But politics, hah, nothing more than back-fence gossip! Just grab hold of your beau, live your life, and ignore the rest, I say." Marthe clapped her hands for servants to serve food in the big dining-room tonight, and Beth let her lead the way.

Dirk came downstairs slower than he would have liked,

but determined to take his place at the table. Hiram took care to treat him with the respect of a grown man, reading the stamp of experiences beyond the youth's years. During the meal, they gently drew him out, encouraging him to talk of his life on the veld. Dirk only vaguely remembered an officer stopping the bayonet-practice, being left for dead, and clambering on that spent horse. He tried to explain, then interrupted himself, "Ag, you wouldn't understand."

"Perhaps not, but I know someone who would," Beth suggested gently. "Harry Lanyard."

He looked at her in long silence, then nodded reluctantly. "Maybe. At least he knows what it was like out there." After her brother went exhaustedly to bed, Beth sat with Hiram on the stoep in the cool of night. "So, are you and Harry going to get hitched, daughter?"

"Well, we've never actually discussed things that far."

"About time the pair of you did, then. This place could do with a no-nonsense guy around to help run things. It's, uh, kind of good timing."

He hummed and hah'd for a minute or two, until she mercifully told him she knew of the change about to take place in his own life and that she thoroughly supported him. It amused and touched her how much he seemed to need her approval. He cleared his throat, and husked, "You think your mother would mind?"

Beth knelt beside him, and put her head in his lap. "Oh, Dada, her spirit's probably been wondering for years when you'd get around to it!" They laughed together, and wept a little, too, and then she went up to bed.

As Hetti showed the way with a candle, they heard Marthe's raised voice, "Hiram, I hope you're not sneaking another cigar out there! It's well past time you turned in." That loving call helped Beth manage to push aside nightmare images of rifle-fire and blood. She went to sleep with a smile on her face.

CHAPTER TWENTY-TWO

Pleasure stayed with her next morning, glowing at the thought of being with Harry in a couple of hours, and hurrying through breakfast to get to the stables. She led the unsteady mare out, holding its bridle firmly, all the while speaking English in a soothing voice, "There's a good girl. Easy does it. At least Simius has started to feed you up, even if he's neglected your grooming."

She tethered it in the paddock, and gently stroked the matted neck. "Still, now." The horse ceased quivering, and stood more calmly, its stare roving the far hills.

"That's better, you'll be seeing him soon enough." Beth unrolled the grooming kit, stiff brushes, curry-combs, and wiping rags. "But first we have to make you look pretty again, don't we?"

She combed out the mane, untangling caked mud and leaves. Then she started brushing hard, sweeping from neck to tail in the direction the hair lay, snagging free clumps from the neglected pelt. The worst cleaned off, she went back again, with a finer comb, brushing and wiping until the mare's chestnut coat gleamed.

"Now, don't you look like a nice surprise?" She made sure there was feed available, as Simius was nowhere to be seen. He was still weak, next to useless since that crack on the head. He and Hetti still could scarcely believe their good fortune that Lt. Lanyard had wangled a hundred pounds' payment to them out of the reward fund.

Dirk and Marthe stood watching from the verandah as Hiram rode away with Petta at the reins. He still hoped to find that some of those missing cows had eluded the rustlers, but took his Winchester along, just in case. Then Beth came with her horse, and Marthe put her hands on her hips at sight of the jodhpurs. Any woman in britches was an abomination to her, and she was never shy of saying so.

"You're not parading around like that in front of Harry, are you? Bad enough you'll be out there with him, un-chaperoned!"

"Oh, come on, Marthe. You know Harry better than that."

"He's a man isn't he? Besides, it's you I'm worried about, not him! Flaunting yourself like that, off alone, and not even engaged."

"Don't be so old-fashioned, Tannie. Anyway, if that's what bothers you, these keep a girl safer than the longest skirt!"

Marthe would not be reassured, and Dirk groaned as the pair raised their voices to bicker over female etiquette, like any true mother and daughter. To escape their squabbling, he took a handful of sugar-lumps and limped away to the paddock. A rat pattered from the barn, then saw him and crouched, not knowing which way to run. He felt none of the old urge, just waved an arm. "Scoot, you!" It darted out of sight.

The mare stood with its neck draped over a rail, restlessly searching the horizon. At first sight of Dirk, she started towards him, then paused, disappointed. She was looking stronger already from the rest and food, and somebody had given her a rub-down. Vaguely, he heard Marthe calling goodbye to Beth, and keep a level head, mind.

He held out the sugar, "Here you, a token of thanks for saving my hide."

The mare munched the sweet cubes from his palm, her eyes still watching the distance. The rich horse-smell brought Dirk a sudden wave of nostalgia for his adventures on the veld, and so many commando brothers who were gone from him forever.

Marthe was at it again, turning her tongue against Simius this time, shouting something about he should have told her earlier. Dirk leaned on the fence, and for the first time began to wonder how he would spend the rest of this life that had been given back to him.

Marthe broke Dirk's daydreaming, bustling to his side, more agitated than ever. "Quick, there's something you must do! Right this very instant!" She looked badly upset, shaking him by the arm when he just stared at her, puzzled.

"Can't it wait 'til we fetch a kaffir?"

"No! This has to be done by you! Come, come!" She pulled him towards the barn. "You're the only one able!"

He grabbed her wrists. "What's got into you, Tannie?"

"That evil Russian, he's back! He must be dealt with!"

"What d'you expect me to do? Ag, let that English policeman tend to it."

"No time!" Marthe darted inside the barn, then halted, and Dirk distinctly saw gooseflesh rising on her bare forearms. She shrugged off her revulsion of the place, and reached behind the manger. She pushed the dusty little .22 into his hands. "It's you who must stop him!"

She gabbled reasons why; that Nikolai intended to foreclose and steal Dirk's birthright, how the Russian had invaded Beth's room, and goaded his bandits to violate Hetti. Anger twisted Dirk's face, but he still hesitated, looking reluctantly from the pop-gun to the spavined horse.

Marthe saw he was not moved enough, and braced herself to say more. "That's not all. Those dirty pigs of his took me in the barn as well. You're old enough to know what they did."

He stared into her agonized expression, reading the shame and stolen pride. Dirk knew he must do this one last thing. He grabbed a saddle and threw it onto the sick horse, ignoring the way it flinched.

"Poor beast isn't much good yet." But he found himself even more caught up in her frenzy, and tightened the cinch. He tried to mount, felt the stitches tear, and slid back, gasping. Marthe linked her hands for his boot, and heaved up, strong as a man.

He gathered the reins, "Where do I find him?"

"Headed straight for the quarry, Simius thinks. You must hurry! Beth is riding there, too, with Harry. You have to warn them. If you can't manage it, maybe he can take care of the Russian."

"No kakie's allowed to do any job for me."

When Beth and Harry had met on the trail, they laughed at how she had to lean down from Swazi to kiss him on the little pony. He looked up at her, the sunlight shining on her spun-gold hair. "Gee, Beth, you look swell!"

"Oh, thank you kind sir." She fluttered a hand over her heart. "But such eloquent flattery might turn a simple Boer country-girl's head!"

"Okay, I should have said you're gorgeous. Pretty as a Gibson Girl." She started to laugh at his floundering. "Damn it, you're the answer to a soldier's prayer!"

"And I can imagine what that would be for!" She chuckled and leaned to give him another fond peck. They cantered along the trail, holding hands at an angle, murmuring as young lovers do, with many a pause for kisses. For propriety's sake, they moved apart when they occasionally met quarry workers straggling along the road home to Spitsdorp.

The men explained they were given the day off to see to their loved ones in the ruined village, and asked her for details about the state of their relatives she may know. Some also quizzed Harry, "Is it really true, Officer, the war's done with?"

"Yeah, it's officially over."

They would nod seriously, and say things like, "Good, so long as the railway doesn't start cutting back on overtime pay."

The last man called, "Maybe now we'll soon see the back of all you soldiers."

When the trail was empty again, Harry said, "This is no darn good." He stopped the horses, and swung up behind

Beth. He put his arms around her waist. "That's better."

She flicked the reins for Swazi to move on, then leaned back with a sigh. "Um, much."

He nuzzled her hair, inhaling the sweetness. "Most of my men can't wait to sail away, but I don't intend to leave here, ever."

"Oh, and what's to keep you?"

"Only the small matter that I love you," he said.

"*Ek het jou lief, skat,*" she sighed. "I have loved you from the moment we first met, darling." She was aware of his strong thighs pressing against her buttocks, rocking with the horse's gait, and felt his arousal stiffen.

His lips caressed her neck, then he groaned, "Soon as I settle things at the quarry, though, I have to take my patrol back to Belfast. Tomorrow."

"So soon?" Then, "Of course, with the wounded."

"Yeah, and I won't be a soldier much longer. My commission being 'For Duration of Hostilities Only', the army will demob me pronto." His lips brushed her neck. "I could be back here in a few weeks. If you want me to."

She leaned into him, "You know I do." His hand cupped her breast, and she reached to hold him there. They rode in silence, enjoying each other's closeness. "I've had to do some stuff out here I'd sooner forget," he said after a while. "But one thing I've never been ashamed of is how much I love you."

She put her hand behind his head, drawing his lips close for a long moment. Swazi seemed to sense something, and halted. Serious as could be, Harry gulped and swallowed, then blurted, "Honey, soon's I come back, will you marry me?"

"Dear Harry, you must know I will!" She kissed him happily. "After all I'd said, I was terrified maybe you'd never want to."

"One way and another, I've been scared I'd never get the chance."

Beth laughed, "Darling, how could we have let a mere war pull us apart?" She clucked Swazi to start walking again, while they clung to each other along the trail.

Both were surprised when they reached the turn-off, and he got back on his pony before they rode in. The quarry was almost deserted, only a few men gossiping around a campfire, and the sound of chopping wood somewhere among the wrecked wagons. They fell silent, watching the pretty woman, and even the unseen axe-man stopped. Harry and Beth dismounted, leading their horses carefully past jagged scrap metal.

A voice hailed, "Hey, if it ain't the Canuck!" Akesson waved from his kitchen chair beside the hut. "And with a mighty good-looking gal in tow, this time!"

From his thick tongue, he had been celebrating for some time. "Come and join the party!" He took a long pull from a bottle, replaced a stogie between his teeth, and stood up unsteadily to bow. Introductions were made, and Bethany's shared American heritage loudly appreciated. "In that case, doubly-welcome, young lady, and sit yourself to home."

At sound of their voices, Dirk stopped about fifty yards from the quarry entrance. The mare's ears pricked forward, and she whickered eagerly, straining to go on despite the bit. He slid off and dropped the reins, expecting her to stay put. Instead, she cantered away into the quarry. Dirk was too weak to catch up, and the horse went far ahead of him. He almost showed himself at the entrance, but managed to duck into some bushes that ringed the pit.

Akesson dusted off another chair for Bethany in the shade. He asked about the peace treaty, and looked disappointed when Harry had no extra details to offer.

"Well, some news does travel up here." The Swede gave a wink, "I hear tell a couple of my fire-crackers came in handy yesterday."

"Yeah, sorry, that's partly why I came. To repay the costs, whatever."

"Ah, forget it. Me and Mister Alfred Nobel were glad to help. Even if his product does blow up one half the world to finance his Peace Prize in the other!" He roared with laughter, "Latest Stockholm joke." Catching Beth's half-frown, he said, "Cheer up, Miss. Your side made a mighty fine effort."

She shook off thoughts of a lost cause, and cheered herself by sharing her glad news. She said proudly, "We've made our own armistice just now. Harry's asked me to marry him."

"Well, I sure hope you said yeah!" Akesson boomed another good-natured laugh. "Hey, really great day! War over, you two getting hitched. Me, I'm giving up booze, quitting this lousy job, and heading back to the good old U.S. of A. 'Calls for an all round gen-u-ine celebration." He belched and wiped his sleeve across the bottle's neck. "Got me some glasses around here someplace."

"Er, thank you, but if you had some water instead."

"Sure thing, Miss. How about you, feller?"

Harry shook his head and strolled away. "Mind if I just look around again? I got to wondering what might be inside that old tank."

"Nah, one of the first places I looked, way back. Nothing but rusty sludge in there."

"What in the hell?" Akesson twisted to stare towards the sudden clatter of hooves. A runaway horse galloped into view, skittered to a halt, then weaved towards the men by the fire. She paused there uncertainly, treading ground, staring around wildly.

Despite her condition, Harry recognized her right away. "Molly! Molly-girl!"

He ran to her, calling incredulously, "Where'd you appear from all of a sudden, huh?" He kept repeating her name, choked with pleasure as he patted her neck and stroked the velvety muzzle. She whinnied, high-pitched ecstacy, tossing her head, bunting Harry's chest

For the moment not caring how Molly had arrived,

Bethany watched, eyes brimming. She turned to the big Swede. "He has her back. Isn't it beautiful?"

Akesson grinned, and lifted the bottle in a toast. He took a long final pull, grass flakes swirling in the clear liquor. Beth saw, and her smile faded. "Where did you get that?"

"Same Bohunk again, rooting through our crappy old junk-carts this time."

She whirled to scream, "Harry, *pasop*! Watch out, he's here! Nikki!"

Lanyard did not seem to hear, still preoccupied with Molly. Beth ran towards him, screaming now. "Take cover, Harry! Nikki's around, close-by!"

Dirk stopped crawling through the thicket when she shouted, and saw the Russian suddenly rise up from the wagon well. He still held a hatchet in his hand. Harry finally heard what Beth was calling. He whirled around, going for his gun, but slowed by his wounded arm. The Russian threw the hand-axe, and it bounced off Molly's saddle.

"Drop it Harry, or Beth gets dead!" Nikki stood with one hand on hip, in elegant target-range stance, the Nagant levelled at her.

The labourers fell over each other, scampering for cover. Akesson jumped up, spraddle-legged. "Oi, none of that in my quarry!"

The long *wacht-en-beetje* thorns snagged Dirk's clothes, and he struggled to wrench himself free of their hooked grip. Barbs tore his hands and face while he tried to raise the little rifle, but it seemed hopelessly entangled.

Harry let the Colt fall, and stepped towards Bethany. "That's far enough," Nikki said. "No romantic last embrace, I'm afraid."

"Why don't you just beat it out of here? The war's over, no charges will ever be laid. What difference will anything make now?"

"What difference in anything?" Nikolai sneered. "My, you sound almost Russian, Harry." He waggled the gun at Bethany. "A poor second choice, when you could have had the genuine article. Me, an aristocrat, not this clod-hopper."

Dirk wrenched the Marlin free of the thorns. He pulled at the slide, trying to jack a round into the chamber. His weak fingers slid on the ribbed wood, unable to squeeze tight enough. He tensed as best he could to force the loading-grip back, willing it to move. Then its catch yielded and the slide double-clicked, forced a cartridge home, and cocked the rifle.

"In the name of God, Nikki, can't you simply leave us be?" She spoke levelly, a straightforward question, knowing it was too late to beg.

"Allow you both to live, you mean? Give Harry the last laugh?"

"Who cares?" Lanyard said, "Anyway, there's a dozen witnesses. You wouldn't get ten miles."

"I won't anyway. My time has run out." The Russian dabbed the blood-poison in his cheek. "Your little whore's done for me already, but she's going to hell before I do."

Dirk raised the gun weakly, pointing at Nikolai's head. The foresight wavered, drifting off target, and he could not line up the rear notch with the aiming-tip. His stomach wounds were agony, and blood and sweat ran into his eyes. He had to lift a hand off the butt to wipe so he could see.

Nikolai said, "No use, Harry, I win this last round. It was here all the time, you know. Right where senile old Muller said. In his wagon, under a false floor."

"You found the gold? So, just grab all you can carry and take off."

Dirk's finger froze, no longer able to do what it had in the past to scores of living creatures from stray dogs to subalterns.

"Is that what I should do, Harry?" Nikki threw back his head and laughed, jeering at them and himself, enjoying the futility. "Hah! Here's our fabled Kruger's treasure! Look!" He threw handfuls of water-rotted banknotes towards them.

Bile rose in Dirk's throat and he sobbed, then half-screamed, "Damn you, anyway!" He pulled the trigger. Too much of a jerk. The muzzle jumped, and the bullet missed Nikolai. Instead, it punched into a naphtha barrel behind him. A thin jet of white flame spurted out, hissing like an angry snake.

Nikki barely flinched. He thumbed back the hammer of his shiny pistol and took deliberate aim at Bethany. "Time to die, you Boer bitch!"

She turned towards Harry, needing him to be the last she would see on this earth. Quite steadily, Beth said, "Darling, I'll always ..."

Harry dived forward, hugging to shield her. The Russian adjusted aim, and shouted a last mockery, "So, two for one bullet!"

His knuckle whitened on the trigger. Then the naphtha barrels ignited with a blue flash. A great billow of red and black flame cremated Feliks Nikolai and blew his shroud of worthless Transvaal banknotes burning into the sky.

CHAPTER TWENTY-THREE

It was a bright bustling morning in Spitsdorp; men hammering and sawing at rebuilding, the street crowded with families chatting alongside the troopers who saddled horses. Busy as he was organizing the departure, Harry took in the clump of Boers around Vilberg on the front verandah.

The cornet's heavily bandaged leg was propped up by a stool. Dirk went over to pay his respects, but saw the talk was serious, and held his tongue. Advokaat Boergaard seemed to be holding court. "To paraphrase von Clausewitz, politics is the continuation of war by other means." The men thought about that, then had a quiet chuckle.

He went on, "The British always win wars but lose the peace. They'll soon leave us to our own devices, running this new corner of their Empire any way we choose. But if we're not careful, the stay-at-home softies in Pretoria will take over the Volksraad at the expense of us who did all their fighting for them."

He looked into each bearded intent face. "It's up to veterans like us to make sure that the right people get elected. Ones holding *'Wit Baasskap'* ideals. Only total white supremacy can keep the kaffirs in their place, and prevent too many uitlanders arriving to thin pure Afrikaner blood. You would be fine as one of our voices, Laurens."

Vilberg shook his head. "All right for lawyers like you, Gabriel, who know the political back-room game. Besides, you came through the war whole." He pointed at his shattered leg. "I'll be lucky to survive the army surgeon's knife. Even then, I'd not be much of a prospect for standing to make speeches."

"Ag, what better badge of honour for a candidate than a battlefield peg-leg? All the more reason for folk to vote for you. We thought enough of you to lead us on the veld, so why not be our elected politician next?" The commandos rumbled their agreement, and pressed forward to urge him.

Ino murmured to Boergaard. "I have to get on my way to Natal now, friend. Before the locals come after me about shooting that two-arsed jackal of a Burgemeester. But if you ever need a strong arm to help at election time, just send for me." He shook hands and slipped away through the crowd.

Glumly, Boergaard watched him go, then turned back to widen his argument. "To see how it's being done, just look at crafty Jannie Smuts. At it already, smarming around Lord Milner, using all the trickery he learned in London. Doesn't let a little detail like having burned his way across Cape Province stop him changing alliances overnight now the war's over." He snapped his finger. "You could get a seat easy as that!"

"Well, let's just see how I feel after the operation." Vilberg nodded at Dirk. "Now there's the sort our country's really going to need. Young men who've proved they have guts. You've a big future ahead, if you put your mind to it, penkop."

"Me?"

"Surely. A good war record, notches on your gun, able to take care of bandits, too. Big land-owner family into the bargain. By what Gabriel says, you're perfect to sit in the Rikstaad one day."

Dirk made a face, but felt suddenly purposeful again. Boergaard said, "Just think about it, the pair of you. We'll talk again."

The commandos made their gruff farewells for now, vowing to stay in touch. They left the verandah slowly, most with no place in particular to go. Vilberg said to Dirk, "If we both end up in politics, man, may the Lord have mercy on our souls." He raised his foot and grimaced, "Meantime, give me a hand aboard Milner's meat-wagon."

Man, his veld-cornet had called him, like an equal. Dirk put Laurens in among the wounded kakies, and went to stand tall beside Hiram at the verandah rail. Marthe was wearing a new kappie, brightly flowered as any young girl's.

Scayles came hobbling down the steps from the von Gliewitz house and Harry gave him an arm to lean on. Deneys and Neave hovered to help, and she said, "You'll be sore for a while yet, but right as rain in no time." She handed a cushion to the MP, and dimpled, "To rest your poor brains on the bumpy ride." He had to clear his throat twice before thanking her.

"Oh, you're entirely welcome, Mister Policeman. But if you're ever stationed in Ireland, you might think of me first before you act rashly anytime." She wiggled fingers to Harry, "Toodle-oo for a bit." Baroness von Gliewitz skipped back to duty inside her cottage hospital.

Deneys looked elegant in a baronial striped shirt and tailored trousers. He offered his palm to Scayles. "Should I be making tracks for a secret hideaway, you think?"

"No need." Glen shook hands briefly. "What you did was as a serving officer in wartime. The MPs'll take no official action against you now."

Deneys helped him settle into the ambulance cart, then Scayles said thoughtfully, "There is one thing, though. I'll have to identify you by name as the spy. Just to clear up the case. Sha'n't cause you any botheration, but it might help boost my record a bit."

Osseboom and Lanyard swapped an amused glance, then shook hands firmly. "You two heading back to Bloemfontein?"

"Yes, I still have to get my OFS army discharge. Besides, Neave's already set on walking down the aisle at Sacred Heart Cathedral." Deneys smiled wryly. "Expect an invite next spring to a ceremony only slightly less grand than the Coronation."

Carolus raised his hat stiffly among his flock, and Harry nodded back. "The Predikant's going to be busy at his altar, too."

"Yes, at least something good's come out of this

madness. Neave and I'll surely come to watch you tie the knot."

"Great, look forward to it."

The ambulance cart was filling up with Boers and soldiers mixed together. McKay lay there gray-faced, but cheerful enough to josh with bandaged Haywood and Bramah about the likelihood of early demob and passage home.

Bethany hitched her blue chambray skirt and stepped up on the hub to reach Lascelles. "He told me what you did, probably saved his life." She kissed him on both cheeks. "I want you to know, if I ever have a daughter, we'll call her Margery."

"Oh, I say, rah-ther! Then I'll jolly-well hop back to see her!"

"Hey, meisie, that's enough canoodling with these rough squaddies. You never know where they've been!" Harry looped his good arm around Beth's waist to lift her down, and held her close. "Time to go."

Bertil handed the pony's reins to him, and he raised a foot to the stirrup. Beth said, "God speed, my love."

He swung into the saddle. "Thanks for taking care of Molly while I'm gone."

"She has a home at Vincennes for life. Besides, it'll give you a reason for coming back." They smiled at each other.

"Then get ready for a long honeymoon. I want to show you off to my folks in BC."

From the stoep, Marthe called, "You better hurry, too. So we can have a double wedding."

"No more'n a month, Lanyard," Hiram growled down at him. "I don't aim to wait any longer making up for lost time." Marthe went pink with pleasure, and linked his elbow.

Bethany whispered, "Quicker you leave, sooner you return to me, sweetheart." Harry scooped her up in his arm, and they kissed for a long moment. His troopers whooped and whistled in their saddles, as townsfolk laughed, clapping.

One boy waved Jiggy's plumed hat, "'Bye, Tommies!"

"Don't forget us 'Canucks too, kid." Bramah called.

"Then, so long, cowboys!"

"Hear that, guys? At least try and behave as if you're still in the army." Sergeant Coveyduck allowed himself a faint smile, and chivvied them into straight column of twos. "Remember now, bags of swank."

Lt. Harry Lanyard looked along their ranks, his last patrol, the finest men he'd ever led. He called, "Let's go! And give us a tune, Bronco."

He snapped up a parting salute to the crowd, then waved his palm ahead. "For-waard!" Ponies snorted eagerly, harnesses jingling, and their hooves padded off down the dusty street.

Black and white alike, people of Spitsdorp found themselves joining in with the Canadians who rode away singing,

"It's soldiers of the Queen, my lads,

Who've been, my lads, who've seen, my lads.

And when we say we've always won, and they ask how it is done, We'll proudly point to every one, of England's soldiers of the Queen!"

THE END.

AUTHOR'S POSTSCRIPT

Kruger's gold really did exist, of course; looted from the Transvaal banks and hidden as I described. Most of it was spent at the time for Boer supplies, but at least seven valuable hoards of the hidden bullion are known to have been found. Even while this book was going to press, over 4,000 Kruger gold coins were dug up by a Zulu family on a farm near Ermelo, Mpumalanga, in June, 2001. It is officially believed that thousands more Kruger pounds could still lie buried on the farm, where they were transported by two wagons in 1900. Other portions probably remain hidden elsewhere in South Africa, still being searched for by hopeful treasure-hunters every year. It is not likely that ex-President Paul Kruger himself profited much from the gold. When he died in Clarens, Switzerland, on 14 July, 1904, Oom Paul's personal estate was worth £35,381.

Howard's Canadian Scouts was also real, one of a score of temporary units raised by the British army for mobile anti-guerilla duties during the Second Anglo-Boer War. My fictional Lt. Harry Lanyard, his troopers, and their Boer counterparts are typical of the redoubtable men and women who took part in that bitter campaign.

In telling their story, I have avoided 'presentism', that trendy urge to impose latter-day politically correct views on people who lived a century ago. Rather, I portray the social attitudes, behavior, and prejudices as they actually were back then, without any retrospective sermonizing. Though the lead characters and the burghers of Spitsdorp, and the town itself, in this novel are imaginary, they are portrayed in as authentic a manner as possible. All historical personages included speak their own style of words, and act as they did in real life. Further background information on them and their era may be found in the bibliography that follows.

KRUGER'S GOLD stems from my own life-long interest in the South African War, starting as a child when I first listened to stories told by elderly veterans. Later, I enjoyed the reminiscences of one-time cavalryman Bill Hawkins, and my wife's indomitable grandfather, ex-Hussar William Collins, Snr. What they shared about old sweats' personal experiences and contemporary views eventually helped enliven this tale.

Of many people who helped me with research, I would particularly like to thank: Denise Ross, Researcher, National Archives of Canada, Ottawa, for ferreting out extra details; Jean Beater, Head, British War Graves Subdivision, South African Monuments Council, Pretoria, who showed me the way to Gat Howard's final resting-place in the Garden of Remembrance at Wakkerstroom; Herman Labuschagne, of Hoedspruit, Transvaal, a proud Afrikaner and descendant of commandos, who was always generously helpful to this *rooinek*; Maj.Gen. Philip Pretorius, Director, South African National Museum of Military History, Saxonwold, for his courtesy and suggestions; Rev. Stowell Kessler, Petrus Steyn, for his unique study of the black concentration camps; John Dovey, University of Stellenbosch, for his knowledge of South African military units; and Ken Hallock, Idaho, a fellow Boer War enthusiast.

Warm appreciation is due the late Ann Melvin, RCMI Librarian, and Gregory Loughton, RCMI Museum Curator, and several fellow-Members of the Institute, Toronto, for those enjoyable chats about the era. I am also grateful to LCol Mike Kampman, Commanding Officer, and Maj. Tim Datchko, Second-in-Command, Royal Canadian Dragoons, for the Regimental Guild's gracious permission to reproduce Peter Archer's vivid painting.

Other people and places that deserve mention are: the wondrous Imperial War Museum, London; National Army Museum, Chelsea; Durham Light Infantry Museum, Aykley Heads, Durham; Royal Roads Military College, Colwood,

BC, which regrettably has since been closed; Canadian War Museum, Ottawa; Australian War Museum, Canberra; Canadian Scottish Regimental Museum, Victoria, British Columbia; University of Victoria Library; Greater Victoria Public Library; Metropolitan Toronto Central Reference Library; Robarts Rare Books Library, University of Toronto; Library Of Congress, Washington, DC; and the resourceful US Army Center For Military History, Carlisle Barracks, PA. As well, I owe a good deal to many previous writers, whose books, newspapers, memoirs, and documents helped me understand things better.

Most of all, thanks are due my ever-patient wife, Beverley, who encouraged me yet again and put up with my long mental absences far away on the veld. My dear friend of 15 years, Molly, our border collie, was part of the book's creation as well. Her merry companionship lightened every hour during its writing, then sadly her bright eyes closed for the last time the day after this manuscript was completed.

Though few people outside South Africa today may know much about the Second Anglo-Boer War, it was of great political and military significance at the time. It warned of coming shifts in world power, and gave the complacent British High Command some sharp shocks. Unexpected humiliations included early defeats on the battlefield, a hard-fought six month campaign to force Boer government troops to surrender, then a further two year struggle against guerilla resistance before full victory was gained.

The experience revealed serious inadequacies in British equipment, training, tactics, and medical services. Such lessons learned at bloody cost forced army improvements in time to be applied in the Great War with Germany just 12 years later. To triumph in South Africa over a much smaller enemy, Great Britain eventually found itself needing to engage almost 400,000 troops and spend £200 million in prosecution of a three-year-long conflict. A further £12 million was spent on post-war reparations and rebuilding of devastated areas.

Immediately the United Kingdom first became embroiled, there were enthusiastic offers of men and money from the white Dominions of the British Empire. Ties of blood and loyalty to the Mother Country were still strong, which at first inspired unquestioning overseas support for its cause, with thousands volunteering to join the fray far away. Lofty generals who were at first reluctant to accept them, soon found that hard-riding Canucks, Kiwis, and Aussies proved more effective than conventional soldiers when it came to irregular warfare against like-minded Boer outdoorsmen.

Considering that over 8,000 Canadians went to fight in South Africa, it is surprising how the conflict has faded from historical memory in this country. Even among those who are aware, there is an apologetic squeamishness about Canada having once supported Britain against Afrikaner independence. In contrast, Australia has a strongly preserved relish of its troops' involvement, perhaps another sign of the sturdy sense of national identity Down-Under.

While Imperial forces were overwhelmingly large, the South African colonial combatants on each side were closely matched in numbers of men under arms. The generally Loyalist population of Cape Province numbered 579,000, and Natal had 97,000 people. Population of the South African Republic (Transvaal) was about 300,000 and that of Orange Free State was 145,000. Their combined forces seldom exceeded 66,000 men in the field. Of them, 30,000 stubbornly fought on after General Cronje's surrender and President Kruger's departure in 1900.

In addition to the British army, Boer republicans faced 56,000 Loyalist troops in 188 local volunteer regiments and units, composed mainly of colonists of British origin but also including numbers of Afrikaners. Even though they played a significant role and suffered over 3000 deaths, these South Africans loyal to the Crown seem forgotten now, strangely little-mentioned in later accounts of the war. Other opponents of the Boers were the National Scouts, Afrikaners serving Britain as counter-guerillas, plus 20,000 burghers in British service. Such "joiners" were detested as traitors by the commandos, who customarily executed any they caught.

Yet where the main opponents were concerned, it could be called "the last of the gentlemen's wars". For the most part it was fought cleanly, both sides usually treating each other's wounded and prisoners with decency. What made the conflict grimmer were the concentration camps and the divided loyalties which fueled a civil war.

Friends and families were torn apart by their differing convictions; one notable incidence being that of Boer General Pieter de Wet, who changed sides after capture and then led the National Scouts against his brother, General Christian de Wet. Eventually, up to twenty percent of Afrikaner males fought for the British, as an increasing number of burghers became convinced that continuing the war was ruinous folly. During the final year, as many Afrikaners were in British service as those who defiantly called themselves "bitter-enders".

That some Boers fought against each other may now seem unpalatable to the folklore of a solidly united Chosen People; lost behind fond tales of unbroken national resistance against countless outside enemies. In reality, the war only aggravated some of the divisions within Afrikanerdom over politics and religion that had existed for decades before the war, and persisted long after. However, all Afrikaners justly celebrate the gallant Commandos, who resolutely carried on their struggle for two years against huge odds. Their name became so synonymous with tough military raiders, it was later adopted by their admiring foe, the British army.

Of all things, Afrikaners are never able to forget or forgive the infamous camps. The British set up 50 "refugee concentration" camps for whites in South Africa, which at peak held 116,572 people, nearly a quarter of the Boer republics' total population. They were established for entirely military reasons: to deny roving commandos of aid, comfort, food, or shelter, and break the will of their resistance, and also to protect the families of handsuppers from bitterenders' revenge. Whatever the original intentions, though, the final consequences were hideously different.

These hellish places stain Britain's national record, but there is positively no evidence of any deliberate intention to exterminate the Boer people. Yet that conspiracy theory is perpetuated, however mistaken. Ground glass in food bowls was lately still being displayed in at least one museum, solemnly labeled as artefacts of English perfidy. False props aside, the harsh fact remains that meager food, lack of sanitation, fatal diseases, and insufficient medical care in the incompetently-run British encampments caused the same horrific results as could have any deliberate malice.

After the enormity was finally exposed by the crusade of Emily Hobhouse and recommendations for changes were made by the Fawcett Ladies Commission, public outrage in Britain brought improvements, though far too late to save many innocent victims. An authenticated total of 27,927 civilian internees died from diseases, exposure, and malnutrition, mainly women and children. Understandably, memory of their martyrdom still rankles to this day, and stands enshrined in the massive Vrouwen Monument at Bloemfontein.

Boer women endured privations with astounding courage, steadfastly loyal to their menfolk who carried on the fight even though it prolonged the suffering of their own families. Boer combatants had far fewer casualties; 7,100 killed in action. An accurate total of their additional losses from diseases on the veld or while held prisoner in Ceylon, Bermuda, Portugal, and St. Helena seems unavailable.

Disease was the big killer of British troops as well, felling two thirds of their total 20,721 dead in the South

African War. Military non-battle fatalities perished from some of the same epidemic diseases that struck hapless civilians in camps. Much retrospective criticism is voiced now against the army medical service, overlooking the reality that no effective cures against tropical diseases even existed back then.

Fuller knowledge has come out recently about the extent of suffering also by black Africans during the war. Destruction of farms and interruption of mining severely affected the livelihood of native labourers and their dependents. About 115,000 of them were forced to take refuge in 66 ramshackle camps for blacks, where conditions were even worse than those endured by Boers. Historians have identified 14,154 black people who died in camps, and estimate that up to 15,000 more may have lost their lives elsewhere through starvation, illness, or atrocities.

Though officially denied, both British and Afrikaners issued weapons to blacks at times. Boers did so far less, as to them the very idea of an armed native was abhorrent. Some 10,000 black after-riders took the field with Boer forces as personal servants, and helped their employers in combat by caring for horses and rifles.

To imagine how things may have gone for Harry and Beth in later life, let us look at what happened afterwards. When the Vereeniging Treaty was signed in 1902, hopes were voiced that the two groups of white South Africans would live in harmony from then on. However, memories of the concentration camps, civil war, and other old scores entrenched a lingering dislike between Afrikaners and Anglos. This mutual animosity diverted their attention from the rising tide of black aspirations and its inevitable future outcome.

In 1910, the four colonies merged into the Union of South Africa, a self-governing member of the British Commonwealth of Nations. Union troops of all origins later fought valiantly alongside Britain in two world wars, led by the remarkable Jan Christian Smuts. A commando general at twenty-eight, he eventually became a British Field Marshal, member of the Imperial Privy Council, and was twice elected Prime Minister of South Africa. Smuts was considered by some to be a hero but a traitor by others of his countrymen, and his internationalism caused him to lose favour after the Second World War. Around the same time, voters of British descent found themselves to be a minority in the Nationalist-dominated South African parliament.

In 1948, Afrikaner politicians exploited long-held historical resentments to elect the Nationalist Party to virtually permanent governmental power, and turned the clock back. Boers took South Africa out of the Commonwealth, imposed the colour-bar regime of *apartheid*, and ruled with an iron hand for over four decades, despite international condemnation. That came to an end in 1994, when the white supremacists were forced by democratic elections to hand political control to the black majority. Free at last to vote, millions of native African citizens elected charismatic Nelson Mandela as their first black president. He led the republic back to rejoin the Commonwealth, and his new era started with a spirit of reconciliation between races in South Africa.

After Mandela's term of office ended, different problems evolved, as some of the newly-emancipated wreak pay-back on their previous masters. A massive increase in violent crime, changing legislation, and epidemic AIDS have created an atmosphere of near anarchy. Numbering less than nine percent of the population and suddenly powerless, whites there can see ahead only radical changes to their status, safety, and property.

Bowing to this shift of destiny, many Springboks are reluctantly leaving their birthplace forever, in a mass exodus world-wide. So, more than 100 years after it ended, the Anglo-Boer War still echoes across the tragic and beautiful land of South Africa.

Sidney Allinson, Victoria, British Columbia, Canada.

Participants and Casualties in the Second

Anglo-Boer War

British Imperial Forces

Total troops throughout	388,749
killed in action	7,582
died of disease	13,139
South African volunteers	57,415
killed in action	1,473
died of disease	1,607
South African Constabulary	
10,000	
deaths	368
Afrikaners in British service	
20,000(est.)	
OFS Burger Corps	448
National Scouts	1,459
Australian volunteers	16,463
deaths	606
Canadian volunteers	8,372
deaths	224
New Zealand volunteers	6,505
deaths	228
India, Ceylon, West Indies	909

Boer Forces

Total throughout	75,000
(est.)	
Regular troops, OFR/ZAR	2,700
ZARP (Police)	1,200
Commandos	59,000
(est.)	
Cape, Natal rebels	13,000
Boers killed in action	7,100

Civilians died in camps	27,927
Foreign volunteers	2,735
American	300
Dutch	650
French	400
German	550
Irish	200
Italian	200
Russian	225
Scandinavian	210
Black African deaths (est.)	30,000

BIBLIOGRAPHY

Numerous books, newspapers, documents, interviews, and letters were researched for authentic background to *KRUGER'S GOLD*. The following sources can interest anyone who wishes to read further:

With The Flag To Pretoria, H.W. Wilson, Harmsworth Publishers, London, 1900.

After Pretoria: The Guerilla War, H.W. Wilson, Harmsworth, London, 1902.

The Boer War, Thomas Packenham, Wiedenfeld, London, 1979.

The Struggle For Africa 1876-1912, Thomas Packenham, Random House, New York, 1991.

The Times History Of The War In South Africa, L.S. Amery, Sampson Low, London, 1903.

Queen Victoria's Little Wars, Byron Farwell, Norton, NY, 1986.

The War In South Africa, John A. Hobson, Nisbet, London, 1900.

The Great Boer War, Byron Farwell, London, 1977.

The Last of The Gentlemen's Wars, J.F.C. Fuller, London, 1937.

The Jameson Raid, H.M. Hole, London, 1930.

The Biograph In War, W.K.L. Dickson, Fisher Unwin, 1901.

The Great Boer War, Sir Arthur Conan Doyle, New York, 1902.

Goodbye Dolly Gray: The Story Of The Boer War, Rayne Kruger, Pan, London, 1959.

The Story Of South Africa In The Transvaal War, J. Clark Ridpath, Guelph, Canada, 1900.

The Last Post, Mildred G. Dooner, Cape Town, 1903.

"Boer War Operations In South Africa: Extracts from reports by military attache Capt. S.L. Slocum", United States Army, Washington, DC, 1902.

The British Case Against The Boer Republics, Imperial South African Association, London, 1900.

Farewell The Trumpets, James Morris, Faber, London, 1978.

Armed & Dangerous: A century of Anglo-Boer War stories, intro. C.N. van der Merne, Ball, Cape Town, 1999.

Randlords, Paul Emden, London, 1935.

The Hinges Creaked, Eric Rosenthal, Timmins, Cape Town, 1951.

There's A Secret Hid Away, Lawrence G. Green, Cape Town, 1956.

The Von Veltheim File, Valery Rosenberg, H&R, Cape Town, 1997.

Road To Infamy, Owen Coetzer, Waterman, Cape Town, 1999.

Paul Kruger: His Life And Times, J. Fisher, New York, 1974.

President Kruger, Johannes Meintjes, Johannesburg, 1974.

The Growth Of Opposition To Kruger, 1890-1895, C.T. Gordon, OUP, Cape Town, 1970.

"Twee Susters" (Three Sisters), Chris Euvrard, Kutra & Kie., Stellenbosch, 1915.

History, Homes, and Customs of the Voortrekkers, Sophia duPreeze, Pretoria, 1974.

White Tribe Dreaming, Marq De Villiers, Penguin, NY, 1989.

The Puritans In Africa: A Story Of Afrikanerdom, W.A. deKlerk, Rex Collings, London, 1975.

With The Boer Forces, H.C. Hillegas, Methuen, London, 1901.

Commando Courageous: A Boer's Diary, R.W. Schikkerling, Keartland, Johannesburg, 1964.

Commando, Deneys Reitz, Faber & Faber, London, 1929.

Circular From Commandant-General Louis P. Botha, 6 Oct, 1900.

To The Bitter End, Emanoel Lee, Viking, New York, 1985.

Three Years' War, Christiaan De Wet, Scribners, NY, 1902.

Diary Of A National Scout, P.J. Du Toit, Human Sciences Research Council, Pretoria, 1974.

A West Pointer With The Boers, Col. J.Y. Blake, Boston, 1903.

The War Dispatches Of Steven Crane, NYU Press, NY, 1964.

Methods Of Barbarism, H.B.Spies, Rousseau, Cape Town, 1977.

With Both Armies In South Africa, Richard Harding Davis, New York, 1900.

Life Of Lord Kitchener, Sir G. Arthur, Macmillan, London,1920.

Kitchener: The Man Behind The Legend, Phillip Warner, Atheneum, NY, 1986.

The General, C.S. Forester, Little Brown, New York, 1936.

The Killing Ground: The British Army, the Western Front, and the Emergence of Modern Warfare 1900-1918, Tim Travers, Unwin, London, 1987.

Anti-Commando, V. Sampson & I. Hamilton, Faber, London, 1931.

Intelligence Officer: On The Heels Of de Wet, Lionel James, Blackwood, Edinburgh, 1902.

History Of The Railways During The War In South Africa, Lt-Col Sir E. Percy Girouard, HMSO, Chatham, 1903.

"Britain's Last Castles: Masonry Blockhouses Of The South African War", R. Thomlinson, S.A.Military History Soc. Journal.

Horses & Saddlery, Maj. G. Tylden, Army Museum, London, 1965.

With The M.I. In South Africa, Maj. F. Crum, Cambridge, 1903.

With Rimington In South Africa, L. March Phillips, Arnold, London, 1902.

With Rundle's 85th Division, T.C. Wetton, Drane, London,

1902.

Scouting On Two Continents, Maj. Frederick Burnham, NY, 1926.

The South African Constabulary: Lessons From The Varsity Of Life, MGen Sir Robert Baden-Powell, London, 1933.

Absent-Minded Beggars: Volunteers In The Anglo-Boer War, William Bennett, Leo Cooper, London, 1999.

The Strange Empire Of Louis Riel, Joseph K. Howard, Morrow, New York, 1952.

I'm Alone, Jack Randall, Indianapolis, 1930.

The Tracer, Dominion Cartridge Co., Brownsburg, Quebec, 1943.

The Colonials In South Africa, J. Stirling, Edinburgh, 1907.

Two Years At The Front With The Mounted Infantry, Lt. Bertie Moeller, Grant Richards, 1903.

The Canadian Contingents, W. Sanford Evans, Toronto, 1901.

With The Infantry In South Africa: A lecture delivered at the Canadian Military Institute, Toronto, 3 February, 1902.

Canada's Sons On Kopje And Veldt, T.G. Marquis, Toronto, 1900.

Royal Canadian Military Institute: 100 Years 1890-1990, Ken Bell and Desmond Morton, RCMI, Toronto, 1990.

No Surrender: The Battle Of Harts River, Carman Miller, Canadian Battles Series, Canadian War Museum, Ottawa, 1993.

Painting The Map Red: Canada And The South African War, Carman Miller, Canadian War Museum, Ottawa, 1993.

Dragoon: the centennial history of the Royal Canadian Dragoons, 1883-1983, Bereton Greenhous, RCD Guild, Ottawa, 1983.

Our Little Army In The Field, Brian A. Reid, Vanwell, St. Catharines, 1996.

The Canadian Contingents and Canadian Imperialism, W. Sanford Evans, Publishers Syndicate, Toronto, 1901.

A Canadian Girl In South Africa, Maud Graham, Wm.

Briggs, Toronto, 1905.

Toronto Globe/Toronto Mail & Empire, 1899-1902.

Victoria Times/Victoria Colonist, 1899-1902.

The Times, London, 1899-1902.

The Australians At The Boer War, R.L. Wallace, Australian War Memorial, Canberra: 1976.

The New Zealanders In South Africa 1898-1902, NZ Dept. of Internal Affairs, Wellington, 1949.

Tommy Cornstalk, J.H.M. Abbott, Longmans, London, 1903.

Scapegoats Of The Empire, George Witton, Sydney, 1904.

Breaker Morant: A Horseman Who Made History, F.M. Cutlack, Ure Smith, Sydney, 1962.

Breaker Morant: Bushman & Buccaneer, F. Renar, Sydney, 1902.

"Butchered To Make A Dutchman's Holiday", Lt. H. Morant, poem written the night before his execution, Pretoria, 1902.

Breaker Morant And The Bushveld Carbineers, Arthur Davies, Van Riebeeck Society, Capetown, 1987.

Sydney Morning Herald, March-April, 1902.

Report Of A Visit To The Camps Of Women And Children In The Cape And Orange River Colonies, Emily Hobhouse, London, 1901.

The Brunt Of War Where It Fell, Emily Hobhouse, Methuen, London, 1902.

To Love One's Enemies, Jennifer Hobhouse Balme, The Hobhouse Trust, British Columbia, 1994.

Parliamentary Report On The Concentration Camps In South Africa by the Committee Of Ladies, Westminster, London, 1901.

Those Bloody Women: Three heroines of the Boer War, Brian Roberts, Murray, London, 1991.

Confidential Print 676, Colonial Office, January 16, 1902.

Return Of Numbers Of Persons In The Concentration Camps In South Africa, June 1901, HMSO, London, 1901.

The Concentration Camps 1900-1902: Facts, Figures, and Fables, Col. A.C. Martin, Cape Town, 1957.

The Concentration Camps In South Africa, Napier Devitt, Shouter, Pietermaritzburg, 1941.

Medical Report by Dr G.R. Woodroffe, Camp Irene, 4 Aug. 1901.

Diary Of A Nurse In South Africa, Alice Bron, Chapman & Hall, London, 1901.

The Medical History of the Anglo-Boer War: A Bibliography, Joan L. Beckerling, University of Cape Town, 1967.

The Medical History of the War in South Africa: An Epidemiological Essay, HMSO, London, 1911.

"An English South African's View Of The Situation", Olive Schreiner, Cape Town, 1899.

The Boer War Diary Of Sol T. Plaatje: An African at Mafeking, Macmillan, London, 1973.

Black People And The South African War, P. Warwick, Ravan, Johannesburg, 1983.

The Black and Coloured Concentration Camps, Rev. Stowell Kessler, Cape Town, 1999.

A Place Called Vatmaar, A.H.M. Scholtz, Kwela Books, Roggebai, 1999.

Ghostriders Of The Anglo-Boer War: The Black Agterryers, P. Labuschagne, University of South Africa Press, Pretoria, 1999.

The Jews In South Africa, G. Saron & L. Hotz, Oxford, 1995.

Roots Of Anti-Semitism In South Africa, Milton Shain, University Press of Virginia, Charlottesville, 1994.

The Jewish War: Anglo-Jewry and the South African War, Richard Mendelson, paper to Unisa Library Conference, Pretoria, 1998.

The Russians & The Anglo-Boer War, A. Davidson & I. Filatova, Cape Town, 1998.

Russia And The Anglo-Boer War, Elizavita Kandyba-

Foxcroft, Pretoria, 1981.

Little Brown Brother: America's Forgotten Bid For Empire Which Cost 250,000 Lives, Leon Wolff, Longmans, London, 1961.

US Congress Philippine Atrocities Investigating Committee, Washington, June, 1902.

Re-concentration Camps In The Philippines, Helen C. Wilson, Boston, 1903.

The American Occupation of the Philippines, 1898-1912, James H. Blount, Putnam's, New York, 1913.

The Balangiga Massacre: Getting Even, Victor Nebrida, Philippine History Group, Los Angeles, 1997.

The Revolt Of The Hereros, J.M. Bridgman, Berley, 1981.

South-West Africa Under German Rule, Helmut Bley, (tr.) 1971.

Rivers Of Blood, Rivers Of Gold: Europe's Conquest Of Tribal Peoples, Mark Cocker, Jonathan Cape, London, 1998.

The British Pro-Boers, Arthur M. Davey, Tafelburg Press, 1978.

The Pro Boers, Stephen Koss, UCP, Chicago, 1973.

The First Casualty: War Correspondents, Philip Knightley, Harcourt, NY 1976.

War's Brighter Side: Correspondents With Lord Robert's Forces, Julian Ralph, Appleton, NY, 1901.

**To enjoy another fact-based adventure tale
by Sidney Allinson, read:**

JEREMY KANE
*A Canadian Historical Novel About The 1837
Mackenzie Rebellion And Its Brutal Aftermath
In The Australian Penal Colonies.*

27779715R00164

Made in the USA
Lexington, KY
23 November 2013